ROSARY ROAD

Robert Chandler

HOBART BOOKS

HOBART BOOKS

ROSARY ROAD

ISBN 978-1-914322-08-2

First Published in 2021
by
Hobart Books, Oxfordshire, England
hobartbooks.com

Printed and bound in Great Britain by Clays Ltd, Elcograf S.p.A..

Rosary Road

By Robert Chandler

Acknowledgements

If I listed everyone who's influenced the creation of this work, this section would dwarf the novel itself. So, a brief thanks to the writers of detective fiction from classic whodunits to tartan (and other) noir who've shaped my view on what makes a great novel.

I'd like to share my appreciation for my friends at the Norwich Writers' Circle, who've helped and encouraged me over many years. I must also credit the Old Library Wood Collective, who've transformed the space from the urban wilderness of "Rosary Road" into a place of joy. Thanks also to the Collective for allowing me to dredge back memories of what the Wood once was.

Kudos is owed to Adam Gardner of Hobart Books for his confidence in publishing this series, and to Amy Custance-Jones for her brilliant cover design. Also to Dr Stephen Carver for his advice. He's helped turn a rough draft into what I hope is now a polished product.

I must mention the city of Norwich, rightly named City of Stories. Its history and character provided much of the inspiration for the Kezia Lee mysteries.

I send love and appreciation to my wife Ann, who allows me to scribble away while she single-handedly keeps the house and my life in order.

And greatest thanks to the people who made this effort worthwhile... you, the readers.

Chapter One

Kezia had written her target's details on a scrap of paper, not that she expected to need them.

But the world is less predictable after dark.

She didn't like the term 'victim'. Guilt was assuaged by calling them 'targets' and telling herself they deserved their fate. Some might even welcome it.

She walked in the footsteps of the damned. Beneath her feet the waters of the River Wensum drifted under the ancient crossing on their curve through Norwich towards the North Sea. In medieval times heretics stumbled where she trod, crossing Bishops Bridge on their passage to the fires of damnation, literally turning their backs on the holy places of the city. Kezia imagined the souls of the martyrs screaming at her to turn round. Sometimes these thoughts were too real, too unprompted. Her mother would claim them as visions from beyond the grave. Kezia put it down to conscience. She shivered and pulled the black hoodie over her head.

No moving vehicles were visible on Riverside Road. Vehicles meant dashcams. She'd checked for CCTV cameras along her route and was confident none would trouble her. Kezia jogged across the street to avoid a couple walking hand in hand towards her, too engaged with each other to notice, let alone remember, a stranger. She wouldn't find a lover in this city. Or the next, or the one after that. She'd too many dark secrets, not enough time.

Kezia crossed the junction with Rosary Road. A hundred yards up the hill, a woman clad in a short skirt stood on the pavement. The pose, the glances left and right indicated she waited for someone. Anyone with desire and cash would do. Kezia wouldn't venture that way. She wasn't nervous about the hooker recognising her. What she didn't relish was a passing punter slowing to suggest business, a witness to her transgressions.

She moved along Riverside towards the railway station, head down. Every approaching car forced her to turn her face away. Voices drifted across the street: holidaymakers on a pleasure boat. People with wealth, people who didn't have to skulk in the shadows. A window to her left taunted her with another vision of the unobtainable – a family huddled together watching television in the warm, safe glow of a lamp.

Chalk Hill Road – the terraced street housing her target. Kezia glanced up the hill before walking the few yards to the start of the alley running behind the houses. Narrow, cobbled, well-lit and deserted. A street with no name, unwelcoming, foliage overhanging the walls on both sides threatening to make the path inaccessible. She bowed her head – she remembered a camera clung to the rear wall of the first house she'd pass. A few steps more and she faced a tall wooden gate. No lock, no problem. Kezia donned a pair of rubber gloves – *unlikely fingerprints would be sought, but you could never be certain.*

She sprayed the hinges with WD40 and waited. Creaks were louder at night. Kezia eased the gate open and stepped into a back yard paved with concrete. She risked torchlight. Everything appeared as she remembered, then…

Bright, blinding lights.

Motion-detected. They weren't there two days ago.

A loud barking from a neighbour's garden…

A wave of irrational fear. *Bloody dogs.*

She hesitated, deciding whether to stand still or run.

A harsh voice helped determine what to do.

'What the bloody hell are you up to!'

The bald head appearing over the fence confirmed the necessary course of action.

Kezia fled.

'Come back or I'll call the police.'

He'd call the police whatever she did. She needed cover. None lay downhill towards the river. Kezia heard her pursuer shout to his dog as she ran, the uneven cobbles bruising her feet.

She tried to dismiss the vague threatening images clouding her mind as the wall to her right gave way to wooden palings. Kezia reached the top of the alley, already breathing hard. The dog continued to bark behind her.

To her left, a passageway led back to the streetlights of Chalk Hill Road. She chose darkness and disappeared into the shadows of Old Library Wood. Adrenaline accelerated her heartbeat as she raced along a path barely visible in the gloom.

Kezia slowed when she reached the exit leading towards the railway station. No-one followed. She held her breath. Silence reigned in the shadow of the trees. She wondered whether her target's neighbour had seen her face, a fear compounded by another unprovoked sensation: the sense her whole body was enveloped in blood, that something terrible lurked nearby.

She took a deep breath and waited.

It was then she knew something else.

She was not alone.

Chapter Two

A phone ringing at seven in the morning is never good news. Especially when the ring tone was 'Another One Bites the Dust'. The phone sat in Detective Inspector David Ross's hand before he was fully awake. 'Yeah?'

'Morning, sir.' He recognised the too-cheerful voice as Sergeant Jimmy Dobbs. The Queen classic warned him the call came from the Bethel Street headquarters of the Norwich East division. Not that Dobbs's joyful greeting was any guide to what was to follow; the sergeant would announce Armageddon in the same manner. 'Body of a young woman found up Rosary Road. In Old Library Wood. You know the area?'

'Sure. Near the station.'

'That's it,' said Dobbs.

He knew exactly where Old Library Wood was. He'd visited it enough times, perhaps every day in his imagination.

The light glaring through a gap in the curtains suggested a bright morning. Good for preserving evidence, lousy for hangovers. *Last night... dry... footprints might not show, but no rain to wash away tell-tale fluids.*

'Forensic team on their way?' Ross's voice carried only a hint of the Glasgow accent he'd brought to Norfolk eight years ago. A dull headache provided a reminder he'd had one lonely glass of malt whisky too many the previous evening.

Old Library Wood... For a moment he contemplated finishing the bottle.

'Yes, Queen Ann and her crew. Might even be there by now.'

'Pathologist?'

'Lord Snooty. Should arrive by ten o'clock.'

Ross put the phone on speaker and stumbled out of bed. 'Who's securing the site?'

'Clifton Walker. Constable. Know him?'

'I think so. Is he the one who looks like that actor? You know, the young black one?'

'Dunno, sir,' replied Dobbs. 'What's he been in?'

'Forget it. Who else is at the scene?'

'Just him. There might be a couple of PCSOs by the time you arrive. We can't spare anyone else.'

Ross searched the jumbled contents of a drawer for a pair of matching socks. His ex would have sorted them in neat pairs, arranged by colour.

'There's five entrances to the Wood,' he shouted at the phone. 'I want the entire area sealed off. We need more uniforms. Sort it out.'

'We haven't – '

The detective killed the call, waited, then made a few of his own. Dobbs would have followed the book as best he could; Ross's superior, DCI Neville Devlin, would be aware; the necessary support services summoned or on call. Ross was responsible for ensuring his team was ready.

He scrabbled about in a cupboard for paracetamol, reflecting on the irony that he was supposed to be proficient in searching for evidence and yet he couldn't find painkillers in his own kitchen.

Half an hour and two coffees later, Ross stopped his Ford Mondeo behind a squad car on Rosary Road, before pulling on his protective suit and shoes. He hesitated between the brick pillars that marked the entrance to Old Library Wood, a pause that would never be long enough to dispel the ghosts of his past.

As soon as he descended into the small park, he didn't need to count the uniforms to realise his hopes for sufficient support were in vain. People were standing in groups on the grassy area to his right, while at the foot of the path Clifton Walker and two PCSOs were too busy shouting at another posse of onlookers to notice his approach. There was no forensic unit.

Ross stopped to survey his surroundings. He noted the houses to his left. Close, but no direct line of sight to where Walker fought off the rubberneckers. A block of flats on the other side of Rosary Road overlooked Old Library Wood, but it was certain the undergrowth would have masked the murder from residents. Nevertheless, every adult living nearby would be interviewed. Even if they didn't see anything, the sound of a scream might indicate time of death.

By day, the wood was pleasant enough, a shortcut for those heading for the city or station, a green playground for dogs and children, but by night it changed as if all virtue fled with the light. He'd already guessed where the body lay: in a dip overlooked by tall trees standing over the spot like mourners around a grave. In the distance, the cathedral spire was an unconcerned observer. It had witnessed worse than this. The murder scene was a vestige of wildwood near the centre of the city, unchanged over centuries.

Ross muttered a few gruff apologies as he barged through the spectators to flash his warrant card at the constable standing on the path. 'PC Walker? Inspector David Ross.' He didn't wait for a reply. 'Why haven't you cleared the area?'

Walker broke off a confrontation with a youth on a bicycle. 'Morning, sir. We've kept them away from the murder scene.' He pointed at the trees behind him. 'At least since we got here. But they keep coming through. Some of them claim they need to catch a train.'

'Yeah, like this is a public thoroughfare,' said the youth, who then adjusted his New York Yankees baseball cap as if he thought it projected an air of authority.

'Not when it's a crime scene,' said Ross. 'On your bike, son.'

He ignored the single finger thrust in his direction before the youth departed.

Walker's attention was already elsewhere. Spectators were holding mobile phones aloft. One had the advantage of a selfie stick. 'Hey, no photographs.'

'Let them be,' said Ross. 'But then get their names and addresses.'

The more photos he had, the better. Experience told him there was a fair chance the murderer lurked among the onlookers.

He pushed back through the throng to where a PCSO stood, arms outstretched like a cut-down pastiche of the Angel of the North, indicating the invisible barrier beyond which lay the body. Ross showed his warrant card to the officer before viewing the corpse, noting ragged brown hair matted with crimson, a black hooded top, and short leather skirt over bare legs.

His first impressions were this was not a frenzied sexual assault. Might not be simple to check – in this area, the likelihood was the dead woman worked as a prostitute. Easy target for a psychopath.

Ross took out his notebook and nodded at Walker. 'What happened?'

Walker produced his own notebook. 'A gentleman called Keith Pritchard was walking his dog around five-thirty when the dog found – '

'Is he here?'

'Sorry, sir. He had to get a train into London. He left us a mobile number if we want to talk to him urgently. Says he'll be back around seven.'

'Did he give any more details? Like checking if she was dead?'

'Just said when he saw the body, he knew she was gone, so he called us.'

'Did he see anyone else?'

'Didn't mention it,' replied Walker. 'He was a bit shocked… or hungover, I don't know which.'

'Anyone else here when you arrived?'

'No sir.'

The dead woman lay in a foetal position on a small patch of grass obscured by bushes and the lower limbs of trees. From above, only her bloody tresses betrayed the impression she could be sleeping. A brief look at her face revealed further injuries. A shattered tooth gleamed on the moss. Ross wasn't squeamish, but he'd no interest in a closer examination, especially when he spotted her shattered eye socket. The CSI team wouldn't thank him for another set of footprints.

'As far as you're aware, no-one apart from Mr Pritchard has been in this area since the discovery of the body?'

'An ambulance turned up. I've got details of the paramedics. They confirmed the woman was dead.'

'Did they say anything else?'

Walker checked his notebook. 'They think she was hit on the head with some force. The other injuries are probably post mortem.' He glanced at the corpse. 'I hope for her sake they were. Rigor mortis has started to set in, so they reckon around six to twelve hours ago.'

She might not have had time to scream.

An elderly man brandishing a walking stick threatened to encroach too close to the corpse.

'Stay back, sir.' Ross knew it was time to make the speech. 'Can I have your attention please?'

The surrounding hubbub continued.

Ross raised his voice. 'Please be quiet!'

Silence – almost.

'This is a crime scene. Unless you have some information pertinent to this incident, then exit the park immediately. If you've taken pictures, please leave your details with the officers. Anyone not complying will be guilty of obstructing the police in the execution of our duty. Is that clear?'

He detected mutterings of protest before the crowd dispersed. The exception was a middle-aged woman with an expensive pink coiffure wearing a matching puffa jacket and black leggings. She peered at Ross through pink-rimmed glasses.

'I have information.'

Ross tapped his notebook. 'Thank you, Mrs...?'

'Consodine, Mrs Sarah Consodine. That's Sarah with an *h.*'

'Thanks, madam. Now –'

The woman didn't let Ross finish. 'Your victim is a whore. I'm sure I spoke to her two nights ago. Foul-mouthed creature. I merely requested she didn't ply her disgusting trade outside my house. She replied in a manner... Well, I have never been subject to such abominable language.'

'Did you discover her name?'

'Do I look like someone who exchanges pleasantries with prostitutes?'

'My apologies.' Ross wondered if she'd ever been pleasant to anyone. 'Can I ask how you're certain it's the same woman?'

He didn't anticipate Mrs Consodine pushing him aside and marching over to glance down at the corpse. If Ross hoped to relish a gasp of horror, a recoil at the bloodied and shattered skull, he would have been disappointed.

She merely pursed her lips in obvious disdain before walking back. 'It looks like her. Long straggly hair, short skirt – yes, I'm certain. We see the same trollops every night. What with them and the drug addicts, a decent woman can't walk outside her own home after dark. I've complained, you know.'

'What about last night? Did you see her then?'

'No, but that's not to say she wasn't there. I don't make a habit of watching these people. As I said, if you'd done your

11

job, this wouldn't have happened.' She touched her hair as if to check it was still in place. 'At least not here, anyway.'

'Did you see or hear anything unusual last night?'

'No. But I want to record that this tragedy would not have occurred if my complaints had been taken seriously. This... this constable must take some responsibility.'

'Mrs Consodine has raised her concerns on a few occasions,' said Walker. 'But – '

'A few! Many times, young man. I've no doubt street walkers are ten-a-penny in Brixton, or wherever you come from, but this is a decent area.'

Ross's dilemma as to whether Sarah Consodine's remarks counted as a hate crime was interrupted by the arrival of Senior CSI Ann Woodhead and her team. A few of his colleagues dismissed Woodhead as inexperienced, but Ross didn't share their view.

'Thank you, Mrs Consodine. We'll be in touch if we need you.'

Mrs Consodine humphed before glaring at the forensic experts.

'Morning, David,' said Woodhead, long blonde hair hidden under the hood of a white paper suit.

'Not such a good one,' he replied, watching Mrs Consodine stomp away, thinking Ann looked good in any outfit. 'Usual gold service required. Treat the area from here to the fence as the crime scene. Everywhere else has been compromised. Unless you or the good doctor surprise me, we're looking at murder. And a nasty one at that.'

Woodhead watched as her team taped off the area and began a preliminary analysis of the site. 'Who's had the chance to mess it up?'

'Guy who found it, ambulance crew, and that bloody woman who just left. Nobody else specific, although God knows who was around last night.'

One of the CSIs called out: 'Ann, fresh vomit over here.'

Woodhead turned away to examine the congealed mass on the ground as if it was a rare orchid. 'Number and bag it,' she said. 'When's P.B. getting here? I assume he's on call.'

Ross nodded. 'Do you mean Lord Snooty? We expect him at ten o'clock precisely.' He pronounced the last word in a mock public-school accent.

She smiled, and Ross wondered if he dared ask her out one day. *Nine years age gap and all the baggage I come with – perhaps not.* 'I'll let you get on with it. I need to start the paperwork.'

He was returning to his car when he saw an Asian woman in a black trouser suit walking towards him, attracting admiring glances from the male spectators clustered near the entrance. She was in her mid-twenties, around five foot three, with long ebony hair – Detective Sergeant Kirsi Mishra, poster girl of the graduate fast track scheme.

'Kirsi, first as usual. It's murder. Ann's working the scene, so not much we can do except wait for Hamish.'

'Who's the victim?'

'It's a young woman. Initial indications are she's on the game. Street prostitute.'

Mishra looked past him at the scene and bit her lip. 'Shit. What a bloody waste of a life. Any idea who did it?'

13

'None as yet. Probably a punter. The guy who found her is off in London, so he's in the frame until proven otherwise. A lot of the locals are a bit tetchy about the toms, but I can't see them resorting to murder.'

Mishra continued to stare at the three CSIs as they carried out a fingertip search of the scene. 'How was she killed?'

'Blunt force trauma, according to the paras. Which worries me.'

'You think it's premeditated, don't you?'

Ross nodded. 'It's the weapon. Strangulation, even a knife... they suggest a spur-of-the-moment crime. I'm thinking robbery here. She'd have carried cash. The odd thing is the level of violence.'

'Could be personal,' suggested Mishra. 'Or someone with a grudge against working girls.'

'Let's hope it's the former.'

Ross saw movement out the corner of his eye and was about to admonish another interloper when he recognised the squat figure of his boss, DCI Neville Devlin, clad as usual in a suit more likely Savile Row than the M&S ones adorning the men who reported to him. Devlin was in charge of Serious Crimes and would assume the role of Senior Investigating Officer when the case was classed as major or destined to result in good publicity for the police.

Devlin patted down his hair in case press photographers lurked in the bushes. 'David, Kirsi... what's happening?'

Ross provided Devlin with the same summary he'd delivered to Mishra.

'Nasty,' said Devlin. 'I'm afraid my workload won't allow me to focus on this, so I assume you've no problem acting as SIO on this one. Put your other cases on hold.'

'Not transfer them?'

'We don't have the manpower.'

We might if you pulled your finger out. 'Yes, sir.'

'We need to close this down fast. It's got all the hallmarks of a serial killer and we can't have one of them on our patch.'

'We could ask the Met to send a specialist team.'

'What? Give our public the impression Norfolk Police can't handle this? I'll give you a week, then I'll take full responsibility. Is that clear?'

'Yes sir.'

'Good. Now what resources do you need? Not sure what we can spare.'

'We'll need a murder room in Bethel Street. I'd like Mishra and McLeod assigned full time, plus three other DCs. I'll require five or six uniforms to carry out house-to-house checks. We'd want an analyst to look at similar crimes across the country and another to identify anyone in the area with form.'

'Three DCs?' Devlin shook his head. 'I can only spare Linda Stevens. She's wasting her time investigating phoney mediums. Or should that be media?' Devlin chuckled. 'Put in a request for the uniforms and analysts and I'll fast track it.'

'I need them now... sir.'

'Can't bend the rules, David. Oh, and I'd like an update. On my desk at noon each day. Starting Monday. Okay?'

'Yes, sir.'

Devlin looked around, nodded, then left.

'Arsehole,' said Ross once his superior was out of earshot.

'Arseholes serve a useful purpose,' said Mishra. 'He bears more of a similarity to what emerges.'

'Only with less appeal,' added Ross.

'He'll be hoping we almost solve it and then he can come along and claim the glory.'

'We'd better solve it quick then. Kirsi, can you hold the fort while I do the preliminaries in Bethel Street? I'll try to get back to entertain Lord Snooty.'

Ross turned to gaze at the body once more. At a distance of a hundred yards and twelve years, another corpse had begged for revenge, one more he'd failed. Already he felt a connection to this woman curled on the ground. He wasn't religious, but some primaeval voice always whispered the souls of the slain couldn't find peace until their killers faced justice. He was her avenger, all she had left. And he didn't boast a good track record.

This is why I've failed to find true love, thought Ross. *I'm too faithful to the dead.*

He turned to walk back to his car. This time PC Walker interrupted his plans. The constable shuffled over and glanced at the ground before speaking.

'Sir, can I have a quick word?'

Ross stared at the CSIs. 'Yeah, sure. Make it quick, though.'

'I've just had a message from HQ. They've asked me to look into an attempted burglary.'

'So? This takes priority.'

'Yes, sir.' Walker hesitated. 'It's just there might be a connection.'

'Okay, shoot.'

The constable examined his notes. 'A gentleman called... James Christie...' He shut the book. 'He lives in Chalk Hill Road. At around half-past ten last night, his dog started barking, and he looked outside. There was an intruder in his neighbour's back garden. He gave chase, but the intruder ran into Old Library Wood.'

'Any description of the suspect?'

The notebook opened again. 'Black top, wearing a hat or a hood, slim build. Mr Christie thought it might have been a girl, but he's not certain.'

Ross glanced at the dead woman. The details matched. 'You stay here, constable. I'll look into it.'

Ross obtained Christie's address, nodded his thanks and went in search of Ann Woodhead. The CSI was talking to one of her assistants.

'Ann, we've got a possible related crime scene. It's just around the corner. Is this a convenient time to check it out?'

She delivered instructions to her colleague before joining him on the path leading to Chalk Hill Road.

'Anything interesting?' asked Ross.

'So far, we've got two used condoms, a needle, and some suspicious spittle and vomit. Plus, the usual collection of cigarette butts and dog shit. We'll keep the lab in business for a few days.'

'Did you see her face?'

17

'What was left of it. It's almost as if the killer didn't want her recognised. He's gone for the eyes, the teeth.'

'But not her fingers,' said Ross. 'If she was on the game, chances are she's in the system. Her attacker should have guessed that. I'm sticking to the angry man syndrome.'

They stopped at the entrance to the alley that descended behind Chalk Hill Road.

Ross pointed down the track. 'We think the robbery suspect ran up here and then into the wood. The timing matches that of the murder.'

'Suspect? Do you think it was the killer?'

'Maybe. But there's a stronger possibility she's the dead woman. And I'm hoping to find a Mr Christie who, given the circumstances, might be in the frame. Hence we say nothing about the murder.'

Two minutes later they were knocking on the front door of a bay-fronted terraced house near the top of Chalk Hill Road. They were greeted by a man in his late seventies, heavily jowled, thin grey hair clinging to a scalp dotted with liver spots. James Christie belonged to the generation who wore a collar and tie at all waking hours. He squinted at his visitors through thick-lensed glasses.

Ross showed his badge. 'Mr Christie, we're from the police. I'm Inspector David Ross and this is Senior CSI Ann Woodhead. We're here in response to your report of a burglary.'

'Blimey, this is a turn-up.' Northern accent rendered hoarse by years of smoking, evidenced by yellow fingers and the smell emanating from the interior of the house. 'I expected a constable, not a bleeding inspector. Short-handed, are you?'

'We were in the neighbourhood,' replied Ross. 'I understand the incident occurred in a neighbour's garden.'

'Right… you'd better come through.' A barking Jack Russell appeared. 'Okay, Winston, enough. Dead good watchdog, Winston. Give 'em a nasty nip if they try anything.'

Ross and Woodhead followed Christie through the hall, accompanied by the stink of wet dog and stale tobacco. Winston trotted behind, growling all the way.

'You've got a bit of a limp,' said Ross. 'Recent injury?'

'Wish it was. Might clear up then. No, arthritis. Price of growing old. Through here.' He took them into an untidy kitchen, at the end of which was a glass door leading to the back garden. 'I was just getting ready for bed when Winston started barking. He'd gone out to do his business. I'd installed some security lights for Phyllis next door. That's Mrs Leadbetter...' He noticed Ross taking notes. 'L-E-A-D, that is. Dead good timing, 'cause I see they're on and I go out and there's this lass sneaking – '

'Sorry, Mr Christie. You said 'lass'. Are you certain it was a girl?'

'Hmm. Happen it was, happen it wasn't. Can't tell these days.' He tapped his glasses. 'The old eyesight's not what it was. I know she was wearing this black hood, so she was up to no good.'

'Was she trying to break into Mrs Leadbetter's?'

'What else was she doing? She had this bag over her shoulder, and she was carrying a long black thing.'

'What else was she wearing?'

'Can't remember.'

Christie opened the back door and led them into the garden, comprising nothing but a small weed-strewn lawn, bare in patches. Ross hesitated before stepping around the dog excrement hiding among the tufts of grass.

'I clear it up every day,' said Christie. 'Anyway, that's Phyllis's garden over there.'

Ross peered over the dark-panelled fence. 'Has Mrs Leadbetter learned about the incident?'

'Thought it best not to tell her otherwise she'd have a right strop. She's just lost her husband. That's why I'm helping her.' He stroked his chin. 'What say whoever it was found out about his passing and targeted her? That's what I reckon.'

Ross pointed. 'Her back gate – do you know if she locks it?'

'No. That way I can help her get the bins out.'

'Where were you standing when you saw the intruder?'

'Just by my back door,' replied Christie. 'Then I went to try to catch her, but she was too quick.'

Ross took three steps back to the entrance to the kitchen. Christie would have had a view of the suspect's head and shoulders, but not her legs – if it was a woman. The intruder might still be the murderer or the victim.

'I heard sirens this morning,' said Christie. 'Anything happening?'

'There's been an incident in Old Library Wood. We're still investigating details.'

'Like a mugging? Bloody Nora, d'you think this girl done it? She looked a nasty sort.'

'I can't comment,' replied Ross. 'I'd suggest you avoid the area for the next few hours.'

'Winston won't be chuffed about that. He goes there for his daily run.'

'Sorry. Would it be best if you accompanied us to meet Mrs Leadbetter?'

'Aye. Good idea. She might get upset otherwise.'

Christie led Ross and Woodhead to the neighbouring house. The small gravelled front garden was free of weeds, the net curtains an immaculate white. A pot of geraniums sat by the side of the tiled path.

Phyllis Leadbetter only released the chain on her door when she recognised her neighbour's voice. She welcomed Ross and Woodhead into her lounge. Every wall was covered in paintings, every surface adorned with China ornaments or black and white photographs in gilt frames.

Ross estimated her age as eighty. Her hair was neat, probably recently permed, and she wore a string of pearls around her neck. Three fingers on her left hand sported an array of gold rings, all except the wedding band enhanced by jewels. She was clad entirely in black.

The interview was brief. Her son, Joe, had come over and left around nine, after which she'd gone to bed. She was unaware of the incident and had little to say except praise for James Christie. She had no problem about allowing the CSIs into her back garden, and furthermore, would try to provide their favourite biscuits if they could supply details.

'Well?' said Ross when they left. 'Any observations?'

Woodhead laughed. 'Elementary, my dear David. Mr Christie's not your killer. He can't walk, and we know he's not faking it, as he's only able to take Winston out once a day, as evidenced by the poop. The merry widow… definite target for a burglar. I'm no expert, but I suspect some of those trinkets are valuable. Plus, I'm certain the pearls and rings are the genuine article.'

'You've left out his eyesight,' said Ross. 'No way can we use him in a line-up.'

They returned to the crime scene. Ross cursed to see a TV crew and other representatives of the fourth estate swelling the number of onlookers – that would only encourage more. Woodhead nodded to the DI before departing to tape off the section of the alley where the intruder made a getaway. Mishra was helping the PCSOs deter anyone from encroaching.

Ross ignored a barrage of questions from reporters. He abandoned his plans to go to Bethel Street, which meant the arrival of Dr Charles Porter-Brown was no inconvenience.

'David, dear boy. We meet again. Always in the most delightful of circumstances.'

'Wouldn't have it any other way,' said Ross.

Porter-Brown was tall, with bushy grey hair either side of a shiny bald pate. He wore a pair of gold-rimmed round glasses and a blue striped tie Ross understood was Old Salopian. The doctor slipped on protective clothing before examining the body.

'Usual speech,' Porter-Brown said on his return. 'Have to get her on the slab, etcetera, etcetera. Unofficially, I'd be putting my money on blunt force trauma caused by a weapon not unlike a hammer. Several blows delivered with a bit of strength. Probably a male attacker, but Mrs Porter-Brown could deliver similar damage if riled. Not that I'm accusing my good lady, of course.'

'You've seen a few of these. Does it look like uncontrolled rage or an attempt to obscure identification?'

Porter-Brown nodded. 'Excellent question. I've not seen any evidence of defensive wounds so it's probable the incapacitating blow was to the back of the head. The blows to the face may even have been post mortem. But, dear boy, that's a preliminary guess.'

Ross grinned. 'You can guess what I'm going to ask next?'

'I'd say time of death was between nine last night and three this morning, but I should be able to narrow it.'

'Any thoughts on the victim?'

'There are no obvious signs of sexual assault but I can't rule it out, given her probable occupation. Lady of the night, I'd guess. She's got extensive needle marks on her arms.'

'Has the body been moved?'

'Again, I'd have to check lividity, but my gut feel is no.'

'How soon can you give me chapter and verse?'

Porter-Brown smiled. 'Chapter at lunchtime Monday. That's if I can get her on the old metal mattress first thing. Verse will have to wait until the lab does all the tests. I predict a couple of weeks at present.'

'Thanks, Doc. We'll put pressure on the lab. Do what you can.' Ross turned to Mishra. 'Kirsi, I'm off to Bethel Street. Wait here till we get more foot soldiers, then meet me at three. Suggest to Ann she joins us. I'm appointing you deputy on this one.'

The detective inspector pushed his way through the reporters and the clicks of cameras back to his car.

'All I'll say is we're treating the death as suspicious,' he told the media.

He wasn't even sure what they'd asked him. Murdered prostitute... clear-up rates were not good, and he'd been given one week to solve it. The history of such events threatened more victims.

At the gate, Ross turned and stared at the path behind him. There'd been too many victims here already.

I didn't bring you justice in eleven years and now I've got seven days.

He didn't believe in miracles, but he needed one at that moment.

Chapter Three

'Murder?' Sabina Romanov slumped down in her chair, her dyed black hair in curlers, the first cigarette of the day poised in her trembling yellowed fingers. She wore a long black wrap and jet beads. Sabina was convinced dark attire made her look slim, a self-delusion her daughter had given up disputing.

Kezia flung open the kitchen-area window. 'God, do you have to smoke first thing? It'll kill you.'

'So what? I'll be among friends. Why didn't you wake me?'

The younger woman sat down and twirled a spoon. 'What would you have done? Worried. And then you'd have slagged me off for not getting any info.'

'Did anyone see you?'

'Some old guy next door to the target. He wouldn't have seen my face.'

'What about the body? Did you touch it?'

Kezia poked the spoon into her cereal. 'I know a corpse when I see one. Felt a bit sick, but I think I kept it in.'

'They'll be looking for you.'

'As long as I stay clear they won't find me. I was here all night. Okay?'

'You avoided cameras?'

'Of course. Maybe you should forget the Leadbetter woman?'

Sabina produced a lighter. 'She's well off. We need her. The spirits tell me it is safe.'

Kezia grinned. 'You trust them? If they're real.'

The lighter hit the table with a bang. 'Stupid girl. You of all people know they're real. You have the visions too.'

Kezia wasn't going to admit her premonition of danger the previous evening. 'If you want, I can do some digging on the daughter. Discover where she went to school, speak to classmates, that sort of thing. If I find out where they used to live before Chalk Hill Road, we'd have something.'

'What about the funeral? He was an important man, so there must be a record. Some of her husband's business associates would've been there.'

'Yeah, okay. When're you seeing her again?'

'Wednesday. That means you haven't got long.'

Kezia poured milk into the bowl. 'I'm off to work in a minute. Somebody's got to earn some money.'

'There'll be a lot more if you can dig the dirt on Herbert Leadbetter.'

'Pity the spirits can't do their job,' mumbled Kezia through a mouthful of bran flakes.

'You understand how it works.' Sabina's voice echoed round the kitchen. 'The curtain isn't clear enough.'

Kezia knew enough not to argue. Her mother's belief in an accessible afterlife trumped all logic. She finished breakfast and left their rented flat to walk along Magdalen Street.

Magdalen Street – the area where immigrants fleeing religious persecution settled in the sixteenth century, the so-called Strangers. A time when outsiders were welcomed. A thoroughfare of fast-food outlets, ethnic restaurants and second-hand shops, the shadows of its prosperous past reflected in the facades of the old buildings above the shop fronts. Elizabeth Fry was born there in the home of the Gurneys, once the richest family of Britain. The moneyed no longer house-hunt on Magdalen Street.

A few hundred yards away lay number nineteen, reputed to be the most haunted building in the city, where the ghost of a murdered woman called Sarah cries out for vengeance on her killer. *Strange Ma has never picked up on her.*

It was a short walk to the vegan café where she worked. Not that Kezia adhered to veganism, but her employers assumed she did.

The café proprietors also believed she spent her evenings getting an arts degree from the Open University. It excused her from social interaction and explained her presence in public houses offering free Wi-Fi, or the central library.

Kezia had lied all her life. It was necessary to survive, but the cost was another layer on the corrosive sense of guilt that never left her. She'd always assumed it would pass, but with every year the feeling grew stronger. Unlike her ability to shut it out when she needed.

She spent the morning as she always did – flirting with the unaccompanied male customers, praising the merits of vegan berry muffins and other delights, cleaning coffee cups in plain hot water – the owners refusing to use washing up liquid as it came in plastic containers.

Despite the aura of normality, Kezia was troubled. What evidence had she left behind? How good a look did the neighbour get?

'Excuse me, miss,' called a girl dressed in a leather jacket and jeans, 'Any chance of another coffee?'

'No problem.' Kezia looked at her watch for the fiftieth time that day. Two minutes to three.

She carried the requested mug over to the table.

'Like your outfit,' said the girl. 'Where did you get it?'

Kezia often wore flowing skirts and T-shirts, describing the style as gypsy punk. Today she'd chosen a combination of blue top with a complementary tartan dress over her black Doc Marten's.

'Small place in Northampton. Can't remember the name.'

It was Oxfam. No need to elaborate.

'Cool,' said the customer.

Kezia's legs buckled. Someone was whispering her name, a voice inside her head, a creature who meant her harm.

'You okay?' asked the girl.

'Sure.' Kezia manufactured a laugh. 'Somebody walking on my grave.'

It was a warning, she knew. Somewhere in the city, the wolves were forming a pack to hunt her down.

***

Ross stood with blue ink marker in hand before a whiteboard in a room without windows. His newly-assembled team sat around a rectangular table on cheap swivel chairs, some dating from the nineteen-eighties. The surface of the table was scarred with scratches and cigarette burns. The walls bore the stains of Blu Tac, ghosts of previous investigations, the floor a patchwork of worn carpet tiles in various hues of brown. In an institution restricted by budget, décor is never the highest priority.

Ross had written 'Unknown female victim' at the top of an otherwise empty surface.

He tapped the word 'unknown'. 'No prints on the system, which surprises me given what we know. Unlikely we can use dental records due to the damage to her mouth. Kirsi, summarise what we've got.'

'Okay, sir. Woman, aged around late twenties, probably killed by a blow to the head with a blunt object. Our current assumption is a hammer. The crime was committed sometime last night. There are no relevant missing person reports, which makes it more likely she might be a sex worker.'

'Pretty obvious,' said Detective Constable Alex 'Hamish' McLeod. McLeod was bearded with a hairstyle that left the world of fashion with the Beatles. A growing paunch hinted McLeod flirted with failure in his next annual fitness test. Despite his nickname, McLeod was Norfolk born and bred.

'Assume nothing,' said Ross. 'Any similar crimes in the last few months?'

Mishra shook her head. 'The only incident of interest was a rape and murder eleven years ago in the same park. Different M.O. and we had a suspect, but he died. We could never establish a case so – '

'Forget it.'

Too curt. He noted Mishra's surprise. *Don't give yourself away.* Stevens merely smiled. *What does she know?* 'It was too long ago. Ann, anything to add?'

Ann Woodhead flicked a finger over her iPad. 'We've got a few leads. In the immediate vicinity we found vomit, condoms, a needle, and five cigarette butts. The ground was too hard for prints. Needle marks on the victim's arms and legs suggest she was a drug addict. Most likely heroin, but we can't be sure yet. We recovered her bag. No ID, money, or mobile. Just make up, a mirror, a pack of three condoms, and a set of keys. She was wearing a locket, and we found what we think is a child's tooth inside.'

'Perhaps she's a mother?' said Mishra.

'Possibly. The P.M. should clarify that. We also found what appears to be a cocktail of saliva and semen near the body. No prizes for guessing what that means. We've sent it to the lab with the other stuff and they'll confirm if the saliva's hers.'

Mishra sighed. 'How could anyone do that?'

McLeod grinned at Mishra. 'It takes skill and plenty of practice. I could run a training course if anyone's interested.'

'Christ, you're sick,' said DC Linda Stevens, Ross's latest recruit. She was in her early thirties with a face that spoke character rather than beauty. Stevens wore a navy-blue trouser suit suggesting she favoured utility over fashion. Her brown hair was pulled back into a severe ponytail.

Ross made a mental note to discipline McLeod at an appropriate time. 'I'm hoping the lab can tell us who the semen belongs to.'

Woodhead nodded. 'If he's in the system. At least the techs should be able to verify whether the condoms predate the oral sex. And don't forget the saliva. In a place like that there's no guarantee it's the victim's. We're checking prints on the bag to see who's handled it. The absence of cash and a mobile might mean a robbery.'

'Maybe the punter didn't pay,' suggested McLeod.

'Good point, Hamish,' said Ross. 'And if so, he's our man.'

Mishra raised a finger. 'Would a sex worker ask for money after the event? Surely she'd demand it up front?'

Stevens's glare answered McLeod's snigger. Ross looked at the whiteboard to hide his own smile.

'Of course, she would.' Stevens continued to lock angry eyes with McLeod. 'It would be bloody dark where she was found, so she'd have got the cash on the street. The punter would've nicked it.'

'It might've been the failed burglar,' said Mishra.

'Thanks, Kirsi. We need to focus on that. Ann, anything from the garden?'

'Hang on,' said Stevens. 'What burglar?'

'Sorry, Linda. There was an attempted burglary at an address round the corner. Chalk Hill Road. The suspect fled into the park during the timeframe when the murder was committed. Our witness thinks she was a girl wearing a black hoodie. We can't rule out the possibility the robber and our victim are one and the same.'

'Or the killer,' said Stevens. 'What house was it in Chalk Hill? It's just I was there yesterday. On my case.'

'It belonged to a Mrs Leadbetter,' replied Ross.

'Phyllis Leadbetter?' asked Stevens.

'The same. Perhaps you should give us a brief summary of your investigation.'

Stevens rose to stand alongside Ross. Her assertive posture belied her junior rank. 'Mrs Leadbetter's son called us. He believes his mother is the victim of a fraudster named Sabina Romanov.' She waited a second to ensure she had the audience's attention. 'Romanov, also known as Sabina Lee,

31

claims to be a psychic. She's promised Mrs Leadbetter she can communicate with her late husband.'

'Difficult case to make,' said Ross. 'Yours, that is.'

'I disagree. Romanov's got form. She left Northampton after a similar investigation. That's when she changed her name.'

'Did they prosecute?' asked Ross.

'They built up a case. But the CPS refused to play ball.'

'Shouldn't Trading Standards deal with that sort of thing?' asked Mishra.

Stevens glared at Mishra. 'They asked us to handle it. Romanov's out of their league. She's too clever.'

'What do you mean 'clever'?' asked Ross.

Stevens paused for a few seconds. 'She just seems to know more than she should. As if she's genuine.'

'Perhaps she is,' said McLeod. 'My old grannie always reckoned she had the second sight.'

Ross was tempted to remark it was clear McLeod hadn't inherited his ancestor's ability, having struggled with the first variant. 'Linda, are you suggesting she was using devious means to get the information?'

'Yes, guv, so there's a case under both the Human Rights Act and Data Protection. Romanov always insisted in a preliminary meeting in her victim's homes so we suspect she may have placed covert recording devices.'

Mishra raised her hand. 'Are you seriously suggesting our murderer is a fortune teller?'

'No way,' replied Stevens. 'Romanov's a forty-something and size somewhere north of twenty. I can't see her running about in a hoodie. But...' A pause for dramatic effect. 'She's got a daughter called Kezia who Northampton thinks may be involved. Bit of a wild child by all accounts. Kezia was a suspect in a murder at one time and earned an honourable mention in a domestic violence investigation. Romanov could be using her to break into her victims' properties.'

Ross raised his eyebrows. 'The daughter was implicated in a murder case?' *We could wrap this one up quicker than I thought.* 'Explain please. Start with this murder.'

Stevens grinned, savouring her moment in the spotlight before replying. 'It was a girl at her school. Kezia and the victim were at one another's throats a few hours' earlier and she was killed near the Lees' home.'

'So why wasn't Kezia charged?'

'It seems they thought the victim was raped,' said Stevens. 'But I got the impression they're reopening the case. New evidence.'

'How was she killed?' asked Mishra.

'A bang on the head,' said Stevens. 'Might not be a coincidence.'

'And the domestic violence?'

'A barney with the boyfriend. He came out worse but refused to cooperate. She's obviously a nasty little cow.'

'Okay,' said Ross. 'Let's not get carried away. Ann, anything to report on the incident in Chalk Hill Road?'

'Whoever carried it out is no mug,' said Woodhead. 'No prints, nothing left behind. The back gate was recently oiled from the outside, probably with a spray-on lubricant. The suspect came prepared with all the right tools, so a hammer isn't out of the question.'

Ross wrote 'Intruder – hammer? – Kezia Romanov?' on the whiteboard. 'The neighbour thought the intruder had something in her hand, assuming of course it was a girl. It's possible it might have been a hammer, she panics, runs into the park straight into the hooker, then she lashes out.'

'Not quite,' said Woodhead. 'She wouldn't have run straight into the victim. Otherwise, the body would have been on the path, or we'd have found bloodstains and drag marks leading into where we found it.'

Stevens clapped. 'Then Kezia must have hidden in the bushes, not knowing the tom was already there. She hears a voice and hits out.'

'Presumably, she took the cash,' suggested Mishra. 'The victim would have just finished servicing a client – no other reason to be there.'

Ross tapped the whiteboard with his pen. 'Why smash up the face? If it was a reactive thing she'd have hit once and run.'

'Simple,' said Stevens. 'Kezia's a violent little psychopath.'

'Okay, we have a person of interest,' said Ross. 'No more at present. And we can't rule out this Kezia being the victim. She matches Christie's description.'

'Bit odd going out robbing an old lady's house with a pack of three,' said McLeod. 'She must have felt lucky.'

Stevens shook her head. 'Give it up, Hamish. It's odds on the little cow is on the game as well.'

Ross added 'Prostitute?' against Kezia's details. 'Let's check if this Kezia is dead or alive before we jump to conclusions. Kirsi, what's the current status?'

Stevens sat down, allowing Mishra to take centre stage. 'We've got uniforms searching Old Library Wood for the murder weapon. We'll extend the hunt to gardens in the vicinity if necessary. This evening we'll begin house-to-house enquiries as well as finding any sex workers who might know the victim.'

'Thanks, Kirsi,' said Ross.

'What about getting the Press guys to release a picture of the victim?' asked Mishra.

'Not a good idea the way she is but the forensic team are working on it,' said Ross. 'Ann?'

'The lab is trying to get DNA from the victim's clothes as well as prints from the bag and its contents. We're also looking at the tooth we found in her locket. It's a fair chance it comes from a relative of the victim. And there's the semen and saliva. We should get the results by Monday.'

Mishra spoke again. 'Should we bring in a profiler?'

'Too early,' Ross replied. 'Devlin won't spend the money until we've exhausted all other avenues.' He raised the pen to the whiteboard. 'Three lines of enquiry. First, Kezia Romanov.'

He wrote the phrase 'Kezia – Linda'. 'Linda, obtain a search warrant and turn the Romanov's home inside out. I realise this is compromising your case, but you're free to look for cameras, footage, anything that might help. After establishing if Kezia is still alive, the primary objective is finding the murder weapon and clothes she was wearing.'

'Will do, guv,' said Stevens. 'One point though – Kezia is still known as Lee. Only the old girl saw the need to change her name.'

'Sir,' said Mishra, 'if Kezia was intending to break in, it might be to retrieve whatever device her mother placed. We should search Mrs Leadbetter's house.'

'Good point, Kirsi. She's met me, so I'll do it. Perhaps bring the neighbour along.'

'Would Mr Christie be able to identify Kezia?' asked Stevens.

'Doubt he could recognise himself in a mirror,' replied Ross. 'Right, second possibility… Murdered by a client.' He wrote 'Punter – Kirsi'. 'Kirsi, hope you've not got a hot date tonight because I'd like you to visit Rosary Road and Rouen Road and talk to the street girls. Show them the victim's picture and see if they can ID her. Ask them about any punters who've shown signs of violence. In the meantime, can you check with the search teams?'

'Don't – ' said McLeod, a smirk vanishing from his face as he decided not to complete a potentially inappropriate comment.

Mishra turned. 'Don't what? I suppose the prospect of me walking the streets has some appeal.'

Ross raised his voice. 'Third possibility. Killer is an unknown intruder.' He wrote 'Burglar – Hamish' on the board. 'Hamish, I want you to identify the usual suspects, breaking and entering with a penchant for violence.'

McLeod grunted agreement. Then: 'What about a fourth possibility? A madman with a hammer?'

Ross smiled as he wrote 'Nutter – Hamish' on the board. 'Excellent suggestion. You can look for anyone released from secure confinement with a history of bopping folks on the head.'

Woodhead broke the ensuing silence. 'David, this could be a drugs deal gone wrong. The victim might have been there to score stuff. Maybe she hadn't got enough cash, so he took his payment in another way.'

Ross nodded. 'Right. I'll check with the drugs boys. The sooner we get the DNA results back, the better. I'm betting once we establish who she is and who provided the semen, we can make an arrest. Anyone else we should consider?'

'What about that woman who stomped all over the crime scene?' asked Woodhead. 'The one who looked like a marshmallow on legs. Classic way of obliterating evidence.'

'Mrs Consodine,' said Ross. 'I wondered about her. Strange woman. No qualms at all about looking at a corpse. Although she didn't really look at it. Just a quick peek as if she wanted to confirm it was still there.'

'Suspicious,' said Mishra.

'I agree,' replied Ross. 'But I can't see her messing up her expensive hairstyle by spraying blood and brains all over it. More likely to freeze her victim with an icy stare.'

Ross dismissed his troops with a sense of foreboding. He'd acquired a team with a chemistry only a bomb-maker would appreciate. The investigation threatened to reopen his old wounds, while his boss demanded quick results with minimum resources.

The detective inspector slumped down at his desk. He rechecked computer records for anything that might drag Sarah Consodine into the picture and found nothing but the litany of complaints she'd generated. In addition to requesting the arrest of prostitutes, she'd raised the issue of illegal parking, insinuated that rubbish thrown into her garden was part of a conspiracy, and reported the theft of a gnome, none of which had been recorded as crimes.

He returned to the never-ending task of paperwork. Who was to do what, why they were doing it, why they weren't doing what was unnecessary? Saturday afternoon… other men his age were playing with their kids, taking part in cricket games, sitting in front of the TV with a beer in their hands… If they did have to work eight days in a row, there was a good chance overtime would be paid. Not at his rank. DCI Devlin would be on the golf course.

Of course, he wasn't a family man. Maybe if things had turned out differently… if *she* was still alive. She was the real reason he sat here.

After a few minutes, boredom kicked in. He googled 'Kezia Lee'. None of the results matched what he knew of the suspect. A quick check of police databases revealed nothing related to the murder and domestic disturbance mentioned by Stevens. No doubt the details mouldered in a dusty box in the archives of Northamptonshire Constabulary. Next, he searched for 'Sabina Romanov'. The first page brought up a plethora of unconnected Facebook entries, so he added 'medium' to his search. He was surprised to find out Kezia's mother had a website.

The layout was simple but effective. The site lacked sophistication, leading him to surmise it had been created by an amateur with basic internet expertise.

He discovered Romanov claimed to be descended from a long line of Romany wise women. Her great-grandfather was a savant related to the Imperial Russian Court who had studied the 'mysterious arts' across Eastern Europe and Tibet. Prospective clients had to fill in a web-based form leaving an address and contact number. There was no other way to reach Sabina Romanov.

The medium's pages contained several testimonials confirming her remarkable paranormal powers, most from women in Northamptonshire. He checked the site ownership. Whoever ran it had set all the privacy markers. The American hosting company would be unlikely to reveal any details.

Ross decided it was unlikely to be relevant to the case. But his guess was the answer would only increase his curiosity about Kezia Lee.

An hour later Stevens appeared.

Ross redisplayed Romanov's web page. 'You seen this?'

The DC scanned the screen. 'She's as Russian as I am. But as for being a pikey, yes.'

'Don't use that word in public,' warned Ross. 'I take it you've got the warrant?'

Stevens nodded. 'Any chance we could get it signed today?'

'You ever tried getting hold of a judge or magistrate on a Saturday?'

'It's just the longer we wait the more chance they've got to dispose of evidence.'

Ross pulled an address book out of his desk. 'Okay, we can try a few of the local beaks. I need to get out of here. Come on.'

The first magistrate's home they visited was a villa in the nearby hamlet of Trowse. It yielded no answer. Ross's next target was a large house near the village of Stoke Holy Cross, four miles away to the south.

'How do you find CID?' he asked Stevens as they crossed over the A47, the dual carriageway skirting the southern edge of the city.

'Very enjoyable. I'm taking my sergeant's exam next week.'

'Where were you before?'

'I started work as an engineer, believe it or not. When I was twenty-five, I was made redundant, and I decided to join the police. I did three years on the beat and applied for the move into CID. Hardly fast track.'

'Slow and steady,' he said. 'We need people like you who've been there, done that.'

'It does piss me off sometimes to see who's been promoted without doing the basics.'

'You mean Kirsi?'

'No, not specifically.' Stevens gazed out of the window at a field full of sheep. 'Who are we trying to see next?'

'Nigel Warder. Magistrate. You heard of him?'

'Christ, soft-touch Warder? We all know him. The prisons would be empty if he was in charge.'

Ross grinned. 'Right, him. He's not so bad. You'd better be nice to him or he won't sign our bit of paper.'

Stevens turned to gaze at him. 'Guv, why did you join the force?'

'Not a lot else to do with an ordinary degree in history from Glasgow. The police or teaching.'

'Yeah, but why here?'

Ross sensed the subtle edge in her question. She delivered it in the way she'd ask a suspect if he was at the scene of a crime, secure in the knowledge she had witnesses to confirm the interviewee was guilty.

'Personal.' *That's all you're getting.* 'Warder's house is somewhere on the left.'

He slowed down until he spotted a large two-storey villa set back from the road, partly hidden by tall trees. The structure was recent, but its architecture paid homage to Art Deco.

Warder was at home. Evidently not alone, as his driveway was so full of vehicles they had to park on the road. A Maserati, two Bentleys and a Rolls Royce sat among the BMWs, Volvos and Audis. A harmony of conversations and jazz music drifted from the rear of the white-walled property.

A tall blonde woman wearing a matching white jacket and skirt accessorised by a diamond necklace and bracelet answered the doorbell. Ross estimated her age as around forty, but carefully applied makeup might have masked a few extra years. Her hair was pinned up, her blue eyes unwelcoming.

'Can I help you?'

'Mrs Warder? My apologies. I'm Detective Inspector Ross from Norfolk Police and this is Detective Constable Stevens. We need your husband to sign a search warrant. I wouldn't bother you, but it's urgent.'

'This isn't very convenient.' The woman switched her scrutiny from Ross to Stevens, her eyes registering disdain at the DC's plain navy-blue suit. 'We're entertaining. Can't you find someone else?'

'We've tried. But we're investigating a murder.'

Mrs Warder aimed a hostile stare at Ross but blinked first. 'I suppose he'll have to. Wait here.'

Stevens waited till the door banged shut. 'She's up her own arse. You'd think she'd have invited us round the back.'

'Probably pissed off we didn't look for the tradesmen's entrance,' replied Ross.

He glanced around at the front garden. If it hadn't been for the slope, the lawn could be mistaken for the eighteenth green at St Andrews. The flowerbeds were immaculate and weed-free. Ross suspected neither of the Warders ever got dirt under their fingers.

Five minutes later Nigel Warder opened the door. Balding, stockily built, fit and tanned, the magistrate exuded confidence and authority. The navy suit and pale blue silk tie enhanced the perception. He was not alone. Beside him stood a woman in her early fifties with short brown hair, wearing a cream outfit and a patronising smile. Ross didn't need an introduction.

'DI Ross,' she said. 'I wasn't aware you had an invite.'

Assistant Chief Constable Alison Forsyth. His boss's boss. Popular with her officers, but not the sort of person you'd want to antagonise.

'Sorry, ma'am, but we need a warrant signed. It's a murder investigation.'

'The prostitute? DCI Devlin mentioned you were acting as SIO on the case. Does this mean you have a prime suspect?'

Ross decided honesty was the best policy. 'I'd prefer to say person of interest. DS Stevens was conducting an unconnected investigation, but it seems one of her suspects may have been robbing a house nearby at the same time and we can't ignore it. At the very least, the girl might be a witness. Or even the victim.'

Warder stepped forward. 'Am I right in assuming you want me to sign your warrant just to satisfy your curiosity over a probable coincidence?'

'Sir, I'd be asking you to sign it even if it just concerned the housebreaking angle. The reason I'm interrupting you on a Saturday is a young woman's dead and we both know the circumstances suggest this murder might be the first of many if we don't close it quickly.'

'Hmm.' Warder glanced at Alison Forsyth. 'One mustn't be seen to be soft on crime. Very well, let me see your warrant.'

Ross handed over the papers and a pen. Warder made a point of scrutinising the document.

'What's your gut feel, David?' asked Forsyth.

Ross noted the use of his first name. He'd escaped the naughty step. 'We think the victim might have been at the scene with a client. The lab is looking at DNA evidence and with luck we'll have a name by Monday. My money's on the punter although there's a possibility this girl saw what was happening and waited for an opportunity to mug the tom.'

'DCI Devlin has assured me the investigation will be concluded without delay.' She smiled. 'Indeed, I'm surprised he's not here instead of you.'

'Busy man, I expect,' replied Ross.

Forsyth shot back a knowing smile.

Warder handed back the signed warrant and pen. 'Let's hope this proves worthwhile,' he said. 'Ali, I need to return to my guests.'

'I'll join you in a second.' Forsyth waited till Warder was on his way. 'I'm tempted to come with you. This is not my idea of a fun afternoon.'

'Sounds jolly from here, ma'am,' said Stevens.

'You're hearing a gathering of the great and good of the East Anglian Conservative associations. We've even got a couple of MPs. Nigel is making a bid to become a candidate in the next election, so he's summoned me as a representative of Norfolk Constabulary to show his commitment to law and order.'

'Sounds like you didn't volunteer,' said Ross.

'The higher power believes we have to suck up to the governing party. God knows why. But no surprise he had a prior engagement, so I have to endure Mr Warder's hospitality.'

'We call him 'soft touch',' said Stevens.

Ross grimaced, waiting for Forsyth to deliver a tirade towards his junior officer.

Forsyth merely laughed. 'Good for you, girl. Mind you, you'll see a different Nigel Warder from now on. Tough on crime. That's what the Tories want. Pity they won't fund it.'

'Have you mentioned the fact?' asked Ross.

'Repeatedly. All I get is speeches on the need for austerity from people with a glass of champagne in their hand. Apparently, we're all in this together.'

Ross laughed. 'I'll remember that next time I have to abandon an investigation through lack of resources.'

'Don't abandon this one, David. Oh, by the way, we've got one of your witnesses here. A Mrs Sarah Consodine.'

Ross tried to hide a grimace. 'Oh.'

'You don't need to hold back. Appalling woman. She spent ten minutes lecturing me on how our standards have dropped. I'm not surprised there's no sign of a husband.'

'Probably keeps him chained up in the cellar.'

'Hmm, splendid idea. I should consider doing the same to Mr Forsyth.' The last remark was directed towards Stevens. 'I don't see why he should enjoy a day's golf while I suffer this lot. Still, one must make sacrifices for the greater good.' She looked back at the house. 'I'd better get back. Best of luck with the investigation.'

Ross nodded a thanks.

'Oh, DS Stevens. Do you mind if I have a private word with the inspector?' She waited until Stevens was halfway down the drive. 'David, are you okay about this investigation? You understand…?'

'Yes ma'am.'

'Do any of your team know?'

'I'm not sure. They haven't mentioned it, but…'

Forsyth placed a hand on his arm. 'They won't hear it from me.' With that she turned and re-entered the house.

'She's okay,' said Stevens when they reached the car.

Ross shook his head. 'Some of the old guys call her the Plum. Soft on the outside, hard as nails on the inside.'

'She probably has to be like that to get where she is.' Stevens looked ahead. 'Being a woman and all.'

Ross should have given Stevens some sage advice about what she needed to do to succeed in the modern police. Play the game, keep the boss happy, that sort of thing. Trouble was he knew he was no expert. He'd achieved the rank of detective inspector by sacrificing any chance of a normal life. No way did it count as a success.

Instead, on their way back to Bethel Street they plotted the arrest and conviction of Kezia Lee, whatever charge was applicable – robbery, extortion or murder. Or even all three.

Chapter Four

Prince of Wales Road, Saturday night. A neon-splashed parade of pubs, clubs, and eateries of all flavours. Bouncers pushed drunks out of doors, a hen party crowded around one of their number vomiting on the pavement, two groups of youths confronted each other across the street. Ross often thought that if the builders of Norwich Castle had constructed a sewer to carry their filth down to the river it would have most likely taken the same route.

Uniformed officers were out in force as usual, in the hope they would deter trouble. They never did, but with help from an army of black-suited bouncers kept it to a level which delivered no serious injuries or sex attacks. Ross was on his way back to the murder scene to meet up with Mishra. He left the crowds and bright lights behind, crossed the river, then drove along Riverside before turning upwards into the silent darkness of Rosary Road. Even a glimpse of the street sign caused him to shiver.

Mishra had parked within sight of the entrance to Old Library Wood. She wasn't alone in her green Fiat 500. A thin, scowling girl sat in the back, picking at her fingernails.

'Evening sir, this is Mirjeta. Mirjeta Bardici. She's got something to tell you.'

The girl smiled, the kind of artificial expression she'd use on her punters. 'I tell him then I go, right?'

Ross recognised an eastern European accent. She had short spiky blonde hair, and a complexion pale even in the gloom of the car interior. The street had hardened her prettiness, although Ross guessed she was scarcely out of her teens.

'Depends what you tell me,' said Ross.

'I not a whore,' the girl said. 'I wait for my friend and she – ' A long dark fingernail pointed at Mishra, 'tell me she bust me for being whore if I not tell you what I know.'

'This friend. Would he be the guy lurking just around the corner smoking a cigarette? Tall, thin, short jacket?'

'I not know.'

'Mirjeta,' said Mishra. 'If he's forcing you to do this we can help. You understand?'

The girl glanced around. The street was empty. 'I not know what you mean.'

Mishra smiled. 'Now, Mirjeta. The offer still stands. David here is an okay guy. He just wants to find out what you saw last night.'

'I not sure. I no trust the police. You arrest me and send me back.'

Ross thought about taking her back to the station. She was scared, and proximity to her pimp wasn't helping. Instead, he tried his kindest voice.

'Mirjeta… I'm not sure if Kirsi told you, but we're trying to catch a killer. Now you say you're not a prostitute, and I have no reason to suspect you are, but the girls who work here are in danger till we arrest this guy.' He glanced at Mishra, who nodded. 'Were you here this time last night?'

'I might be. With… Trixie…'

'Trixie?' *The victim might have a name.* 'Sorry, carry on, Mirjeta.'

'Trixie was here too. She pick up man called Kendz. Horrible man.'

Ross maintained his friendly tone. 'Why do you say that, Mirjeta?'

'I – Some girls, they talk. They say he likes rough, he hurt them.'

'He's violent?'

'Yes. Girls no want to go with him. Only Trixie. She need quick money. He want me first. I say no.'

'Did you notice anyone else?' asked Ross. 'Around the time Trixie disappeared?'

'I saw some people.'

'What about someone in a hoodie?'

'Yes, I saw girl. At bottom of road.'

Ross continued to turn round to stare at Mirjeta. Through the rear window he noticed a brief flash of light. The pimp had reappeared and lit another cigarette. 'Do you know Trixie's second name?'

'No.'

'You didn't see her again after she vanished with this Kendz?'

A hesitation... 'No.' Mirjeta bit her lip. 'I think Kendz kill her. He very drunk.'

'Why do you think it was Trixie?' asked Ross. 'Did you find her body?'

'No.' Mirjeta was shaking. 'I not go to park. I... I just know. Please let me go meet my friend.'

'Kendz is still out there, Mirjeta,' Mishra said. 'Can you come back to the station with us and give us a description?'

'No, I meet my friend. Please. I tell you, Kendz ugly. He have scars. One eye.'

'Sorry, Mirjeta,' said Ross, 'but I'm going to insist. I promise you won't be arrested.'

'But my friend...'

'Kirsi, take her to Bethel Street. I'll speak to the... friend.'

While Mishra executed a three-point turn, Ross approached the figure who'd been watching them, but now was intent on walking away.

'Excuse me,' called Ross. The man continued to trot towards a block of flats.

'Police, stop!'

Ross's shout achieved its objective. His quarry took four more steps, hesitated, then turned around. Ross noted the short brown hair, the thin face seeming to grow even thinner towards the jawline, the eyes reminding him of a weasel.

'Have you any identification?'

The man mumbled, took out a bulging wallet, extracted a driving licence. 'I done nothing wrong,' he said, handing the card to Ross.

'Ardian Dragusha?' Ross peered at the man. The photograph resembled the figure in front of him; the licence seemed genuine. The address was Unthank Road – a fair walk. He guessed Dragusha had a vehicle parked nearby.

'Yes, I am refugee from Kosovo. I am legal. I done nothing wrong.'

'What brings you here at this time?'

'I look after Mirjeta. It is not safe for a woman on these streets.'

'So why does she go out? Is she a prostitute?'

Dragusha pulled the cigarette out of his mouth and threw it to the ground.

Ross noted where the butt landed. 'Well?'

'She likes to go for walk at night. I protect her. That is all. Why have you taken her?'

'She saw someone who may have been a murderer. We need her to identify him. Would you like me to take you to her?'

Dragusha took out another cigarette. 'No. You bring her home, right?'

'Where's home?'

The pimp didn't answer.

Ross tried again. 'Where should we drop her off?'

'Here. I take her home.'

'Of course. Were you here last night?'

A long pause before Dragusha spoke again. 'Yes, but I see nothing.'

'Are you sure? All night, looking after Mirjeta, and you saw nothing?'

'I watch Mirjeta. I no look anywhere else.'

'Do you know Trixie?'

'No.' Dragusha peered at the pavement.

'Try again, Mr Dragusha. She worked the street alongside Mirjeta. Long brown hair. Probably wearing a dark top and a mini-skirt last night.'

'I maybe see her. But she is whore. I do not speak to whore.'

Ross glanced in the direction of Old Library Wood. If someone like Dragusha committed murder, would he hang around afterwards? Would he leave Mirjeta alone to follow Trixie? *Unlikely in both cases, but...*

'Well, thanks for your time, Mr Dragusha. I'll let you get along now.'

Another inaudible mumble preceded Dragusha walking past Ross and back down Rosary Road. The detective waited until the man was out of sight before taking an evidence bag out of his pocket and carefully scooping up the discarded cigarette.

Ross found an address in his notebook by the cold light of a streetlamp. He didn't need to read the street name – St Leonards Road. *She lived halfway up. She was heading this way when...*

Focus on the present... the guy who found the body.

He fought memories all the way to a cream-washed terraced house a few score yards up on the left. The door opened to reveal a young woman with a barking dachshund at her feet. She wore designer jeans and a white T-shirt with a glittering heart motif. Ross would have found her attractive were it not for a hardness around her dark eyes.

'Mrs Pritchard?'

'Not yet,' she said. 'I'm Jane Nolan, Keith's fiancée. Are you from the police?'

52

'Is it so obvious?' He produced his badge. 'Detective Inspector Ross. I assume Keith's home?'

Keith Pritchard appeared behind her – a thirty-year-old wearing a Jimi Hendrix T-shirt and jeans. In spite of the rockstar clothing, he still looked like a banker. 'I was expecting you.'

'Sorry it's so late.'

'No problem.' He stood aside to let Ross enter the front room. Bookshelves covered every wall. Every shelf was full.

'Do you work on a Saturday?'

'Big takeover deal.' Pritchard tapped the side of his nose. 'Can't tell you anything more.'

Ross scanned the books. In addition to science fiction and classic novels, the main subjects were travel, photography, and two shelves dedicated to international company law. 'Talk me through the events of this morning.'

Pritchard sat down on the settee opposite Ross. Nolan perched on the arm. 'I was taking Merkel for a walk. The dog, right? Then she started barking. She'd found the body.'

'What time was this?'

'Around half five. No later. I had my phone, so I called it in. I waited for a quarter of an hour, then the policeman turned up. You know, the black one?'

Ross nodded. 'PC Walker.'

'Right. I gave him my details and left.'

'Did you touch the body? You must have considered the possibility she was alive.'

Pritchard glanced at Nolan. 'I – I saw the mess her head was in. I–'

'Keith might have thrown up,' said Nolan. 'He was in shock when he came in.'

'But you still went to work?'

'Jane ran me to the station. I needed to get away, like take my mind off things. I've never seen a dead body before.'

'Where were you last night?'

'God,' exclaimed Pritchard, 'you don't believe I did it?'

'I need to ask.'

'We went out for a meal,' said Nolan. 'At the Belgian Monk in Pottergate.' She cast a knowing look at her fiancée. 'I'm sure the staff will remember us.'

'What time did you get back home?'

The couple again exchanged glances.

'Around ten,' said Nolan. 'Then I took Merkel out for a few minutes.'

'Just you?' Ross turned to Pritchard. 'Didn't you go with her?'

Ross noted another brief unspoken interaction between the couple. *They're hiding something.*

'Um, I was a bit tired. Heavy day and all that.'

Ross turned to Nolan. 'Where did you take Merkel?'

A telling hesitation…

'Along the riverside.'

'Did you spot anything suspicious? Anyone in a hoodie, for example?'

She shook her head.

'What time did you return to the house?'

Another bout of eye contact... 'Um, perhaps half ten,' Pritchard said. 'The news had just finished.'

'Mr Pritchard, we'll need your DNA for elimination purposes.' Ross pulled a kit from his inside pocket.

'Is it necessary?'

'We found some vomit near the body. I recall you mentioned you might've thrown up. We'll need to check DNA, because if it's not yours, it could be the murderer's.'

Pritchard allowed Ross to swab the inside of his mouth. Ross thanked the couple and returned to Bethel Street. His first task was to look up the name Ardian Dragusha on the system. No criminal record; listed as living in Unthank Road. He didn't fancy starting any more paperwork, so he decided to find Mishra.

She was sitting at her desk typing up a report. 'Sorry, sir. Mirjeta wasn't very cooperative. She couldn't describe this Kendz apart from his scars and a missing eye. We've let her go back to Rosary Road to meet her friend.'

'Couldn't or wouldn't?'

'I'd say 'wouldn't'. She's frightened.' Mishra tapped at her mobile and turned it so Ross could observe the screen. 'Check out these. It's her arm. I'm thinking old cigarette burns.'

'Nothing recent?'

'Nothing visible. Could be she's learned her lesson. She wasn't too happy about me taking this picture.'

'Did you get her address?'

'Funny that. She hadn't a clue. All she said was it was past the cathedral on the hill. I reckon she means the Catholic one. Any luck with the boyfriend?'

'Something's not right,' replied Ross. 'I'm surprised he's not on the system. I've got his DNA, so that might tell us different. One thing though… he lives in Unthank Road, which is probably where we'd find Mirjeta. I saw Pritchard as well. There's something not kosher there either.'

'Pity the search couldn't turn up the murder weapon. We'll extend it tomorrow. This Kendz sounds a likely suspect, doesn't he?'

'A person of interest, no more. He might like rough sex, but it's a big jump from that to smashing somebody's brains out with a hammer. Who carries a hammer around with them, anyway?'

'You still reckon this Kezia Lee is prime suspect?'

'Or whoever the burglar was. I'm not assuming anything at this point. We'll find out more tomorrow. And in the meantime, sod off home. It's late and we need you fit in the morning.'

Ross walked back to his desk. He sensed the metaphorical finger of bureaucracy pointing at his incomplete paperwork. In his imagination he raised a single middle digit towards the pile. He then drove to his empty flat, his goal two real fingers of ten-year-old Laphroaig.

Chapter Five

Sunday morning, eight o'clock. Not early enough to qualify as a dawn raid, but it woke Kezia from a troubled sleep on the sofa in the room serving as her bedroom, lounge and kitchen. A hammering on the door, a screamed, 'Police. Open up!'

She pulled on a T-shirt and jeans before staggering to the door. Even with glazed eyes she could see the man wasn't unattractive. Probably early thirties, but she suspected lack of sleep and a poor diet didn't flatter him. She observed his brief and troubled intake of breath when he first saw her before her attention was diverted to the scowling woman behind him, and at her back, two uniformed constables.

'Yeah,' Kezia yawned. *Why were they here? What had she left behind at the house in Chalk Hill Road?*

'Are you Kezia Lee?' asked Ross.

'That's a bloody hard question to start with.' *I remind him of someone.* 'Yes, I am she. So?'

'We have a warrant to search these premises.' Ross held up a piece of paper while he scanned the room. A blue jogging top, white bra and knickers lay on the floor next to an old brown leather couch covered in a blanket. A table wedged in the corner beside an oven, two cups sitting on top. Further along was a shelf supporting a microwave, next to that a sink. Facing him were two doors, side by side. A portable clothes hanger sat in front of the far wall, on which were hung coats and some brightly coloured skirts. An aroma of incense and cheap tobacco pervaded the flat.

'Stinks like a Turkish brothel,' said Stevens.

'You'll be the expert,' said Kezia, thinking about slamming the door in their faces, but Stevens was past her too quickly. The four police officers donned rubber gloves.

'Where's your mother?' asked Ross.

'Bit old for you,' said Kezia. 'And she doesn't like rude men.' She spun round to observe Stevens carefully picking up the clothes from the floor. 'Or women. This isn't a jumble sale.'

Sabina emerged from the left-hand door, hair in curlers, the first cigarette of the day wedged between her fingers. 'Who is it?'

Kezia turned to her mother. 'Goldilocks and the three little pigs. Too early for the party.'

Stevens stomped across the room until her face was six inches from Kezia's. 'Be very careful what you say.'

'Wise advice,' snapped Kezia. 'I shall treasure it.'

'Kezia,' said her mother, 'be civil. We must always cooperate with the custodians of law and order.' She smiled at Ross. 'How can we help you, officer?'

Ross decided these two were trouble. 'Madam, we have reason to believe your daughter was in the vicinity of Rosary Road on Friday evening. She may have witnessed a serious crime.' He watched for a reaction. While Sabina stayed calm, a split-second of nervousness showed on Kezia's face.

'What time, officer?' asked Sabina.

'After ten o'clock.'

'Then it wasn't her. You were back by seven, weren't you, sweetie?'

'Right. I was tucked up in bed by ten. Bit of a headache.'

Ross gently pushed Stevens aside. 'Miss Lee, suppose I said I had a witness who could place you in the back garden of a house in Chalk Hill Road.'

'Then he'd be a liar.'

'How do you know it's a *he?*'

She'd made a slip. Cool it, girl. 'If it lies, it must be a man.'

Ross beckoned to the two uniformed officers. 'Jim, take the bedroom. Harry, bathroom. You know where to look.'

'I need a pee first,' protested Kezia.

Stevens answered with a triumphant grin. 'Try crossing your legs.'

Kezia and Sabina looked on as every item in their home was examined, picked or rolled up, shaken, and in some cases bagged. Stevens showed particular enthusiasm over Kezia's black hoodie, trainers, and a can of WD40 found under the sink.

'Okay,' said Ross. 'Go pee.' He looked at one of the uniforms. 'No way out of there, is there?'

Shake of the head.

Kezia disappeared into the bathroom. The privacy gave her a chance to hide the android tablet she'd stuffed down the back of her jeans when the police entered.

Ross turned to Sabina, who now occupied most of the sofa. *Are these two really related?* 'Mrs Romanov, can you please tell me where you and your daughter actually were on Friday night?'

'Here.'

'All night?'

'Kezia got back from work at seven. Then she studied until ten.'

'Studied? At college, is she?'

'Open University. She's doing a degree in psychology.'

Stevens was examining a notebook. 'Mrs Romanov, there's an entry here marked *Phyllis Leadbetter*, with some nonsense written underneath. Can you explain?'

'I'm a psychic consultant. Mrs Leadbetter is one of my clients.'

Kezia reappeared and squeezed herself onto the sofa beside her mother.

Ross smiled at Kezia before asking: 'What's a psychic consultant?'

Sabina assumed a smug expression. 'I have supernatural gifts, you know. I contact the recently deceased.'

'You're a medium,' said Stevens.

'No.'

More a large, thought Ross. 'What's the difference?'

'A medium is merely a channel for the dead to communicate. They have no control over the conversation. I speak to the departed.'

'You're a fraud,' said Stevens. 'Come on, speak to my old granny. Her name is Phoebe. Ask her what her dog was called.'

Sabina sniffed. 'It doesn't work like that. When our souls depart our bodies, we go into the wilderness of transition.

60

There the soul remains until it is ready to move through the second veil into the unknown land beyond.'

Kezia's mother stared through the small window over the sink as if the unknown land lay in the upper floors of the neighbouring multi-storey car park. Ross suspected this was a well-rehearsed speech. 'The soul cannot move on until it is at peace. That is why the unburied, those who seek justice, those whose conscience will not let them rest, and other troubled spirits, remain to produce the phenomena we call ghosts.'

Stevens grunted. 'So, granny's moved on?'

Sabina smiled. 'I hope so, my dear.'

'What does this stuff mean?' asked Stevens, stabbing at the notebook.

Sabina's infuriating grin remained. 'It's the language of the spirits, my dear.'

Ross moved his chair forward till he was a foot away from Kezia. 'Where's the hammer, Miss Lee?'

Kezia made eye contact and kept it. *I trouble him in some way.* 'What hammer?'

She's a good liar. 'The one you used when you broke into Mrs Leadbetter's.'

A brief hesitation… eye contact lost for a split second… 'I don't know what you're talking about.'

Not that good a liar. 'Okay, I'd like both of you to come with me to the station to provide fingerprints and DNA.'

'Do we need a lawyer?' asked Sabina.

'Not if you're innocent,' replied Ross.

Nobody spoke as they travelled along the inner ring road to Bethel Street. Not that Kezia remained ignorant of the inspector's thoughts: a confusion of intrigue, desire, suspicion, and nervousness. Ross left the pair with a female officer who swabbed and inked them. He made a few phone calls. Afterwards he and Stevens sat across a coffee-stained table from Kezia and her mother in a small interview room.

Ross stared at both of them for twenty seconds. 'Anything you'd like to say before we let you go home? How about the truth?'

Kezia mumbled at the table. 'We've told you the truth.'

'Speak up for the recorder, please,' said Stevens.

Kezia looked up. 'We've told you the bloody truth. Did you get that, or do you want to fetch a megaphone?'

Ross glanced at his notes. 'I've been doing some checking. About this degree you're doing. The Open University, isn't it? They've got no record of you.'

Kezia wondered how he'd found out on a Sunday. She tried to read him, check if he was bluffing. *Why can't I tell if he's lying? Maybe there's a database the police can access listing every student at every university. On the other hand...*

'I'd ask them to check again. Who did you speak to?'

Ross blinked. 'I can't remember.'

Porky. Kezia stared at the two detectives. Okay, she'd called his bluff – a pyrrhic victory. She tried to read Ross again. *He's far more interested in me than the enquiry justifies. As for Stevens...* Kezia saw a growling dog that wouldn't let go. Neither of them would resist the temptation to phone the OU when it opened on Monday.

'Okay, I just want to get a GCSE. I tell people it's Open University 'cause it sounds better.'

Stevens leaned across the table. 'You're lying.'

Kezia decided to take the offensive. 'I'm not. Not now, anyway. And, hey, like what are you accusing me of? Studying without a licence?'

'Breaking and entering,' answered Stevens. 'And conspiracy to defraud.' She looked at Sabina. 'Both of you.'

'So, what part of me learning stuff is a crime?'

Sabina patted her daughter on the shoulder. 'I'd like to understand why I'm here. You seem to be intent on framing poor Kezia, so why do I have to provide DNA and fingerprints?'

Stevens sat back, arms folded. 'Because we think – '

Ross held up a hand. He didn't want the pair to guess they suspected Sabina had planted a bug. 'It's routine, Mrs Romanov, that's all. I can promise if you haven't done anything wrong, we'll purge you from our records.'

Kezia wasn't detecting sincerity. She said nothing. *Antagonising these two any further won't be a wise move.*

Ross had used a fib to persuade Kezia to confess an untruth once already in the interview. He tried again.

'Now, Miss Lee. You say you arrived home at seven o'clock on Friday and didn't go out again. Suppose I told you we've got you on CCTV leaving the Rosary Road area around quarter to eleven.'

Definite lie. 'That's impossible. It must have been someone who looked like me.'

This time her victory was absolute.

'We're pretty sure it's you,' said Ross.

Even Pinocchio could hide an untruth better than this.

'Well, I can assure you it's not.' Kezia wasn't going to explain she knew the location of every camera on her route.

Ross ended the interrogation. He refused Sabina's request for a lift home and returned to the interview room.

Stevens looked glum. 'Pair of liars, guv. Should we put a tail on them?'

'No point. The old girl'll stay put and I've a feeling that Kezia lass is clever enough to give us the run-around. No, Linda, we've got to be patient with those two. One of them will slip up before long.' He could see Stevens was disappointed. 'But Linda, it's your case. It's your decision what to do next.'

***

At two o'clock Ross sat alone at his desk staring at the whiteboard. The door-to-door enquiries, the extended searches, revealed nothing. McLeod had identified four possible leads who'd been released, but one had moved to Newcastle and the other three had rock-solid alibis.

Ross was now convinced the hammer lay under the Wensum's muddy waters. Devlin wouldn't pay for divers to search the meandering watercourse between Bishop's Bridge and Fye Bridge – the likely route Kezia would have taken. And the river would have contaminated any DNA or fingerprints on the weapon.

Nobody called 'Kendz' with the right profile existed in their online files. Ross had allowed his team the rest of the day off. Unlike him, they had lives outside of the police.

He didn't even know who the victim was. There wasn't a likely 'Trixie' in the system either.

The board showed seven suspects: Kezia Lee, 'Kendz', Ardi Dragusha, Keith Pritchard, Jane Nolan, Sarah Consodine, and A.N. Other. He could do nothing until time and forensics allowed.

His thought drifted back to Kezia's eyes: blue, beautiful, dangerous. Eyes that summoned ghosts. Windows into a world he couldn't understand.

Most certainly a person of interest.

Chapter Six

Kezia left the flat at half-past seven on a grey Monday morning, worried about what a forensic investigation would discover on her hoodie and shoes. What had she touched? She'd been careful on her way towards the Leadbetter house, but once the neighbour had spotted her she'd… *perhaps not panicked… more acted without thought*. Hell, no, she'd panicked.

Egress from their temporary home required her to descend a metal stairway into a courtyard behind a shop. Kezia reached halfway down when an image crashed into her brain – *a dark creature, malevolent, piercing eyes…* Evil lurked nearby and it shadowed her. She looked around but saw nothing out of the ordinary.

Perhaps she should seek psychiatric help to stop the visions? Except they weren't random. She hadn't been alone on Friday night, and now she reaped the consequences. She'd sensed the police closing in. And now? Something else stalked her. And not just a guilty conscience.

The sensation never left her as she walked to work. Every so often she turned around, only to see nothing suspicious save slight movements as if her pursuer hid in doorways, anticipating when she would glance back.

She reached the café and helped lay the tables. Then she saw him… or her. A black hood, a face in shadow on the other side of the street. The invisible eyes stared at her, and the voice in her head was screaming…

Those eyes have seen you before.

***

Ross again nursed a minor hangover. He'd consumed one glass of Islay malt too many, and not eaten enough, as he digested the Sunday papers. At nine o'clock on a Monday morning, he again stood in the small room at Bethel Street addressing his team.

McLeod brought in a copy of the *Eastern Daily Press*. The murder had made it to the front page, accompanied by a photograph of Sarah Consodine looking cross.

McLeod waved the paper at Ross. 'Says here this Mrs Consodine reckons it's all our fault, because, and I quote, we allow prostitutes to ply their trade freely in front of her house.' He grinned and looked at each of the others. 'Didn't appreciate they were giving it away for nothing these days.'

Ross seized the paper and read the article again. 'Bloody Mrs Consodine.'

'She's got a point though, guv,' said Stevens. 'Soliciting in a public place is illegal, so why don't we do something about it?'

Ross handed the paper back. 'Try proving it in court. You can't touch them for simply standing on the pavement.' He tapped the whiteboard. 'Our job is solving a murder. I've got DCI Devlin's agreement to release an artist's impression of the victim to the local media. Hopefully, someone will recognise it.

'Linda, I'd like you to go to Northampton. Speak to the detectives who failed to prosecute Sabina Lee or Romanov or whatever she calls herself. Look at their evidence, in particular anything they've got on Kezia. Signs of violence, especially. Hamish, check out every CCTV camera, public or private, between Magdalen Street and Rosary Road to see if we can pick up Kezia. I'm certain this story about getting home at seven is a pack of lies.'

He nodded at Mishra. 'Kirsi, show the victim's picture around sexual health clinics and local GP surgeries. Chances are she's visited them on a few occasions.'

The breakthrough came at quarter past nine. The front desk called to say someone waited in reception asking to speak to the officer in charge. They'd had a few time-wasters – this one appeared different.

Ross and Mishra went down to discover a man in his early twenties standing in reception, reading the two brass memorials to officers killed in the wars. He was thin, with heavily tattooed arms. His brown hair was swept back from his forehead, accentuating half-closed eyes in a pale face that bore all the signs of recent heroin use. He sported flesh tunnels in both ears.

Sy Mercer, as he introduced himself, soon sat in an interview room, recorder running, hands trembling, eyes darting between Mishra and Ross.

'Yeah, like I'm her boyfriend. Gotta be, see. She didn't come home. Like maybe she scored a trick, so I'm not worried, but – '

'Sorry, Mr Mercer, can – '

'Call me Sy. Mr Mercer, no like.' Mercer's entire body began to shake. 'Hell, can I have some water or something?'

'DS Mishra is leaving the room at nine twenty-two,' Ross told the recorder. He said nothing until she returned with a glass and a case file.

'DS Mishra has returned at nine twenty-four. Now, Sy, have a drink and calm down. First, what's your girlfriend's name?'

Mercer drained the glass before replying. 'Um, Suze. Suze Smith.'

'Not Trixie?'

'No… well, like maybe she calls herself Trixie when she's working.' Mercer took a gulp of water. 'So, does that mean you've found her? Like she's dead?'

'Why are you sure it's her?'

'Like I said, she didn't come home. An' she worked up Rosary. Shit, this is bad.' He drained the glass. 'So, do I get compensation?'

Ross glanced at Mishra, who opened the file. She slid the artist's impression of the victim across the table.

Mercer gagged, eyes were wide with fear. 'Shit… Yeah, that's her. Like what am I goin' to do?'

'Do you need more water?' asked Ross.

Mercer nodded and Ross sent Mishra for more, the recorder being apprised of her journeys.

'Where were you Friday night? Between nine and midnight?'

'Shit, I don't know. I might've been on the street. Maybe I was home. Hell…'

Mishra came back with yet another manila folder in addition to the glass. She passed the folder to Ross. It contained a single sheet of paper.

'Sy, it appears you're no stranger here. May the seventeenth this year. Domestic disturbance. Officers called by the neighbours, Susan with bruises on her face, refused to press charges.'

Another swig of water. 'So? Like it was just an argument. Fucking cow next door should mind her own business.'

'April the sixth. Breach of the vagrancy act in Gentleman's Walk. You accepted a caution.'

'So fucking what?'

'June the thirteenth. Appeared before the magistrates on a charge of begging. Let off on a technicality.'

'You lot got it in for me, see. Like I'd no money to get home. So I ask a few people, then I get busted.'

'You live in Mile Cross. You could've walked. Not sworn at everyone who passed by.'

'I was sick. Should've got treatment. Medicines 'n stuff.'

'Are those needle marks on your arms?' asked Mishra.

'So? You won't find any stuff on me. I'm clean, see.'

Ross shuffled his papers. 'Did Susan have a mobile?'

'Yeah. Dunno why. Nobody called.'

'What sort?'

'Dunno. Cheap one from Tesco, maybe.'

'Do you remember the number?' Mercer nodded. 'Then can you please write it down?'

Ross placed a pen and paper in front of Mercer.

Ross closed the folder and watched Mercer slowly scribbling the victim's number. The quality of the writing would have earned a six-year-old extra tuition. 'How do you feel about your girlfriend having sex with other men?'

Mercer wiped his nose on his sleeve. 'We need the money.' He sniffed and knocked back the last of the water. 'When do I get the compensation?'

'Can't be nice,' said Mishra. 'Don't you ever wonder about what she's doing? What she's thinking? Perhaps the punter's better looking than you, a bit of money, a bit of class. She might reckon, wow, this is cool, I could do this for free with this guy.'

Mercer scratched his left forearm. 'Like I don't think about it. You got a boyfriend?' His voice raised half an octave. 'How does he feel about you hanging around with this old guy? Same thing, innit?'

Ross sensed Mishra wanted to punch Mercer.

Instead, she took four deep breaths and smiled. 'Look, Sy, we understand how upset you are. The DI and I want to clear this up as soon as possible, don't we, sir?' She acknowledged Ross's nod. 'I mean, nobody will talk about compensation until we establish it is murder, and you didn't do it.'

'Like–' The voice still high.

'We need to prove that. So why don't you let us take you home and have a look at your place? Find out if Susan left any clues? Okay?'

Mercer nodded. Ross grinned. They wouldn't need to bother Nigel Warder or any other magistrate in order to search their new suspect's place.

Ross organised a team outing – Stevens continued her investigations in Northampton, so McLeod and Mishra accompanied him along with two uniforms and a photographer.

The terraced house in Mile Cross turned out worse than they feared: dark, untidy, a smell of cheap food and poor hygiene, a jumble of unwashed clothes and black rubbish bags. Used needles lurked in unexpected places. Whatever services Susan Smith provided, they didn't include housekeeping. What they couldn't find were drugs or a hammer. They did uncover a T-shirt with ominous stains on the front. It didn't take a major leap of imagination to assume the garment belonged to Mercer, the blood Susan Smith's.

They took the T-shirt away, but Ross didn't jump to too many conclusions. Kezia and the mysterious Kendz remained ahead in the suspects list. He couldn't see Mercer killing the goose that laid his golden eggs… probably more golden brown than anything else.

His next task comprised writing a report for DCI Devlin. Terse, lacking in detail, merely a list of their potential leads, which now included Sy Mercer. The more effort required, the less Devlin would wish to be involved.

Ross's superior didn't let his DI off lightly when he delivered the report in person. Devlin should have been based at the Force HQ in Wymondham but chose to retain an office in Bethel Street. The DCI sat back behind a desk empty of everything bar a gold fountain pen in a holder, no doubt an award of some kind. Ross couldn't see an inscription but imagined it read 'tosser of the year' or something similar.

'The ACC tells me you thought it necessary to interrupt a private function to obtain a signature. Was it worth it?'

'She didn't seem to mind. Sir.'

'The ACC's views are incidental. More to the point is our relationship with the local bench. We mustn't alienate those on whom we rely to dispense justice. Is that clear?'

'Perfectly.'

'Good. Now please tell me this search proved worthwhile.' Devlin scanned the single-page report. 'Which of these miscreants did it relate to?'

'Kezia Lee. We seized some items that might have been used in the execution of a crime, plus some clothing the subject may have been wearing on the night of the murder. We're waiting for forensics. Whatever the outcome, I'm convinced Lee is lying. She knows something she's not saying.'

'Hmm. Let's hope your confidence isn't misplaced. I'm sure the ACC will show an interest in the outcome.' Devlin scanned the report again. 'What's your next move?'

'Depends what the good doctor comes up with. But as things stand, we need to verify Pritchard's story.'

'Good, I look forward to your next update. That's if you haven't apprehended the killer by then.' Devlin waved a pen in a gesture of dismissal.

The encounter didn't improve Ross's mood. His headache returned before he left the police headquarters. Mishra knew better than to enquire about the cause as they walked past the rear of the city council offices. Their destination was the seventeenth century building in Pottergate housing the Belgian Monk restaurant.

Their luck was in. They were introduced to Laura, who'd served the couple on Friday. The noise in the bar forced the waitress to talk to them outside.

'I won't forget them,' she said. 'They had a blazing argument at the end. All about how much he'd drunk. He'd only had four beers, but they were the nine percenters and she refused to let him drive her home. She stormed out before he'd paid the bill.'

'He did pay, didn't he?' asked Mishra.

Laura smiled. 'Yes, and he tipped well. I guess he was a bit embarrassed.'

'What time did they leave?'

'Gosh, I'm not sure. Lateish – around quarter to ten? You should be able to find out from his credit card details.'

Ross promised Laura he'd visit the restaurant as a customer in the future. He would if he ever found someone to take.

'Celebration here if we nail this one?' asked Mishra.

'My leaving do if we don't.' They were now walking up Lower Goat Lane on the scenic route back to Bethel Street.

'How does that stack with Pritchard's story?' asked Mishra.

'Doesn't help his case. Or hers, for that matter. Sounds like he was over the limit, which might explain his suspicious manner.'

'Also, why he was so quick to throw up,' said Mishra.

By now they'd reached the outdoor market. Ross was too caught up in his thoughts to notice the surrounding activity. *A young man affected by drink, abandoned, albeit temporarily, by his lover – would he seek solace from a street prostitute and then hit out in his shame? Did he have a hammer in his car?*

Charles Porter-Brown waited in reception. 'Afternoon, old chap. Thought I'd pop round and deliver my report personally.'

'Any surprises?' asked Ross.

'Depends on your level of incredulity. Death occurred between half-past nine and eleven o'clock. Blunt force trauma, and the weapon was almost certainly a hammer of the bog-standard claw variety. As anyone with a single brain cell would suspect, not a virgin. She shows no evidence of defensive injuries. Penetrative sexual activity within three hours of her death, and signs of fellatio a few minutes before she expired. I assume you understand what that means?'

'Yes,' said Ross. He guessed Mishra knew as well, although not from personal experience, so he didn't need to explain. 'She wasn't raped when she was murdered?'

'Difficult to prove either way,' replied Porter-Brown. 'Whoever performed in the missionary manner used a condom, so unless you find it, I can't help you. But I'd be somewhat gobsmacked if it's the same chap who allowed her to play his pennywhistle. Her clothes have gone to the lab so you might be in luck. I've also sent mouth swabs to the ladies in white. She had heroin in her system. The poor girl showed extensive signs of drug use. She was finding it hard to hit a vein. I identified bruising around her face and rib area incurred a few days before. Plus a healed fracture of the left arm.'

'What about her last meal?'

'She hadn't eaten for at least eight hours. What about dental records? Do you need information on which teeth remained?'

'We know who she was,' said Mishra. 'Her name is Susan Smith, and she lived in the Mile Cross area with her pimp.'

'I'm not sure our friend Sy carried out even the basic duties of a pimp,' said Ross. 'Anything else?'

'One minor fact that might be interesting. She'd had a caesarean. A few years ago.'

'That ties in with the child's tooth in the locket we found,' said Mishra. 'I wonder what happened to the kid.'

Ross grimaced. 'If it had Sy Mercer as father, then God help it.'

'Well, lads and lassies,' said the doctor, 'I'll leave you my report. Best of luck.'

Ross reached his deck and called Ann Woodhead. 'Ann, could you spare someone to accompany McLeod this evening?

I need you to search for a listening device.' McLeod would appreciate a night out with a CSI – better than looking at CCTV images, which Ross soon learned had been a fruitless exercise.

'Sure, I can spare Jim Eaton,' came the reply. 'He's perfect. At least for Hamish. They can swap dirty jokes. And hot news, we've got the first results back from the lab. You're going to love this.'

'I hope you're not being sarcastic,' he said. 'Shoot.'

'Right, bad news first. No match on the vomit.'

'No problem, we're pretty sure we know whose it is.'

'Good news. We've identified the semen. It belongs to someone called Jeremy Kendal, usually referred to as Jez.'

Or possibly Kendz... 'Why's he in the system?'

'Conviction for assault. He served a year and was released last December.'

'Excellent.' He now had a prime suspect. 'Anything else?'

'The syringe probably lay on the ground for a week. We found one cigarette butt that could have been left around the time of the murder, the others show signs of damp from rain the previous day.'

'DNA?'

'We got a match for that. Probably irrelevant, but it belongs to an asylum seeker. Name of Ardian Dragusha.'

Bugger. Make that two prime suspects. 'Thanks Ann.'

'Oh, and the lab'll send you through a separate report, but they said to tell you the black hoodie had traces of WD40. No blood, though. Plus the trainers have deposits of mud and grass consistent with Old Library Wood. Am I right in assuming they belong to Kezia Lee?'

'Right first time.'

Ross ended the call and summoned Mishra and McLeod to stand before the whiteboard.

'We're getting close,' he said. 'One of these people killed Susan Smith. We have irrefutable physical evidence confirming three of them visited the murder scene, and the odds are another was in the vicinity. Jane Nolan's unlikely.'

'There might be another two suspects,' said McLeod.

'What?'

'I did a search on our records for Susan Smith. Her name came up in a stalking case. She'd complained about a guy called Walter O'Donnell back in 2007. He'd been hanging round outside her flat, calling her at odd times.'

'Long time ago… is it relevant?'

McLeod read his notebook. 'We warned O'Donnell off, but he didn't stop. He received a caution only to have another go. He went inside in 2008. Got out after six months.'

'And? Did he start again after that?'

'No, sir. But we should check him out, shouldn't we? He's obsessed with her.'

'Does he still live in Norwich?' asked Mishra.

'Wymondham,' said McLeod. 'Close enough.'

'It doesn't make sense,' said Mishra. 'She's a sex worker. Why raise her head over the parapet by complaining about a stalker?'

Ross wrote 'Walter O'Donnell' on the whiteboard. Not that he needed another suspect. 'Kirsi, find out what you can about Jeremy Kendal. Hamish, who's the other possibility?'

'I've got the numbers from her mobile. There's only one number she calls regularly. Pay-as-you go, and no record of the owner. She called it at six o'clock the night she died.'

'Okay, Hamish – get the techs to track her phone and that number and then let's go visit Walter.'

***

Wymondham, the town where Robert Kett started his doomed rebellion against church and state in 1549. Ross had a secret admiration for Kett, often viewed as Norwich's version of Robin Hood. That moment he couldn't escape the symbolism that Kett's army gathered in the hills above Rosary Road before sweeping into the city and embarrassing the authorities.

Walter O'Donnell was not at home. His mother, Margery, came to the door of their terraced house in a grey dressing gown, perched on a zimmer frame. She was frail, but her grey eyes glowed with resentment at the arrival of the two detectives.

'Why can't yer stop plaguin' us? My Walter's a good 'un. It was that trollop what got him in trouble.'

She led Ross and McLeod into a front room whose walls were decorated with garish flowered wallpaper, every surface covered in photographs – most of the same male at various stages of life. No doubt Walter. No evidence of any other Mr O'Donnell.

'Can you please tell us where Walter was on Friday night?' asked Ross.

'Why?'

78

'We're investigating a murder. The sooner you answer questions, the sooner we leave.'

'Friday he goes to his club. He come home after half eleven, drunk as a newt. The lummox can't get work, after the trouble.'

Ross heard the front door open. Walter O'Donnell came into the room wearing a tattered 1990s Norwich City top. He was overweight, with a round face. His vacant expression suggested any attempt to join Mensa would be a waste of time. Susan Smith's one-time stalker had arranged his few long strands of hair over an otherwise bald skull.

'Who's this, Ma?'

'Police. They think you killed somebody.'

'Please sit down, Mr O'Donnell,' said Ross. 'Your name has come up in an enquiry, that's all. A loose end we need to tie up, nothing more.'

'It's about her, in't it?'

'Who?'

'Trixie.'

'Trollop,' added Mrs O'Donnell.

'What's she said? I in't been near her. Honest.'

'Where were you Friday night?'

'I tell yer,' shouted Margery O'Donnell.

Walter put a hand on his mother's arm. 'It's all right, Ma. I was at the club. I left afore eleven, came home.'

McLeod opened his notebook. 'They'd remember you, would they? Any names?'

'Old Joe – he's the barman. He'd say I'd had enough. Who's dead?'

'We believe it's Susan Smith,' replied Ross. 'You know her as Trixie.'

Walter's hand flew to his mouth. 'Jesus. I love her. If she'd listened to me, she'd been all right.'

'She's a trollop,' said Margery. 'She led yer astray.'

'It wasn't her what complained.' Walter's voice threatened to break. 'It was that boss of hers.'

'What boss?' asked McLeod.

'Walter done wrong,' said Margery. 'He goes to this club in Norwich. Naughty Step – '

'Hot Steps,' said Walter.

'Dreadful place. This trollop latches onto him, then this man, Tim something – '

Walter corrected her again. 'Tom Vickery.'

'That's him. He gets the law to keep Walter away.'

Ross glanced at McLeod. 'Let me get this right. Susan Smith, or Trixie, worked at Hot Steps for Tom Vickery.'

'Right,' said Walter.

'Well, Mr O'Donnell, Mrs O'Donnell, thank you for your time. We'll verify your alibi, of course, but hopefully we won't be bothering you again.'

'Not now the trollop's dead,' said a triumphant Margery. Walter scowled at her through tearful eyes.

Ross decided Walter didn't have the persona of a violent killer, but procedures dictated he had to confirm the alibi. They walked the four hundred yards to the local social club, a nondescript brick building squatting at the end of a large car park. They entered to find a man in his late seventies cleaning glasses behind the bar.

'Are you Joe?' asked Ross.

'Who wants to know?'

Ross showed Joe his warrant card. 'Police. Do you know anyone called Walter O'Donnell?'

Joe put down his tea towel. 'Why?'

'Please answer the question.'

Joe folded his arms. 'I know Walter. Anything else?'

'Do you remember if he was here last Friday night?'

A scratch of the head. 'Cor, blast me. One day seems the same as any other. I in't sure, but I think he was here.'

'Can you think of anyone else who might remember him?'

The arms folded again. 'If I in't remembering Walter proper, then I in't remembering anyone else what was here. But, Friday... hold you hard... Walter was here. Yeah, he had a skinful and I told him to go home.'

Further questioning revealed nothing. As they left the club Ross glanced back. 'Hardly convincing, was it?'

'Sounded okay to me, guv,' replied McLeod. 'Besides, how could Walter get back from Norwich? There's no sign of a car, and even his old mum said he was drunk. He doesn't look the sort that can afford a taxi.'

'And he's a loner,' said Ross. 'Otherwise, he'd have someone else backing him up instead of a geriatric barman with a dodgy memory. So no mates to drive him.'

'We can rule him out then, guv.'

A turquoise bus rolled past. Number thirteen.

'Hamish, find out when the last one of those rolls in on a Friday. And if it's in the timeframe, get hold of the CCTV if they have it.'

Ross wasn't sure if he'd needed to write the stalker's name on his whiteboard. Some might assume the investigation was flowing along nicely.

But the merest hint that Tom Vickery might be involved had pitched his enquiry into the murkiest of waters.

Chapter Seven

'Tom Vickery.'

Ross banged the whiteboard with his pen. 'Kingpin of crime in Norwich during the noughties and beyond.'

'Is he a Norfolk version of Professor Moriarty?' asked McLeod.

Ross grinned. 'That's close. Except Moriarty kept himself in the shadows. Vickery will never be that shy.'

'Why do you reckon he's involved?' asked Mishra.

Ross sat on the corner of the table. 'Nobody crossed Vickery.' He glanced at the door to check if anybody lurked outside and lowered his voice. 'This place wasn't immune from his influence. He was the subject of a hundred investigations and zero prosecutions. Witnesses tended to change their story or even disappear. Evidence conveniently vanished or ended up compromised. Victims withdrew complaints.'

Mishra's perplexed impression remained. 'But why should he murder Susan?'

'We suspected Hot Steps – that's the club he owns – doubled as a high-class knocking shop until a few years ago. If she was one of his toms, he wouldn't be too happy about her going independent. Plus, she'd have known stuff he didn't want revealed.'

Mishra folded her arms. 'She hasn't just left, has she? I mean, why now?'

'Good point. But maybe she's making more than the girls in the club. Suppose she swans up and talks to them, saying they're working too cheaply.'

'You suggested he was active in the noughties,' said McLeod. 'What about now?'

'Allegedly, and I'll repeat, allegedly, he's gone legit. Hot Steps is now a highly respectable lap dancing club – '

'Is there such a thing?' interrupted Mishra.

Ross grimaced. 'Okay, I'll say 'legal'. He also has a flourishing building business. Some have muttered he finds it easier to get planning permission and buy council land than his rivals, but I'm not commenting.'

Mishra raised her hand. 'Bribery and corruption?'

'As I said, no comment. But Vickery uses other means. Pictures of kids leaving school with a noose drawn over them would do it in some cases. He understands his victims and their weak spots.'

Now it was McLeod's turn to ask: 'If he's legit, why risk it by murder? He might be recognised.'

'He won't get his hands dirty. He used paid muscle in the past. We've got a few names on file that might be worth checking out.' Ross tapped the victim's name, then sat down on the edge of the table. 'Kirsi, what have you found out about Susan Smith?'

Mishra opened her notebook. 'She was born in Great Yarmouth in 1987 to a single mother. Social Services took her into care at the age of three. She spent most of her childhood in a children's home near Yarmouth, relocated to Norwich when she was sixteen. Went on the pill but somehow got pregnant at the age of twenty-one. Moved – '

'Whoa,' interrupted Ross. 'I understood kids stayed in care till they reached eighteen? She should still have been in the system. Kirsi, you need to find out about her social workers. See what they remember.'

Mishra nodded. 'Will do, sir.'

'Thanks. Carry on.'

'Okay. She moved to Nottingham where she gave birth to a daughter. Susan made two visits to an STD clinic, then her child died in 2015. Susan suffered from depression and her shrink prescribed happy pills.' She looked up. 'Dr Porter-Brown's description, not mine. He obtained her medical records, which I'm not sure we should have.'

'We can get them legally if we want,' said Ross.

'Fine, sir. Susan returned to Norwich last year. She paid one more visit to an STD clinic, when they noted early signs of heroin abuse. In November she broke her arm. The hospital suspected it was a domestic, but she said she fell over.'

'Poor girl never had a chance,' said Ross. 'Sounds as if she might have been on the game in Nottingham.'

'Could that be significant?' asked Mishra.

'I doubt it. I'm guessing whoever caused her death is based in Norwich. We could check with the Nottingham force to establish if they have anything, but for now we focus closer to home. The bosses want this one shut down quickly and Kendal ticks all the boxes.'

Ross took a step up to the whiteboard. 'Okay, tonight, six o'clock. Stevens should be back by then, so we'll hit Kendal's house. We've enough to arrest him so no warrant required. In the meantime – '

A female civilian knocked on the door. 'DI Ross, I've got Linda Stevens on the phone. Do you want me to patch her through?'

Ross nodded and waited for the ring. 'Okay Linda, you're on speakerphone. Things are moving but I'll fill you in when we get back. What have you found?'

'Right, the Romanov-Lees. They've been active in Northampton and Brackley. The old girl's good. Half her clients are still convinced she's the genuine article. In fact, one of the guys here reckons she believes it herself, but she needs a bit of window dressing from the daughter.'

'What about the other half of her clients?'

'A few complaints. The main investigation here concerned Kezia. She's a devious little bitch by all accounts. She uses every trick in the book to dig up information. She's been reported going through bins, even intercepting mail. She'll trace people who remember the deceased and press them for info. The guys here reckon she's a hacker to boot.'

'Any use of violence?'

'She was expelled from a couple of schools. Both times for fighting. Ma Lee tells everyone Kezia's a gypsy, and it seems some of the pupils tried to bully Kezia. Bad move. Then along comes the incident at Brackley.'

'The famous incident at Brackley.' Ross laughed. 'Fill us in.'

'Not that funny, guv. When Kezia was thirteen, she came into class, sat down, then suddenly told everyone one of the girls had been murdered. Girl – her name was Hester Boswell – hadn't turned up at school. Her father found her body later that day, and the police never solved the crime. It looked like she was raped, and the cause of death was blunt force trauma.

Kezia never explained how she found out, and the police couldn't build a case against her.'

'Any other incidents?'

'A few tantrums. Left school at sixteen with six good GCSEs but been doing odd jobs to supplement what she gets from mum.'

'So she's smart. What about the father? What happened to him?'

'Her dad was called Byron Lee. Cambridgeshire had him down as involved in a murder in 2006 during a robbery, but they couldn't prove anything. In the end, they got him for receiving. He died in Wellingborough jail following an assault when Kezia was ten. One odd thing – the very same day, she went ballistic and broke a window in her primary school, then attacked another pupil before the headmistress had a chance to break the news of her dad's death. The school called the police, but they took no action due to the circumstances.'

'History of violence, wouldn't you say?'

'Prime suspect, I'd say, guv.'

'Have to disagree. If you can get back here by six, you'll hopefully meet the main contender. Thanks, Linda.'

Ross turned to Mishra and McLeod. 'Phew. That's something to ponder on. Right, Kirsi, I'm going to be sexist and keep you away from Vickery. Believe me, it's for your own good.'

'No problem,' said Mishra, her reply unconvincing.

'Kirsi, what I would like you to do is put the pressure on Miss Lee. The address of the café where she works is in the file. Linda and I have pissed her off. She might respond to a more sympathetic approach. Hamish, with me.'

Tom Vickery's company had office space in an upper floor of the Union Building in Rose Lane. The large sign 'TV Investments' projected an air of prosperity. A tall blonde receptionist wearing an electric-blue designer suit led Ross and McLeod into the inner sanctum.

Vickery stood up. Six foot two, bald with a large forehead, piercing blue eyes. Ross understood how lesser men could be overawed in his presence. Through the window, the DI observed the tall spire of Norwich Cathedral. Prince of Wales Road, that modern Slough of Despond, lurked hidden from view between Vickery's office and the sacred edifice.

'Sergeant Ross, it's been a while.'

Vickery damn well knew Ross's rank. Ross recognised it as a warning.

'Detective Inspector now, Mr Vickery. This is DC McLeod.'

'Call me Tom. I apologise for my error. Your promotion is no doubt deserved. How is DCI Devlin? You must give him my regards.'

Ross wondered about Vickery's relationship with Devlin. Hopefully nothing – yet another attempt to intimidate him.

Vickery sat down in a large, padded leather office chair. 'What can I do for you? I've a meeting at three, so I'm a little pressed for time.'

'We're investigating the death of a Susan Smith. You might remember her as Trixie.'

'Ah, you have an identification now. I attended Nigel Warder's function on Saturday when you called. Nigel didn't seem too happy about your gate-crashing his party.' Vickery rubbed his chin. 'Trixie, you said? The name is familiar. She might have been a dancer at one of my clubs. So long ago, though.'

Vickery ran in the same social circles as Alison Forsyth. The warning bells continued to ring.

'I've been told she worked at Hot Steps. We're just wondering why she left.'

'If it's the Trixie I recall... Eight years ago... Hmm... Right, we had to let her go. Drugs, if I remember. We found out she used heroin and we've got a strict policy.'

'She worked as a prostitute when she died. I'm wondering if she was on the game when she worked for you.'

Vickery put on a good impression of someone who felt insulted. 'I don't tolerate such behaviour. If we suspect any of our hostesses or dancers are using their position to indulge in immoral activity, then we'd show them the door. Am I making myself plain, officers?'

'Certainly, Mr Vickery. Did she establish relationships with any of your staff?'

'We dissuade our people from becoming entangled, but human nature being what it is... You understand. However, I don't remember Trixie being involved with anyone.'

'Could you provide us with a list of club employees when she left?'

'You'll understand that in our business some of the girls are a little reluctant to allow their details to be published. If you can obtain the appropriate legal documentation, we will certainly attempt to comply but otherwise I can't. I'll provide you with our lawyers' contact numbers.'

'This is a murder investigation, Mr Vickery.'

'I appreciate that, but I have a duty of care to my people.'

Ross and McLeod left the Union Building shortly afterwards. Vickery's answers told him two things: the club owner knew exactly who Trixie was, and what's more, he'd concealed something about the murdered woman he didn't want to share with the police.

***

Kezia stood outside the café in Magdalen Street with Mishra. She worried what the proprietors might think. She needed the money if not the job. She didn't expect Mishra's next statement.

'Sorry if my colleagues gave you a rough time yesterday.'

'Yeah, well, they're doing their job. Look, I can't stay out here too long.'

'No, I understand. I just wanted to meet you, find out what your mum does.'

'She's a psychic consultant. She brings comfort to the recently bereaved.'

'She talks to the dead?'

'I wouldn't say talk. Communicate, that's a better word.'

Mishra moved out of the way of an onrushing mobility scooter. 'Does she have special powers?'

The policewoman didn't fool Kezia. Mishra was trying to lull her into saying something that would incriminate her or her mother. 'I suppose you could say that.'

'Is it hereditary? I mean, do you think you'll take over?'

'I doubt it.' Kezia looked over her shoulder. 'Look, I'm supposed to be working.'

'It's just I heard about what happened at your old school. You remember, when the girl was murdered?'

Kezia saw it again – the black creature, the devil's eyes... Briefly, Mishra, the passers-by, the buildings, the whole city vanished, and she stood alone in a wasteland with only that dark shape lurking a few yards away...

'Sorry...' Kezia stared towards the entrance to the Anglia Square shopping centre. A black hood vanished into the throng.

'The girl at your school... the one who was killed. You had some sort of vision.'

'Yeah... right... That was a long time ago. I can't remember.'

'You must. If that happened to me, I'd be having nightmares.'

'Well, I don't. Please let me go back inside.' Kezia sensed whatever stalked her still prowled a few yards away.

Mishra handed her a card. 'Kezia, you're troubled. I can see that. Give me a call if you want to talk. Okay?'

Kezia pocketed the offering and grunted a thanks. She darted back into the café.

'Problems?' asked Lydia, the co-owner.

'Following up an old case where we used to live. I was a witness.'

Lydia smiled, but Kezia's mood didn't improve. What motivated the police to rake over these long-dead coals? Hester Boswell had bullied her, and Kezia swore revenge. She'd imagined the thrill of seeing the girl's corpse lying bleeding at her feet. Death was never as sweet, she understood that now, and the guilt she felt over her classmate still haunted her. Perhaps her stalker was not a living human, but an avenging ghost from her past?

***

At five o'clock that evening, Ross had the misfortune to meet DCI Devlin. His superior was leaving after a full day of looking busy.

'David, how are things going? Any of the leads looking good?'

'We're going to make an arrest tonight. Former soldier by the name of Jeremy Kendal. We found his semen at the scene and he's got a conviction for assault. He works as a carpenter for a local builder so he's more likely to be carrying a hammer than the average punter.'

'Excellent. Sounds like you've got your man.'

'We've still got another couple of leads. There's the girl called Kezia Lee who was up to no good in the area – '

'Doesn't strike me as a girlie crime. And?'

'Tom Vickery's name's come up. Susan Smith used to work in his clubs. He claims he sacked her for using drugs.'

'Word of advice, David. Stay clear of Vickery.' He raised a hand to stop Ross objecting. 'Vickery may have been a bad lad in the past but as far as I'm aware he's a reformed character with access to the movers and shakers in the county.'

'There's a pimp who might have been at the scene. Not the victim's, another tom's. We found a cigarette butt.'

'Circumstantial. That park is like a hot desk for hookers. This Kendal – you reckon we can build a case?'

'Should be easy,' said Ross. 'Given that he'll own a hammer, means. Motive is he's short tempered. Opportunity – alone in the dark with the victim.'

'Then charge him, that's an order. Ex-squaddie – sort who'd do a runner if he suspects we're onto him. Call the CPS straight away. We don't want the public to suspect we're twiddling our thumbs.'

Ross stared at his departing boss, imagining the DCI retiring to his large house to spend a fascinating evening of thumb-twiddling.

***

The time: six thirty in the evening. The place: a bay-fronted terraced house in a quiet street off Thorpe Road, conveniently situated half a mile from the station, suspiciously located a similar distance from the murder scene… No blue lights, no sirens, just three unmarked cars including Ross's Mondeo and two squad vehicles. Ross deployed McLeod and two uniformed officers in the lane running behind the houses in case their quarry tried to escape in that direction.

Ross saw the net curtain twitch before he knocked on the solid red door. It was answered by a short woman with a long waistline. She wore a mauve outfit with padded shoulders; a string of large black beads hung round her neck. Her nose reminded Ross of a sparrow's beak, her mouth narrow and lipsticked.

'Yes,' she said.

'Mrs Eve Kendal? Police.' Ross showed his warrant card. 'Is your son at home?'

A gasp, then: 'Why? What's he done?'

'We'd like to speak to him. Can we come in?'

93

Mrs Kendal crossed her arms and took a step forward. 'Not without a warrant you don't. We don't want trouble. You lot have fitted him up before and I'm not standing for it.'

'Mrs Kendal, we don't need a warrant if we're conducting an arrest. Please stand aside.'

'What is it, Ma?' Ross saw Jez Kendal for the first time as the ex-soldier limped down the stairs. The suspect stood a foot taller than his mother. His face was scarred, and it was obvious one eye was false. The right ear was a misshapen lump of flesh.

'Jeremy Kendal, I am arresting you on suspicion of the murder of Susan Smith on Friday the fourteenth of July. You – '

'You're not taking my boy away!'

'do not have to say anything. But it may harm your defence if you do not mention when questioned something – '

Eve turned and pushed her son. 'Jeremy, go to your room. I'll call a lawyer. I'll – '

'which you later rely on in court. Anything you do say may be given in evidence. Do you understand?'

'I didn't kill anybody,' Jez shouted.

'See, he's telling the truth. You can't take him.'

Ross was reluctant to push the woman aside. Stevens took the initiative and squeezed past, grabbing Jez Kendal by the arm. Their target didn't offer any resistance. Eve Kendal seemed to shrink as two policemen barged in and helped Stevens bundle the suspect out of the door and into one of the squad cars.

'Don't say anything till the lawyer gets there,' were Eve's final words to her son.

Ross followed the now weeping Eve into her front room. He noticed an array of 'In Sympathy' cards above the fireplace. She allowed Mishra to make a cup of tea as she sat, dabbing her eyes with a handkerchief.

'You're wrong. My Jeremy wouldn't hurt anybody. Who's this Susan Smith, anyway?'

'You might have heard it on the news,' said Ross. 'The woman found dead in Old Library Wood.'

'The prostitute! Well, there you are. My Jeremy wouldn't go near one of them. The very thought!'

'Mrs Kendal, we've got evidence placing Jeremy at the scene. We have witnesses who saw him with the victim. I realise he's had problems, and the best thing you can do is be honest so we can get him the help he needs.'

'Well, your evidence must have been planted. And who's the witness? Someone reliable?'

Ross hesitated, his eyes lighting on a leaflet promoting a local spiritualist church. Kezia Lee and her mother invaded his thoughts.

'I thought not,' said Eve. 'Another prostitute, or some other criminal. Probably the murderer.'

'Tell me about Friday night. What time did Jeremy come home?'

'He was with me all night.' The tears gone; arms folded again.

'Mrs Kendal, I'd ask you to tell me the truth. If we find any part of your story is a lie, we'll assume the rest is, and that's not going to help Jeremy, is it?'

Mishra appeared with a tray. 'DI Ross's right, ma'am. I understand you're certain your son didn't do it, so please help us find out what actually happened.'

Eve deposited three spoonfuls of sugar into her cup. 'Very well. He came home late. He'd been at the pub. He sometimes goes to the Compleat Angler, but it depends where he's working.'

'How did he seem?' asked Mishra.

'He was… I'm sorry to say, he came home very drunk. I've told him so many times. He wasn't like this before his accident.'

Mishra touched Eve on the arm. 'Afghanistan, wasn't it?'

'Yes. His truck hit a bomb.' The tears had returned. 'He spent weeks in hospital. It ruined his life.' She wiped her eyes. 'He was engaged, you know. Horrible girl. Soon as she saw what he looked like she broke it off.'

Mishra shook her head. 'That's awful. He must have been angry.' A quick glance at Ross who nodded his approval. 'You said we'd fitted him up over his conviction. What did you mean?'

Eve took another sip of tea. 'I'm sorry. It wasn't the police. I blame the army. He was a hero, and they just threw him out without any help. Some thug bullied him, and he lashed out.'

They let her finish her tea before Ross resumed his questioning. 'When he got back on Friday, did you observe any marks on his clothing?'

'No blood, if that's what you mean. His clothes were filthy. He works on a building site after all. I washed them first thing Saturday morning.'

While Mishra and Ross talked to Eve, McLeod led the search of the house. Jez's bedroom was the main focus, although the potential prize would turn out to be a bag of tools left in the hall.

Eve continued to explain the injustice of Jeremy's earlier conviction when McLeod interrupted. 'Sir, something here you should see.'

Ross followed the detective constable into the hall. A uniformed officer held up a hammer so Ross could observe the dark marks near the point where the head met the handle.

Experience told Ross he stared at blood.

Chapter Eight

'Richard Carpenter?'

Ross almost spilt his coffee.

He'd just been informed by the desk that the aforementioned solicitor had breezed into Bethel Street and demanded to meet his client.

'Bad news?' asked Mishra.

'He's the sneakiest solicitor in the city if not Britain. He'd have got Hitler off at Nuremberg on a technicality.'

'Hitler wasn't tried at Nuremberg,' said McLeod.

'Carpenter wasn't there either, so my remark stands. What's he doing representing a low-life like Kendal?'

Mishra laughed. 'You mean how can Kendal afford him?'

'Yeah, right. Legal aid wouldn't pay for thirty seconds of Carpenter's time. I'm getting warning bells here. Carpenter is the go-to brief for Tom Vickery. We've often wondered about his role in convincing witnesses to change their statement at the last minute.'

'You suspect there might be a connection between Vickery and Kendal?' asked Stevens.

'They're both vicious thugs. Different leagues, though.' Ross gathered his files. 'Anyway, here goes. Kirsi, with me.'

Carpenter and Kendal sat side by side in the interview room. It wasn't difficult to tell them apart. The disfigured Kendal slumped in a police-supplied track suit, two sizes too big. The handsome dark-haired Carpenter smirked in a navy-blue suit, a light blue shirt and matching tie held in place by a pin crowned with what Ross guessed was a diamond. A silk handkerchief of the same colour poked from his top pocket. A gold Rolex adorned his wrist.

'My client may assert his right not to answer questions,' were Carpenter's opening words. 'Suffice to say he is not admitting guilt and wishes to understand the evidence against him.'

Ross opened his file. A photograph of the corpse lay on top. 'Mr Kendal, do you deny you were in Old Library Wood on Friday night?'

Kendal spoke before Carpenter could raise a restraining hand. 'Where? Never heard of the place.'

'The small park off Rosary Road.'

'Nah. Wasn't there.'

'We discovered semen at the site. We've identified it as yours. We're awaiting results of semen found inside the dead woman's mouth. If we get a positive match, that's two separate pieces of evidence pointing to you indulging in sexual activity with Susan Smith.'

'Excuse me,' said Carpenter. 'May I have the chance to consult with my client in private?'

Ross nodded, then motioned for Mishra to follow him out of the room. 'We'll be outside.'

They only detected Kendal's voice through the door, initially loud then fading to inaudible. After six minutes

Carpenter opened the door and invited the pair back into their own room.

'My client is prepared to admit he performed a sex act with a prostitute. He apologises for misleading you, but he is naturally ashamed of his actions.'

Ross pulled out a second photograph: Susan Smith on the slab. Dr Porter-Brown had closed the mouth and blindfolded the victim to hide the damage to her eyes. 'Is this the prostitute?'

Kendal stared, mouth open. 'Jesus Christ!'

'You recognise her?'

Carpenter laid a hand on his client's shoulder. 'Mr Kendal can't be expected to identify anyone in this state.'

Kendal's eyes never moved from the photo. 'Trixie. Her name's Trixie.' He stared at the picture for several more seconds. 'I'm sure it's her. I know I was pissed but I couldn't do that.'

'Why did you attack her?'

'I didn't! I –'

Carpenter's restraining arm… 'My client refuses to answer.'

Ross placed the photo back in his file and brought out one showing the murder scene. 'You killed her with a hammer. You can see the wound here.' He jabbed the picture. 'Messy.'

Kendal glanced at the image, then looked away. He shook his head vigorously. 'No! No!'

'We found a hammer at your house. In your tool bag. There are stains on the handle we've identified as blood. The splatter marks are consistent with a vicious assault. We've sent it to the lab for analysis. Chances are it's Susan Smith's.'

Kendal's eyes locked onto the photo again.

Ross moved closer. 'Why hit her after she's dead? What did she do? Say? She made fun of you, right? You wanted to shut her up.'

Kendal covered his eyes.

Ross brought his fist down on the photograph. 'That's it. You weren't sure you'd finished her off. So you hit her again. And again. But she'd mocked you. You needed to stop her talking, calling you inadequate. You hit her in the mouth. Then her eyes. Or was it the other way round?'

The ex-soldier kept his hands over his face. 'No! No! No!'

Carpenter cast a glance at Kendal. 'I'd like another chance to speak to my client.'

Ross and Mishra once again stood outside the room. They made out Kendal's raised voice: 'There was this bloke... no fucking way... set me up...'

Mishra moved closer to the door. 'I'd love to hear what Carpenter's saying.'

'I can guess,' replied Ross. 'Carpenter probably believes Kendal did it. He'll try to plead diminished responsibility or loss of control. A poor wounded hero suffering from post-traumatic stress taunted by a thoughtless slut. Kendal, on the other hand, was so pissed he can't or won't remember, and is in denial.'

Carpenter's opening remark confirmed Ross's opinion.

'Until you've got the results back, I've advised my client to remain silent. He was by his own admission slightly the worse through drink. His memory is therefore unclear, although he remains convinced he did not commit the murder. I would remind you his condition directly results from the injuries he suffered in defence of our country, and you should treat him with the respect he is due.'

Kendal turned to his lawyer. 'What about – '

'Okay, Mr Kendal Let me handle this.'

'Kendz, mate. Call me Kendz, remember.'

Kendz – Ross now knew for certain Jeremy Kendal was the punter who propositioned Mirjeta Bardici.

'My client believes he saw someone in the vicinity after he left Miss Smith. Alive, I would add. I suggest you seek this person out as they may prove to have important information.'

'Okay, Mr Kendal. Describe this person.'

Carpenter nodded at Kendal.

'He wore a hood. I couldn't see the face. Yeah, he said he'd found my hammer.'

'What do you mean – 'found my hammer'?'

'Yeah, well like I said I was pissed. This bloke says I dropped my hammer or something and he hands it back.'

'Where was this?'

'Christ, I can't remember. Might have been just after I left the park.'

'And do you remember dropping your hammer?' asked Ross.

'Dunno. I thought it was in my bag all the time.'

'And you were in possession of your bag the whole time?'

Carpenter held his hand up before his client had a chance to reply. 'I suggest we can assume my client left the bag unattended while he was engaged with the lady.'

'Are you sure the person who returned your hammer was a male?' asked Mishra.

Kendal scratched his head. 'Like I says, I was pissed. I think it was... hell, I don't know. It was fucking dark, and I was out of it, right? He... she... was English. I remember that. Local, even.' He looked up, a flicker of hope in his eyes. 'Yeah, it might've been a woman. Maybe another hooker?'

Carpenter wasn't slow to pick up what lay behind Mishra's question. 'Why do you doubt it was a man, sergeant? I hope you're not withholding evidence that would clear my client.'

Mishra blushed. 'I'm just trying to get the facts right.'

Ross intervened. 'Mr Kendal, I'm going to terminate this interview now. You will be held here tonight pending an appearance before the magistrates tomorrow. Please accept my assurance we'll look into your story about the hooded man.'

A uniformed sergeant led the prisoner down to the cells. Ross's team gathered for their final briefing of the evening.

'Sorry, sir,' said Mishra. 'I scored an own goal there.'

'You've learned a lesson. Count to ten before you ask a question. I'm not sure you've ballsed it up as much as you fear.'

'How so?'

'Carpenter will want to stop the jury hearing about Kendal's previous conviction. He'll get away with it, unless Kendal gives evidence, thus permitting the prosecution to assert he's got a temper and bring up the assault charge. And the only way he can introduce the hooded man is by putting Kendal in the witness box.'

'Would anyone believe him?' asked Stevens. 'Violent thug like him? How the hell could a hammer fall out of his bag without him knowing?'

'Someone might have taken it out,' suggested Mishra.

Stevens laughed. 'No bloody way!'

Ross didn't share the detective constable's view. Kendal was drunk. No way would he mention it in front of two female colleagues, but…

To paraphrase Ms Austen, it is a truth universally acknowledged that a man in possession of a bellyful of drink must be in want of a longer time than usual to achieve ejaculation. Long enough for a hooded figure to slip a hammer out of a bag, wait till the climax had passed, and then beat a hooker to death.

Kezia Lee was back in the frame.

Chapter Nine

Three magistrates frowned down on a disconsolate Jez Kendal, flanked by two policemen. The case against him was now stronger, although Kendal submitted a 'not guilty' plea. The lab had worked overtime – they'd confirmed the blood on the hammer belonged to Susan Smith, the semen in her mouth identified as Kendal's. They'd also proved the blood on Mercer's T-shirt was Susan's, but it had been there for several days before the murder.

The court refused Carpenter's half-hearted plea for bail to the surprise of no-one except Eve Kendal. Her son's plea of not guilty was duly recorded in the court's records. In Ross's view, they'd witnessed another pointless waste of public resources.

His musings on pointless waste continued when he emerged from the courtroom to find his superior facing a group of reporters and cameramen.

'I'm pleased to say my investigations into the tragic murder of Susan Smith have been successful, and the suspect will now face trial.' To describe Devlin as smug was like calling the Himalayas a trifle hilly. 'I still don't understand why Jeremy Kendal committed this terrible crime, but the women of this city can now walk our streets safe in the knowledge that under my direction my officers have almost certainly removed a monster from our city.'

Ross pondered if the reference to the women of Norwich indulging in streetwalking might be inappropriate given the circumstances.

A female reporter from the BBC thrust a microphone at Devlin. 'How confident are you that Jeremy Kendal is the killer?'

'We have witnesses and evidence placing him at the scene. In addition, we discovered a bloodstained weapon, with the victim's DNA, in his possession. I'd remind you this case is now *sub judice* and reporting should reflect that.'

Ross walked back to his car, doubts swimming in his mind. The facts screamed Kendal was the killer. His gut kept whispering 'Kezia' and 'Vickery'. He remained so caught up in these concerns he failed to spot the imposing figure of Nigel Warder standing by a large Mercedes.

'DI Ross. A successful few days, I gather.'

'Mr Warder. You've played your own part.'

'An open and shut case, if ever I've seen one. You must be ready to celebrate.'

'Not until the killer is locked up. We've still got work to do.'

Warder smiled. 'I thought we'd just ensured the killer is locked up. Have you any doubts Kendal did it?'

'His story leaves a few loose ends. We need to tie them up.'

'Probably a good idea if you're to best Richard Carpenter. I'm amazed he's taken a case like this. I'm sure you'll have the loose ends tied up tight in a couple of weeks. Anyway, it's me keeping you from your business. I'll bid you farewell.'

Ross watched the Mercedes disappear out of the car park. Warder had invited Tom Vickery to his event on Saturday.

Vickery was too close to Devlin. Devlin seemed too enthusiastic about pinning the murder on Kendal. The investigation had quietened, but his copper's metaphorical gut grumbled louder than ever.

***

Kezia left work at half-past five and made her way to the Lollards Pit pub, built near the spot where heretics were burnt at the stake. The hostelry lies opposite Bishops Bridge, close to the entrance to Rosary Road. It was the first time she'd been back to the area since the night of the murder.

Vague visions of ravenous beasts haunted the edges of her mind; she wasn't sure why. Her mother might have argued it was because she sensed the ghosts of the persecuted unbelievers, or because her ancestors were trying to reach her – for a few years the once-shunned site hosted the largest gypsy camp in the city. Kezia feared there might be another, more immediate, reason.

She never used the same place twice in a row. People might get too friendly, too nosey. She bought a lemonade then connected to the free WIFI using her tablet. After she checked her mother's website for enquiries, she logged onto Facebook under an alias and searched for 'Joe Leadbetter'. A result – Leadbetter proved a prolific poster. Kezia found out about his schools, places of work, and best of all, his summer holidays. 'Mum and dad stayed here in the fifties and loved it.'

Sabina could say: 'He's talking about Sorrento… a wonderful time… does that sound right?'

More posts: 'Had to help Mum with council tax, they tried to rip her off.' Another potential Sabina revelation.

Then one she didn't expect: 'Worried about Mum. She's found this psychic woman called Sabina Romanov. I think

107

she's one of the ones mentioned in the Victims of Phoney Mediums group.'

Kezia followed the provided link to the group's site. It was closed to non-members, so she fired off a request in a false name to join after failed attempts with potential Joe Leadbetter logons. Hopefully, the administrator wouldn't recognise her.

This was serious. She wouldn't tell Ma, but she'd keep a watching brief. Joe Leadbetter had become a threat. Kezia looked at his pictures – only one showed his face up close. *Good looking in a rugged sort of way, if you ignored the birthmark on his cheek.* Other pictures showed Joe in judo suit, Joe playing rugby. *Not a man to trifle with.*

She returned to her original task.

The Ancestry website, accessed via stolen credentials, was an excellent source of information. It amazed her how many people created family trees containing personal information on relatives, such as date of birth. Kezia discovered Phyllis Leadbetter's grandfather worked as a gas stoker in Salisbury. Phyllis might not know about the site, so it was the sort of information that built integrity.

She jotted down every pertinent revelation in a notebook, written in a variation of shorthand developed by her mother: *'the language of the spirits'.*

At eight o'clock she left the pub. Untroubled by vegan guilt, she bought a kebab and made her way home over Bishop's Bridge. A figure lurked in the corner of her mind. Threatening, but not close. Not yet.

Perhaps she suffered a flashback to the horror in Old Library Wood. Or possibly the ghosts of the long dead... Or...

It's him.

Kezia kept glancing back. Nothing. Dare she take the shortest route or head for the cathedral? She could use the riverside path, but it was too risky. She increased her pace along Bishopsgate before skirting the cathedral grounds on the direct route to the flat. The shadow skulked in the fringes of her imagination.

He's keeping a safe distance.

She was close to the Adam and Eve, the city's oldest pub, when the images transformed.

He's close... The wolf, the dark pursuer...

Kezia sped up as she turned into St Martin-at-Palace Plain. She sensed he was still behind her, perhaps closing the gap. A quick glance round confirmed her fears – a hooded figure, perhaps seventy yards back. To her left, a high flint wall blocked access to the cathedral grounds. *As if she was a sinner refused entry to heaven.* She reached Whitefriars, then passed the building hosting the Magistrates' and Crown Courts. Her pursuer was closing the distance with every step.

St Martins-in-the-Plain Church offered no sanctuary before she broke into a run, darting down Bedding Lane past the Wig and Pen pub. Two smokers slouching outside the front made indiscernible comments as she dashed past. Ahead she could see the path leading to the river.

Even after two hundred yards, she was out of breath with an ache in her side.

Kezia didn't care. The wolf had gone.

She turned to look up the empty lane. Satisfied there was no pursuit, she paused to gather her breath. The evening sun glinted on the Wensum as she strolled along the path towards Fye Bridge, fear now reduced to a cloud of doubt, as if something still menaced her.

Doubt changed to alarm. Blood swamped her mind.

He'd avoided the pub. Too many witnesses. Instead, he must have kept going on Whitefriars and ducked down the next lane leading to the Wensum, knowing she'd pass that way. Her arm came up to shield her face just before he came in sight. She felt the sting of the acid as it splashed on her hand, heard the fizz as it burnt through her clothes.

Kezia screamed and instinctively staggered towards a short flight of steps leading to the river. She'd closed her eyes and failed to notice the chain across the entrance. Off-balance, she tumbled headfirst into the chill Wensum. For a second there was silence, as if she'd entered another world. The sounds of shouts, of running feet, soon echoed through the muddied waters. She broke the surface and dared to look. People ran towards her. Some were intent on saving her, others to film her predicament on their phones.

Hands reached out from the bank, a kaleidoscope of faces, a cacophony of voices, some soft, some harsh. Kezia saw them as if in a dream – they were all on the margins as she searched for the dark wolf in the fog of her confusion. He'd gone, and she returned to a strange reality, being pulled from the water by friendly arms.

'Has anyone got a blanket?' A man's voice, someone who wanted to be in control.

Kezia searched for her bag. A girl in a red coat had pulled it from the water and handed it to her, water dripping from the brown leather. She feared her tablet was damaged beyond repair.

'Why did you do it dear? Is life that bad?' A kindly, well-meaning woman.

'She was attacked. Didn't you see?' A girl, bobble hat, observant.

Kezia seized bobble-hat by the sleeve. 'Did you see him?'

'Yeah, but it was too quick. I mean he was coming for you, then you jumped. He was wearing dark stuff. I mean, that's if it was a bloke. Might've been a woman.'

'You should get a shot,' said Well-Meaning-Woman. 'You don't know what's in that water.'

'Don't worry,' said Controlling Man. 'There's fish in the Wensum. You'll be okay.'

Somebody, somehow, brought a blanket. A flask of coffee appeared from nowhere. She looked inside the bag. Her tablet appeared dry, although her notebook lay warped and damp.

'Don't move, the ambulance will be here soon,' announced Controlling-Man.

'And the police,' shouted a youth in a yellow Norwich City shirt.

Kezia shivered. 'Look, I'm okay.'

'You're not,' said Well-Meaning-Woman. 'You're in shock. Best thing to do is drink your coffee and wait for help.'

Kezia recoiled at the scrum of bodies surrounding her. Half the clientele of the nearby Ribs of Beef seemed to have wandered across Fye Bridge Street to enjoy her predicament. Some clutched pint glasses in their hands. Her only way to escape them would be to plunge back into the river, except she suspected a smaller crowd was gathering on the opposite bank. She surrendered to her fate, and within minutes a female PCSO appeared wearing a high-vis jacket.

Would-be witnesses enveloped the woman, and it took several minutes before she was able to crouch down next to Kezia.

'Are you okay?'

Kezia looked at her hand. There were a couple of red spots, but otherwise it seemed most of what had been thrown at her failed to penetrate skin before the balm of the Wensum came to her aid.

The PCSO touched Kezia on the arm. 'Your sleeve looks like it's been burnt by acid or something.'

Kezia saw the damage. 'Shit. I liked this jacket.'

The crowd parted to allow a paramedic access. Kezia couldn't spot an ambulance, so the odds were he'd arrived by motorbike. She allowed him to remove her jacket, before replacing her blanket with a foil one and examining her left arm. All the time she fielded questions from the PCSO.

'What's your name?'

'Kezia. Kezia Lee. Look, I'm fine. I'm – '

'Where do you live?'

'In a flat behind a second-hand shop on Magdalen Street. I'm not sure of the actual address. It's – '

'Hang on.' The PCSO spoke into her radio. 'Kezia Lee. Right, I'll hold.' She stared at Kezia, a forced smile on her lips. Kezia saw trouble ahead as a full minute passed before the officer nodded. 'Sounds like her.'

Kezia struggled to free herself from the medic's embrace, 'I need someone to tell my Ma.'

The paramedic held on to her hand. 'Miss, we need to check you. Until we confirm the substance isn't toxic, we can't let you go home.'

'That's right,' said the PCSO. 'It's for your own good.'

Lie.

Blue flashing lights appeared on the bridge. Kezia's first reaction was that the paramedic had summoned an ambulance. She was wrong. Two police cars waited over the Wensum.

Uniformed officers materialised, one male, one female. The woman wore sergeant's stripes. They were followed by two constables who shepherded the crowd away from the scene.

The police created order from the chaos. They identified where the attack occurred, taped off the area, spoke to the relevant witnesses. The paramedic helped Kezia walk up the slope to Wensum Street, after which the sergeant led her towards the nearest police car on the bridge.

Kezia struggled to free herself from the firm grip of the policewoman. 'I've got to get home. My Ma will be worried.'

'We'll let your mum know you're okay,' came the reply. 'I've got orders to bring you back to headquarters.'

'Shit, I'm the victim here. I've told you all I know.'

Her protests were in vain. Fifteen minutes later she sat in an interview room in the Bethel Street HQ facing Mishra and Stevens. They'd taken her fingerprints and DNA, allegedly for elimination purposes. Her jacket, notebook and tablet were God knows where, no doubt being pored over by men in white coats. The walls were bare, the only furniture a stained table and four chairs. Mishra brought in a pitcher of water and three plastic cups.

Stevens turned on the recorder perched on the edge of the table. She opened a file and began reading:

'This interview is being recorded and may be given in evidence if a case is brought to trial. We are in an interview room at Norwich Bethel Street Police Station. The date is the eleventh of July and the time by my watch is nine-fifteen pm.

I am Detective Constable Linda Stevens. The other police officer present is Detective Sergeant Kirsi Mishra.'

'Whoa. Am I being arrested?'

'Please state your full name and date of birth.'

'I'm not answering any questions until you tell me why I'm here.'

Stevens glared at Kezia. 'You've got questions to answer. Please state your name and date of birth.'

'It's bloody Kezia Lee, and I was born on the bloody ninth of June 1997. I've answered your questions. Can I go now?'

'Do you agree there are no other persons present?'

Kezia made a point of looking around. 'Well, you're a bloody good detective spotting that. You don't need any help from me.'

'Before the start of this interview, I must remind you that you are entitled to free and independent legal advice either in person or by telephone at any stage. Do you wish to speak to a legal advisor now or have one present during the interview?'

'Why would I need a lawyer? Are you going to arrest me?'

Stevens slammed the file shut and took a drink of water. 'Possibly. Depends how honest you are.'

Mishra glanced at Stevens. Kezia spotted hostility between the pair.

'Kezia,' said Mishra. 'Tell us what happened.'

'I was doing a bit of studying. On the internet.'

Kezia analysed the two women sitting on the other side of the table. *The younger one has a higher rank, while the older one is aggressive, probably ambitious, and resents her companion's status. The constable's clothing is unfashionable, and she's made no attempt at makeup. The sergeant's outfit looks expensive, and she's wearing eye shadow and lip gloss. Neither wears a ring.*

Mishra continued: 'Where?'

'Lollards Pit. You know, the pub on Riverside.'

Stevens leaned forward. 'The gay hangout? Why there? Nowhere closer?'

'I like to explore the city. Find new places, you know. Besides, there are gayer pubs. The – '

'Sounds like you're a dyke,' said Stevens. Mishra fired a shocked glance at her colleague.

'Like that's my business,' replied Kezia. 'I'll tell you this. If I was, you're not my type.'

Stevens looked down for a split second. *Is she gay? Maybe bisexual? She doesn't want the others to find out, that's for sure.*

'Thank God for that.' The detective constable took another drink. 'This desire for new places – some might think you didn't want to be remembered.'

Mishra's turn: 'You left the pub. What then?'

'I got a feeling someone followed me.'

Stevens: 'What do you mean a feeling? Did you see anyone?'

'No… I don't think so, I'd gone in for a kebab – '

'Kebab?' Stevens laughed. 'And you a vegan?'

'Who says? I work in a vegan café. So what?'

Mishra: 'Carry on, Kezia.'

115

'I'd gone past the Wig and Pen – '

Stevens: 'Hang on – what route did you take? Were you on a bloody pub crawl? Where else did you go?'

'I was trying to shake the guy off.'

Stevens: 'The guy you couldn't see? You expect us to believe that? Jesus, you're – '

Mishra: 'Sorry, Kezia, you were by the river. Then what happened?'

'I'm walking along when he rushed out of Pigg Lane and threw the stuff in my face. I realised what's happening and managed to get my arm up in time.'

Stevens: 'How the hell did you react so quickly?'

'I see things. I can't explain. Call it a premonition if you like.'

Mishra: 'Are you sure it was male?'

'I don't know... I get these images... it felt male.'

Stevens: 'You felt it? You touched his prick, did you?' Another sip of water.

Mishra glared at Stevens. 'It might have been a woman?'

'Yeah, maybe.'

Mishra: 'You're doing fine, Kezia. What do you remember about your attacker?'

'Not a lot. My arm was up in front of my face. I never saw his.'

Stevens threw the contents of her cup towards Kezia's eyes. She'd no chance to react.

Mishra grabbed Stevens by the arm. 'Why did you do that?'

'Don't you understand? She never saw it coming. All this crap about premonitions and visions. She knows damn well who attacked her and why.'

Kezia wiped her face. 'I don't. Honest.'

Stevens: 'You're lying. Who was it? One of your victims? Someone you and your old mum have scammed with the phoney medium trick?'

Mishra: 'Get her a towel, Constable Stevens.'

Stevens' mouth dropped open. 'Eh?'

'I ordered you to get a towel for Miss Lee. And an apology wouldn't be out of place.'

Stevens clenched her fists. 'What? You're joking.'

Mishra: 'I'm pulling rank. Constable, please get Miss Lee a towel. Now.'

Stevens opened her mouth to object, but the only word that emerged was 'Jesus!' She rushed from the room.

Mishra addressed the recorder. 'For the tape, Detective Constable Stevens has left the room after throwing water at Miss Lee. The time is... twenty past nine. I am switching off the tape until DC Stevens returns.'

The recorder paused. Mishra turned to Kezia. 'Look, if you want to raise a complaint, I can help you. That's not the way we behave.'

'No problem. You'd only get shit from the other cops if you ratted on someone like her.'

'You really didn't see who did it?'

'No. But...'

'What?'

Kezia remembered her experience in Old Library Wood. The sensation of not being alone. She was convinced the presence she sensed then was now too familiar. To admit her fears would be to confess her presence in Phyllis Leadbetter's back garden.

'Doesn't matter.'

Mishra turned on the recorder again. 'Detective Constable Stevens has re-entered the room at nine twenty-three.'

Stevens threw a roll of paper towels onto the table. 'Wipe whatever you want.'

Mishra: 'Please continue your questions, constable.'

Stevens shot Mishra a hateful glance, transferring the same evil eye to Kezia. 'Let's try again. Hester Boswell. Remember her?'

Kezia shivered. *The ghosts from the past wouldn't leave her alone.* Hester was crouching somewhere in the corners of her mind, whispering, 'You killed me.'

'Right, you do. They never proved who did it. Only they had a damn good idea. You.'

Kezia sat back, arms folded. 'Screw you. I was fourteen. And she was raped.'

'So they thought at the time. Now they're looking at you again. Teenage angst and all that. Hester bullied you, didn't she? Called you a pikey. You threatened her in front of witnesses. Then you announce to the entire class you killed her.'

'I didn't kill her.' Kezia was trembling. 'I… I just knew she was dead.'

Stevens kept twisting the knife. 'Don't you remember what she did to you? She saw the way you freaked out when your father got topped. Did she laugh at you back then? Call you a weirdo? A freak?'

A tsunami of memories flooded Kezia's mind.

Stevens's voice grew even louder. 'Her family blamed you, didn't they? They found out the truth, if we didn't. How you butchered Hester. How long did it take to wash the blood away?'

'No. You're lying.'

Except Kezia could no longer tell. Angry ghosts gnawed at her sanity, once forgotten voices screamed abuse and accusation.

'Hester's father and brother swore revenge, didn't they? You remember what they looked like? Seen either of them recently?' The DC was shouting now.

Kezia clenched her fists. A grey mist descended. The walls of the room began to close in…

'Stop it… stop it!'

Stevens walked round the table and stood behind Kezia. 'You're a killer, Kezia. Admit it. You want to.'

'No!' More of a scream than a statement.

'You took a brick and beat her to death. Remember the blood? Her screams?' Stevens was a vulture, tearing at the flesh of her prey, exposing her guilt to the world.

Mishra sat open-mouthed, powerless to stop the slaughter.

Memories… hatred… jealousy… teenage angst and half-remembered visions, all drowning in a sea of blood.

Kezia collapsed on the floor in a foetal pose, her hands round her head.

'Look what you've done,' screamed Mishra.

Stevens stood over the quivering body on the ground. 'She's faking it.'

'Interview terminated at half-past nine,' shouted Mishra. 'Get a doctor here. Quick.'

Chapter Ten

Ross glared at his in-tray through early morning eyes and decided to get a cup of machine coffee. A host of burglaries, drunken assaults, and internet scams lurked in the manila folders, every one threatening to spawn a hundred pages of accusations, explanations, and finally excuses why they merited no further action. Many of them never met the criteria of 'serious crimes' but had been reclassified to spare his peers in other sections. He needed a stamp with the message 'No can do, not enough resources' he could pound on ninety percent of his paperwork.

That human dam buster DCI Devlin had lifted his embargo on Ross's other cases and the flood threatened to engulf him. Faced with the tsunami of unsolved offences, a retreat to the coffee machine offered an obvious, albeit unappetising, solution. At least he might acquire some company in contrast to the emptiness of his flat.

Mishra was already there. 'Morning, sir.'

'I notice you didn't say it was a good one. If you've got the time, there's some stuff you can help me with.'

'Remember the shoplifting gang operating in the city centre? I assumed you wanted me to work on that. I've also got a domestic in Costessey to finish up. And I'm still trying to find out who Susan Smith's social worker was.'

'Bugger. Forgot your other cases. When Hamish turns up, we'll reprioritise. I'm not sure we can get Stevens – the case of the phoney medium carries on.'

'About that, sir...'

'Go on.'

'Kezia Lee was in here last night. She'd been attacked.'

Ross experienced an unexpected ripple of fear. 'What? Is she okay?'

'Um, yes. She was lucky. But Stevens and I interviewed her, and it all went... well...'

'Tits up?' Ross smiled, then caught himself. 'Sorry,' he said.

'Literally. Kezia collapsed. Stevens pushed her too far.'

Ross ignored the full plastic cup awaiting his collection. Instead, he pointed at the nearest meeting room. 'In here.'

Mishra provided Ross with a description of Kezia's interview.

'Bloody hell,' was Ross's reaction. 'Did you get a doctor?'

'She perked up after a cup of coffee. Demanded we let her go.'

'She walked home?'

'We couldn't stop her.'

Ross paced to the far wall and back again. 'Who's running with the attack? We're treating it as a serious assault, aren't we?'

'Uniform are dealing with it for now. Stevens is pushing for it because she thinks it ties in with her case. Either that or an old investigation her mates in Northampton screwed up.'

'She can't treat the victim as a suspect.' Ross sat down, drumming his fingers on the table. 'Okay, I'll take it on. I'll need your help to make progress on the other shit I've got to shovel. But there's something else we should do.'

'What's that, sir?'

'The Susan Smith case. Devlin wants us to stop work on it, but something's niggling me. Especially now Richard Carpenter's got involved. What's Carpenter's motivation?'

'Eve Kendal's got money,' said Mishra. 'She wants to do the best for her little boy.'

'I'll suggest another reason Carpenter's taken it. Vickery's involved somehow. He needs to steer the defence away from finding out the truth.'

'Why would Tom Vickery want a street prostitute dead? If it's something in their past, why hasn't he moved before now?'

'We won't find out unless we can uncover something else,' replied Ross. 'We need to search her place.'

'What's the point? We've done that and couldn't find anything.'

'We were looking for evidence of murder. Now it's the something else. Anything connected to Vickery. Do we need a warrant?'

'The place was in her name. My understanding is the landlords have been trying to evict her so if her boyfriend's still hanging around, he's a squatter. I'll organise a couple of uniforms and we'll go this afternoon.'

They returned to their office area just as McLeod arrived.

'How did you get on at Mrs Leadbetter's?' asked Ross.

'Bloody pain in the arse,' was McLeod's reply. 'The old bird wouldn't let us in, so we had to go next door and get the neighbour. Then the son turned up and slagged us off for not arresting Sabina Romanov.'

'Did you find a bug?'

'No, but Jim reckoned if it was a small one the battery might've died. We looked in all the obvious places. That Joe Leadbetter's a bugger, though. Gave his mum as much grief as us.'

'What do you mean?' asked Mishra.

'They had an argument about psychic Sabina. He said she was trying to get hold of his mum's money. At least he didn't stay too long.'

Mishra remained curious. 'How long did he stay?'

'Got there about half eight, left at nine on the dot. Not exactly the loving son.'

'So?' Mishra said. 'At least he goes to visit her, makes sure she's okay.'

'Makes sure his inheritance is okay, more like,' said McLeod. 'Old man Leadbetter was worth a lot of money when he died. She told us. He used to run an insurance broker.'

'Okay,' said Ross. 'We can't do Joe Leadbetter for being an arsehole.'

'There is something else, guv,' said McLeod. 'Something you ought to see.'

They followed McLeod over to his desk. He punched a couple of buttons on his keyboard and his screen displayed what was clearly the interior of a bus.

McLeod pointed. 'There.'

Slumped half-way along the lower deck was the unmistakable figure of Walter O'Donnell.

'This is taken on the ten forty-five bus from Norwich to Wymondham.'

'Shit,' said Ross. 'This puts O'Donnell back in the frame. He had time to kill Susan and get up to Castle Meadow to catch the bus.'

McLeod pressed another button, and the video speeded up. 'Have a look at this.'

They watched O'Donnell slowly standing up, collapsing down, and then succeeding in staggering towards the front of the bus.

'He's incapable of killing anyone in that state,' said Mishra. 'It's a miracle he got off without breaking his leg.'

Ross had to agree. There was no way O'Donnell would have walked up to Rosary Road in that condition. He hated leaving loose ends, but... 'Okay, let's park the Smith case for now and focus on these burglaries.'

The three detectives settled down to the task of identifying which stolen items might be easily fenced in the second-hand shops along Magdalen Street. The outcome would be even more paperwork to add to the pile, which in Ross's mind was growing like a fatberg in a sewer.

***

Sabina was gathering clothes into a bag in preparation for a trip to the laundrette when the front door swung open.

'Kezia! You're back.'

'It's half day. Have you forgotten?' snapped Kezia.

'My mind's all in a tizzy. I saw Phyllis Leadbetter this morning. I think she's impressed. The spirits guided me well.'

'I don't suppose my notes helped any. Sorry if they were a bit wet.'

Sabina, who proclaimed to be adept in picking up psychic emanations from beyond the grave, somehow missed the sarcasm in her daughter's voice. 'Never mind. The news just gets better. We've got another client. She's minted.'

Kezia threw her newly purchased jacket onto the sofa. She'd heard of retail therapy, but it hadn't done her any good. Limiting her scope to the stalls of Norwich market possibly wasn't the most efficacious approach. She was still shaken by her treatment at Bethel Street, especially the realisation that Hester Boswell had risen from the grave to torment her once again.

'Ma, I thought we'd agreed to chill it. The cops're still buzzing around like wasps round a jam sandwich. Talking about that, I'm hungry.'

'Have you felt him today?'

Kezia didn't want to tell her. At ten o'clock she'd seen the shadow of a wolf passing by the café, pausing, then walking on. 'No.'

'You're lying. Be careful.'

How does she know? 'He won't dare attack me again. It was some random nutter. Who's the latest mug, anyway?'

'Client, Kezia. We help people, don't forget it.'

'Yeah, bloody Red Cross of the paranormal, that's us. Who is it?'

'It's a lady called Eve Kendal. I first saw her at the church.'

'Church is on Sunday. How come you've just signed her up?'

'I met her this morning in Anglia Square. The spirits told me she was troubled. Indeed, I believe they led her to me.'

'Who's dead? The husband?'

'Her grandfather... and talk about happy coincidences.'

A sense of dread enveloped Kezia. 'Shoot.'

'You remember the body you found? The prostitute?'

'I'm not going to forget it, am I?'

'Her son's been accused of the murder!'

Kezia slumped down on the sofa and stared straight ahead. 'Shit! I am not happy. That is not a happy coincidence. It's a fucking – '

'Kezia!'

'I don't care. We've got the cops up our arses and you want us... Jesus!'

'Look, I promise this will be the last for a while. We'll go on holiday. Somewhere nice. Greece, you've always wanted to go there, haven't you?'

Kezia sat, fists clenched. 'In case you've forgotten, I'm twenty years old. If I go on holiday, I'll go where I want and I'll go alone. I am not spending the next few years sitting in jail for obstructing the police, or worse. That cow of a detective Stevens thinks I killed the hooker as well as Hester Boswell.'

'The spirits have spoken, Kezia. They've told me Mrs Kendal's son is innocent. You were near the body at the time of death. Her spirit will try to talk to you. Together we can find out the truth.'

'No.'

'The police won't bother us. They've stopped investigating. All I need is something that belonged to the murdered girl, then we can commune together. Combined, our powers – '

Kezia hammered the table. 'I have no powers. Neither do you. We've just got some... I don't know... intuition... gut feeling... hell, whatever it is.'

'They are messages from beyond. You must learn to control them.'

Kezia sat staring straight ahead, her whole body shaking, the bones of her knuckles quivering and straining against her taut skin.

Sabina put an arm round her daughter. 'Kezia, please. One more. Just get me something the girl owned and touched. You can do it.'

Kezia's eyes never left the far wall. It was blank, a uniform magnolia, but she imagined the entrance to Hell.

***

Kezia knocked on the door. The neighbour's curtains twitched – a brief glimpse of a woman's face. Kezia's grin caused the curtain to fall back into place. It hadn't been hard to find the house. The *Eastern Daily Press* had printed the murdered hooker's address.

'Yeah?' Sy Mercer stood in the doorway wearing a vest and shorts. A blast of curry and unwashed clothes hit Kezia.

'Hi. Like, I'm a friend of Susan's and she said I could keep something to remember her if anything happened.'

Mercer looked her up and down. Kezia was wearing a tight T-shirt and a long blue dress. His eyes settled on her chest area. 'Yeah, come in.'

He forced Kezia to squeeze past him into the murky interior. The stench was far worse inside the house. Gangsta rap music thumped from upstairs.

'Anything'll do,' she said. 'Like earrings, or a hairbrush.'

'Sure, babe. Try the bedroom.' He pointed at a door at the end of the hall.

Voices were muttering inside her head. She had to get this done quickly.

He shuffled behind her, never letting her beyond arm's length. 'You're fit, anyone tell you? I can help you make some cash. You get what I mean? Bit of fun, nothing serious.'

Kezia ignored him, opened the door and scanned the room. The curtains were closed, but were too short, providing sufficient light to reveal the untidy swirl of stained bedclothes. Clothes lay on the floor, including a bra, so he hadn't tidied since the murder. A moth-eaten teddy bear leant beside the bed. *Not his. Without doubt something Susan Smith would've kept for years. Why? Was it her child's?*

'You hear me, babe. Like I need someone new. I've got connections, right? You could do worse.'

He's a ram, fired up at the sight of an available female. Be very careful. 'No thanks. Mind if I take the bear?'

'Cost you'. She felt his hand squeeze her bum.

Kezia stepped out of his grasp. 'I'll give you a fiver.'

'You'll give me more than that.'

Mercer caught her round the waist and tried to throw her onto the bed. Kezia anticipated the move. She squirmed away and swung round. He grabbed her neck and pulled her towards him. Kezia brought her knee up between his legs. As Mercer doubled up, she swung an elbow into his face. He fell to his knees, at which point Kezia aimed her right boot at his head. Mercer flopped backwards. Her heel slamming into his groin completed the job.

She stepped over the groaning, crumpled heap on the floor and ran with her prize into the street.

***

Mishra pointed out of the car window. 'Isn't that Kezia Lee?'

Ross spun round. 'What's she holding? A teddy bear?'

'What's she doing out here?'

'She's weird,' said McLeod, who was driving. Ross had failed to find any spare uniformed staff. 'Nutter.'

They pulled up outside Susan Smith's house. Mercer tumbled out of the front door, blood streaming from his nose.

Mishra was first to reach the man who now knelt on the pavement. 'What's happened?'

'Some bitch broke in and attacked me. She stole Susan's bear. Like she might've nicked other stuff.'

Mishra looked at Ross. 'Should we go after her?'

Ross grimaced. 'Tell you what, Mr Mercer. I'll ask my colleagues to accompany you inside and have a good look. See what else we can find.'

'I want compensation for this as well, know what I mean? I reckon she took all my money.'

They decided to leave Mercer sitting on the tarmac. Mishra and McLeod vanished to conduct what proved to be a fruitless and nauseous search of the house.

Ross took the car in search of a girl with a teddy bear.

***

Kezia sensed the proximity of the vehicle and identified who was inside. She changed her route back, weaving a path through alleys and one-way streets to minimise the chances of him following her. By the time she reached Magdalen Street her senses told her there was no immediate danger. Nevertheless, when she reached the passage providing access to her home, she paused... *Nothing.* She climbed the steel staircase and stood by her door, listening to any noises, be they outside or inside her head.

Finally, she put the key in the lock. 'Ma! I've got something.' She walked in. 'Even I can feel it's what you're after. Are you – '

Ross sat on the sofa, her mother sitting behind him by the table.

'Hello, Kezia,' he said. 'Beaten up any drug addicts lately?'

Kezia stood still, teddy bear clutched under her arm. *Why hadn't she sensed him? Had her recent traumas finally dispelled whatever powers she had?*

Ross was beaming. 'Before I arrest you, can you provide me with your version of events?'

She looked at her mother, who replied by staring at the floor. Behind her was the door. *Had Ross set his troops to intercept any escape?*

'There's no point running, Kezia,' he said.

Why can't I read him? 'The bastard attacked me first.'

'You seem to have emerged unscathed. Try again.'

'Come on. He's a sleaze ball. He wanted to rape me.'

Ross kept smiling. 'It's his word against yours. A violent drug addict versus a con artist who steals teddy bears. Tough call.'

Sabina finally found her voice. 'My daughter is not a con artist.'

'Perhaps artist isn't the right word. You two have made a science out of it. Give me the bear, please.'

Kezia handed over the stuffed animal.

Ross examined the toy. 'Mrs Romanov. Do you own a pair of scissors? The nail variety would be ideal.'

A minute later Ross was cutting the stitching at the back. He plunged his hand into the bear's torso and rummaged about in its innards. Apparently satisfied, he sniffed at the padding.

The DI laid the bear down beside him. 'Right, no drugs, no secret papers. Why did you take this?'

Kezia remained tight-lipped.

'Okay, you give me no choice. Come with me, please.'

'Am I under arrest? Don't I get a lawyer?'

'If you need one, we'll get you one. I'll take teddy.'

Kezia crossed over the room and squeezed her mother's hand. 'Don't worry, ma. It'll be okay.'

Sabina clasped her daughter's hand with both of hers. 'Tell him the truth, Kezia. We've done nothing wrong.'

Kezia was in no mood to tell Ross anything. She glared at her mother and grabbed her jacket. She walked beside Ross in silence until they reached his car.

'Where are we going?' she asked.

'Somewhere we can talk. Not the station.'

Kezia stared out of the window as the car made its way out of the city. She wasn't picking up on what the policeman was thinking or feeling. It was as if some psychic force field enveloped him. Except…

Maybe I'm getting something I don't expect.

Ross turned off the southbound road to Lowestoft just after its junction with the A47. Twenty minutes later they reached a riverside pub in the village of Surlingham.

'You're buying me a drink?'

Ross grinned. 'Right, but it's not a date. It's a nice day. We can sit outside. More private. What do you want?'

'If you're buying, I'd like a large white wine.'

Still puzzled, Kezia found a table in the garden and sat down. The River Yare sparkled a few yards away. An expensive cruiser was moored on the riverbank, white decks gleaming. Across the water she noticed more boats of a similar size. Half the other tables were occupied, all save one by couples. Two loud middle-aged men entertained a pair of giggling women at the other, almost certainly passengers on the cruiser.

The DI returned with a glass of wine and a pint of beer.

'You allowed to drink on duty?' she asked.

'Who says I'm on duty? Besides, I might be going under cover.' He took a sip of the beer. 'Okay, tell me the truth.'

She raised her glass and tasted. 'Wine's nice. Thanks.'

'Right,' said Ross, 'let me put it this way. I'm investigating a murder. Circumstantial evidence puts you in the vicinity. Some of my people think you did it. Their idea is you were fleeing a failed robbery, Susan Smith steps out in front of you, you panic, hit her. You get the picture. I don't buy it.'

He took another drink. 'Your average housebreaker doesn't carry a hammer. There's no motive at all. You'd have pushed

Susan out of the way, not hit her several times. No connection. But then I find you visiting her house and stealing stuff.'

'Why haven't you arrested me then?'

'You say you're psychic.' Kezia was about to object, but Ross's eyes dissuaded her. 'Perhaps not psychic, but you've got unusual... sensitivities, shall we say? Me too. I can smell a killer, and you're not one. Now, let's start with Mr Teddy. Why were you prepared to risk the advances of a druggie to get hold of him?'

Tell the truth, her mother said. *No problem with this one...*

'Okay. You won't believe me. My mother has got it into her head she can help Jez Kendal. She met Kendal's mum.'

'Kendal's mum's into all that spiritualism stuff? Funnily enough, I do believe you.'

'Yeah. So Ma wants something belonging to Susan Smith so she can contact her spirit.'

'Can she?'

'The truth... no effing way. Like, maybe I've inherited powers from her, but with me it's the living I connect with. I somehow know when there's trouble about, that sort of thing.'

'Which is why you looked so surprised when you saw me.'

'Yeah, right... I should've known.'

'Maybe it's because I'm not dangerous.'

Kezia stared at Ross. Truth was a double-edged sword. 'Convince me.'

'Tell me about the night you found the body.'

She looked again. *Was he wearing a wire?* Her gut said no. *You can trust this man...*

She wondered if all her guilt had built up to the point where she needed to confess. *I've got a conscience after all. He's no priest, but then I'm not a practising Catholic.*

'Okay, what do you know about me? What I do for Ma?'

'I'm guessing you've no intention of doing a degree at the Open University. What I reckon is you're trying every trick in the book to find out about the mugs your mum is targeting. Social media, breaking in – '

'Whoa. I never break in. Least, not into houses. I go for the bin. Recycling material. I'm looking for stuff like letters, bills, holiday brochures. Anything with personal information. You can't do me for taking rubbish.'

'Right, so you visited the Leadbetter house to raid the dustbin. The bloke next door chases you off, then what?'

'I ran into the park. I kinda thought there was something there, so I waited, then shone my torch, and...'

'You saw the body. Anything else?'

'No. Although... Yeah, it was weird. I felt something evil before I found her. Same feeling I had when I was attacked.'

'If you passed whoever it was in the street, would you recognise them?'

Kezia took another sip of wine. 'I don't know. I mean, I'm not sure if I pick up on the people or their intentions.'

'Okay. What can you say about me?'

She laughed, then stared at him for thirty seconds.

Then she smiled. 'Right, you're not living with anyone. Or if you are, they don't care.'

'Carry on.'

'I'm guessing you live in a flat. Either that or you're a workaholic. You got divorced in the last few weeks, not that you wanted to. Your eyesight isn't perfect, but you don't like wearing glasses.'

'Bugger me. I'm sitting with the reincarnation of Sherlock Holmes. How did you do it?'

Kezia winked. 'My secret.'

'You've been spying on me. Rummaged through my refuse.'

'You wish. Your complexion's a bit pale. The last couple of weekends have been sunny, so if you lived in a house you'd have been outside. Unless of course you've been working. You've still got the mark of a wedding ring, but it's fading. So you're not married, but if it was a divorce and you were the one pushing for it, you'd've ditched the ring ages ago.'

'You said I was living alone?'

'Your shirt collar's a bit frayed. There's a mark on your jacket. A wife or live-in girlfriend would've picked that up.' She giggled – the wine was taking effect. 'On the other hand, you might be married to a slut, so you take your ring off as soon as you leave the house in case you get the chance to pick up a young redhead and ply her with drink at a riverside pub.'

'And the glasses?'

'Faint mark on the bridge of your nose. You're not wearing contacts so I'm guessing you're long sighted otherwise you wouldn't be driving.'

'You're good. What else?'

Kezia picked up her glass and swirled it round.

He wondered if she was using it like a crystal ball.

'When you first saw me,' she said, 'you reacted as if you knew me. And then a split second later I felt sadness. You lost someone who looked like me, right?'

Ross stared at the river. 'Go on.'

'I'm guessing it wasn't your ex.' *This is hurting him.* 'Someone before. Not a relative. A girlfriend, maybe.'

'We could do with you in the police. Ever thought of joining up?'

That's right, change the subject. 'Can't see me in a uniform. Besides, first thing you'd ask me to do is bust Ma, isn't it?'

Ross laughed. 'You could give her a caution.' The smile faded. 'These… feelings you get. Is it just evil or sorrow? What else can you pick up?'

'You mean if a guy likes me?' She paused and saw him blush. 'I can tell if someone's lying… well, most of the time.'

'Funny that. I always reckon I could detect untruths. Facing Jez Kendal in the station… Everything says he's guilty. But… I don't know. He's coming out with this unbelievable shit about somebody finding his hammer, and yet...'

'You think he's telling the truth.'

'It's possible. But I'm not getting the chance to investigate. My bosses think it's done and dusted.'

Kezia watched a blue boat drift past, a laughing couple sharing the wheel, no doubt also sharing their lives.

'I'd like to help,' she said. 'Maybe you should let Ma keep the bear.'

'You and your Ma have an interest in this. Suppose we cleared Jez Kendal, would that be worthwhile?'

'Yeah, sure.'

'Okay. For starters, why don't you visit Kendal in prison? Look him in the eye – shouldn't be hard, he's only got one. Tell me if he's lying.'

'Okay. Two conditions.'

'What are they?'

'One. I get my tablet back. Two. Ma gets the teddy bear.'

Chapter Eleven

Ross's first call on Thursday morning was to Tom Vickery's office. Accompanied again by McLeod, he waited for half an hour before Vickery's receptionist, now wearing a white skirt a shade short of normal business etiquette, led him into her employer's inner sanctum.

Vickery didn't shake the offered hand but instead sat back in his chair. He picked up a pen and began twirling it. 'DI – did I get that correct? – Ross… and your bagman. I can't say it's a pleasure to see you. I'm rather busy. Architect problems. Please be brief.'

'The Susan Smith business. I – '

'I understood the case had been closed. You've got your man, haven't you?'

'I'm just tying up loose ends. Richard Carpenter's representing him. You must have come across him – clever lawyer. He'll squeeze through the smallest loophole.'

'You know damn well I've got him on a retainer. Don't treat me like an idiot.'

'You said you sacked Susan for using drugs. Was that true?'

'As far as I remember. It was, what, eight, nine years ago?'

'Are you sure it wasn't because she was pregnant?'

Vickery stiffened – ever so slightly. Ross recognised he'd touched a nerve. *Where was Kezia Lee when he needed her?*

'Perhaps. I've sacked a few girls over the years. Maybe the old memory's playing tricks. So?'

'She left town and went to Nottingham, where she'd no connections. Almost as if someone paid her to go.'

'She was a tom. I expect she spotted a business opportunity. You're not accusing me of being the father?'

'No, sir.'

'I expect you've checked. I'd imagine you've subjected the poor little brat to DNA testing. Then compared her DNA to mine. I'm certain you've got it on file.'

First mistake. 'You said 'her'. Why was that?'

'Figure of speech. Was I right?'

'Yes, except the kid died. That's when she started on drugs.'

Vickery tapped his pen on the desk. 'Tragic.'

'Any idea who the father was?'

'I imagine it could have been anybody. Except me, and I hope you and your good constable here. Knowing what I do now, I wouldn't be surprised if she was on the game when she left Norwich. I'm not naïve, inspector. I regret the reality that a few of the girls can't resist boosting their income. We sack them if we find out. But if Susan was high on drugs, promiscuous... I need not spell it out, do I?'

'And she didn't try to contact you in the last few months?'

'No. I'd have remembered.' Vickery stood up and gazed out of the window towards the cathedral. 'I believe we're finished here, detective.'

Ross nodded to McLeod, thanked Vickery, and returned to his car, more convinced than ever the club owner was hiding something.

***

Later that morning, DCI Devlin invited Ross in for a 'little chat'. Little chats were never good news; they usually resulted in a considerable amount of work or a threat of disciplinary action.

'David,' Devlin began. His informality ruled out disciplinary matters. 'I met DC Stevens yesterday. Had a little chin wag about her work. Good girl, sort we should encourage, eh?'

'Yes, sir. I'm just a little concerned – '

'The force has to be seen to provide equal opportunities. You and me, we came through the ranks. None of this fast-track nonsense. DS Mishra's adequate, helps us meet our ethnic minority quotas, but I'm worried her liberal attitude might get in the way of good policing.'

'Has this anything to do with Kezia Lee?'

'Ah, yes. Apparently, Miss Lee came in here and feigned a panic attack, which persuaded DS Mishra to send her home. Stevens was denied the opportunity to carry out an interview that might have led to a conviction in a fraud case if not a cold murder investigation.'

'Sir, I understand the reason Miss Lee came here was because she was the subject of a vicious attack. She'd been traumatised and should have been treated in a sympathetic manner.'

'I share Stevens's view that the girl brought her troubles on herself. Stevens also made what I consider a serious allegation against you.'

Ross didn't reply.

'DC McLeod informed her that Miss Lee carried out a vicious assault of her own during the execution of a robbery. You told DC McLeod and DS Mishra you'd apprehend the young lady concerned, but I've checked the charge sheet and see no mention of an arrest. Can you please explain?'

'I interviewed Miss Lee. She claims she was defending herself against rape. I took the decision that her story had more credibility than the ramblings of a heroin addict with a conviction for violence against women.'

'Hmm.' Devlin placed his hands together as if in prayer. 'Some might argue that's a decision for the Crown Prosecution Service. What about the robbery angle?'

'Mercer, he's the addict, confirmed the only thing she pinched was a teddy bear. I can't see us making a case in court.'

'I understood she stole money as well.'

'She denied it. Any money Mercer had would be converted into drugs in an instant, not left around the house.'

'Hmm.' Devlin sat back. 'This Kezia Lee. Pretty girl?'

Ross put on his poker face. 'Some might find her attractive.'

'Be careful, David. You wouldn't be the first, you know. Beautiful woman taking your eye off the ball. I don't want to lose a good officer.'

'No danger, sir.'

'No.' Devlin placed both palms on his desk. 'Stevens also told me Miss Lee was prime suspect for a murder in Northampton.'

'They'd no evidence. Apparently, the victim was raped.'

'Perhaps not. Stevens has put forward the suggestion this might persuade us to reconsider Miss Lee as a suspect in Susan Smith's murder. Miss Lee's visit to Smith's home reinforces this. I remain convinced we've got the right man, but we need to rule Miss Lee out before Mr Carpenter starts pointing the finger. Consequently, I'm taking you off the case... for your own good, you understand... and handing it over to Mick Alder. You'll provide Mick with your files – including a write-up of your last interview with Miss Lee. I assume you taped it.'

'I thought I might make better progress outside the station.'

'A bad mistake, David, a bad mistake.' Devlin glanced at the ceiling. 'I'm going to make Stevens an acting sergeant and assign her McLeod to carry on the fraud investigation. If Stevens or Mick ask for your assistance, you will provide it, but otherwise please stay away from Kezia Lee and her mother. The same goes for DS Mishra. Do you understand?'

'Yes sir.' *Understood, yes. Accepted, not a snowball's chance in hell.*

Ross left the office as if nothing happened, turned the corner, then kicked the wall. 'Bastard!'

As if summoned like the devil, Detective Inspector Mick Alder appeared.

'Dave, I was hoping to catch you. The DCI wants me to take over your investigation. Can't think why.'

Yes, you do. 'No problem, Mick. It's done and dusted, anyway. There are a couple of lines I was pursuing. Might be worth a punt.'

'I bet one's the pikey. The DCI mentioned her.'

'No. The key one is Tom Vickery. He lied about knowing Susan Smith.'

Alder put up his hands in a gesture of surrender. 'Whoa! Vickery's got nothing to do with this. He's had no contact with the victim for eight years.'

'Okay. I'd double-check if I was you. Then there's Walter O'Donnell. He stalked Susan Smith, and he was in Norwich the night of the murder.'

'Fine, I hear what you say. But as far as I'm concerned, the killer's up the hill, and the only thing we need to do is make a few enquiries in case he tries to use this hooded man defence, or his brief blames the pikey.'

Ross spotted an opportunity. 'Mick, I know Devlin's keeping me off the case. But there were some leads I wanted to pursue.'

'No point, now Kendal's likely to plead guilty. Carpenter apparently told Devlin.'

'Are you certain it's not Carpenter playing games? He gets us complacent, then his client changes the plea in front of the jury, and he brings up all the possibilities we didn't investigate.'

Alder shrugged. 'I suppose we should close all the gaps.'

'Devlin just wants me to lay off Kezia Lee. If I keep you in the loop, will you back me if I do a bit of digging?'

'No problem.' Alder peered at his watch. 'Gotta rally the troops. I understand you've got an interview to write up. Any chance I can see it before we haul in Gypsy Rose Lee?'

Ross grunted and returned to his desk to write a partly fictitious account of his meeting with Kezia. He confirmed she'd been sent by her mother to obtain something belonging to Susan; Mercer attacked her after allowing her to take the toy animal. He left out details of her finding the body. He made a point of suggesting any follow-up should start by interviewing

144

Eve Kendal to establish whether Sabina was assisting her to prove her son's innocence.

With luck, Alder would lose interest in Kezia, and he could persuade Devlin to drop the investigation into Sabina Romanov.

***

'Ask not for whom the bell tolls...' Kezia had not read Donne's oft misquoted work, but the relationship between a bell and her mortality wasn't far from her mind. Not so much a toll, more a tinkle from the device that alerted the staff of the Green Haven Café to a customer who'd walked through the front door.

Genuine customers weren't her concern. Lydia had left Kezia with an empty café and a greater sense of unease. Her dark wolf was prowling outside – she was a little pig in a house of straw. *If only Lydia fitted CCTV... If there were witnesses sitting at the tables...*

She sat behind the counter, staring at the door. If he came, one option would be to retreat to the storeroom and flee through the fire exit at the back. That would put her in a courtyard with a ten-yard dash to a back gate padlocked against intruders. She could take the key...

It wouldn't work. He would be on her by then. Unlocking the padlock in advance would only create another potential entry point.

She'd have to fight. She walked over to the nearest table and removed a knife, hardly ideal for the task with its rounded end. A steak knife would be better... vegans never thought about the downsides of their philosophy.

A shadow at the door... a grey hood... the bell sounded.

No nightmare visions in her head...

145

'It's you,' she said.

'Normally is when you think about it,' replied Ross, throwing off the hood. 'You okay?'

'Yeah.' She scrutinised his outfit – the grey top was complemented by matching track suit bottoms. 'Why are you dressed like that?'

Ross leant against the wall between the door and the window, ensuring he remained invisible from outside. 'I'm not supposed to be here. We've got a problem. I've been banned from contacting you.'

'What do you mean 'we'?'

'I'm off the case. DC Stevens has been given the go-ahead to chase you. I might be able to head her off, but I'm giving you the heads-up.'

'Just 'cause you're off the case, why can't you talk to me?'

'Never mind. I said I've been officially banned; doesn't mean we can't talk. I have to make sure we're not seen.'

'Christ, sounds like we're having an affair.'

Ross needed to change the subject. 'You sure you're okay?'

'I don't know. I've just got this... It's hard to explain... like a sensation... He's still out there. Somewhere close, watching. Oh shit – '

Lydia walked in.

'Kezia, why are you standing with a knife in your – ' Lydia realised Ross was lurking beside her. She screamed.

'It's alright, I'm a policeman.'

'I don't believe you. Where's your badge?'

146

'Back in my flat. Kezia'll back me up.'

Lydia's eyes flicked back and forward between the pair. Her gaze finally settled on Ross. 'I'd like you to leave, please.'

Ross grimaced. 'Certainly, ma'am. Kezia, be seeing you.'

Lydia waited till the tinkle of the bell died down. 'Kezia, please tell me what happened here. Was that a policeman?'

'Yeah, it was about me being attacked the other night.'

Lydia shuffled from one foot to another. Kezia realised she was about to hear something bad.

'Kezia, I've been a little concerned about your attitude lately. On several mornings you've come in tired. I'm not going to pry into your social life, but it's affecting your work.' Lydia paused, as if trying to remember a badly rehearsed speech. 'I appreciate you had a traumatic experience on Tuesday, but I've noticed you were acting oddly before then, and I'm afraid some customers have mentioned it.'

'I'm sorry. I'll – '

Lydia was in full flow now. 'I don't care what that... that man said he was, but he didn't appear like a police officer to me. Slouching against the wall, and you with a knife in your hand. You see...' Another hesitation. 'My sister's girl wants a job. She can start tomorrow. It might be best if you left us. If you stay till five, I'll pay you for the rest of the week.'

Kezia didn't intend to beg. 'Fine. In fact, not fine. I've had enough of your effing café and your effing vegan food. I'm going now, and I'll probably head up to McDonalds and get a double cheeseburger.'

'Kezia!'

Too late. Kezia stormed into the back room, grabbed her jacket, then marched out the café without a goodbye. She'd reached the downmarket shopping area that was Anglia Square when a hand clutched her sleeve.

'Christ! You scared me.'

'Didn't see that coming, did you?' Ross released his grip. 'I was checking the area. What's happened?'

'I quit. Or I was quitted. Take your pick.'

'My fault?'

'Nah. Or maybe it was. Shit, who the hell cares? I've got to get another job now.'

'Minimum pay?'

'Yeah, nothing new. That cow Lydia wouldn't pay me any extra, always spouting on about helping the third world and the oppressed, then expecting me to run her bloody café for six quid an hour.'

'I thought the minimum was seven?'

'Not if you're twenty. It goes up when you're twenty-one, which is probably why she gave me the boot.'

Ross led her into the dark tunnel separating the shops from Magdalen Street. 'Suppose I gave you seven. Cash in hand. Would only be temporary.'

'What're you after?'

'Information. I've asked you already to visit Jez Kendal. You've missed the Thursday and Friday slots. There's something else I'd like you to do. Might mean an overnight stay.'

She smiled. 'Oh, yeah?'

Ross guessed what she was thinking. 'Alone. If you're not, that's your business. I need you to go to Nottingham and check out an address. The place where Susan Smith lived. Ask the neighbours if she ever let on why she left Norwich. And more important, why she came back.'

'Okay, no problem.'

'If you find anyone who remembered her, ask if the name Tom Vickery means anything. But be careful. Just slip it into the conversation.'

'Who's this Tom Vickery?'

Ross feared he'd told her too much. 'Someone dangerous. Someone you don't want to mess with. He runs a place called Hot Steps. That's the club where Susan Smith used to dance.'

'Okay, I've seen it. It's a strip joint in Prince of Wales Road, right?'

Ross nodded. 'Vickery prefers 'American-style gentleman's lounge'.'

'Full of gentlemen, is it?'

Ross grinned. 'I wouldn't bet on it.'

'How do I pay for this trip? Me and Ma don't use credit cards.'

'I'll fix you up with train tickets and I'll give you a couple of hundred cash. Please get receipts in case I can ever justify claiming the money back. Have you got a mobile?'

'No. I'm the only gal in the country without one.'

'How do you keep in touch with your friends?'

'Ain't got none.'

A PCSO came into view. Ross turned so his face was obscured. 'Okay, I'll get a couple of pre-paids. You have one, I'll keep the other. When could you go?'

'Today if you can bring the stuff.'

'Too soon. Tomorrow's the soonest you can go. I'll bring everything you need round to your place tonight. About eight. Okay?'

'Cool. When do you start paying me?'

'Tomorrow. Eight hours… seven… let's say you get sixty a day. And don't forget this is helping you and your Mum sort out Eve Kendal.'

Ross left Kezia to return to his flat. There would be too many questions if he turned up in Bethel Street wearing a tracksuit. Kezia took the long route back to her place, never shaking off the idea that something evil was close by.

***

'Guv, can I have a word?' Stevens approached Ross's desk.

'What?' Ross didn't look up from his keyboard.

'I can see you're busy, but… I just wanted to apologise if DCI Devlin gave you the wrong impression.'

'Depends what impression you thought the DCI gave me.'

'He…' Stevens bit her lip. 'He might have suggested I raised a complaint about you.'

Ross stared at her, playing the role of interrupted-and-angry man. 'And did you?'

'Not a complaint. I just said I was surprised you didn't take Sy Mercer's claims seriously.'

'And was I wrong?'

'We should take any claim seriously. Just because he's a…'

'Drug-addled, money-grabbing, violent little bastard. Is that what you were going to say?'

'Kezia Lee's no angel.'

Ross pointed at his in-tray. 'See this pile?' Stevens nodded. 'This heap of shit is only a fraction of the cases Devlin wants me to investigate. If I cloned myself twice, and all three of us worked twenty-four hours a day, seven days a week, I still couldn't convert half of these into successful prosecutions.'

Stevens continued to stand in front of the desk.

Ross maintained his cross face. 'There are two approaches I could use. Start at the top and work through them. Only that would mean I might spend a disproportionate time on misdemeanours and ignore the nasty stuff. Or I can weed out the minor ones or those that would never stand up in court and focus on serious offences. Which approach do you consider better serves the cause of justice?'

'The second one.'

'Right.' He finally allowed her a glimpse of a grim smile. 'So where does an allegation by a low-life like Sy Mercer fit in the spectrum of easy wins for the prosecution?'

'I understand, guv,' she said.

'Good,' he said, his attention returning to the keyboard.

Stevens didn't move. 'I visited Mrs Romanov this morning. She's confirmed Mrs Kendal asked her to stick her nose into her son's case.'

Ross stared at the screen. 'That explains her daughter's visit.'

'I suppose. The woman's a charlatan. And that Kezia's just as bad.'

'You still working that case? Best of luck.'

Stevens folded her arms. 'I can make it stick. Anyone who peddles the supernatural is a con artist.'

Ross's gaze didn't shift. 'Has anyone told you the Bishop of Norwich and his notorious gang of vicars have been extracting money from the gullible for years by claiming a Jewish joiner rose from the dead and can somehow forgive everyone's sins? You going after him as well?'

'DCI Devlin says – '

'Best of luck. Oh, and there's a guy called Pope in Italy running the same racket. Better contact Interpol.'

Stevens stood tight-lipped.

'Any progress on the attack on Kezia Lee?' asked Ross.

'The lab says he used sulphuric acid. We're working on the assumption it was a random nutter. Or an ex-boyfriend, but neither she nor her mother will admit to anyone. Uniform are mounting extra patrols in the area.'

'I'd be checking out friends and relatives of her so-called victims.'

'Yes, guv. I'll check it out. Anything else?'

Ross shook his head.

'Thanks, guv. Sorry to bother you.'

McLeod had been eavesdropping. 'Sir, I was thinking.'

'Yes, Hamish, first time for everything.'

'Wouldn't it be better if you started at the bottom of the pile? Then you'd get the cases in the right order.'

Ross grinned, then returned to finding the cheapest online open return train fare between Norwich and Nottingham.

***

The last notes of the *EastEnders* theme echoed round the flat. Kezia didn't hear it.

She removed her headphones. 'How can you watch that miserable shit?'

Sabina turned the sound down. 'I could ask you why you listen to *that* shit. Boom, boom, that's all I hear.'

Kezia contemplated turning up the volume on her small radio. Then…

A terrifying image returned.

'Quiet!'

'You shouldn't shout if you want me to shut up.'

'No.' Kezia reduced her voice to a loud whisper. 'He's near. Find a weapon.'

She wedged a dining chair under the front door handle. Storm clouds moved in her head. Something was approaching. Kezia ran to the sideboard and retrieved a carving knife. Her mother held a rolling pin.

She sensed the wolf again. Red eyes, sharp teeth, climbing the cold metal steps outside.

A distant voice – Kezia couldn't tell if it was in her head or for real… the sound of feet on steps… a yell… a cry of pain… another shout.

Sabina raised the rolling pin. 'What's happening?'

Kezia dropped the knife to the ground. She pulled the chair away and flung the door open.

Ross was crawling up the stairway. Even in the darkness Kezia could see the blood.

Chapter Twelve

Kezia stared out into the blackness of the yard below before slamming the door. Behind her Sabina carefully lowered Ross onto the sofa.

The older woman recognised the face behind the blood. 'It's that policeman.'

'Yeah, his name's David. He's cool. We need to call an ambulance.'

'No.' Ross tried to sit up. 'Nobody can discover me here.'

Sabina walked over to the sink and filled a bowl with hot water. 'What happened?'

'I spotted a guy climbing up the stairs. He'd got something in his hand – I'm guessing a baseball bat. I shouted, then he turned and attacked me. I managed to – ouch!' Ross flopped back, holding his side.

'You might have cracked a rib,' said Sabina, as she wiped Ross's face. 'And broken your nose. You need to see a doctor.'

Kezia kneeled down beside Ross. 'Did you see his face?'

'Too dark. He wore a hood. I'm wondering if it was the same guy who attacked you earlier.'

'It is. I recognised him. I can sense him even now. He's out there watching.'

Ross touched his nose, curious how Kezia had witnessed the attack through a closed door. It didn't feel broken, but blood still soaked his handkerchief. The prowler had landed a punch after Ross grabbed the baseball bat. Ross pondered how close he'd come to death. His attacker could have swung the weapon one more time but instead chose to flee.

The face… okay, it was dark, but he'd noticed something – a darkness on the left cheek. A birthmark? Or perhaps simply a shadow, a trick of the light? He'd managed a powerful kick against his attacker's shin, but it was unlikely any useable DNA ended up on his shoe. Gloves meant no fingerprints. The book said he should call it in, instruct the CSIs to scrape the ground for traces, order his troops to check CCTV and potential witnesses. The book and Devlin also said he should never pay clandestine visits to a suspect with the means to permit said suspect to flee the city in his pocket.

Ross recognised he couldn't leave these two alone. If Kezia was right, and their stalker hovered in the shadows, his departure might encourage another attack. He wasn't in the best shape to fight off an attacker, but the hooded man wouldn't guess that.

'It might be best if I stayed.'

'You want to search the house again,' said Sabina. 'You'll be planting bugs and secret cameras.'

Kezia looked at the ceiling. 'Ma, the guy can't walk.'

'Then call an ambulance. I'm not having him here, especially if you're off to Nottingham first thing.'

Kezia put a hand on Ross's shoulder. 'He's not supposed to be here. He's helping us. Who do you think's paying me to go to Nottingham?'

'I've told you not to trust coppers. They fitted up your Pa, remember.'

Ross struggled to sit up. 'Mrs Romanov. You have my promise I will not touch anything, go anywhere, except of course your bathroom facilities. I'll leave with Kezia in the morning and try never to darken your door again.'

Sabina refused to acknowledge the detective. 'Where's he going to sleep?'

'Where he is,' said Kezia. 'I'll kip with you tonight.'

Sabina uttered an inaudible gypsy curse. 'I wanted to watch TV this evening. You usually go in my room and read a book. I'm not having him in there alone with you. Not under my roof.'

Kezia looked upwards again. 'Jesus!'

For the next hour, the three sat on the sofa watching banal comedy shows, Nobody laughed. At ten past ten, Sabina announced she was going to bed and expected Kezia to join her without delay.

Ross allowed Kezia to cover him with blankets. 'Sorry to cause trouble.'

'No problem, I know why you're doing it. It's appreciated.'

'What was that about your father? That stuff about the cops fitting him up?'

Kezia grimaced. 'I dunno. It's like, well, I was nine when he went inside. The caught him handling stuff pinched off church roofs. All I remember is a bastard called Boswell shopped him.'

Boswell? Ross recalled the schoolgirl Kezia was suspected of murdering was named Boswell. He couldn't risk antagonising her. *Not yet.*

'Was he a good dad?'

'Yeah, I reckon so. I remember him perching me on his knee and calling me his little princess. He took me with him in his van when he went to buy stuff. Then I recall going with Ma to visit him in Wellingborough when he was inside. He was always happy, never moaned.'

'He died in jail, didn't he?'

'I'll never forget that day. Ma had to identify his body. They wouldn't let me see him, touch him. I begged and begged, then just sat there and cried.'

'Did they ever find out who killed him?'

'No. Although they claimed he started the fight.' She bit her lip. 'I've never believed that.'

They sat in silence for a few seconds before Ross spoke. 'I've got something for you. Fetch my jacket please.'

Kezia complied.

'In the side pocket.'

Kezia pulled out her tablet and an envelope, from which she extracted three hundred pounds and two train tickets.

'Expenses and payment in advance,' said Ross. 'I hope the tablet's okay.'

Kezia checked the device. 'Looks fine to me.'

Ross struggled to sit up, only to collapse back in pain. 'Now try the inside pocket. Padded envelope.'

Sabina screamed from the bedroom: 'What are you doing?'

'Sorting out tomorrow,' replied Kezia, before finding the package and opening it. Inside was a silver mobile phone.

'It's only an iPhone 5,' said Ross. 'You ever used one?'

'My ex had one. Cost him a bloody bomb. He let me use it sometimes.'

'You know how to make calls, send texts, take photos?'

'Sure. Like how hard is it? Have I got web access?'

'Yeah, but don't hammer it 'cause I've only put thirty quid on the account.'

'No mail?'

'No. Mail's easy to track.' Ross took a deep breath that caused a wave of pain to flow through his body. 'You got any painkillers?'

Sabina stuck her head round the door. 'I'm not waiting any longer.'

'Jesus, Ma, if you're trying to protect my virtue, you're too bloody late. Go to bed.'

Kezia then found some ibuprofen tablets. Ross consumed three.

'Thanks.' He breathed deeply before continuing. 'The phone... there are two contact numbers...'

Kezia examined the mobile while Ross massaged his side.

'The one... Teddy... that's my burner.' He grimaced. 'Ouch... sorry. Then there's the other. I've put doctor.' Another flash of pain. 'Shit.'

'I see them. It's a Norwich landline, right?'

'Right. But listen carefully. The number bit, you have subtract one from each digit. Then reverse it. And then double it. Got that?'

'Eh?'

'It's my... home number. Emergency only. If anyone finds the phone, I don't want then linking it back to me.'

Kezia did the calculations in her head. She'd remember it – if she'd ever need it.

'You're okay with what you have to do tomorrow?' asked Ross.

'Sure. Find the address, ask if they remember Susan, why she left, all that shit.'

The pain eased enough for him to sit up. 'Right. I've been doing some checking. There's a woman called Cheryl Jackson listed on the electoral roll who's been there for the past ten years. She would definitely have known Susan. Plus, Cheryl appeared on the radar of the Notts vice squad for a while.'

'No longer?'

'God knows why. Perhaps she's a reformed character. Or she's given someone a reason to stop looking. But please take care. I don't want any comeback from the Nottingham cops.'

'I'll be cool.'

Ross just smiled and bade Kezia goodnight, ignoring his gnawing suspicion over why Kezia's murdered classmate shared the same name with the man who helped destroy her beloved father.

***

Ross couldn't sleep. Pain and an uncomfortable bed made sure of that. Kezia rose to provide an early morning cup of strong coffee, delivering enough consciousness for him to limp through the town centre to his flat in the old hospital building. He retrieved his car and paid a quick visit to Bethel Street, hiding his embarrassment as he returned to his vehicle with a large toy bear under his arm, before returning to Magdalen Street.

Sabina clutched the teddy as she would a long-lost relative. 'I can feel her pain already,' she gasped.

'Probably rheumatism,' whispered Kezia to Ross.

In a quarter of an hour, Ross stood on the station concourse, scrutinising the other passengers boarding the 8.57 train, fearing his attacker followed them from the flat.

Kezia didn't share his concerns. As she headed west, she felt the darkness receding with every mile. She settled down with Agatha Christie's *Sad Cypress*, in which a detective fights to save a woman accused of murder. She smiled at the notion Ross might be her Hercule Poirot, albeit a little less dapper and minus the carefully trimmed moustache. Just after half-past eleven, the train reached its destination.

After a quick lunch at a nearby café, she allowed herself the luxury of a taxi ride to the northern edge of the city. She made sure her stated destination lay several numbers away from her objective, a bay-windowed terraced house pebble-dashed in white with brand new PVC glazing. An estate agent would have described it as in excellent condition – not what Kezia expected of a brothel.

The door opened to reveal a woman with long brown hair and grey eyes. Her complexion belonged to a twenty-year-old. The wrinkles around her eyes suggested otherwise.

Kezia smiled. 'Hi, Ms Jackson, sorry to bother you. I'm trying to find out about someone who lived here a couple of years ago. Name of Susan Smith. She might have called herself Trixie.'

A reaction – a momentary expression of shock mingled with shame. The woman regained her composure in an instant. 'I'm sorry. It's just me and my daughter live here.'

Kezia hadn't travelled over a hundred miles for nothing. 'I know Susan lived here. She was on the electoral roll.'

'Who are you? A journalist?'

'No.' *The woman radiated fear.* 'I'm a friend.'

'I never heard her talk about any friends. If you were a real friend, you'd know all about her.'

The woman made to shut the door.

Kezia's foot stopped her from succeeding. 'She's dead. Did anyone tell you?'

Now the expression turned to pure shock. It lasted slightly longer. 'What's that got to do with me? You're not police, are you?'

Time for the truth, albeit stretched. 'They're accusing me of killing her. I'm trying to clear my name.'

A neighbour emerged with a shameless stare.

'You'd better come in.' *The woman didn't want to share her lies with next door.*

Kezia walked into a neat front lounge. Cheryl Jackson had taste. The look was modern, probably Scandinavian flat pack. Flush-mounted ceiling lights, a forty-inch TV with tall external speakers. A photograph of a girl around nine years old sat on the sideboard. The room smelt of tobacco and air freshener.

Jackson removed a pink hippo from a cream sofa. 'How did she die? Not drugs, I guess. That's how I assumed she'd go.'

Kezia sat down in the space vacated by the fluffy toy. 'Beaten to death in a park.'

Jackson sat down opposite Kezia. 'Christ.' She picked up a cigarette packet. 'Trixie was still on the game then?'

Kezia nodded. 'She lived a shit life. Abusive boyfriend, heroin…' She made a point of looking round. 'I mean this looks cool. Why did she leave?'

'You a working girl too?'

'No.'

'Keep it that way. I'm one of the lucky ones. For every one of me there's a hundred Susans. What's your name, anyway?'

'Jenna. Jenna Taylor.' A rarely used alias, but the truth remained too dangerous.

Jackson lit a cigarette and offered one to Kezia. 'Fag?'

'No thanks.'

'Christ, you're a fucking saint.' Jackson took a long drag on her cigarette then turned her head away to expel the smoke. 'I keep meaning to switch to e-cigs. My boss keeps bringing these in. Smuggled.' A pause as she examined the Arabic writing on the packet. 'Sorry, you asked why she left. I chucked her out, that's why. Let me ask you something.'

'Okay.'

'She's killed in a park, so I can assume it's late at night. They suspect it's you, and even if it's not, they must have some grounds for pointing the finger. I'm wondering if you were there as well, so if you're not on the game, what were you doing?'

Kezia wondered if she'd met someone else who could read minds. 'Would you believe going through dustbins?'

'You're homeless?'

Kezia laughed. 'My Ma's... Well, like she helps people. She needs to find out about them, so I rummage around for letters and stuff.'

'Do the cops know that? Doesn't sound legal.'

'It's not.' Kezia took out a notebook. 'Mind if I take notes?'

'No problem.'

'Why did you chuck her out?'

'It's a long story, and I'm not proud. 'Specially now I find out she's dead.' Another lungful of smoke. 'Okay, let's start from the beginning. I used to work in Norwich. In a place called Hot Steps. Some of us saw an easy way to make more money.'

'That's the club run by Tom Vickery?'

Jackson stiffened. 'You know Vickery? You don't work – '

'Nah. The guy who gave me your address mentioned his name. He might be involved.'

Jackson stubbed out her cigarette. 'Shit. You should leave. I'm not saying anything that might get back to Vickery.'

'I don't want to know about him. Just why Susan pissed you off.' *Mentioning Vickery was a mistake. Get Jackson back on side.* 'If you're sorry about Susan's death you should tell me something.'

'Who gave you my name and address?'

'A friend.' She needed to leak a little more truth. 'He's a cop. He's been frozen out of the case.'

Jackson popped a trembling cigarette into her mouth. 'And you a suspect?'

'Yeah. Which is why I'm here instead of him. He can't come and I have to.'

'Is he fucking you?'

'No.' *God, I might be blushing.*

'Okay. I'm not bad-mouthing Vickery. He doesn't like his girls going freelance.' Jackson kept glancing at the window. 'I knew another girl who moved here, so I joined her. My aunt died and left me enough to buy this place. We worked together, then the girl moved out. A week later Trixie's knocking on the door. She's pregnant, and she's carrying a heap of cash. She said the other girl gave her my details.'

'Did she say where the cash came from?'

The cigarette shook in her hand. 'I'm guessing a pay-off. Or maybe she put the squeeze on a punter, threatened to tell his wife. She never said. I was already a mum, so it was good to have another working girl round the place. She had a daughter... called it Cheryl after me.' A tear formed. 'We could look after each other's kids and sometimes do a threesome. It was going fine until Cheryl got meningitis. Just before Christmas as well.'

'That's a bummer.'

'Yes, a real shitty bummer. The kid died after a few days. Susan went to pieces. She got hooked on anti-depressants, but she needed more. She started on the hard stuff. The punters stayed away. The on-line reviews bombed. She kept bursting into the room when I was doing business and demanding cash so she could score.'

'Did Trixie mention anyone from her past who might want to harm her?'

165

'Not that I remember. Although she had some guy who stalked her. She used to call him Softy Walter, like the wimp in Dennis the Menace. You ever read that?'

'No.' Kezia added 'Walter' to her shorthand notes. 'Have you got a picture of Cheryl?'

Jackson wiped her eyes. 'Yes. Hang on.'

She left the room to return a few minutes later with a photo album.

'That's her. With Susan and me and my daughter Chloe. That's taken the day we visited Cadbury World. Cheryl looks nothing like Trixie. Must have got her looks from her father.'

The picture showed a pretty, smiling, dark-haired girl between two women. The child's eyes suggested an intelligence, a bright future cut short by tragedy. Jackson wiped more tears away.

'Mind if I take a picture?' asked Kezia, pulling out her phone.

'Only if you promise to cut me out of it.'

Kezia used Ross's mobile to capture an image of Susan and her daughter. She showed Jackson the result, receiving a nod in reply.

'Why did Trixie go back to Norwich?' asked Kezia.

'She reckoned she could get her old job back. Working for Vickery. No fucking chance.'

'She ever name the kid's father?'

'She never found out his name, that's if she could narrow it down. Trixie was a scatty cow at the best of times. Might have forgotten to take the pill. Although she once claimed he was a freemason.'

'A freemason?'

'I suppose. She mentioned a lodge. Bunch of rich men and a bucketful of secrecy. God knows what they got up to. It was like she was scared to tell me much about it.'

'What happened to the kid? I mean, like where's Cheryl buried?'

'Cremated. I've no idea where Trixie scattered the ashes. It was weird. She burnt the girl's clothes in the back garden. All she kept was Cheryl's tooth in a locket.'

'Have you given up… you know… the business?'

'Too true. It's not what it was. Too many east Europeans coming in. Trafficked, most of them. These days I work in webcamming. The money's not as good, but it's safer. You got a job when you're not doing this?'

'I'm doing this full time now,' Kezia lied.

Kezia left shortly afterwards. She walked to the end of the road and rang Ross.

'A mason?' he asked when she'd finished her report.

'Sounds like it. All you cops are masons, aren't you?'

'I'm not. I don't know many who are. Perhaps in the 1960s you wouldn't make DI without a rolled-up trouser leg, but not now. I'm wondering if Tom Vickery's a member. It would fit with his move into respectable society.'

'Anything else I need to do here?'

'No, come back when you're ready. You've done well.'

Ross rang off and eased himself into his chair. He's just returned from a lengthy visit to A&E where they'd diagnosed cracked ribs. His colleagues thought he'd fallen over.

McLeod didn't give him a chance to get comfortable. 'Hi guv, the results from Susan Smith's phone company have come back.'

'Shoot.'

'Her phone hasn't been used since the murder. The number she called is a pay-as-you-go.'

'Have you identified whose?'

'No, but we've tracked it. It's usually static in one location. The Nest Lane estate.'

The Nest Lane estate, west of the city centre, rated by some as being in the bottom ten percent in England in terms of affluence. 'No surprise there. Can we get an actual address?'

'Not with any accuracy. We can narrow it to a few houses. I've checked our records and there's one that sticks out. It's where Red Stibbons hangs out.'

'Who?'

'Red Stibbons. His actual name's Alfred. He's got a couple of convictions for possession. The drugs boys have him down as a low-level supplier and he's on a watch list.'

Ross winced as his ribs spasmed again. 'He sounds like her dealer. Chances are he supplied her on the same day she called. Sod the drugs boys, tell Mick Alder to drag him in.'

Ten minutes later Ross was reaching for another couple of painkillers when Stevens appeared at his desk.

'Guv, we're about to start an interview. Thought you might like to observe. Not that I suggested it, okay?'

A few moments later Ross stood before a monitor watching an interrogation. The subject was a man in his late forties, square face, eyes a little too close together over a pugilist's nose. The hair was cropped short, only accentuating the dark birthmark on the left cheek.

DI Mick Alder and Stevens sat opposite.

'Why the hell am I here? I only came in here to find out whether you lot had done anything. I need to get home soon.'

Alder sat back in his chair. 'Simply routine, Mr Leadbetter. You did ask to speak to me.'

Joe Leadbetter, Phyllis's son. Ross now understood why he'd been summoned.

It wasn't hard to distinguish Leadbetter from Mr Happy. 'Only because this... sorry, Sergeant Stevens... she couldn't tell me anything.'

Stevens didn't correct his promoting her. 'I did tell you we'd not found any evidence of wrongdoing. So far Mrs Romanov has only offered to help your mother contact your late father. If she actually claims to have talked to the dead, then we can do her under the Unfair Trading legislation.'

'You people are stupid. It's bloody human rights, isn't it? Everyone knows when you're dead, you're dead. And what about the daughter?'

Alder leant forward. 'The daughter?'

'Right. There's a Facebook group called 'Victims of Phoney Mediums' and I found someone who reckons the daughter is in on it. She steals things.'

Ross wondered why Stevens hadn't mentioned the site before.

Alder sat back again. 'Interesting. What do you do for a living, Mr Leadbetter?'

'I work for Lewinski's off Salhouse Road. Will this take long? I have to go home and pack. We're flying from Gatwick tomorrow.'

'Laboratory suppliers, aren't they?' Alder's question was too nonchalant. 'Chemicals and stuff?'

Leadbetter reached for a glass of water. His hand shook. 'So?'

Alder edged forward again. 'Do you handle sulphuric acid?'

'We might have some in stock. Why?'

'What were you doing Tuesday night?'

'I – I – Why do you need to know? You trying to fit me up?'

Too nervous. If Ross had been in there, he'd have pressed harder. Alder was content to sit back.

'Please answer the question, Mr Leadbetter,' said Stevens.

'Okay. I went home, then at half eight I popped out to check on Mum. Got there a quarter of an hour later, left at... I don't know... I usually leave at quarter to ten and arrive back home just after ten. My wife'll back me up.'

'What about your mother? Would she remember?'

Leadbetter's hand shook as he took another drink.

'Yes... she's a bit... you understand... forgetful... but you could ask her. Look, I promised my wife I'd be back by five so we could get going.'

'Where are you off to?' asked Stevens.

'Tenerife. Two weeks.'

Ross was curious as to why the time Leadbetter claimed to have left his mother differed from the one reported by McLeod. He also questioned why an innocent man would have reacted so strongly over Alder's interest in his whereabouts on Tuesday evening.

Alder addressed his suspect's concern. 'You see, somebody attacked Mrs Romanov's daughter on Tuesday night. Anything to add?'

'The cow got what she deserved then,' snapped Leadbetter.

'Her attacker used sulphuric acid. Nasty. Not something you can buy from Tesco.'

'Jesus… Wasn't me. I mean, if I'd gone for anyone it would have been her mother.'

'We're still reviewing CCTV,' said Alder. 'If it was you, we'll track your movements. Best to confess now, sir. Make things easier.'

Leadbetter gazed down at the table. *Keep pushing,* thought Ross. *He's going to crack.*

Too late. Alder had given Leadbetter a chance to compose himself. 'Where did this attack take place?'

'Near Fye Bridge,' said Stevens.

'I wasn't anywhere near there.'

Further questioning revealed nothing. Ross returned to his desk only for Stevens to appear.

'What did you think, guv?'

'He's lying. I'm guessing he visited his mum, but not for as long as he says. When I saw her, she said he left at nine on the Friday so no reason to be different on a Tuesday, especially as that's when Hamish said he vanished. Are you checking CCTV like Alder suggested?'

'We've had a look,' she replied. 'What little there is suggests a figure in a hood is following Lee, but we never get sight of his face. It could be Leadbetter, but there's no way of telling.'

'Come on. Kezia started from the Lollards Pit. Leadbetter's at his mums, a few hundred yards away. Why is Alder letting him go?'

Stevens shrugged. 'No choice.'

'Means, motive, opportunity.'

'Alder can't see the motive. Leadbetter's right. Why go after the girl?'

Ross had already asked himself the same question. The best, if not welcome, answer was that Kezia's investigations had revealed more about the son than the mother, and she'd tried to blackmail Joe Leadbetter. Not a suggestion he intended to share.

Instead, Ross just said, 'Yup. He's got a point.'

'And if it was him, he's aware we're onto him. He won't dare bother her again.' Stevens grinned. 'Much as she deserves it.'

'You set up that Facebook site, didn't you?'

'Guv?'

'Victims of phoney mediums. You're trying to coax other mugs out of the woodwork, aren't you?'

Her grin remained. 'You won't find me admitting it.'

'If something happens to Kezia Lee, it could be your fault. Did you consider that?'

'Wouldn't lose any sleep… guv.'

Don't let her wind you up.

Ross dismissed Stevens and pulled the first case file off his in-tray. He opened it but thought of nothing but Kezia. Had she deceived him? Was Leadbetter the man who attacked them both? Would he be sitting by the pool in Tenerife plotting further attacks? If it was Joe Leadbetter, she'd be safe for a fortnight.

Mishra appeared beside him, clutching a piece of paper. 'Sir, you got a minute?'

'Sure,' he lied. 'Shoot.'

'You remember you asked me to find out about Susan Smith's social worker?'

'Yeah. Any luck?'

'Depends what you mean. Have you heard of Operation Bane?'

'I got involved. Joint investigation with Suffolk into kiddie porn.'

Mishra placed the paper on his desk: a screenshot showing a photograph of a middle-aged man wearing glasses. 'Leonard Cooper, decision made not to prosecute as others in his office had access to his computer. He was Smith's last known social worker.'

'And? I assume you'll have looked into this.'

Mishra nodded. 'Social Services put Cooper in charge when Smith absconded from the children's home. They asked us to help, but then Cooper said she'd found lodgings with her cousin and he was happy she was safe.

'The chief warden of the home allegedly met with Susan who swore the woman she shacked up with was her relative.' Mishra stared down at Cooper's photo. 'Perhaps we should recheck that. They didn't look after her, did they?'

'Somebody should,' said Ross. 'Is Cooper still working?'

'He left. By mutual consent, and I got the old privacy excuse when I tried to find out more. I've obtained Cooper's present address if you decide it's worth a shot.'

After Mishra left Ross stared at Cooper's image. The epitome of a kindly old uncle. Children would trust him. He might of course be innocent, the victim of a devious colleague. Ross's gut dismissed the possibility as unlikely before pointing out that, if guilty, Cooper had a motive for silencing his former charge.

His thoughts were cut short by his phone: Devlin. 'DI Ross, you put in a request to detain an Alfred Stibbons, did you not?'

'Yes, sir. Person of interest in the Susan Smith case.'

'I thought we'd already arrested the murderer? And I recall I took you off the case.'

'Most likely, sir, but we need to tie up loose ends. Mick's happy with me helping him.' *Or he will be once I've spoken to him.*

'I've spoken to DI Kemble. Stibbons is under surveillance as part of a drugs operation. We will not take him off the streets merely to satisfy your curiosity. Understood?'

'Yes, sir. Do you know if he was under surveillance the night of the murder?'

'No idea. You'll have to speak to Fliss Kemble.'

Ross guessed the answer before he dialled the DI in charge of the narcotics operation. She'd no idea where Stibbons spent that Friday night. And she wouldn't let him find out either.

***

Kezia arrived back in Norwich just after half-past eight. She wondered if she should call Ross but decided against it.

She felt strangely content as she returned to the flat. Even though the light was fading, a darkness seemed to have vanished from the world.

Chapter Thirteen

The wolf might have slinked off into the far recesses of Kezia's mind, but the ghosts of the past had slithered into its place. She'd spent Saturday morning looking for employment, deliberately avoiding anywhere she'd have to wear a uniform. A greasy spoon on Dereham Road met most of the requirements, not the least being they wouldn't seek a reference from Lydia, or anyone else come to that.

Sabina had confessed that despite emanating an aura of pain, the teddy bear had not disclosed the identity of Susan Smith's killer, although she claimed it told her Jez Kendal was innocent. She remained adamant, however, that Susan's spirit insisted she had never seen the murderer before. Kezia expressed her doubts about this assertion, but she recognised Sabina was totally convinced of this communication, more so than some of her 'spiritual revelations' in the past.

Now Kezia walked the final two hundred yards towards Norwich jail. Memories of visits to Wellingborough prison flooded back, the strongest being that tearful day when she knew she could expect no more embraces from her cold, murdered father. She agreed with her mother that Jez Kendal should not be told of the reason for her visit. Instead, Ross invented a charity supporting ex-servicemen awaiting trial.

She called Ross from the visitors' centre outside the prison after they'd verified her ID. In truth she was delaying the inevitable, the return to a place of incarceration. He expressed satisfaction with her progress.

'Oh, Kezia, one more thing. The guy who attacked you...'

'He's gone. I'm sure. Don't ask me how.'

'We're confident we've found out who it was. We can't prove it yet. But he's left the country for two weeks. We'll watch him when he returns.'

'He's gone forever. Trust me.'

'He's coming back, Kezia. Hopefully he won't try it again now he knows we're onto him.'

If the wolf lurked anywhere on the planet, I would know. Surely? Kezia wondered again if her powers, if she could describe them as such, had diminished. Could her feelings for Ross be the cause?

She couldn't stay outside any longer. Inside, the smell and echoes were painfully familiar. Kezia considered turning back, but within half an hour she sat opposite the man accused of killing Susan Smith.

'I'm Kezia,' she said, offering her hand.

He held it just too long – against the rules.

'No physical contact!' The guard glared at her.

It didn't matter anymore. She'd touched him... connected.

'Call me Kendz,' he said. 'My mum says you can help me. You're from some charity, right?'

She gazed into his one good eye, gleaning his unspoken thoughts. 'That's right. We need to find out if you're happy with your legal representation.'

'That Mr Carpenter, he's all right, but... He wants me to plead guilty, says I can claim diminishing responsibility or summat, but I says I'm innocent.'

He's telling the truth. 'Tell me what happened.'

Kendal looked down. *He's embarrassed about something.*

'Look, Kendz, you can talk to me. I'm not easily shocked and I keep secrets. You'd be surprised what I've heard in this job. You don't tell me the complete truth, I can't help you.'

'Okay. I leave work and have a few beers in the Angler. Then I fancy… you know…'

'A shag. Carry on?'

Kendal's eyes opened wide. He clearly hadn't expected this level of frankness from a charity worker. 'You got a boyfriend?'

'Sorry, yes.' *A lie and I feel bad about it.* 'You wanted a shag. What did you do?'

'You've got to understand. I can't get a girl.' He pointed to his false eye. 'Not like this. I've got needs like any other guy.'

Kezia reflected on her own self-pity. Only her lifestyle and guilt stopped her from finding a partner – if not a soulmate. She could ditch her Ma, sleep around until she found someone close to Mr Right. She'd be in control. Jez Kendal lay trapped in another place. 'I understand. Really, I do. What happened after you left the pub?'

'I head up Rosary Road. I meet the foreign blonde bit, but she's not interested.'

'Why not?'

'Dunno.'

You're lying now. You won't admit you've been a bit rough in the past.

Kendal's sad eye fixed on hers. 'This boyfriend, is it serious?'

'Yeah, we've been together years. Almost married.' She broke off eye contact. 'Sorry, the blonde's not putting out. What next?'

'Then I see Trixie. She reckon I haven't got enough for the... you know...'

'Shag.'

'Yeah, well...' Kendal's shame showed through again. *Susan offered him some service...*

'She offered you a hand job.'

No reaction. Try again.

'Sorry, I remember now. It was a blow job.'

'How do you find out?'

'We've got someone inside the cop station. Did she take you into Old Library Wood?'

'Where?'

'The park off Rosary Road.'

'Why are you asking me all this? I can't see why a charity wants to know.'

'Do you trust your solicitor?'

'My mum picked him. Cost her a packet. He's the best.'

'We need to ensure he is the best. That sort, they often take the money and run. Like, if you went to Eton or Oxford, they'd give you a hundred percent, but an ex-squaddie... Not saying he's going to shaft you, but we like to be sure.' She smiled at him. 'When you got to the park, did you see anyone?'

'No. Not then. Anyway, Trixie does the business – ' He put his head in his hands.

'Back up, Kendz. You had your tool bag with you, didn't you?'

'Yeah. Always carry it. I put it down while she... you know...'

'You being pissed, I expect it took a bit longer.'

Kendal gazed at Kezia for five seconds before replying. 'Yeah... Sure, but Trixie's good. Sorry, was good. It didn't take that long.'

She wondered how close he came to not getting it up at all. Perhaps he wasn't as intoxicated as he claimed.

'Where did you leave your bag? Close by?'

'Fuck me, I can't remember. Few feet away, maybe.'

'Okay. She's done the business. What then?'

'I pick up the bag and walk home. Then this bloke come up and says I dropped my hammer. He give it me.'

'What did he look like?'

Kendal shrugged. 'Christ, I was pissed, and it was dark. He wore black clothes, a black hood.'

The wolf crept into her imagination. 'Do you remember nothing about him? His voice?'

'Shit, now you're asking. Growly – like he's trying to disguise it.' His one eye fixed on Kezia. 'Could even have been a woman.'

Dangerous. If the police took him seriously and looked for a woman in a black hoodie, she might be in the spotlight again. *Time to stop digging...*

'They treating you okay in here?'

'So-so. It'd be nice if you could visit again. If your fellow's okay about it, that is.'

Before she left Kezia asked him about his time in the army and his recovery from his wounds, then shared the problems of living with mothers.

As she left the gloom of the prison, her thoughts drifted to Jez Kendal sitting in a cell, denied the late afternoon sun now warming her face. Although Kezia's brief employment with Ross had ended, her mother still needed her help. But she now had another motive to keep digging...

She felt a kinship with Kendal. They shared so much: both lonely outcasts from society, both had suffered pain and rejection. The difference was that he was accused of a crime he didn't commit. He'd nothing to feel guilty about.

She'd have to find someone else to take the blame.

***

Ross persuaded Mishra to accompany him to a terraced house in the coastal town of Gorleston, on the trail of another loose end. Leonard Cooper, a former social worker, was at home. They heard his shuffling footsteps on the other side of the door before it opened to reveal a stooping figure, wispy white hair clinging to his skull. His eyes were rheumy, his skin mottled. Ross found it hard to believe he'd located the same man whose photograph had appeared on his desk, especially as records put Cooper in his late fifties.

Ross flashed his warrant card. 'Leonard Cooper?'

'So? What d'you want?' The voice sounded hoarse, angry.

'I'm Detective Inspector David Ross. This is Detective Sergeant Kirsi Mishra.' He paused while Mishra showed Cooper her own card. 'We'd like to ask you about Susan Smith.'

'I don't remember anything,' muttered Cooper. 'You've wasted your time.'

'Can we come in please?' asked Ross.

'Suppose. She's dead, isn't she?'

Cooper led them into a drab front room No pictures, no photographs. A worn sofa and matching chair. A sideboard with shelves holding nothing but dust and documents. A smell of bad body odour and frying. He grunted as he moved newspapers from the settee to allow his unwanted guests to sit down. Ross looked at the pile of correspondence on the table: a letter from James Paget hospital confirming an appointment with the oncology department; a tourist brochure promoting the Philippines; a reminder from British Gas.

Ross's suspicions worked overtime. 'You were Susan Smith's social worker, right?'

Cooper's gaze flitted between the two detectives. 'Only for a few months.'

'Three years according to Norfolk Social Services,' said Mishra. 'One year overseeing her progress at the children's home, two years checking she remained safe until she reached eighteen.'

Ross picked up the brochure. 'Why did she abscond?'

Cooper's eyes fixed on the document in Ross's hand. 'She was trouble. I wasn't shocked when I read she'd been murdered.'

'Trouble?' said Ross. 'I imagine you'd describe a lot of the kids as troubled. That's why Social gets involved. You need to give me more.'

'Improper relationships with boys, that sort of thing. Staying out late. She might've been on drugs. She always argued with the staff.'

'Why did they allow her to leave the home?' asked Mishra. 'She should have been there till she reached eighteen.'

Cooper continued to stare at the brochure, rubbing his nose at the same time. 'She ended up with her cousin. She seemed happy, settled. We decided it was in her best interests.'

'There's a slight problem,' said Mishra. 'I checked. The woman she stayed with wasn't her cousin. She left the same home three years earlier. You should have realised that.'

Cooper made eye contact with Mishra. 'You don't understand. Have you any bloody idea what our workload's like? We don't have time to check everything. Susan swore it was her cousin, so I believed her. I checked to make sure it was a comfortable home. Safe.'

Mishra stared at Cooper. 'The woman had a conviction for prostitution. You should have checked that.'

Cooper looked away and grabbed loose skin around his throat. 'The police didn't tell me. You lot were supposed to get her back, not leave it to me.'

Mishra leaned forward. 'Why did you leave Social Services, Mr Cooper?'

'Stress. You bastards didn't help. You tried to fit... fit me up. Said I had... you know, stuff on my works computer.'

Ross nodded at Mishra. 'Where were you on Friday the fourteenth?'

'Here. I don't go out. I'm a sick man.'

'Well enough to go to the Philippines,' said Ross. He nodded to Mishra. 'Strange choice of destination. I wonder what the attraction is?' The DI turned back to Cooper. 'Can anyone confirm your movements?'

Cooper's voice began to break. 'I live alone, so why bother asking?'

Mishra took over. 'Have you had any contact with Susan in the past two years?'

Cooper looked at the floor. 'No.'

'Are you sure?'

'No. I mean yes. I never seen her.'

'Do you ever go into Norwich?'

'Sometimes. Not often.'

'When did you last visit the city?'

Cooper now visibly trembled. 'I haven't a bloody clue. May... June. Why do you want to know?'

Ross feared Cooper would clam up. He guessed the man was guilty, but not of murder.

He tried a change of direction. 'Just routine, Mr Cooper. Tell me, what do you know about Susan's early life? I mean, why did she end up in the home?'

Cooper sat back in his chair. 'You'll have to ask Social Services. I recall her parents were alcoholics, if she even had a proper father. She'd been in the home from the age of seven or eight. I know that.'

'No other relatives you're aware of?'

'Only her cousin. But then you're telling me – '

'Not a cousin. She had no-one else?'

'That's right.'

'Okay, Mr Cooper. That's it for now. Only thing left is to take a sample of your DNA.'

'Why? What are you accusing me of?' Cooper clenched his shaking fists. 'Don't I have a right to refuse?'

'Of course.' Ross smiled. 'But then we'd be suspicious, and we'd have to get a warrant, take you back to Norwich and then ask all the neighbours about your movements.'

The former social worker grumbled, then allowed Mishra to obtain the sample. It gave Ross a chance to glance around the room. Another brochure, this one advertising Thailand, a photograph showing a younger Cooper with three other men, a couple of menus from local takeaways.

'Well, sir,' said Mishra when they arrived back at his car. 'What do you reckon?'

'You tell me first.'

'Okay. He's lying about something. I suspect he has talked to Susan. And I can't accept he didn't have suspicions about the so-called cousin.'

'Is he our murderer?'

'Can't see it somehow.'

Ross steered the car onto the road back to Norwich. 'I agree. But he's a first-class kiddie fiddler. Did you see his holiday choices? He's a sick man, being treated for cancer. He might be in remission if he's contemplating a trip abroad. Do you want to hear my theory?'

Mishra nodded.

'Okay. I think either he assaulted Susan when she was under his care or she had proof of what else he was up to in the home. Fifteen-year-olds might be a bit too mature for him. Suppose when she goes, she blackmails him into confirming her story about the cousin.'

'Sounds plausible,' said Mishra.

'Good. And I agree with you, he's seen Susan recently. Perhaps she tried to put the squeeze on him again. But I can't see her getting anything. He'll need every penny he can grab to fund his perverted fun in the Far East.'

'What do we do?'

'We tell the child protection people about our suspicions. We run his DNA through the system. I doubt we'll get a match with the Susan case, but you never know what else might pop up.'

'She never had a chance, did she?' said Mishra.

'Life dealt her a dud hand, that's for sure. But she didn't take it lying down.' Ross realised what he'd said. 'Bloody awful choice of words. But she's tried to turn what little she had to her advantage.'

'Didn't turn out so well…'

'Perhaps not. But apparently, she had a load of cash when she left Norwich, almost certainly provided by Tom Vickery. If I'm right she's forced Cooper into a lie that could have ended his career.'

'How did you find out about the cash from Vickery?'

Damn, I can't tell her about Kezia. 'Just a piece of info someone called in. Somebody who met her in Nottingham.'

'Who was that, sir?'

186

'Some woman she shacked up with. No matter. The key thing is it suggests Susan was happy to use a bit of blackmail to get her way, and it's possible that's what got her killed.'

No way would he reveal it, but in Ross's mind Tom Vickery seemed the most likely target of that blackmail.

***

When night fell, Kezia retraced her initial steps of the previous Friday. This time she did not avoid Rosary Road. Her target now was the woman with spiky blonde hair standing on the pavement in a short skirt and high heels.

'Hi, I wonder if you can help me?'

'No. Piss off.' The woman looked away, readying herself for the next car.

'It's about Susan Smith. You know, the woman who got killed.'

'Piss off. I know nothing.' Still no eye contact. Kezia sensed fear and lies.

'Please, there's a killer out there. Beats people like you to death. You should help.'

Now Mirjeta Bardici showed interest. 'You cop?'

'No. I'm somebody who cares.'

Kezia heard footsteps behind her. A thin man in a leather jacket and jeans marched towards her, a cigarette hanging from his mouth.

'What do you want?'

Kezia still had some of Ross's cash left. He couldn't grudge another expense.

'I want a bit of girl-on-girl action. You gotta problem?'

The man shrugged. 'She pay, you do. Okay?'

'I no go with women,' protested Bardici.

'You do who I say.' He turned to Kezia. 'Fifty pound. Okay?'

Ross would baulk at that. 'Twenty – maybe just a hand job?'

'Give me.' The pimp threw down the cigarette and held out a hand.

Kezia gave him a twenty-pound note.

'You be quick,' the man said.

A nervous Bardici led Kezia towards the Old Library Wood. Kezia looked behind to make sure the pimp didn't follow. She'd seen violence and cruelty in his eyes.

Once they were out of his sight Kezia placed a hand on Bardici's arm. 'No hand job, right? I need information.'

'I know nothing.'

Kezia fought the dark memories of her last visit to this wilderness in the heart of the city. 'Don't worry, you're safe. I'm not a cop.'

'Then who are you?'

'I'm a friend of – ' *No, the girl doesn't like Jez.* 'I hunt down killers.'

'Ardi don't like me talk to strangers.'

'Ardi's not here. Let me ask questions. If you can't answer, just say. Okay?'

Bardici looked round to check her pimp hadn't appeared. 'Sure.'

'How well did you know Susan?'

'I call her Trixie. She my friend. Ardi no like her. He want other girls, his girls, on street.'

'Do you believe he might have killed Susan?'

'No. Kendz killed her. Police say so. But Ardi kill me if I cross him, I know.' Another fearful glimpse around.

'Was he with you on Friday night?'

'He leave me here then I go with Brian in car the night I last see Trixie. Ardi not there when I come back – he turn up later.'

'Who's Brian?'

'He a punter. Nice man, treat me good. Take me to place other side of Mousehold. He work there and we go to first aid room. Most Tuesday, every Friday. But he on holiday so I no see him this week.'

'What time did you go with Brian?'

Bardici shrugged. 'I never bother with time.'

'Jez asked you for business first that night, didn't he?'

'Who Jez? You no mean Kendz? Kendz bad man. He rough, hurt me. I glad he in jail.'

'Right, Kendz. How did he seem? Drunk?'

'He very drunk. Make him worse.'

'Did you see anyone else? Anyone following Trixie?'

'No.'

'How did Trixie seem that night? I mean, did she act odd, happy, excited, that sort of thing?'

'Same as before. I sorry she dead. She say she leave business soon.'

'What do you mean?'

'She say she find way make lot of money.'

'She tell you what?'

'No. But...'

'But what?'

'I tell Ardi. He want to know bad. Now I go. Please no tell him I speak.'

Bardici fiddled with the front of her skirt as she walked away. Kezia smiled with admiration. The streetwalker was taking no chances. She needed the smell of a woman on her hands.

***

Kezia curled up on the sofa in a rare, contented mood. The wolf had vanished from her thoughts. She had enough to tell Ross the case against Jez Kendal was flawed. Tomorrow she would call him and begin the process that would see the accused man walk free.

She slept peacefully, until...

Seven o'clock, Sunday morning. A bang on the door. More visions of beasts, close, snarling... 'Open up, police!'

Kezia pulled on a T-shirt and jeans and staggered to the door. A female officer and a man in his forties wearing a grey suit waited outside. At the foot of the steps, Linda Stevens

190

stood with a triumphant grin, another suited middle-aged male by her side.

The man on the threshold nodded to the woman who produced a pair of handcuffs. 'Miss Lee, I'm Detective Inspector McNab from Northamptonshire Police. I'm arresting you on suspicion of the murder of Hester Boswell on the fourteenth of September 2011. You do not...'

Another nightmare began.

Chapter Fourteen

Ross stood in front of a monitor, Stevens at his side. The screen showed Kezia facing two men in their late fifties. Despite the poor quality of the video feed, he recognised Kezia's nervousness.

'Thought you'd like in on this, guv.'

'Like' wouldn't be the first word that came to Ross's mind. He guessed the visitors had requested the room – narrow, windowless, claustrophobic, a cold fluorescent light flickering every so often.

'Who are they?'

'I understand it's DI McNab and DS Easton from Northamptonshire. Cold case unit.'

Ross could only see the backs of the two men's heads. The light reflected off McNab's bald spot, and when he turned Ross noticed a beard. Easton sported a mass of grey hair with long sideburns.

McNab led the questioning. 'Care to explain, Miss Lee?'

Kezia began to shake.

Stevens pointed at the monitor. 'She's going to do her falling over act.'

McNab stared down at his notebook. 'Miss Lee. You announced Hester Boswell's death before her father found her corpse. I put it to you that you'd only possess such information if you'd already seen the body.'

'I've told you. I just knew.'

'Why hasn't she got a brief?' asked Ross.

'She told us she didn't want one.' Stevens shot him a knowing smile. 'Asked whether you were around, though.'

Easton tapped the table with his pen. 'Come on, Kezia... Do you mind if I call you Kezia? It will be so much better if you tell us the truth. You were a teenager, hormonal and all that. Explain what really happened and we'll make sure the court treats you lightly.'

Kezia glared at Easton. She'd wrapped her arms round her chest, no longer trembling.

He just smiled back. 'We found your earring. The lab will verify the blood's yours. I'm guessing you and Hester fought. I expected you acted in self-defence. Any court will treat you lightly if you only confess.'

'God, they're using the good cop, bad cop routine,' said Ross.

'They stole both of them a few days before.' Kezia looked up at the camera as if she was aware Ross observed her ordeal. 'Her and those other bitches. They ripped my earrings out of my ear. I bled. Ask them.'

'We spoke to Darren Kemp,' said McNab.

'So?'

'Darren Kemp. Your first boyfriend. You had the hots for him, didn't you?'

'I was a kid. You're falling in love every other week. So what?'

'Hester Boswell moved in, didn't she? Darren reckoned you weren't as... how shall I put it... accommodating... as Hester.' Ross imagined McNab grinning. 'Said you turned out to be a frigid little cow.'

Kezia sat back, folded her arms, stared at the edge of the table in front of her. Ross recognised she was fighting her demons, desperate to take back control. 'Hester was a slut. Like she'd put it out for anyone.'

Stevens nudged Ross. 'She's lying, guv.'

McNab shuffled through his notes. 'Miss Lee, the DCI who investigated this case before assumed it was stranger rape. We know different now. You remember what happened. There's this bunch of kids in the woods near your house. You probably hid behind a tree, watching them having fun. You might have seen Hester and Darren doing it. Making love on a blanket.'

He stopped, waiting for a reaction. 'Sorry, a poor choice of words. Fucking.' Another pause. 'Darren admits he wasn't very experienced, hadn't understood the finer points of foreplay. I suppose you weren't a very good teacher. He got a bit rough. He claims the sex was consensual and Hester's not going to say otherwise, is she?'

Kezia trembled again, her gaze never leaving the table.

'We've got witnesses who say Darren left with his mates after they'd had sex. Hester walked off alone. Probably with a big, satisfied smile on her face.'

'Darren was a bastard.'

'What about Hester? She seduced your boyfriend. You probably looked forward to a nice big virgin gypsy wedding. You're all gypsy stock, aren't you?'

Stevens laughed. 'Bet he's dying to say pikey.'

Ross said nothing. No emotion on his face, his fists clenching tighter by his side.

McNab sat forward. Kezia's agitation became more evident.

'It must have been terrible. Maybe you thought he was a virgin, saving himself for your wedding night, and there he was, banging away with a girl you hated.'

Kezia slumped forward, her hands over her ears in a desperate attempt to block out the noise. Ross imagined the DI as a matador going in for the kill, his victim's anger exhausted.

'Here's what I believe happened. Here's Hester all on her own. The girl who stole your boy. Plus, she's the daughter of the man who put your father in jail. Got him killed, even though I hear your old man started the fight.'

McNab moved even closer to Kezia. 'Streak of violence runs in your family, doesn't it? Bad genes, I reckon. You run out, confront her, she rips out your earring, you pick up a brick and hit her with it.'

'No.'

'Must have freaked you out. Losing the earring. I can picture you scrabbling on the ground looking for it.' His voice rose. 'Isn't that the way it was?'

'No.'

McNab lounged back and had another peek at his notes. 'Don't like sluts, do you? You seem to have been around when the hooker got done last week. Bit of a coincidence?'

Kezia sat up. 'I wasn't anywhere near.'

Ross knew she lied, and her body language didn't contradict him. He slammed his right fist into his left palm. 'Why are they looking at our case?'

'Worth a punt, guv,' said Stevens. 'Especially now they've got new evidence on the Boswell killing.'

McNab leant forward again. 'Come on, Miss Lee. The cops here have got the hoodie you wore the night you killed Susan Smith. There's evidence linking you to the scene. You even visited the victim's house and assaulted her partner. Was it because she's a prostitute? A cheap tart, like Hester Boswell?'

'No.' Her eyes now flicked between the table and the camera.

'We checked our records again. We dug up a domestic in Northampton. A flat belonging to a Danny Wilby. Two officers called and sorted things out. We didn't raise any charges.'

'Please stop. This is crazy.' Kezia finally looked at her accuser, panic in her eyes.

'Seems you threatened to kill him. Apparently, he'd been to a stag party in Budapest and had a little bit of a frolic with the local ladies of pleasure. He brought you back a souvenir. A dose of chlamydia, was it not?'

Kezia stood up, fists balled. 'None of your fucking business!'

Another nudge from Stevens. 'Ooh. Touched a nerve there.'

'You struck lucky there,' continued McNab. 'Got off with a warning. It shows why you don't like whores.' He closed his folder. 'Question is – do we take you back with us or let the locals grill you on the hooker murder? What do you think, Mike?'

Ross couldn't see Easton's expression, but he imagined a gleeful smile. 'Take them in order, sir. We got there first. What do you reckon, Miss Lee? If you can convince us you didn't mean to kill Hester, we'll go easy. Perhaps reduce the charge to manslaughter.'

'Fuck you,' snapped Kezia. 'Fuck, fuck, fuck, fuck you.' She stared at the camera, her eyes flashing hatred. 'And fuck you, Ross. I trusted you... you bastard.'

Her gaze remained fixed for around five seconds. Then she turned and clutched her head again.

'Anything you'd like to say, guv?' Stevens walked away before he found an answer.

Ross stumbled back to his desk. His ribs hurt, but he felt a deeper pain. They'd broken Kezia. And she held him responsible.

Protocol says you can't whisk a suspect out of the reaches of a force who's given you every assistance and might have an interest in said suspect for what arguably was a more serious offence. Easton and McNab therefore agreed to leave Kezia in the Norwich custody cells for the next few hours.

Devlin was not a happy man, as he made plain to Ross from behind his large and almost empty desk.

'David, this is a right mess. We had Jez Kendal bang to rights for the Smith murder and now this fresh evidence has come to light. Miss Lee appears to have motive, opportunity, and if we accept Kendal's story, the means. And worse, I understand she claimed you two had some sort of relationship.'

'Kendal still looks like our man.'

'Hmm. I must say I agree with you, but... The most important thing is to keep any mention of this complication from the media.'

'Yes sir.'

'Can I ask about your relationship with Miss Lee?'

'Purely professional, sir. I wondered if the acid attack might be linked to the murder. Someone might be worried she saw something and tried to stop her talking.'

Devlin shook his head. 'A good story. David, I'm going to assume you felt sorry for her and perhaps she mistook your kind nature for something else. Stay away from her, okay?'

'Yes sir.'

The ache in Ross's side grew worse. He trudged back to his flat and drank whisky, listened to Coldplay. At six he forced himself to eat a ham sandwich. At ten he'd had enough of wallowing in untidiness and misery. His apartment in the old Norwich and Norfolk hospital might have been a place of healing once, but it hadn't done him any good.

He walked back to Bethel Street.

'I'm not here,' he said to the custody sergeant, and received a nod in reply.

He found Kezia sitting in her street clothes: red T-shirt and long matching tartan dress. Her ankles and feet were bare. Tights and shoelaces represented a suicide risk.

Kezia welcomed him with a curt 'Fuck off.'

'Thanks. By the way, I didn't shop you. I'd no idea Northamptonshire were looking at you. Stevens stirred up a pot of shit when she went there.'

Kezia stared at the wall. 'Yeah, and you're covered in it.'

He sat down on the bench beside her. 'I need to know.'

She wouldn't look at him. He grabbed her chin and turned her round to face him.

'Ouch. You bastard. That's assault. I'll – '

'Just shut up. I want you to look me in the eye and tell me you didn't kill Susan Smith.'

Now she looked at him. Stared. Pure anger sparked from her eyes. 'I didn't kill her. I didn't kill her.' She clenched her fist in his face. 'How many fucking times do you want me to say it?'

'What about Hester Boswell?'

'Fuck you.' Her stare never wavered.

'Tell me. Did you kill Hester Boswell?'

He sensed the anger dissipating.

'No. Those bastards won't believe me.'

'I watched the interview.'

'I felt you.' Her gaze stayed on him. He wondered if she could hypnotise him.

Perhaps she had. Maybe he couldn't trust his gut anymore. But then, what else did he have?

He smiled. 'I believe you.'

'I'm not sure I believe you anymore.' She blinked. She did believe him, even though he still qualified as a bastard. 'In case you're interested, Jez Kendal's innocent. And that foreign blonde hooker's boyfriend wanted Susan Smith to move on and he hasn't got an alibi. And... Susan reckoned she could get off the game – she had some source of funds.'

'Thanks. What I need from you is the names of the girls who helped Hester Boswell steal your earring.'

'Why?'

'Why do you think?'

Surely, he wouldn't investigate Hester's killing? 'Judith Keaton and Courtney O'Brien. I doubt they're called that anymore.'

'Okay. One more thing… I haven't been here.'

They stared at each other for a full five seconds. Then Kezia clutched his hand. 'Sorry.'

Ross felt sorrier, but he wouldn't tell her. He'd have ended up making promises, and he wasn't sure he could deliver. He'd try, no doubt about that. Tomorrow he'd claim the pain was too much to come into work and instead head down the A11 towards Northampton to investigate somebody else's case.

Death had other plans.

Chapter Fifteen

Ross packed a case. He expected to be in Northamptonshire for a couple of days. He guessed Kezia would follow him in the company of Easton and McNab, although the Norfolk cops would try to keep her confined in the city.

'Another One Bites the Dust' sounded as he lifted his phone to call in sick.

'Good morning, sir.' Sergeant Jimmy Dobbs. Nobody else sounded so happy on a Monday morning.

'Morning, Jimmy.' He added some extra hint of pain to his voice. 'I was just about to ring – '

'Sorry sir, getting to be a bit of a habit this. There's been a suspicious death up on Gertrude Road. Uniform called it in.'

'How suspicious? Can't uniform deal with it?'

'Clifton Walker thinks CID should have a gander. I've summoned the CSIs.'

'Jimmy, the thing is I'm in a bit of a bad way. I need to take a couple of days off. I concede I'm the go-to DI, but what about Mishra?'

'She's off duty. Mick Alder's working on the Rosary Road job. Dave Smythe's on holiday. And Walker's nervous about this. Looks like an accident but he's got suspicions.'

'Okay, give me the address.' Damn Clifton Walker. A tragedy, and he wants it to be more. Never mind, Ross only had to turn up, groan, stagger around, pronounce the scene as death by misadventure, and hand the lot off to uniform before slinking off to the Midlands.

The alleged crime scene proved to be a semi-detached ex-council house in the north-east of the city. Behind lay the extensive woodlands of Mousehold Heath.

Ross had learned a little of the history of the Heath: the gathering place of rebel armies through the ages preparing to attack Norwich. The corpse of a twelve-year-old boy, canonised as Saint William of Norwich, was found there in 1144, his killing blamed on the Jews – targets of false accusations and persecution down the centuries. The same applied to gypsies. Kezia Lee had become the latest in a long line of such victims.

A battered pickup truck sat outside the house. Neighbours, mostly women, either stood in the gardens or talked in small huddles on the pavement. The splintered frame of the blue front door told Ross the last person to enter didn't hang about for an invitation. The front garden was unkempt, patches of bare earth interspersed with coarse grass. An old car engine lay rusting beside the path. Clifton Walker had taped off the entrance and now stood next to a middle-aged red-faced man in a boiler suit that failed to hide a substantial paunch.

'Morning, sir. This is Mr Carter. Mr Carter, DI Ross.'

'It was me what found him.' Carter didn't wait for the courtesy of a handshake or questions. 'Supposed to do a job. Demolition out in Sprowston. Kev, he's normally up and ready. When I saw he in't, well, I got a funny feeling so I go round the back and check in the kitchen window and there he is lying on the floor. Bugger me, I say, so I go and call an ambulance then I think he might need help now, 'cause you knows what ambulances be like. My sister had to hang around –'

Ross: 'Did you smash the front door?'

'Course I did. I mean he might be dying so I in't breaking in or anything. I give it a good kick and it doesn't budge so I get the crowbar – '

'Was it locked when you got here?'

'Of course it was. Do I look like an idiot? Of course, it were locked, otherwise – '

'Did Kev have any family?'

'He never mention it. Might've been a wife way back.'

'Thanks, Mr Carter. I'm sure Constable Walker's got your details, so we'll come back to you if we need more information.'

'I in't told you what happened when I go inside.'

'Did you see anyone or move anything?'

'No, I go to check on Kev and I know he were dead straight away. I reckon it were a heart attack, maybe down to the heat in there, and I went to phone the ambulance but then I think to myself, hold you hard, 'cause of what happened to my sister, so I ring 999 and ask for the police – '

'Thank you, Mr Carter. You can go now.'

Ross watched Carter saunter away, turning round every few seconds in the hope he would be asked to contribute something else.

'Okay, Constable Walker, let's have a more succinct version of what's in there.'

'The dead man's called Kev Connor. Not that I'm a medical man, but from his colour it looks like carbon monoxide poisoning. I've opened the back door – '

'It was locked, right?'

'Yes, sir. The key was in the lock.'

'Okay, Constable. Why did you bother dragging me in? Case like this, it's a uniform responsibility unless the medical people tell us different.'

'It's the heating, sir. It was full on. Bit strange for July, don't you think? Mr Carter claims the kitchen door was shut when he came in, and that's the room the boiler's in.'

'Perhaps this Connor likes it hot?'

'He's wearing a T-shirt and shorts.'

Ross's annoyance with Walker had evaporated. No matter how much inconvenience he'd caused, the guy had a point. This death had suspicious written all over it. He sent Walker round the back while he waited for the CSIs.

Ann Woodhead and her team turned up with a gas engineer who ensured the supply was switched off and the level of carbon monoxide in the house reduced to a safe level. By this time, Charles Porter-Brown had parked his aged Jaguar outside.

Ross had no interest in viewing the body. He wanted somebody to pronounce this a tragic accident so he could hand the investigation onto the Health and Safety Executive. Two PCSOs now assisted Walker in guarding the property, which allowed Ross to talk to the neighbours.

'We keep ourselves to ourselves here,' said an elderly woman wearing an apron who'd been standing gossiping to her friend in the next-door garden since he arrived.

'Did Mr Connor have many visitors?'

'That his name? Never knew. There were a few people. Couple of tarts and some blokes. Dodgy types, if you ask me. Then there's the man with the lorry, him what came here earlier, always blocks my view.'

'Anyone else in the past couple of days?'

'Might have been someone on Friday. Late on. Just after that man with the lorry dropped him off. I was doing the weeding, and I seen this man going in. Didn't see a face. Wearing one of them hoodie things. Weird, I say to myself, because it was warm, so why do he have to cover up?' She looked at the CSIs walking in and out in their paper suits. 'Ooh, is it murder? Like on the telly?'

'Probably an accident,' said Ross. 'Was it definitely a man you saw?'

'You know, I'm not sure. Like I told you, Mr Connor – that his name? – had tarts coming in sometimes. You know the type – short skirts and dyed hair. They always left after an hour. Could've set your clock. Sixty minutes every time. But I couldn't describe them any better. Like I say, I keep myself to myself.'

'If any of your neighbours knows anything relevant, please ask them to call me.' He handed her a card. 'And you are?'

'Mildred Catchpole.' She looked at the card. 'Ooh, a detective inspector! It is like the telly.'

'This man you saw. Did you notice when he left?'

'Funny. I never seen him come out. I go in at half five for my tea so he must have went after then. Ooh, d'yer reckon he's the murderer?'

'As I said, Mrs Catchpole, we're not sure it is murder.'

Mildred dashed off, no doubt to tell her neighbours she'd help solve a killing.

A large woman atop a mobility scooter scattered the spectators along the pavement. 'Has something happened to Mr Connor?' she asked when she reached Ross.

'I'm afraid he's been involved in an accident,' replied Ross. 'Was he a friend, Mrs...?'

'Mrs Johnstone. He wasn't a nice man. Always very rude to me. Him and his friend used to leave their lorry on the pavement so I couldn't get past.'

'Did you see anything suspicious over the last few days?'

'No. I don't go out much. Arthritis and heart problems – that's what I've got. Not to mention my haemorrhoids. They took me into the Norwich and Norfolk only last week.'

Ross expected he would endure a history of her medical problems. He was right. He tried to bring the conversation round to the matter in hand but eventually decided rudeness might be his only option.

Then: 'Once my knees packed up, I couldn't do my lawn. Then Mr Potter next door to me, he says he'll do it and he cuts my grass every week. You should speak to Mr Potter – he's always in his garden if he's not doing mine. A lovely man.'

Ann Woodhead emerged from the house, clipboard in hand. 'We might not need your sleuthing skills. The engineer reckons it's a dodgy boiler that hasn't been maintained for a couple of years. There's a half bottle of whisky and a single glass in the kitchen. Looks like he got pissed, passed out, and then the gas killed him.'

'Humour me, Ann. Dust the place for prints.'

She grimaced. 'Dust it? Have you seen inside? The place is a tip. God knows how many prints we'll find.'

'Okay, at least dust the bottle, glass, and any controls related to the heating. And the door handles. Oh, and it might not be a bad idea to bag the bedclothes.'

Dr Porter-Brown joined them. 'Terrible business, eh? Sad single bloke, past the first flush of youth, living alone, turns to whisky, doesn't bother checking basic safety whatsits, and bye-bye blackbird.'

Too close to home. Ross tried to remember when he'd last had his boiler checked.

'As usual,' continued Porter-Brown, 'I'll need to do a post-mortem, but I'd bet the house on carbon monoxide poisoning. Died where he fell, and I'd guess sometime between early Friday morning and Saturday midday.'

Ross decided he'd better look at the scene. He donned his own paper protection and entered the late Mr Connor's house.

It was, as Woodhead had stated, a tip. The furniture was cheap, the carpet worn, the wallpaper faded. The most obvious and incongruous feature in the room was a sixty-five-inch curved screen TV. No photographs, nothing suggesting family or friends. A pile of paper lay on a Formica table: betting slips, fast food offers, receipts, final reminders. Ross examined the slips. Connor didn't stint when it came to the bookies. The average stake seemed to be around £100. All in the past few days.

He checked the receipts. A couple from Aldi, one from Tesco, and another from Hughes. The last stood out. It was for the television – top of the range Samsung, cost nearly a thousand pounds. Dated last Monday. Paid in cash.

The white-suited CSIs bustled around him as he entered the kitchen. The body lay face-down on the floor. A stocky man, muscled, military haircut. A skull and crossbones tattoo decorated the back of the neck. More tattoos adorned the bare legs. The skin was unnaturally red.

Porter-Brown followed him in. 'Sad way to go. I can turn him over if you like.'

Ross nodded, although he didn't relish staring into the dead eyes of a man whose lifestyle mirrored his own.

The doctor struggled to pull the corpse onto its back. Ross forced himself to look at the body.

Connor's T-shirt celebrated Motörhead. The shorts were stained with oil. His nose was that of a boxer.

Ross hardly registered such details. His focus was on the tattoo shaped like a lightning bolt running from the man's left cheek to his ear. He was sure he'd seen it before.

Ross looked down at the victim's right shin.

'Doc, is that a bruise just above the ankle?'

Porter-Brown bent down to examine the corpse. 'I think you're right. Mind you, it's a couple of days old so probably not relevant.'

More relevant than you could imagine, Doc.

Ross knew for certain he was staring at the man who attacked him on Friday night.

And he also accepted he would not be visiting Northampton that day.

Chapter Sixteen

Mishra arrived to assist in the search. Woodhead appeared perplexed when Ross insisted she checked anything that might have contained sulphuric acid.

Ross spotted the baseball bat hidden among tools at the back of the shed. Only he suspected its possible significance and he dare not share his suspicions with anyone. The jam jar on the shelf above fell into a different category. A brief sniff burnt his nostrils.

He called to Ann Woodhead, who was dusting the back-door handle. 'Ann, there's an empty jar in the shed. Please photograph and bag it. And treat it carefully.'

She strolled up the garden towards him across what once might have been a lawn, now bare earth, baked hard by the sun. Two plastic chairs lay upended halfway down. 'Why?'

'It smells like it contained acid at one time.'

Mishra stood next to Woodhead. 'Sir... is there something we don't know? I mean, this has all the hallmarks of an accident and I'm guessing you're linking this to the attack on Kezia Lee.'

'Call it gut feel,' he said. 'We've got someone here who's clearly had access to a lot of cash in the past few days. His death is suspicious. Why does he drink in the kitchen when he's got a brand-new TV in the front room?'

'Why search the shed?'

'I expected to find stolen goods or drugs. How does someone like this suddenly acquire a lot of money?'

'Stop lying, David,' said Woodhead. 'You asked me specifically to look for acid. You're guessing this is connected to the Kezia Lee incident.'

Christ, these two women were too good. He'd been caught in a pincer of feminine intuition. 'Can I trust you?'

'Depends,' said Woodhead.

'Perhaps,' said Mishra.

'That's a ringing endorsement. Okay, I decided to see Kezia on Thursday night.'

'After Devlin told you not to,' said Mishra, while Woodhead responded with an audible intake of breath.

Ross shrugged. 'Whose side are you on?'

Woodhead took over the assault. 'Are you and this Kezia an item?'

'No.' Ross wondered if he'd sounded genuine. 'I'm not dropping the Susan Smith investigation just because that prick Devlin doesn't want to upset Tom Vickery.'

Mishra's phone rang. Saved by the bell.

'Okay,' she said. 'What? You're joking… The boss will love that.' A quick glance at Ross. 'Six months ago? Who was in charge?' A nod. 'Alder. Makes sense.' Whoever spoke on the other end sounded unhappy – Ross could hear the tone if not the words. 'No way. He kept that quiet.'

The call ended.

'Okay,' said Ross. 'Show me the love.'

'I asked the crew to check up on Kev Connor. They're going to send you a dossier. He's a very naughty boy.'

She was teasing him in her own way. 'I guessed that. Go on.'

'For the last few years, he's been boosting his income working for Dodgy Derek Forbes. Remember him?'

'Loan shark,' said Ross. 'Alleged.'

'Right. In February, Connor appeared before the beaks on a charge of assault, supposedly linked to debt recovery. He got a suspended sentence – they reckoned there were mitigating circumstances. Alder had nothing on Dodgy Derek, although he certainly ordered Connor to rough the woman up.'

'Surprise. What were the mitigating circumstances?'

'The woman hit him first. Allegedly. Alder couldn't prove otherwise.'

'I'm not loving that. Come on, Kirsi, give me the big news.'

'Okay. Connor's got real form. Five years ago, he did time for housebreaking. Served a year. But before then he worked as a bouncer at a lap dancing club.'

'Let me guess. Hot Steps.'

Mishra nodded. 'Sorry, sir.'

'Any convictions during that time?' asked Ross.

'Apparently we had him on a charge of assault in 2011. Our main witness failed to appear in court and the magistrates dismissed the case.'

'Quelle surprise,' was Ross's reaction. 'When did he start at Hot Steps?'

'Six months before the assault charge.'

'Before then?'

'No idea,' said Mishra.

'I'm missing something,' said Woodhead. 'Why's that a big deal?'

'Because it links Kev Connor to Tom Vickery. And hence to Susan Smith.'

Woodhead wasn't convinced. 'But you're saying Connor's got some association with this Lee woman?'

'Okay, when I visited Kezia I spotted someone trying to attack her, armed with a baseball bat. Which you'll find next to the acid. That's how I cracked my ribs. I only caught a glimpse of his face, but as soon as I saw Connor today...'

'Sorry, sir,' said Mishra, 'but why would Connor try to assault Miss Lee? Unless he suspects she killed Susan, and it's a revenge attack. He does appear to be involved with prostitutes, and he might know Susan from Hot Steps.'

'Because someone believes Kezia is a witness to Susan's murder. He's hired muscle.'

'You're calling her Kezia,' said Woodhead. 'Bit familiar.' She shook her head and headed for the shed.

'She's jealous,' said Mishra. 'I think she fancies you. Watch out. A woman scorned and all that.'

Ross watched Woodhead disappear into the outbuilding. 'It's not her I'm worried about. How do I explain this to Devlin?'

'The link to Kezia... Might it be connected to what her mother does?'

He wouldn't share his fears there might be another connection between Kezia and Connor. 'Possibly.'

'I suppose the odds have just shortened on murder.'

Ross nodded. 'If it is, it's clever. This is a million miles from thumping somebody over the head with a hammer.' A dog howled in a neighbouring property – Ross thought of a wolf mourning its dead mate. 'I'll call in extra help. I want this place searched for anything linking Kev Connor to Tom Vickery. Ask the neighbours if they saw anyone go into the house Friday or Saturday. Make sure you speak to someone called Mr Potter. He seems to spend a lot of time in his garden.'

'Sir...'

'Something on your mind, Kirsi?'

'You remember what I said about a revenge attack?'

'Right? So what?'

'I read Kezia Lee's file last night. She had a fiancée called Danny Wilby.'

Ross nodded. 'Dumped him in 2015 after she discovered he'd misbehaved on a stag weekend. Your point?'

'Were you aware Wilby worked as a gas fitter? I'm wondering if he's back in the picture. Suppose Kezia and Connor were an item, Kezia drops Connor for Wilby, Connor gets jealous and attacks Kezia so Wilby kills Connor. It fits.'

Her logic was impeccable. Except he was certain Kezia didn't have a boyfriend. Certain might not be the right word. Perhaps 'hopeful' might have been better.

'Or,' continued Mishra, 'Wilby taught Kezia about boilers. It's possible she had the expertise to fix the heating system. Connor might have been clingy, and she had a better offer.'

He clenched his fists, trying to fight anger and jealousy. 'Interesting theory. Why don't you check on Wilby? Establish his movements Friday and Saturday.'

'Will do, sir. What about Kezia? Should I look into what she did on Friday?'

'Leave it to me.' *Sorry, too sharp. I don't want you knowing I paid her to visit Nottingham.*

Ross drove back towards Bethel Street. He interrupted his journey outside another ex-council house a few streets away.

The architecture might have been similar, but nothing else here resembled Connor's hovel. A royal blue BMW 5 series gleamed in the driveway, alongside a luxurious weedless lawn fringed with flower beds. Ross's closer examination revealed the grass was artificial. A stylish door of glass and varnished wood had replaced the council standard version attached to most of the dwellings.

A woman came to the door: bleached blonde, black leather trousers, low cut silk blouse with a pearl necklace. Her static rouged cheeks betrayed a Botox injection. She looked at him with long-lashed eyes heavy with suspicion and mascara.

'Yes.'

'Mrs Forbes? Is your husband in?'

'He might be. Whom can I say is enquiring?' She couldn't hide a Norfolk accent.

Ross flashed his badge. 'Police. I'd like a word.'

'Police.' She spoke loudly, no doubt to warn Dodgy Derek. 'It may be inconvenient. I will consult him to see if he's available.'

'Tell you what, madam, I can't put you to any trouble. I'll consult him myself.'

He squeezed past her, ensuring there was no contact with her substantial bosom, and walked into the front lounge. A man who weighed at least twenty stone lay on a bright red leather sofa wearing a white T-shirt with a flower motif and Bermuda shorts. His long blonde-streaked hair and fake tan gave him the air of a has-been pop singer from the seventies. Ross looked around the room. Hummel figures stood on every surface, except the one housing the forty-inch flat screen TV. A large photograph of an airbrushed Mrs Forbes semi-clad in a sheepskin rug hung above the fireplace.

'Hi Dodgy, you've been a bit quiet lately. I'm getting worried about you.'

'It's Mister Forbes to you, inspector. I trust you've brought a warrant to cover this unjustified intrusion.'

'He pushed his way in,' wailed Mrs Forbes.

'You run along, Pearl. Fix me up a Martini so I can celebrate the inspector's departure.'

Mrs Forbes slammed the door before Forbes muted an American cop show.

The homeowner grinned. 'I like 'em passionate. And now, inspector, your warrant, if you please?'

Ross smiled. 'I thought I smelt dope. I haven't got a warrant, so you don't need to worry about my seizing your loan book. The truth is I wanted to ask you about a mutual friend.' Ross had his attention. Now to watch for a reaction. 'Kev Connor.'

Forbes blinked. 'Who?'

'Oh, come on. Are you suffering from Alzheimer's? Kev Connor. Rent-a-thug. Goes round collecting donations for your favourite charity.'

'I am not acquainted with the gentleman.'

'Oh dear, it seems your memory is definitely fading. We've got some photos back at the station with you standing next to him. Then there's the record of a party we raided in 2016 when both of you were present.'

'You're lying. Connor wasn't there.'

'Oh. Now you remember the names of everyone at the party. Let me make this easier. Kev Connor is dead.' Ross noted Forbes' reaction. *Shock, perhaps.* 'Probably murdered, which means if you're lying, you're guilty of obstruction, if not being an accessory.'

'Okay, okay. I know Kev. There might've been a couple of times when people owed me money and refused to pay. Kev offered to help me. When I found out he used strong-armed tactics... well... I was most disappointed. I told him in no uncertain terms he should no longer act on my behalf.'

'In other words, you paid him off to stop him shopping you.'

'I resent that accusation. How did he die?'

'No comment at this stage. When did you dispense with his services?'

'February. I believe he attended the magistrates' court as a consequence of the incident.'

Ross looked at the TV. 'Nice telly, Dodgy. Of course, Kev just bought an even better one. Seemed to be a bit flush in his final days.'

216

Ross interpreted Forbes' reaction as puzzlement. He wasn't looking at the source of Connor's latest cash. 'Any idea what he got up to after you ditched him?'

'I'd heard he moved into the demolition business. His murder... Do you have a prime suspect?'

Ross guessed Dodgy Derek wasn't the killer. His reaction just confirmed Ross's view that the manner of the murder, if it was murder, was far too sophisticated for the overweight creature slouching before him.

'No, and we're not a hundred percent sure it was murder. Did Kev have any close associates? Lady friends?'

'Kev? Bit of a loner. He'd pick up drunk scrubbers on a Saturday night and kick 'em out Sunday morning. Wasn't amiss to the occasional prozzie if he had a dry spell. Nobody liked him, but you wouldn't say it to his face. Don't see what else I can tell you.'

'No problem, Dodgy. Probably one of your old clients getting the first instalment of revenge. Hopefully, they'll leave more clues when they come after you.'

Forbes now looked very worried. Ross felt better. He'd upset another villain, as well as further reducing the odds Tom Vickery was behind at least one murder.

***

Kezia had nothing to feel happy about. She slumped in the rear of an unmarked police car, WPC at her side, handcuffs around her wrists. Easton drove, while McNab sprawled in the passenger seat. The detectives talked about rugby for two hours, while the WPC remained silent. Kezia's discomfort increased when their route took them past the mothballed Wellingborough jail.

McNab broke off his doom-laden predictions regarding Northampton Saints' prospects for the coming season to acknowledge her existence.

'Remember that place, Kezia? Your old man died there. All down to the Boswells. Wonder where you'll end up?'

'Piss off.'

'A confession might persuade the court to treat you lightly. PMT and all that. Temporarily nuts. What do you say?'

The WPC's consequent raised eyebrows were accompanied by a sympathetic smile.

Kezia stayed silent. In twenty minutes, she sat in another cell. She'd sussed out McNab: results-driven, unimaginative, lazy. Not the sort who'd bother trying to find Judith Keaton and Courtney O'Brien. And even if he did, those bitches were quick to point the finger six years ago. They wouldn't lift those same fingers to help her now.

She wasn't expecting salvation elsewhere. Ross was bound by jurisdiction and professional etiquette. If he did try, he'd get no cooperation from the Northamptonshire force. Escape might represent her only hope.

They gave her an hour alone before the custody sergeant reapplied the handcuffs and brought her through to an interview room. McNab and Easton were already sitting on one side of a table. A woman in her late twenties wearing a navy-blue trouser suit sat opposite them. Her perfectly cut short blonde hair and complexion wouldn't be out of place in a moisturiser advert.

'This is Karen Unwin,' said McNab. 'She's our duty solicitor. If you want her to leave, just say, but my advice is to let her help you.'

'I'd like a couple of minutes alone with Kezia if you don't mind,' said Unwin. She glanced at the camera in the corner. 'Preferably not here.'

McNab grunted confirmation and led the pair through to an adjoining room. Unwin waited until the detective's footsteps faded away before opening her briefcase.

'You're new,' said Kezia.

'Does it show?'

Kezia smiled. 'You've no empathy with those two. And you're nervous.'

Unwin fumbled in her bag, pulled out a file. 'I understand you were reluctant to seek legal help in Norwich.'

'Yeah. Can't afford it and I'm innocent.'

'You'll get legal aid.' She scanned the contents. Kezia knew she'd read them before – a good sign – she cared.

'I was supposed to start a new job yesterday. Will I get compensation?'

'Kezia...' Unwin spoke slowly, a serious tone, the way a doctor would tell a patient they had six months to live. 'The case against you is strong. We may have to agree on a mitigation strategy.'

'Piss off. I'm innocent. If you're any good, you'll get me off.'

'Okay. Let me outline what they've got. On the fourteenth of September 2011, Hester Boswell and three friends went out late at night. The others were Darren Kemp, Sharon Kitchener and Murray Ledger. Know any of them?'

'Not that well. Except Darren Kemp. Bastard.'

'Right, that's what I thought. About you knowing him. Kemp and Kitchener were fourteen, Ledger fifteen. They didn't come forward at the time of the murder because Ledger had borrowed his brother's car and already had a conviction for driving underage. Hester's father, Patrick Boswell, also known as Taff, last saw his daughter at nine o'clock. According to Miss Kitchener, the three picked up Hester and took her to some nearby woods. Kemp admitted that, after drinking cider, the two couples separated, and he and Hester had sex.'

Kezia repeated her allegation concerning Darren's parentage.

'Miss Kitchener says when Kemp and Hester came back, they were arguing. Hester seemed upset.'

'So why aren't they arresting him? He must have done it.'

Unwin shook her head. 'All three are sticking to the story that Hester refused to get in the car and insisted on walking home. The others drove back into Brackley. Consensus is they reached the town around one o'clock. It seems implausible Kemp could have returned in time to murder Hester.'

'I haven't heard me mentioned yet.'

'You and Hester both lived at Dunroamin Park, a static caravan site in Whitfield near Brackley. Kemp claims he had a relationship with you, and you'd been to the same woods on a couple of occasions.'

'Yeah, well, I can't deny that 'cause I don't know which woods you mean, and I never had sex with him. Least not all the way.'

'That night your mother was away providing...' Unwin flicked over some papers, 'psychic counselling. That suggests you haven't got an alibi. Kitchener claims Hester taunted you at school that morning, telling you she and Kemp were going out that evening. You knew where they were headed, and the prosecution will claim you went there to spy on them, and when you saw your chance, you beat Hester to death with a brick. The police found your earring at the murder scene, as well as your skin under her fingernails. They reckon she put up a fight.'

That was unexpected. 'She scratched me that morning. Cow didn't even wash her hands before going out. And she'd pinched my earrings the day before. Her and them other two.'

'Because of bruising in the genital area, the police linked the killing to a spate of unsolved sexual assaults in the vicinity. You were briefly a person of interest, but they were convinced the killer was male. Until the cold case team re-interviewed Kemp.'

Kezia sat back. 'That's all they've got? You just need to find Judith Keaton and Courtney O'Brien. Put the screws on and they'll 'fess up about the bullying, you know, like pinching my earrings and stuff.'

'They'll corroborate Janet Gibson's story. You remember Janet? Probably called her Mrs Gibson. She taught you English. Apparently when Hester didn't turn up for the first class of the day you said, and I quote: 'The bitch has been murdered. Hooray'.'

'I probably said 'fucking hooray', but I'm not denying it. I just knew she was dead.'

'Murdered?'

'Yeah, like there's a difference. I just saw this picture in my head.'

'There was bad blood between the Lees and the Boswells, wasn't there?'

Kezia scowled. 'Not before the old bastard stitched up my Pa.'

Unwin shut the folder. 'Bottom line is, Kezia, you're screwed. Your only hope is two girls who you say bullied you and won't admit it in court. Your DNA was found at the scene, you have a double motive, opportunity... You're going to end up with a barrister on legal aid up against a seasoned prosecutor who'll push the tempestuous gypsy angle.'

'Find the two girls, then.'

Unwin resumed her six-months-to-live expression. 'Kezia, we haven't got the resources. I'll try, but I can't guarantee I can get them on board, or even find them. If I were you, I'd be thinking about pleading self-defence. Perhaps you confronted Hester, there was a fight, you thought she would strangle you... you picked up a convenient brick...'

'Where did I get the brick?'

Unwin looked at her files again. She hadn't read them that thoroughly. 'Um, here we go. There was a pile next to one of the homes in Dunroamin.'

'And am I correct in saying the body was found a few hundred yards up the road?'

'Right. Okay, I see what you're saying. It was premeditated. Are you trying to convict yourself?'

'No. I'm saying you need to find me innocent. If you want help, call Inspector David Ross at Norwich.'

'Why should he help?'

'He will. He's got to.'

Chapter Seventeen

DCI Devlin was not amused.

'Inspector Ross. There is no way I'm going to approve a warrant relating to Tom Vickery. You're not even certain this is a murder. All the evidence points to an accident.'

'Not all the evidence, sir.'

'A man drinks in his kitchen with the door closed. He likes his house warm. And yet you think that justifies your continued infatuation with Vickery? I'm handing this over to the HSE. Unless they tell me this is not an accident, I'm not wasting any time or money on this case.'

'What about the acid?'

'Circumstantial. There could be any number of reasons why the jar was in the shed. I suppose you think this links to Kezia Lee. Even if there is some strange connection between Connor and Miss Lee, I don't see it's relevant. Unless of course Miss Lee killed Connor. We know she's capable.'

Ross wasn't going to admit Kezia had a partial alibi, courtesy of himself. There again, she'd told him the man who attacked her had gone forever. One indisputable fact about Connor's demise: if it was murder, the killer didn't have to be in the house at the time of his death.

'I've looked at your notes on your informal interview with Derek Forbes. Connor was a misogynist, don't you agree? No respect for women. The fact that he was up for assaulting a woman speaks volumes.'

'Sorry, sir. Your point?'

Devlin leant back and twiddled his thumbs. 'Damn obvious. Best form of defence is attack. It's an affair gone wrong. Miss Lee fears Connor will come after her, so she goes to his house, drugs him, fixes the boiler.' He sat up. 'But damn hard to prove without a confession. If the Northants boys can do their job, she'll be inside for a few years and out of our hair. No-one's going to mourn Connor, so I suggest we stick to the accident theory for now.'

'Sir, I can't believe – '

'David, I want you to stick to the burglaries. Solve them. You've been skating on very thin ice lately, and I'd hate to lose you. Understood?'

'Yes, sir.' Ross hesitated, looked at his feet. 'Sir... I've perhaps been overdoing it lately. I've got leave due. How about I take a week off?'

'Hmm. I suppose the burglaries can wait. We need you at your best. Fill in the necessary paperwork and I'll consider it.'

Ross returned to his desk.

Mishra called across. 'Sir, I'm just typing up the witness interviews from the Connor death. Anything else you need?'

'DCI Devlin's decided it's an accident. Just stick to the basics and put them in the file.'

'Why's he so quick to shut down the investigation?'

'If I was a cynic, I'd say it was because Vickery might be involved.'

Mishra stood up and walked across to his desk. 'Danny Wilby's in the clear. You remember – Kezia's boyfriend.'

Ross experienced another unexpected twinge of jealousy. 'Why?'

'He joined the army. He was running around on manoeuvres in Norway when Connor died.'

'Fine.' He reached for the top manila folder. Anything to divert Mishra from her theory about Kezia's involvement in Connor's killing.

'I looked into Connor's background,' said Mishra. 'He moved to Norwich in 2010. Before that he was in Dagenham.'

'Sounds like it's unlikely he met Susan Smith.'

'Doesn't look like it. I think you should speak to Bill Potter. You remember, the neighbour you wanted me to talk to?'

'Why?'

'He just seemed a bit nervous. He denied seeing Connor during the two days before the death. Perhaps it's the Kezia Lee influence, but I've got this feeling he's hiding something.'

'Copper's instinct, Kirsi. Don't knock it.'

Nice Mr Potter, good Samaritan of Gertrude Road. Another database search – no information other than that he purchased the house in 2013. A model citizen, albeit one who displayed nervousness during a routine enquiry.

So what? Possibly he was a month late paying his television licence. Perhaps he'd watched too many TV programmes about cops stitching up the innocent. Devlin was probably right – everything pointed to an accidental death.

His focus on Kev Connor was about to diminish even further. His phone rang.

'DI Ross, my name's Karen Unwin…'

Ross reached Towcester at half past ten. Finding Judith Keaton had proved impossible. Locating Courtney O'Brien, on the other hand, was the proverbial piece of cake. He'd tracked her to a modern semi-detached house sitting in a row of identical properties. Now Courtney Ledger, she answered the door with a small child tottering at her heels, pink chewing gum poking from her mouth. She wore an ill-fitting, stained, light-blue tracksuit.

'Mrs Ledger, I'm with the police.' He flashed his warrant card, hoping she wouldn't notice which county he was from.

Courtney stopped chewing for a second. 'Oh my God, is it Murray? Has there been an accident?'

Murray Ledger? *One of three who accompanied the murdered teenager on her trip into the woods.* 'No, nothing like that. It's about something else. The Hester Boswell murder.'

'Have ya caught him?' Normal chewing resumed. She smoothed down her straggly long brown hair.

'No. May I come in?'

'Sorry… yes. The place is a bloody mess. Sorry.' The interior smelt of used nappies and the previous night's curry. She led him into a dark front room, throwing open the curtains to reveal a toy-strewn floor and clothes rails covered in baby garments. A large white teddy bear dominated one corner. Three smaller bears looked down from the mantelpiece.

'How old is he?'

'She. Thirteen months.'

'Nice kid. You remember the events back then?'

Courtney placed the child inside a playpen. 'I'll never forget it. She was my bestie, her and Judy. We were tight.'

'What happened to Judy? I couldn't trace her.'

The child whimpered, forcing Courtney to make soothing noises before continuing: 'Went to Ibitha'n shacked up with a DJ. Lucky cow. Better'n this.'

'Do you remember Kezia Lee?'

Courtney laughed, revealing the garish pinkness of her chewing gum. 'The didicoy? She was spooky. D'ya know she knew Hest had been killed? Weird.' She glanced at the child. 'Mummy's busy, Zoe. Be nice.'

'Why did you call her a didicoy?'

'Hest did. Hest was a real proper gypsy, not like Kez. Kez's mum was Russian or something.'

Ross held up his mobile. 'Do you mind if I record this? Just so I remember right?'

Courtney nodded.

Ross was about to press the right buttons. Literally and figuratively. 'Tuesday July the eighteenth. DI Ross speaking to Courtney Ledger, nee O'Brien. Courtney, just to put you in the picture, Kezia Lee is now a suspect in the murder of Hester Boswell. Any thoughts?'

'No way! Hey, like it all makes sense now. All this freaky psycho stuff she came out with. That's how she could tell us, isn't it?'

'We think so.' *Kezia would spot I'm lying. I hope Courtney doesn't.* 'We're trying to establish motive. We've discovered Kezia didn't like Hester, but why would she kill her?'

227

'Cause she's weird.' Courtney twirled her right index finger around her ear to emphasise her opinion. 'Nuts.'

A green stuffed monkey flew out of the playpen. Courtney retrieved it and returned it to the child. 'Be nice to Cuddles, Zoe.'

Ross watched Cuddles execute another escape from captivity. 'Yes, but why Hester? Had Hester done anything to upset Kezia?'

'They fought in the morning. Real kicking'n scratching.'

Ross tried not to smile. 'Was that about the boyfriend?'

Courtney recaptured Cuddles. 'Yeah, well, like it might have been. But Darren ditched Kez ages before. Could've been about the earrings.'

'Earrings?' Ross did a good job of looking surprised.

'Yeah. The day before, Kez dissed us. So Hester'n me, we taught her a lesson. She'd got these gold hoops what she thought were wonderful, so we ripped them out. I mean, she started it.'

'What happened to the earrings?'

'You're not doing me for assault? Like I said, Kez kicked it off.'

'No, I can promise you won't be charged. What happened to Kezia's gold hoops?'

The child whimpered again. Courtney stuck her tongue out, pulled a dummy out of her pocket, thrust it into the infant's mouth. 'Hest kept one'n she gave me the other. Judy didn't want none of it.'

'What happened to yours?' Ross was on a roll... *please... please...*

'I kept it. Like I might need the money sometime.'

Jackpot. 'Mrs Ledger, the earring is stolen property. I appreciate I said you won't be prosecuted, but you'll need to let me take it.'

Courtney scowled. 'Watch Zoe, will ya?'

Ross handed Cuddles back twice to its whimpering jailer before Courtney returned with a matchbox.

'In here,' she announced.

Ross took the box, opening it just enough to confirm it contained a small gold circlet. He dropped it into an evidence bag.

'Thanks, Mrs Ledger. You've been a big help. Hopefully, we won't bother you again.'

'Like won't ya want me to give evidence? Ya know, when Kez gets up before the judge.'

'We might. We know where to find you.' He nodded at the child. 'Nice kid. You look after her.'

Twenty minutes later he reached Northamptonshire Police HQ. Karen Unwin waited for him in reception.

'Karen?'

'You must be DI Ross. Thanks for coming. Did you locate either of the two girls?'

He smiled. 'Better than that. I've got one of the earrings and confirmation Hester Boswell took the other the day before she was killed.'

Unwin wasn't as grateful as he'd hoped. 'The real killer is the DNA under Hester's fingernails. DI McNab won't give up with what you've found. If anything, it just adds to motive.'

'Listen.' He played the interview with Courtney Ledger, pointing his finger at the mobile when she described the fight on the morning of the murder.

Unwin still wouldn't smile. 'This is promising. Kezia's not out of the woods yet. Her motive just gets stronger and stronger.' Finally, a faint sign of a grin. 'I don't think they've got enough to justify a prosecution.'

'Call McNab then. Let me take her home.'

McNab didn't show Ross the same courtesy Norfolk had shown him. After Ross briefed him on his conversation with Courtney Ledger, he called the Norwich detective into a meeting room and slammed down several files on the desk.

'This is the case against Kezia Lee. You've got shit. Even if there was a fight. Big fucking deal. It just reinforces how much Lee hated Hester. It's bloody obvious she killed her. What the hell are you doing interfering in our investigation?'

Ross said nothing, instead thumbing through the paperwork in front of him. It was well-organised, so he knew where to find what he wanted – the autopsy.

'What the hell are you doing?' McNab grabbed at the remaining files.

'Just checking. Aha, here we are. Analysis of clothing. One pair blue jeans. Mud stains, also blood splatter. Contents of pockets – keys, three pound coins and two ten pence pieces. One gold circular earring.' Ross threw the file on the table. 'The earring was in her pocket. It couldn't have fallen out in a fight as you claimed. That's sloppy police work. Do you want your failings exposed in court?'

'That's shit. They fought. Hester grabs the earring, sticks it in her pocket. Lee grabs a brick and thumps her.'

'So why didn't Kezia get back the earring if she's that upset about losing it?'

'She panicked. Bloody obvious. She's horrified at what she's done.'

Ross laughed. 'Just think about it. Okay, Kezia found out where Hester and Warren are going. But she couldn't guess they'd leave separately. Are you telling me she'd pick up a brick outside her home and walk several hundred yards on the off-chance she'd catch Hester alone?'

'Whose side are you on?'

'It took me a minute to find a major flaw in your case. Are you happy to let me spend an hour or two going through this?'

McNab banged the desk. 'Your fucking DCI will hear about this.'

'In that case so will yours. And his boss as well. I suggest you let me take Kezia back to Norfolk.'

'The rumours are right. You're giving her one.'

Ross would normally have laughed the allegation off. 'Don't talk shit.'

McNab sat glaring at Ross for a full minute. 'Tell you what. Let me have one more go at the bitch. Then she can suck your cock until we find enough to drag her back.'

'Unwin sits in, right?'

'I'll let you sit in if you keep your gob shut. Hopefully it'll show you what a lying, vicious little cow she is. Deal?'

Ross wasn't going to refuse. A few minutes later he and McNab sat opposite Kezia and Unwin. Kezia smiled when she saw Ross. He grinned back and winked.

If McNab felt outnumbered, he didn't show it. 'Miss Lee, further information has come to light. We guessed you hated Hester. Only we didn't appreciate how much. DI Ross here has uncovered evidence you launched an unprovoked attack on Hester earlier in the day.'

Kezia glanced at Ross, who shook his head and held a finger to his lips.

'No comment,' she said.

McNab produced the matchbox and emptied the contents onto the desk. 'Remember this?'

Kezia's eyes widened. 'My earring!'

'Right. You loved this, didn't you? Hester took it from you and wouldn't give it back. How badly did you want it, Miss Lee? Enough to kill?'

Kezia stared at the jewellery. 'Did Hester have this on her when she died?'

'Yes. Why couldn't you find it? Was it the shock of knowing what you'd done?'

Ross wanted to tell Kezia it wasn't the right earring. *What would be the point?* It was one of a pair.

Kezia seized it and shut her eyes. She began shaking. 'Bears. White bears. I saw white bears. Polar bears.' The earring dropped from her trembling hands. 'Blood on their fur. Fresh blood. Dead white bears.'

'Are you okay?' asked Unwin.

'She's gone loopy,' said McNab. 'She's remembered killing Hester and it's too much.'

'Why?' Kezia was weeping, now banging her fist on the polished wood. 'Why?'

'Stop this interview,' said Ross. 'She's – '

'Tell us, Kezia,' shouted McNab. 'Make it easy on yourself.'

Kezia held her head in her hands. 'No… why?'

'Why what, Kezia?' McNab sounded triumphant. 'Why did you kill her?'

Kezia calmed down. She stared at the earring as if it was something from another planet.

Ross couldn't stop himself. 'Kezia. It's not the earring Hester had. I got that from Courtney.'

'It doesn't matter,' she said. 'I don't do the dead. I do the living.'

'What the hell was all that about?' screamed McNab.

'It was a memory. This brought it back. Something I felt at the time but tried to suppress.'

McNab wasn't going to give up. 'About you killing Hester?'

'No.' Kezia looked at him and grinned. 'About who killed her.'

Chapter Eighteen

Old memories clawed at Kezia's mind as she climbed the three familiar steps before knocking. She hadn't returned to Dunroamin since the day of her father's funeral. She must be strong, push the nightmares aside, and focus on what she had to do.

The door of the static caravan opened. A man filled the space, the aroma of bad whisky and cheap tobacco wafting around him. For a second she recalled the great white bear of her previous vision. She forced the image away.

'Remember me?'

He smirked, his mouth a graveyard of broken teeth. 'No, but come in, darlin', an' help me remember.' His speech was slurred, emphasising the smell of alcohol.

'I'm Kezia Lee.'

The smile faded. 'Mother of God, it's Byron's daughter. Why are yer back?'

'I found out what you did.'

'What'd I do? Eh?' His grin returned.

'You killed Hester. I saw you doing it.'

'You're lyin'. Bag o' shite like yer Pa.'

'She came back. You had a row about where she'd been, what she'd done. She walked out. You ran after her, grabbed a brick, and bashed her brains out.'

The bear returned, fierce and hungry. She should have heeded the warning, not ignored it. A gnarled hand grabbed her T-shirt and pulled her inside the caravan. Kezia lost her footing and struck her head against a table. She turned to watch him shutting and bolting the door.

That wasn't in the plan. She was weak, stunned from the collision. Taff Boswell pulled a large knife out of a drawer.

'My boyfriend's outside. He knows I'm here. He'll call the police.'

Boswell took a step towards her. 'To hell with him. I'll gut him after I gut yer.'

'I'm right, aren't I?'

'There's a code, yer knows. The code we live by. Us, not didicoys like you.' He waved the knife like a conductor would a baton. 'She was to marry my cousin's lad, an' he wasn't havin' her if he'd known what a little slut she was. She tells me she's been fuckin' that Kemp boy an' she says she's leavin'.'

Kezia shuffled backwards on the sticky grimy floor, looking in vain for a means of escape. 'How come the cops didn't arrest you?'

''Cause Betsy backed me up, God bless her soul. Betsy lived by the code, so she did.'

She looked for a weapon, anything she could use. *Where were the others?* Boswell was standing four feet away, the point of the knife inches from her face.

Kezia tried to appear defiant. 'She was frightened of you, that's what.'

'You really seen me?'

She kept inching back. 'Nah. I guessed. Combination of common sense and my imagination.'

'Well, yer goin' ter pay for it.' He licked his lips. 'Mebbe in more ways than one. You ain't got no boyfriend.'

He loomed over her. Kezia's back was now against a wall. The front door shook as someone tried to break it down. Boswell swivelled round.

Kezia swung her leg at the drunk man's ankles. He tottered. She drove her heel into his shin. Boswell fell to his knees as she scrambled to her feet.

'You fuckin' bitch!' The knife came forward.

Kezia grabbed his wrist. He was strong but off balance. The weapon scraped her side, and she toppled backwards. She stabbed two fingers into his eyes and rolled away.

'Damn yer ter hell.' Temporarily blinded, Boswell thrashed out. He stumbled into the table, swinging the knife back and forward.

Kezia looked down. Blood already seeped through her T-shirt. She scrambled to her feet and aimed a kick at Boswell's groin, striking him on the thigh instead. He tried to slash at her legs, missing by millimetres. The pain in her side increased as she stumbled to the door and unbolted it. Boswell heard her and staggered towards the sound.

'I'll kill yer, you didicoy slut.'

Kezia stepped aside. The door flew open. Ross burst in, followed by McNab. The unseeing Boswell cursed and swung the knife again. Ross caught the drunken man's arm and delivered a punch into his midriff.

Easton ran through the door and handcuffed Boswell, now again sunk to his knees, gasping for breath. Hester's killer screamed and swore as McNab pulled him to his feet by his collar.

Ross put his hands on Kezia's trembling shoulders.

'Christ, that wasn't supposed to happen.' He looked down. 'Jesus, you're hurt.'

Kezia tried to hide the wound. 'It's nothing.'

Blood trickled through her fingers. Ross turned to McNab. 'Find a clean cloth. Now.'

After a frenzied search, McNab pulled a stained faded dishcloth out of a drawer. Ross looked at it – hardly a shining example of good housekeeping, but it didn't appear dirty. He grabbed the cloth and pressed it against Kezia's side.

'Sort things out. I'm taking her to hospital.'

'Nearest A&E is Horton at Banbury,' said Easton. 'A43 then A422. Best of luck.'

Ross led Kezia to his car. Her side was hurting more.

'Keep the cloth over the wound,' he said.

She felt the blood ooze through her fingers. Suppose the wound was serious? Kezia turned to glance at Ross. She found concern. There was more, but she couldn't read this man like the others. Surely, he didn't still like her? She'd revealed her chlamydia, the doomed intimacy with Darren Kemp, her poisonous relationship with Danny Wilby and her weird hallucinations.

Ross made it to Horton hospital in fifteen minutes, courtesy of an up-to-date satnav and a speeding violation. He'd fight that later. Monday night is not the worst choice to attend Accident and Emergency, and Kezia was released after three hours and ten stitches.

Kezia hadn't spoken on the way to Banbury, too worried about her wound. Now she was curious.

'Where to now?'

Ross was keeping well within the speed limits. 'Norwich. I'm taking you home.'

'Won't I be needed to give evidence and that stuff?'

'There's no reason. You were wearing a wire. McNab heard everything that went on. Okay, perhaps if Boswell goes on trial, they'll want you back.'

'If? What d'you mean... if?'

Ross kept his eyes on the road. 'He didn't admit he killed Hester. He hinted it, yes, but he never actually said it. And as for attacking you... Well, old man late at night, and a stranger comes to the door. Announces she's the daughter of a man she's convinced he sent to jail. He's nervous she might even be the person who murdered his Hester and is now after him.'

'He threatened to kill me!'

'Who says? The defence will try to get the wire recording deemed inadmissible. If so, it's the word of three cops with a prejudice against gypsies and the prime suspect in Hester's murder who'd say anything to escape prosecution.'

'What was the bloody point?'

Ross turned to gaze at her for the first time. 'The point was proving you innocent. Just because a jury wouldn't find him guilty doesn't mean McNab isn't convinced.'

Kezia pictured Boswell as another wolf joining the pack hunting her down. She stared out at the Northamptonshire night.

Ross understood Kezia well enough not to expect thanks or conversation. He turned on his CD player. Travis's 'The Man Who'. If she didn't like it, she'd have to speak up.

Travis began an encore as they reached the edge of Cambridge. Ross hit the off button.

'Okay, I give in,' he said. 'What was all that nonsense about white bears? I noticed a load of white bears in Courtney Ledger's house. I'm guessing there's a connection.'

Kezia had been wondering if she really wanted to go back to Norwich and a life serving her mother's delusions.

'No,' she said.

'What do you mean 'no'?'

'Like there's no connection. I never really knew Courtney. She was just a sheep who followed Hester around.'

'Okay, I'm asking again. Why the bears?'

'It's… hell… you wouldn't understand.' She gazed out the window again. The lights to her left were those of another travellers' site. She'd stayed there with her mother for a week when they'd fled Northamptonshire.

'Try me.'

'Even my mother can't understand.'

'I realise you're something special.' As soon as he said it, he wondered how she would take it.

'I sometimes see people as animals.' She wouldn't look at him. 'Not all the time. Like it's not even people, maybe their emotions, their thoughts, and then only when they're directed at me or really strong. And they don't even have to be close by. Like I saw the guy who was stalking me… he was a wolf.'

'Native Americans think everyone has a spirit animal,' said Ross. 'It's not a new concept.'

'Yeah, well, whatever. I can't control it. Like it happens without warning. I didn't even get it when I was young. It's like a fit or something.'

Ross wasn't getting polar bears. He still had an hour's drive ahead. *Plenty of time.* 'When you noticed the bears, which one of us was it? McNab? Me?'

Now she turned to gaze at him. 'Neither. It was a memory. The earring brought it back. When I went to school the morning after Hester was killed, I passed the Boswells' caravan. I imagined polar bears. One grown, and a bloodied dead cub. Male polar bears eat their young.'

'And you didn't understand what it meant back then?'

'No. I'm getting better at it now. I get the meaning even if I can't control it. The other stuff is even easier.'

'Other stuff?'

'Yeah, like if I'm in real danger I feel like I'm soaked in blood. Like when the guy threw the acid. And when I was in the park off Rosary Road when Susan was killed.'

'You were in danger in Old Library Wood?'

'I must have been.'

He accelerated past a couple of trucks heading towards an early morning ferry from Felixstowe. 'It's a useful skill.'

She looked away again. 'Is it? To recognise what someone's thinking?'

'You'd make a fortune playing poker.'

'It wouldn't work with the high rollers. Too calm. I need raw, powerful emotions. You only get them with stuff like love or hate. Maybe jealousy or lust.' She looked straight ahead. 'Sorrow, joy.'

'Still, it must be valuable.'

'It messes up relationships. I think someone loves me, and I sense… I don't know… a dove. Suddenly the dove's gone and I don't get anything until he looks at a girl and I'm seeing a dog ready to fuck whatever comes to hand. I can pick up lies as well, guilty lies.' He detected anguish in her voice. 'I'm always waiting for the next vision, worrying, angry. I don't want to be alone, but I can't handle the fucking menagerie that comes with somebody else.'

Ross feared she read him at that moment. 'What about your mum's ability? Her being able to speak to the dead.'

Kezia laughed. 'She can't. Thing is, she thinks she can. But she's the same as me. What she's picking up is the emotions of the relatives.'

'So why do you help her?'

'Because she really helps people through their grief. She's like a psychiatrist. One of them who gets the punters on the couch and charges them a fortune for rabbiting on about their childhoods. Difference is she's a lot cheaper.'

Ross's Mondeo headed east, its occupants again drifting into silence, finally broken by Kezia. 'The guy you reckon threw the acid – who was he?'

'Can't tell you.' *And I'm not ready to find out if you and he were lovers.* 'And I'm still not sure if he attacked you. There's someone connected to the con you and your mum're working who remains in the picture.'

Kezia seized on the obvious suspect. 'Joe Leadbetter?'

241

'Not saying. I've told you too much already.'

That's a yes then, decided Kezia.

They reached the Thickthorn Junction, the roundabout where the London-bound A11 meets the A47 on the outer edges of Norwich. Ross headed straight ahead towards the city.

Kezia couldn't stand the latest silence any longer. 'That girl you lost. She's dead, isn't she?'

'You know she is. It's none of your bloody business.'

Kezia sensed an unexpected guilt, not anger. 'Okay. I'll change the subject. I suppose you want to discover what animal I see you as?'

He didn't. 'I'm thinking I'm a carthorse, plodding along, doing my job.'

'I imagine you as a stag, prepared to fight the other stags to keep your females.'

It was Ross's time to laugh. 'What females? The last one I had ditched me a year ago.'

'Why? You're not that bad.'

'Why do you think? You've seen the hours I work. I've ducked out of birthday parties, cancelled weekends away. What woman's going to put up with that?'

'Come on. What about Karen Unwin? You fancied her. She likes you.'

Ross had found Unwin attractive, true. 'Nonsense, I've only just met the woman. Besides, cops and defence solicitors aren't a match made in heaven.'

'You're lying. There's always the other copper, the Indian one.'

'Kirsi? She'll most likely end up in some arranged marriage. Besides, I don't date co-workers. Never shit on your own doorstep. Anyone told you that?'

'You're screwed then,' said Kezia. 'You can't hook up with cops or lawyers, and you've decided nobody else'll put up with you. Only chance you've got of getting laid is to pay for it.'

Ross stared ahead, stayed silent. Kezia had set out to needle him, but instead she'd stabbed him with the dagger of truth. She'd clearly ruled herself out of any romantic attachment with him, and she'd moved his thoughts back to the doomed existence of Susan Smith and her ilk on Rosary Road. And probably the one woman he'd really loved, the one he'd lost.

She shut her eyes and feigned sleep. She'd lied. She'd never seen Ross as a stag, and she was now forced to endure the pain emanating from the man beside her. Kezia couldn't shake her visions and no way in hell would she share them.

Kezia wished she hadn't spoken. Another reason to wallow in guilt.

Chapter Nineteen

Kezia didn't share her mother's joy when she opened the door to their flat. Sabina insisted on hearing a full account of the arrest of Taff Boswell. It was nearly four o'clock when Kezia settled down on the sofa. Her job at the greasy spoon was a no-hoper, so she was resigned to tramping the streets seeking alternative employment.

She feared she'd hurt Ross to the extent he wouldn't want anything to do with her. After her dig about his love life, his conversation reduced to monosyllabic grunts, and a muttered 'take care' when he dropped her off.

At eleven o'clock on a sunny Tuesday morning, she woke up for the second time. The first occasion was when Sabina announced she was off to the city centre. This time it was a sensation that roused her, a strange combination of joy and fear.

Someone knocked on the door. Kezia pulled on a pair of jeans. She already recognised her visitor before she opened it.

'Inspector Ross.'

'David. I'm off duty. Do you mind if I still call you Kezia?'

He was acting odd... embarrassed? She was still finding it hard to read him, as if a grey curtain was in the way. 'No, that's okay. D'you want to come in?'

'Yeah, okay.'

He walked in. Her clothes from the previous night covered the floor, even the bloodstained T-shirt.

She scooped up the garments, starting with her discarded bra. 'Sorry, I couldn't be bothered to tidy up.'

'That's understandable.' He waited till she'd picked up the final sock. 'I came to apologise. About last night. I wasn't very sociable.'

Shapes moved in her mind, but she couldn't make them out. She had to clear her head and focus.

'I wasn't nice either,' she replied. 'Coffee?'

'Yeah, thanks. Milk, no sugar please.'

She busied herself getting the drinks. 'You didn't come to apologise.'

'I forgot you could read minds. I've got good news and a proposition.'

Kezia smiled. 'Been some time since I've had one of those. Good news first, please.'

'Good news. Hope it is. Taff Boswell has confessed. McNab showed him a picture of his daughter and he broke down. He claimed it was an honour killing, that sort of thing.'

Kezia steadied herself.

So what if Boswell isn't coming after me? I'd wanted Hester dead, he obliged, and now I've sealed his fate. Will I have to face him again? Okay, he'd threatened to kill me and possibly more, but he was drunk, his soul devoured by the cancerous guilt he'd carried all those years. I hated both generations of Boswells. Did I will him to slay his daughter and in doing so destroy himself? Am I guilty of Hester's death after all?

'That's cool,' she said, pouring boiling water into the cups. 'Now, what's the proposition.'

'I pay you three hundred to work for me until Friday. Three and a half days, say eight hours a day, that's over ten quid an hour.'

'Depends on the work,' Kezia replied. 'You're not hiring me as a waitress.'

The irony wasn't lost – she was at that moment providing him with a coffee. 'No. And don't be scared to tell me if you don't want to do it.' Ross took a sip. 'My boss won't let me near Tom Vickery. I have to understand why Susan Smith found it necessary to leave Norwich.'

'What do you expect me to do? Like I said, I can only pick up on the living.'

'I realise that. The first thing I'd like you to do, well… You're a young woman, right?'

Kezia clasped her cup in both hands and laughed. 'Hey, like you're no ordinary detective. You're the new Lord Bloody Peter Wimsey working that out. How d'you do it?'

He grinned. 'Okay. If I go into Hot Steps and ask to speak to the girls, I'll get thrown out, and that's before they even discover I'm a cop. You've got a better chance.'

'Whoa, big boy.' She held up her hands. 'You expect me to get a job as a stripper? That's offensive. It's demeaning. In fact, it's such an insult I'd want a thousand quid.'

'You're saying you'd be willing to do it?'

She smiled. 'No fucking way. But I reckon even you would be unwilling to pay a grand to see my tits.'

For a split-second Ross thought about making the offer. Common sense intervened. 'Only joking. All I want you to do is connect with a couple of his girls. Work out who was there when they started, and whether they remember anything about Susan Smith or the freemason angle.'

'Why don't I just be nice to Mr Vickery?'

'No way. Vickery's dangerous. I've seen what happens when you put yourself at risk. I'm not contemplating taking you to A&E a second time. Any trouble, you're straight out of there. If Vickery takes too much interest, you're off. Understood?'

'Fine. Anything else?'

'If you get the chance, speak to a girl called Jane Nolan. She lives in a street off Rosary Road. Her partner is the guy who found Susan Smith and his whereabouts are a bit of mystery at the time of her death.'

He jotted Nolan's address in his notebook.

Kezia watched his hand shake as he wrote 'St Leonards Road'. *Something about that address is hurting him.*

He tore out the page and handed it to her. 'This is her house number. The boyfriend works in London and doesn't arrive home till about seven. See if Jane has any suspicions about what he was up to.'

'No problem. I keep the same phone, right?'

'Right. I'll put another fifty quid on the account. You might require web access and I don't want traces left on your tablet. Call me if you need anything.'

Kezia sat nursing her cup in both hands. 'Um... David.' She smiled at him. 'Not Dave?'

'I prefer David.'

David, not Dave? Is that his subconscious avoiding intimacy? 'Okay, David. Look... I never really, like, thanked you for getting me out of jail and taking me to the hospital. I understand how much you did, what risks you took.'

'That's okay. My job's to find the guilty.'

Not the whole truth. 'Yeah, but I'm not that innocent.'

'I shouldn't have snapped at you when you asked about… You know.'

'No sweat. I shouldn't be nosey. It's… Well…' She touched him on the arm. 'The girl you lost. It feels like it's eating you up. Like a cancer.'

'So, what do I do? Cut out my heart?'

'Share it.' Her hand stayed where it was, her eyes pleaded.

Her gaze smashed any vestige of reluctance. 'We met during my second year at university. Her name was Heather. It was at a Christmas party in a mate's flat in Glasgow. She'd been studying psychology at the UEA and came home for the holidays. Heather looked…' He stopped, worried about how she would react.

'She looked a bit like me, right? I worked that out.'

'Right. We fancied each other straight off. Even sneaked off for a weekend alone at the Easter break. Aviemore.' He tore his eyes away and stared at a lost memory on the far wall. 'Her mum phoned to tell me what happened the day after I'd finished my second-year exams. I called the cops in Norwich, but they weren't willing to talk to me.'

Kezia waited. She knew better than to ask questions.

'I had to travel down here on buses to find out what happened. She was raped and murdered… In the same park where we found Susan Smith. She lived up St Leonards Road. Easy to get to uni from there on the 25 bus.'

Kezia squeezed his arm.

'Alison Forsyth was a DCI then. She was in charge of the investigation. She even interrogated me. I can't blame her, as it must have been suspicious me asking questions and getting in their way. In the end, one of the DIs fucked up. Contaminated the evidence or something. They suspected who killed her, but the bastard walked.'

'And that's why you joined the police?'

'Yeah, I never stayed on for the honours year. I got out after three with an ordinary degree. I applied straight to Norfolk, and they accepted me.'

'Weren't they worried…?'

'What, about me seeking revenge? The guy who attacked her died before I joined. Brain tumour, so they claimed. No, I only wanted to make things better. Get justice for people like Heather.'

'And Susan?'

He grinned, but there was no warmth in his expression. 'Right. And so far, I've failed. Three murder investigations and one conviction. Four if you include a suspicious death by carbon monoxide poisoning. And the conviction was an old guy who slipped his wife a few extra sleeping pills when she got dementia and messed up topping himself. I've put away a few burglars and thugs, but…'

'You haven't failed her.' She squeezed his hand. 'So why did you get married?'

'God knows. I found a woman who seemed to fancy me. You know that Bob Dylan line? "I gave her my heart, but she wanted my soul." A month after the wedding she asked me to quit the force.'

'You'd unfinished business, right?'

Christ, this girl is something else. He'd never talked about Heather to anyone, even his ex-wife. As far as he was aware, Alison Forsyth was the only copper who connected him to a twelve-year-old crime. But Kezia was different. *Perhaps she's too like Heather, seducing me into believing I can regain what was lost?* But if Heather was unattainable, happiness might still be in reach.

Should he, could he, make some kind of advance? He told himself to take it slowly. The girl was an enigma, maybe twelve years his junior. She inhabited a world he couldn't understand. And yet...

'Kezia, I wanted – '

The door opened to allow Sabina, weighed down by carrier bags, to stumble in.

'What's he doing here again?' the older woman said. 'Last time we helped him, his friends barged in and arrested you.'

'He's cool. He's given me a job for the rest of the week.'

Sabina snorted. 'He's filth. They've never been good news for people like us.'

'Mrs Lee,' said Ross, 'I can assure you my intentions are honourable.'

A snigger from Kezia, whose internal lie detector activated again.

'It's Mrs Romanov to you. And what sort of job?'

'Checking stuff out,' replied Kezia. 'Like on the internet. Help you hook Eve Kendal.'

Ross decided he should drink up quickly and disappear. After he'd left, Kezia helped Sabina unpack the groceries and cheap clothing she hoped her mother had paid for. She was fully aware that in lean months, some of Sabina's acquisitions didn't go through the till.

After lunch, Kezia announced she was going out. She assumed Ross hadn't yet loaded the mobile account, and she needed access to the Web. A few minutes later she sat at the back of the Ribs of Beef, making sure nobody could see what she was doing.

Vickery's club was advertising for dancers: 'Hot Steps needs energetic and enthusiastic performers to join our existing team. Whether a beginner or professional, we want to hear from you...'

I can do energy and enthusiasm.

'To start the application process, simply complete stage one by filling out the short form to the right and uploading two recent photos (examples below).'

Now she was moving into unfamiliar territory. The first photo was of a beautiful, flawless blonde's head and shoulders. The second example showed a tall, slim, confident woman wearing a bikini.

Kezia closed the window and sat back, reviewing her options. Maybe Plan A wasn't such a good idea. Plan B comprised hanging around outside the club and follow anyone who resembled a dancer. That would mean standing in Prince of Wales Road at some unearthly hour in the morning at the mercy of every lecherous drunk staggering out of the many bars and clubs. Odds were her quarries would hop into a taxi outside the door.

Plan C seemed the simplest. *Tell David to stuff his stupid job.*

It wouldn't help Ma or Jez Kendal. But who cares about Ma and Jez? Or even David Ross?

No brainer.

She went back to the flat.

'Ma, help me pin this sheet up against the wall.'

'Why?'

'It's background. I'd like you to take a couple of pictures.'

'We haven't got a camera.'

Kezia waved the mobile supplied by Ross. Within a few minutes they'd covered wallpaper and the bathroom door with a light blue bedsheet. Kezia started the camera app and taught her mother how to use it.

'Right, head and shoulders shot.' She watched Sabina aim the phone.

'It's bust,' said Sabina. 'There's a big pinky-black bit.'

'Your finger's over the lens. And stop wobbling.'

'Right. Smile.'

Kezia looked at the result. 'Christ, my teeth look awful. They're not straight at the bottom. And they're a yucky grey.'

'You never complained before. Besides, they're fine.'

Kezia kept her mouth shut for the next attempt. She rejected it because she thought she looked ill and borrowed her mother's make-up to enhance the third try.

'That'll do. Looks more like a wanted poster than a glamour shot.'

'What do you mean 'glamour shot'?'

'Nothing. Okay, let's do the second one.'

Sabina's eyes and mouth widened in unison as Kezia stripped to bra and knickers. 'Why are you doing this?'

252

''Cause I haven't got a bikini. Just take the picture.'

'No. I realise what's happening. I wasn't born yesterday.'

'I guessed that. Please just take the bloody picture.'

'I'm not having my daughter selling her body. I'll get a job if it stops you becoming a prostitute.'

'Jesus. Ma, you have my promise I am not going to be a hooker.'

'It's that policeman. He wants to ogle you. I told you we shouldn't trust him.'

'It's not. Trust me. Please click the bloody button.'

Sabina muttered a final protest. Kezia assumed the pose she'd seen in the example – right hand on hips, right knee bent, pouting lips, left arm strategically placed to hide her stitches.

'God, what a minger,' was Kezia's comment when she saw the result.

'So now tell me,' demanded Sabina.

'I'm applying to be a lap dancer.'

Sabina's scream could have rattled windows three streets away.

***

Ross had topped up the pay-as-you-go mobile, allowing Kezia to complete her application form, including the two photos. Her finger had paused over the 'send' option for several seconds. She'd never respected women who flaunted their bodies, and here she was, a wannabe sex object, volunteering to expose herself in front of strangers. She told herself she'd back out, flunk the audition. Who was she kidding? How

253

would she feel when the reply arrived, confirming she was too ugly to be of any interest?

She'd used the name Mary Malone. Three years ago she'd acquired a fake driving licence using Mary's identity – a favour for supplying a false alibi for a second-cousin who'd been accused of housebreaking. She wouldn't share that with Ross. Mary the Minger, trashy lap-dancer. Not that it would be needed, but she created a Hotmail account in the same name. A Facebook account already existed. Mary was born in the Irish Republic – the country's records weren't as easy to access as the UK's.

Her finger descended. Whatever the verdict would be on Mary Malone, she wouldn't like it.

***

Ross regretted his success in cancelling the rest of his leave. Instead of shuffling through the increasing pile of reports, he was standing in ACC Alison Forsyth's office. The walls were covered in certificates and commendations. Two photographs, one of Forsyth with a man whom he guessed was her husband, the other a group shot from some conference of senior officers.

DCI Devlin sat beside the assistant chief constable, a smirk on his face.

'Inspector Ross,' she began. 'You've given me a problem.'

'Ma'am.'

'I've received a thank you from the Chief Constable of Northamptonshire Constabulary. It seems you've helped them solve a cold case.'

Ross guessed he wasn't about to receive a medal.

'Normally, I'd see that as a reason for celebration. But it appears in doing so you've enabled a person of interest in three of our cases to walk free without informing the appropriate officers.'

'Kezia Lee.' Devlin was always quick to state the bleeding obvious.

Ross stood to attention. 'I don't believe the evidence is sufficient in those cases to detain Miss Lee.'

'It's not your call,' said Forsyth. 'DI Alder is the SIO. He's found more evidence damning Miss Lee.'

'May I ask what?'

'She visited Jeremy Kendal in prison,' said Forsyth. 'What do you think that indicates?'

'No idea, ma'am.'

Devlin laughed. 'Really? And you call yourself a detective? She raids the victim's house. She's linked to the man who undoubtedly carried out the killing.' He glanced at Forsyth, the epitome of smugness. 'The one weakness in our case against Kendal is motive. We've got him bang to rights on opportunity. His fingerprints were on the murder weapon. But why did he do it? We assumed Susan Smith had somehow upset him. But...' He paused like a compere announcing a reality TV show winner, 'suppose he's acting under orders?'

'Eh?' Ross grinned. 'You think Kezia Lee is some kind of criminal mastermind?'

'Perhaps not a mastermind,' said Forsyth. 'A messenger. We think it's drugs.'

'Best of luck proving it.'

Devlin coughed. Ross recognised this was usually the prelim to a pretentious announcement.

'DI Ross,' said the DCI, 'I've warned you before about your relationship with Miss Lee. Too close, I fear. I took the precaution of checking the whereabouts of your mobile phone over the last few days. I found to my disappointment that, after you'd been told to stay clear, you appear to have spent last Thursday night with her. All night, may I add.'

'It's not what it looks like.'

Devlin opened his mouth, but Forsyth stopped him.

'I'm sorry, Inspector Ross,' she said, 'but you leave me no choice. I'm suspending you until Professional Standards complete an investigation. Please surrender your warrant card and keys. You may keep your mobile in case we need to contact you.'

'Ma'am, is it possible to have a private word with you?'

Forsyth looked at Devlin before turning back to Ross. 'Inspector, we have a chain of command in this force which I must respect. If you have a complaint about DCI Devlin, then please state it now.'

'No, ma'am.'

'Fine. I think we're finished here. Your warrant card and keys please, inspector?'

Ross handed the items over and left the ACC's office. He stormed out of Bethel Street grim-faced, cursing Devlin, fearing Kezia's liberty might be short-lived. His route took him past the Forum towards the Theatre Royal where he pulled out his own burner phone.

'Kezia, it's David Ross. Listen, I've been suspended. They've got some stupid notion in their heads you're in cahoots with Jez Kendal. Just watch your back, okay?'

'Do you still want me to look into Hot Steps and the other thing?' said Kezia.

'Yeah. But be very careful. Only way I'm going to come out smelling of roses is if we clear you and Jez.'

'Fine. I'm on it. I've applied for a lap dancing job.'

'What?'

Several passers-by turned round to check what the shout was all about. Ross nodded to them and resumed his expression of horror. 'You can't do that. I didn't want – '

'Well, I have, but like I'm such an ugly cow they won't hire me.'

'Christ, Kezia, whatever you are, it's not ugly. I don't want you to do this. I forbid it.'

Bad move.

'To hell with you, Inspector Ross. You don't own me. Bye.'

She hung up.

He gazed at the mobile in shock, contemplating ringing back. His other phone stopped him: 'Why Does It Always Rain on Me'. A mobile number he didn't recognise.

'David?'

Alison Forsyth's voice. *David*. This was a turn up.

'Ma'am?'

'You wanted a private word. Now's your chance.'

'I don't trust Devlin. I think he's Vickery's pet.'

'Be careful what you say. Suppose I tell you Vickery is Devlin's pet?'

'Vickery's no-one's pet. He's a snake, and a venomous one as well.'

'Vickery's ours. We realise he's been a naughty boy in the past, but we've reached an accommodation. He was an old-time crook. Protection rackets, prostitution, illegal gambling. That was before the eastern Europeans and the London boys moved in, bringing organised drug and people trafficking with them. Vickery's gone legit, and he gives Devlin a heads up whenever he knows of something we'd be interested in.'

'What about bribery and corruption?'

'Lobbying and corporate entertainment, you mean? It's a thin line, and Vickery knows how close he can go.'

'What about murder? You going to let him off with that?'

'You've got nothing. Susan Smith was a prostitute who worked for him long ago. Every crook with a past in this town has an association with Tom Vickery.'

'What about Kev Connor? Two years ago, he was Vickery's thug.'

'An accident, so the gas man says.'

'You're telling me to lay off Vickery.'

'No, I'm ordering you to lay off Vickery. I'm telling you to lay off Kezia Lee. She sounds like a nasty bit of stuff, and she'll ruin you.'

'Fine. Please humour me. When I saw you at Nigel Warder's, did Vickery find out anything about the warrant?'

'To be honest, I don't know. He and Nigel were deep in conversation immediately after you left. I didn't eavesdrop. I can't imagine Nigel telling him. Or anyone else for that matter.'

'Thanks.'

'David, I'm warning you. I can't help you if you persist with this infatuation with Kezia Lee. You might have gone too far already. I want you back, so please be careful and stay away from that girl.'

He pulled out the burner phone but thought better of it. Kezia was a free spirit. There was less chance of her following his advice than him kowtowing to ACC Forsyth.

***

Kezia regretted her outburst at Ross's request to cease her table-dancing application. All he wanted to do was protect her. She spent a miserable few hours musing on whether she should apologise. But if she did, he would only attempt to persuade her to hold back, and she dare not risk another confrontation. Instead, she wallowed in self-pity until six o'clock. Hot Steps hadn't contacted her, so she decided to visit Jane Nolan.

Her press on the doorbell was answered by a series of barks. She took a step back, nervous about encountering the dog. Nolan came to the door, her foot blocking a dachshund.

Calm down. It's a sausage dog, not a bloody rottweiler. 'Miss Nolan?'

'Yes.'

I'm picking up suspicion, fear… a hint of jealousy. And she wonders if I'm Pritchard's secret girlfriend. 'I'm from the Psychological Review. Have you heard of us?'

'No.' Hardly surprising, it was a specialised American publication.

'We're conducting a study on the indirect victims of murder.'

'Sorry, I'm not quite…'

'We work in conjunction with the police. That's how we got your information. You see, no-one really understands the impact of a murder on the witnesses, especially those who find the body.'

'Right. You should come back later. It was my fiancée who found the woman.'

Kezia smiled, trying to ignore the dog's growls. 'We've found when we've interviewed people like your fiancée, they hide the true effects of their trauma. It's their loved ones who spot the hidden signs.'

'Well, I'm a bit busy right now.' She pointed to the dachshund. 'Merkel needs her walk.'

'No problem. Why don't I accompany you for a bit? It won't take long.'

Nolan didn't like the idea, but she couldn't find a reason to refuse. 'Okay, I'll get my coat.'

The two women walked along Rosary Road, Kezia ensuring she kept well clear of Merkel. She guessed their destination was Old Library Wood.

'D'you normally come this way?' asked Kezia.

'Not late at night. We walk along Riverside after sunset. Too many weirdos crawl out of the woodwork when it gets dark.'

'Pity. It's a nice area.'

Jane talked about how convenient it was to get to the city centre and how lucky they'd been to purchase their house.

Kezia shared in banal social chit-chat before getting down to business. 'Have you two been together long?'

'Ten years now. We met at Nottingham University.'

Ross would value that snippet. Kezia wondered why they hadn't yet tied the knot. 'Were you out the night of the murder?'

'Why are you asking?' Jane betrayed concern.

'I'm just thinking. I mean, like you might have seen the murderer. It wouldn't have registered at the time, but in view of what happened, you know...'

'Well, I didn't.'

Kezia noted her use of the word 'I'. Not 'we'. *He wasn't around.* 'What time would you have gone?'

'We went out for dinner. Supposed to have been a celebration. We took Merkel up to the park about seven. Then after I got back...'

Kezia took note of the word 'supposed'. 'You took Merkel out again. Just you, not Keith?'

'So what? I'm not sure I like these questions.'

Kezia reckoned she'd pushed Jane too far. 'Sorry, my natural curiosity. That's what you get with psychological training.' As if she'd know. 'The morning Keith found the body, how did he react?'

They'd reached the entrance to Old Library Wood. Bloody images of death permeated Kezia's thoughts. She swept them aside.

Jane let the dachshund off the lead. 'He was stunned. I didn't see too much of him. After he called the police, he'd

261

only enough time to grab a biscuit before I ran him to the station.'

'And has he seemed normal after the incident? Any changed behaviour?'

Jane watched Merkel squatting down a few feet away. 'Not that I've noticed.'

As the woman bent down to pick up Merkel's gift to the grass, Kezia mused Jane probably had to deal with a lot of shit courtesy of her boyfriend. Since she hadn't seen Jane along Riverside on her way to the bins of Chalk Hill Road, she couldn't rule out the possibility Jane had risked a trip to the Wood to check if her fiancée was there.

Kezia fired a few more questions, the kind that might be expected of the Psychological Review. She left Jane when they emerged from the park, pondering if the events leading to Susan Smith's murder lay in the antics of an undergraduate in Nottingham. Perhaps she wouldn't have a career in lap dancing after all.

Chapter Twenty

Kezia was nervous as the mobile fired back into life. She kept telling herself other people's opinions didn't matter. She was comfortable in her own skin; she was not a sexual object.

A message from Ross: 'Be careful.'

She should let him know about Jane Nolan and the Nottingham connection. He might tell her to get back on the train, check up on the university or see if Cheryl Jackson remembered either. If so, she wouldn't have to open her mail.

Hell, she needed to settle the issue that nagged her. She logged on to Mary Malone's Hotmail account. One message. Admin@hotstepsclub.co.uk.

'Hi Mary,' it started. 'We've seen your photos and, wow, you might have what it takes to be one of our artistes. Call me to arrange an interview.'

It ended with a smiley face emoji next to the name 'Mandy Stewart, Dance Director' and a Norwich phone number.

Wow, indeed. Kezia dialled the number.

'Mandy speaking.'

'Hi, I'm Mary Malone. You sent me an email.'

'Mary. Wow, you got back quick. Enthusiasm, that's what we need. Can we fix a time to see you?'

'I'm free anytime.' Kezia wondered if her response sounded too desperate.

'How about four this afternoon at the club? Bring some ID. Mr Vickery's coming in around then and he'll want to see you. You don't have a problem doing a strip, do you?'

'No, that's great.'

Great, she thought when the conversation ended. *Ross will love that. I'll call him and tell him Vickery's going to gawp at my tits and possibly my fanny then check my fake driving licence. What can possibly go wrong?*

Kezia walked into the city with a sense of guilty elation. If she was going to do this, she had to do it right. A rummage through her underwear drawer confirmed nothing she owned could be described as glamorous. Ann Summers or Marks and Spencer? She wasn't an Ann Summers girl. She left M&S with matching red padded bra and knickers, plus some other necessities.

Ross called her as she was leaving. 'Kezia, it's David. What are you up to? You're not going ahead with this lap dancing stunt, are you?'

'Nah. Decided against it. Silly idea. Thought I'd trawl round the dance academies in town, speak to the people to check if they remember anyone who used to work at Hot Steps. That okay?'

'Fine. Just be careful. Any joy with Jane Nolan?'

'Right. One. They met in Nottingham. At the university. They lived there the same time as Susan Smith. It sounds like her and the boyfriend weren't together around the time of the murder and she might have been near the park walking the dog.'

'Nottingham? Your gut instinct... could Jane be the killer?'

'Doubt it. Although she's hiding something. Like maybe she suspects the boyfriend.'

'Makes you wonder what Pritchard got up to at uni.' Ross thought for a second. 'How do you feel about getting up early?'

'Like how early?'

'On the morning after Susan's murder Pritchard called the police just after five thirty when he walked the dog. If you got hold of a dog, you could engage him in conversation. I could wait nearby in case you had a problem.'

'Tomorrow morning? I refuse to get a dog, but I'll improvise.'

'Phone me before you do anything. Okay?'

'Cool.'

Fine, that got Ross off her back for a few hours. She'd need them to make herself beautiful.

***

Ross arrived at the UEA Pathology Department looking for answers, running out of friends, and fearing he might lose another.

Dr Charles Porter-Brown showed no signs of alienation when Ross entered the Queen's Building on the university campus. 'David, an unexpected pleasure.' Handshake completed. 'I've heard strange rumours of your suspension. DCI Devlin, no doubt?'

'Precisely. I've strayed into forbidden territory.'

'Ah, the red lines the thin blue one cannot cross. And does your gardening leave permit you to visit me?'

'Probably not. You're welcome to throw me out. Particularly when you discover what I want to ask.'

Porter-Brown laughed. 'I doubt it. Fire away.'

'You're a mason, aren't you?'

'I may have let my darkest secret slip out in the past. Why? Would you like to join?'

'Not yet. Were you a member seven years ago?'

'Fifteen years man and boy.' Another laugh. 'Although we can't talk about the boys. Why do you want to know?'

Ross had rehearsed his next question; he still wasn't sure how to ask it. 'Seven years ago, was there any organised contact with prostitutes in the Norwich branch?'

A horrified expression crossed the doctor's face followed by a broad grin. 'What?'

Ross took a deep breath and asked again. 'Did you ever hear of lodge members indulging in… well, a bit of fun with prozzies?'

'What do you know about freemasonry?'

'I know it's all secret. Supposed to be a boys' club doing charitable works and all that, but – '

'Correct, dear boy. It is secret, in as much as what happens in the lodge stays in the lodge. And yes, it is a boys' club. Which is why we don't invite women except occasionally as guest speakers. Not PC, as they say these days, but we pride ourselves on upholding standards, and that doesn't embrace prostitution.'

'Okay, I apologise. It's just we had a report suggesting Susan Smith had something to do with the lodge in Norwich.'

'Dear boy, let me put you right on another point. There are several lodges in Norwich. I am a member of just one.'

'Suppose one of the lodges went off message. Would you notice?'

Porter-Brown maintained a patronising smile. 'We meet at the same venue. Ladies of the night might be spotted.'

'Okay, Charles. Bear with me. Perhaps some members of one of the lodges got together for some off-piste activity. Were there ever any rumours?'

'Sorry, David. Can't help. I can't think of a single member who was ever suspected of paying for sex. Apart from alimony as a consequence of the act – if you grasp my meaning.'

'Too well. One last question. Can you think of any members who might be associated with Tom Vickery?'

'If you mean the new Tom Vickery, entrepreneur, leading light of our city's commercial community, then I suspect many of our brethren would meet that criteria.'

'What about the old Tom Vickery?'

'Ah, I'm afraid I must fall back on my oath of secrecy. I would suggest you trawl the worldwide web and seek illumination regarding the secretary of the Lodge of Integrity.'

Ross's first act after reaching his car was to google freemasonry in Norwich. A few clicks later he was able to access public information on the various lodges and their officers.

The secretary of the Lodge of Integrity was listed as Richard J. Carpenter. The man trusted to clear Jez Kendal. More significantly, someone else who nestled in Tom Vickery's pocket.

**

Kezia stepped out from the sunshine of Prince of Wales Road into the gloom of Hot Steps. The interior smelt like the downmarket pubs she'd worked in over the past few years – a mixture of sweat and alcohol. On her left, a shiny metal pole ascended from a raised stage. In front sat several tables each surrounded by four padded chairs. A long bar faced her, while to her right were several alcoves, some obscured by black curtains. Each visible alcove contained a single chair. She felt like a French aristocrat enjoying her first glimpse of the guillotine.

A woman in her fifties pushed a vacuum cleaner with little enthusiasm over the stained carpet.

'Hi,' said Kezia. 'I'm looking for Mandy Stewart.'

'Nie mówię po angielsku,' muttered the woman.

Kezia didn't appreciate it was Polish, but guessed the woman couldn't speak English and she'd just communicated the fact in her native language.

'Mary?' A woman's voice, coming from a doorway next to the bar.

Kezia didn't react. She assumed the woman was speaking to the cleaner.

'Mary Malone?'

Shit, that's who I'm supposed to be. 'Sorry. You must be Mandy.'

Mandy Stewart was in her late thirties. Short auburn hair, a face a little too heavily made up, a body maintaining the physique of a dancer.

'Thanks for being early. Mr Vickery's waiting in his office.'

Kezia followed Stewart through the door and then into a windowless room, hazy with smoke, reeking of after-shave and tobacco. Tom Vickery sat behind an antique desk, his bald head reflecting the light from a tall standard lamp which provided the only illumination. A half-smoked cigar smouldered on an ashtray, the only item on its polished surface.

The walls were covered with black-and-white head and shoulder pictures of attractive young women. The floor was wood parquet.

Stewart sat down in the only other chair in the room, identical to those surrounding the tables in the main arena, and nodded towards Kezia. 'Mary Malone.'

Vickery smiled. *If he'd had a moustache, he'd have been twirling it.* 'Okay, Mary, let's see what you've got.'

He pulled a remote control out of a drawer and pressed a button. From a hidden speaker Lenny Kravitz kicked off 'American Woman'.

Vickery opened his hand to indicate she should start her performance.

Kezia wore her usual T-shirt and long tartan skirt. She commenced by wiggling her hips and then slowly unpeeling her top.

Smile, she thought. She assumed a broad toothy grin and with some effort yanked the top over her head. *He'd see nothing more if I was wearing a bikini.* The smile didn't listen and morphed into an embarrassed gurn. Kezia forced the corners of her mouth up again, executed a quick swing of her hips, and dropped her skirt to the floor in a single motion. Now her eyes betrayed fear and hesitation. *Should I go further?*

Vickery aimed the remote. 'Enough.'

Lenny stopped singing. Vickery looked at Mandy and shook his head. His eyes then wandered around Kezia's body.

'Mary,' he said at last. 'That was bloody awful. Ed Balls looked more erotic on *Strictly.*'

Shit. She'd spent a fortune on lingerie, embarrassed herself, eroded her self-esteem, and all for nothing.

'Good news is I've seen worse. At least the end product is worth waiting for.' He pointed at the stitches on her side. 'Boyfriend trouble? That doesn't augur well.'

'I was mugged,' Kezia said. 'Some bastard tried to steal my bag. The doctors say you won't notice it in a few weeks.'

'Bit of makeup'll soon fix that. As long as you don't bring your personal problems into the club.' Now he was staring at her lace-lined breasts. 'Mandy, give the lass the spiel.' He picked up the cigar and nodded to Stewart.

'Okay, Mary,' the woman said. 'What Mr Vickery means is we like you. But...'

Here we go, thought Kezia. *Don't call us, etc.*

'Your dancing's crap. We can sort it. It's not as if you need to learn much. We're not the Bolshoi Ballet. Here's the deal. We hire you on a freelance basis. You go round chatting to the guys. Get them to buy you a bottle of champagne, you earn five pounds. Anything else it's a quid. Don't waste time with any of the punters, unless they offer to pay for that time. Don't settle for less than a tenner, and if they stump up, we get half. There are cameras everywhere so don't try to cheat. You charge twenty quid for a private dance, and we get ten. If the punter tips you any more, you get to keep it. Okay?'

Kezia nodded.

'Twice a night you'll do a ten-minute stint on the pole, free of charge. Before you start, you'll go to a lady called Vicki. She'll train you. There's a couple of girls booked in with her on Monday morning, so one more shouldn't hurt. Can you make it?'

Another nod.

'If you're still crap at the end, she tells us and you're out. If you make the grade, you refund the costs. So, you only get a fiver a dance until you've paid off three hundred. How does that sound?'

Appear interested... 'How many dances do I do a night?'

Stewart shrugged. 'That's up to you. The punters like you, you'll be turning them down. Some girls can do thirty in a good night, and they're the ones who get the big tips as well.'

Kezia suppressed a cough – the cigar smoke was getting to her.

'Suppose they ask me for something more?'

Vickery placed his cigar back in the ashtray. 'Then you tell them to fuck off. This is not a knocking shop, and you're not here to be a tart. Everything you do will be on film. We've got rules.' He nodded to Stewart and retrieved the cigar.

'The guys can't touch you,' said Stewart. 'If you touch them, okay, but no hands or mouth down there, and – '

Vickery interrupted. 'And if we see their Brightons...'

Kezia raised her eyebrows. 'Brightons?'

'Tom's idea of rhyming slang,' said Stewart. 'Brighton Rock – '

'Cock,' explained Vickery. 'They're out the club headfirst. Turn round.'

Kezia obliged.

Vickery pointed with his cigar towards Kezia's left shoulder. 'You've got a tattoo.'

'It's a rose,' she said. 'Only one I've got.'

Vickery looked at Stewart. 'No problem. Football teams, names of boyfriends or kids, political parties, wouldn't have them. A few decent tattoos are good. They suggest you're up for it.' He took one last leer at her cleavage. 'You can get dressed now.'

Once she was clothed, Vickery showed no further interest. Stewart shot a cursory glance at her fake driving licence as they walked back towards the entrance.

'I'll send you a mail with Vicki's details. Nice meeting you.'

Kezia blinked in the brightness of Prince of Wales Road. She was unsure the expedition had been a success. Tom Vickery had been adamant prostitution wasn't on offer at Hot Steps.

Her burner phone rang. She readied her lies about where she'd been.

'What the hell are you doing?' She wasn't expecting an angry tone in Ross's opening line.

'I'm in town. I was going to the library to check up on dancing classes.'

'I damn well know you're in town. You're nowhere near the fucking library. You're on Prince of Wales Road. And you've spent the last half hour in Hot Steps.'

She looked round. *Where was he?*

The truth dawned... 'You've been tracking my phone.'

'Yes. And it's not your phone. Kezia, I need to be sure you're safe.'

'Shit, you've been stalking me. You don't own me.'

'I'm employing you. That means you do what I say.'

'I do what you need. I use my initiative.' Kezia spun round to make sure nobody was listening. 'You want to tell someone how to do this job, hire a fucking performing monkey.'

Silence. She wondered if he'd hung up.

Then: 'Kezia, I care what happens to you. Tell me what happened in there.'

'I saw Vickery and some woman. They – '

'Jesus! You met Vickery. Does he know who you are?'

'Relax. It's cool. He thinks I'm called Mary Malone.'

'It's not cool.' Ross paused, calculating potential consequences. 'Okay, tell me the rest.'

Kezia waited till a couple walked past. 'I had a quick audition and they've offered me a job. I've got to see some woman in Wroxham first. She's going to train me. Like she might remember what happened seven years ago.'

'Hang on, they offered you a job? What address did you give them?'

'The flat. What else?'

Silence for five seconds. 'Kezia, there's a possibility a guy called Kev Connor attacked you. Does that name ring a bell?'

'Never heard of him.' Her matter-of-fact tone reassured him. 'Have you arrested him?'

'He's dead. He might have worked for Vickery.'

'So? If he's dead, it explains why I had the feeling he'd gone.'

'You're missing the point. Connor found out where you lived. Therefore, Vickery might know. And if he recognises the address, you'll be a target.'

'How did Connor die?'

'Carbon monoxide poisoning. The current theory is a malfunctioning gas boiler, but my gut says it was murder. My bosses want it to be an accident. All I'm saying is, please don't carry on with this dancing idea.'

'It's cool. Vickery's not going to look too closely. He just wanted to ogle me. Some woman called Mandy Stewart's doing the admin.'

Kezia was mistaken if her assertion that Vickery had leered at her half-naked body was going to make him any happier.

'Give me those names. Mandy Stewart, right? Who's the woman in Wroxham?'

'Vicki Mayweather.'

'Right, go there. Keep your phone on. Do not return to Hot Steps. Is that clear?'

'Crystal.'

Kezia pocketed the phone and looked back at the club. If she did return, Crystal would be an excellent dancing name.

Chapter Twenty-one

That early in the morning, even the late July sun struggled to raise the temperature on Rosary Road. Only a few braved the chill: a couple of commuters en route to the station, a man walking a dachshund, and a panting young woman in a black tracksuit jogging along the street.

She sprinted past the dog-walker just before he entered Old Library Wood. He was surprised to find her sitting on the path clutching her ankle.

Kezia picked up a hint of desire mixed into Keith Pritchard's concern when he approached her. 'Are you okay?'

She rubbed her leg and slowly got to her feet. 'Ouch!'

'You don't sound okay.'

'It's an old injury. Flares up every so often. I'll be fine.' She took a step and doubled up in apparent pain.

Pritchard needed no further excuse to put his arm round her waist. 'Just take it easy.'

'Thanks.' *He's providing a little too much support.* 'Hell, this is worse than usual. Sorry to interrupt your walk.'

'No problem. You be okay for a second?'

She nodded. Pritchard loosened his grip and released the dachshund from its lead. Kezia was relieved to see the dog run towards the trees at the far end.

'Nice dog. She likes it here, doesn't she?'

Pritchard's arm snaked further round her waist. 'Merkel? Loves it.'

'I'm okay now, I can manage.'

'Are you sure?' He kept holding her.

'Positive.'

His hand slid away, maintaining contact as long as possible.

Kezia gave him her sexiest smile. 'Dangerous place, this park. Wasn't there a murder here the other week? I read it in the paper.'

'You won't believe this. I was the one who found the body.'

'Wow. So cool! I mean, like it must have been horrible, but hey, what a story. God, like I can't imagine how I'd cope. You didn't see the murderer, did you?'

Pritchard fell for the faux hero worship. 'No. Just as well. The police reckon she was killed the night before. Funny thing is, most nights I'd have been around here, taking Merkel for her last walk, but that evening I went out for a meal.'

Kezia watched Merkel running around, then stopping for a minute, before darting off. Pritchard made no attempt to check if the dog had left a souvenir of its visit.

'Bit dodgy here at night, isn't it?' asked Kezia.

'The street's not too bad. There's a couple of girls… you know… but they're used to me. I even stop and have a chat sometimes. I wouldn't go in the park late at night. Too many druggies.'

Kezia laughed and sparkled her eyes at him. 'Doesn't your wife get a bit worried, you being pally with ladies of the night?'

'I'm single,' he said, allowing Kezia to ensure her internal lie detector was functioning normally. 'What's your name by the way?'

'Mary,' she said. 'Mary Malone.'

'I'm Keith. Do you need any help getting back?'

Kezia assumed a moderate limp. 'No, I can walk the rest of the way. Thanks for your help... Keith.' One last seductive smile.

She slowly made her way to the junction with Hill House Road. Forty yards away Ross was waiting inside his Mondeo with a flask of coffee. The car smelt of the previous night's chips.

'Well?' He poured her a cup.

'He's a first-class creep,' she said. 'But he's not a murderer. He claims to have been mates with the hookers. You know, saying hello and all that.'

'Perhaps I should have another conversation with him. Find out if Susan said anything.'

'Jane might have had suspicions.' She grinned. 'And not without good reason.'

'You think Jane might have killed Susan?'

'Doesn't seem likely.' She took a sip. 'Thanks for this. I need it. I had to run at least two hundred yards.'

'You should join a gym.'

'Yeah, right. Are you going to pay for it?'

Ross sat holding his cup, staring straight ahead. Kezia saw a troubled man.

'Kezia,' he said at last. 'This arrangement we've got...'

'You want out,' she said.

'I've put you in danger. I'm sorry.'

'I'm in this for my Ma as well. You're paying me to do what I'd do for free anyway.'

'This isn't a game. This freemason angle... there's a name I've found linked to Vickery. Guy called Richard Carpenter. He's secretary of one of the Norwich lodges. He's also Jez Kendal's lawyer. If he finds out you're sniffing around Kendal, it'll get back to Vickery.'

'Vickery thinks I'm called Mary, remember.'

'Kezia, please. I don't want you to do this anymore.'

'I need to do this. You won't understand.' *He wouldn't. Nobody could realise how the years of guilt and lies had affected her. She needed to balance the karma. Saving Jez Kendal, getting justice for Susan Smith – perhaps if she achieved those she could move on. She mustn't let her feelings for Ross get in the way.*

Ross cursed his curiosity. He should have been patient, not pressed Kezia to get involved. If something happened to her, it would be his fault. Just like it was when he'd let Heather come down here alone. Everything he'd done so far had only dragged Kezia closer to danger. If he really wanted to help her, he'd move out of her life.

'We have to stop seeing each other.'

Kezia knew it was already too late. She pulled out the mobile. 'It's cool. Here's your phone.'

Ross stared at the mobile. *I should take it. Sever every connection I have with her.* Instead he said, 'Keep it. If you're in trouble, call me.' He continued to stare ahead. 'I can't help you much more. That bastard Devlin's suspended me.'

Kezia wanted to touch him, fool him into thinking everything would be fine. 'Because of me?'

'Not really.'

He's lying. 'Will you lose your job?' she asked.

'Unlikely. Might end up as a constable. At least I'll get paid overtime.'

She forced a smile. 'Can't see you with a pointy hat. Who's Devlin anyway?'

'My boss. Neville bloody Devlin.'

Kezia could tell how much her presence was troubling him. 'I can walk back.'

'I'll drive you. Least I can do as a thanks.'

Ross took her back to her flat. Neither spoke.

Kezia opened the door, then swiftly turned and kissed him on the cheek. 'Bye, David,' she said. 'Take care.'

Ross wanted to seize her, press his lips to hers, tell her how he felt. Pragmatism stopped him. He simply nodded and drove away, feeling lonelier than ever.

***

Kezia crawled back onto the couch, once more wallowing in self-loathing. Sabina appeared at eight o'clock and woke her daughter. Kezia finished breakfast then *Sad Cypress* before heading off to find another Wi-Fi-enabled pub. Even though she still had the mobile, she was reluctant to use it for any purpose other than to contact Ross or communicate with Hot Steps. Anything else would seem to be akin to infidelity.

Following the successful consultation with Phyllis Leadbetter, Sabina had acquired several potential clients, so Kezia focused on her search for interesting information. She anticipated Ross would quickly become a memory, a vivid dream of a life she could never aspire to. She'd continue to have an interest in the Susan Smith murder if only to find anything that might help confuse the case against Jez Kendal.

***

Ross's brief return to indolence was about to expire. As he slumped down on a chair to contemplate the debris of the previous night's takeaway, his phone rang.

'DI Ross, DCI Devlin here.' A subdued Devlin – this was going to either a humble apology or terrible news. 'The ACC has been speaking to the Commissioner about you.'

The Commissioner... unexpected. Were his transgressions that serious?

'It appears your accomplishments in Northamptonshire have earned you a rather flattering reputation.' Devlin's flat tone suggested he was reading from a script. 'The Commissioner feels if our reasons for suspending you were misconstrued as being connected to your success in apprehending the murderer of Hester Boswell... Well, the press would have a field day. Consequently, we have asked Professional Standards to terminate their investigation, and we would like you to resume your duties.'

'Thank you, sir.'

'Subject to certain conditions. You will cease contact with Kezia Lee and will play no part in the investigation of the Susan Smith murder. Furthermore, you will not make any allegations about the death of Kevin Connor which we are treating as a tragic accident.'

'I understand, sir.' Ross could live with those. He'd walked away from Kezia. If Connor attacked Kezia, then justice had been served.

An hour later, Ross returned to Bethel Street. His in-tray had grown by an inch. Illegal dog fights, car thefts, and a gang targeting cash machines now jostled with organised shoplifting and robberies for his attention.

Mishra had made progress on the shoplifting. She'd recognised one of the suspects and now waited for phone records to establish who else might be in the gang. Ross checked the forensics reports on the ATM raids – nothing of any significance. The vehicle was dark red, the paint database suggested a Range Rover. Exactly what the CCTV revealed in addition to the number plate. Not that the registration was much use. The car it belonged to had been stolen from a driveway in Holt the night before.

Dog fights – something for Hamish to get his teeth into.

Delegation left Ross with the burglaries. He had twenty-four reports from across the city with information on a further fourteen within a fifteen-mile radius.

They wouldn't be all related. Most of the break-ins on council estates would be down to residents of nearby properties. He should get a list of the usual suspects living in the area, wait till the next report, and send uniformed officers round with a warrant. Three estates were affected, and fifteen reports could be attributed to those districts.

That left nine in addition to the out-of-town ones. Of those, three appeared to be opportunistic – unlocked front doors or windows. *Best of luck with the insurers.*

Six left, all from large houses. He read the details. The first one detailed graffiti sprayed on walls, faeces left on front room carpets – drug addicts without doubt.

The other five... interesting. Most burglars went for the obvious – jewels, cameras, computers, money. Those featured among the stolen items, but the inclusion of pottery in the lists was unusual. He checked two of them online: Clarice Cliff wind-bells wall plaque, price £500; Pair of Staffordshire white and gilt dogs, cost £260. Whoever took them knew what he was doing.

Next step was to check the police's online records for a robber with expertise in ceramics. Pottery, dishes, antiques – he tried every search term he could think of without success. Ross recognised he had one more option...

Sergeant Jimmy Dobbs was at his post.

'Jimmy, you ever come across a villain with a penchant for antique pottery?'

Dobbs laughed. 'Doesn't sound likely. I mind old Percy Walsh used to call everyone 'me old China' – you heard of him?'

Ross shook his head.

'Called himself the Crafty Cockney, but he wasn't so crafty. Tried to pass off forged fivers in Barclays Bank.' Dobbs stroked his chin. 'Mind you, there was Wedgwood Willy.'

'Who?'

'Wedgwood Willy, aka William Pickersgill. He used to work for a dodgy antiques dealer. Stole stuff to order. Mainly operated in the Kings Lynn area, although he did a couple of jobs in the city and we caught him. Must have been, what – 2006? Put away for a spell.'

William Pickersgill – Ross checked the name on the database. Released from Highpoint Prison in 2010. Current whereabouts unknown.

He decided he would visit a couple of houses where robberies had taken place. He wouldn't learn anything new, but it would assure the householders Norfolk Police were serious about their misfortune.

Ross was about to commence the necessary paperwork when his phone rang.

'Ross speaking.'

It was a female voice, cultured: 'DI Ross, I'm Alex Thomas of the UK Border Force. Your DCI has given me your name as someone who can help us.'

Thank you, Devlin. My in-tray is about to become the highest point in Norfolk and you've dumped more shit on it.

'What's it about, Miss, or is it Mrs...?'

'Call me Alex. Anyone listening in?'

Ross glanced around. The office was empty. 'No, carry on.'

'We're investigating a human trafficking operation working out of ports in East Anglia. We suspect the ringleaders and most of the gang members are Albanian. There's a few locals involved, mainly crewing the fishing boats that bring in the illegals.'

'How can I help?'

'We need backup. We're certain it's not just smuggling. They're bringing in a lot of girls and we've got evidence some end up as prostitutes. We suspect the gang might be shifting drugs and weapons as well.'

'How come this is the first time we've heard about this?'

'We're protecting our sources. What we plan is a coordinated series of raids. My people will wait for the boat to come in. Your role is to raid a suspected brothel in Norwich. You'll probably need armed officers.'

'Okay, send me the details.'

'Better we meet,' said Thomas. 'We must keep this on a need-to-know basis. I'll come up to Norwich. Are you free this afternoon? Say three o'clock?'

***

Kezia sat in the Edith Cavell café in Tombland, utilising purloined IDs on sites such as 192.com and Ancestry to search for address and family details of her next targets. She mused on the irony that with every hour passing since her separation from a policeman, she'd further retreated into lawlessness.

Every few minutes the subjects of her enquiries changed from recipients of psychic consultation to former employees of Hot Steps. She soon realised that in a world where every facet of some people's lives is documented on social media, certain aspects are immune from recording for posterity. Working in Tom Vickery's club was one of those.

Reviews of the club didn't mention any dancers by their full name. Kezia turned her attention to the freemason Ross had mentioned: Richard Carpenter. She soon discovered he was a lawyer, and an expensive one to boot. He had a LinkedIn account and a Facebook page, neither of which contained anything of any interest.

Time for what a former American boyfriend – an exaggeration, they had one date – had referred to as a 'Hail Mary' – a last, desperate attempt with little hope of success. She accessed Mail.com and created a new email account: richard.carpenter@solicitors.com.

Kezia then composed a message to the Master of the Lodge of Integrity stating someone had accessed the home addresses and other details of the freemasons in the lodge and there was concern they were at risk of physical harm. She, or rather the false Richard Carpenter, asked the Master if he believed the members should be informed. The sender also pointed out his new email address – set up as he feared his old one had been compromised.

No chance, she thought. *No one would fall for such a dumb ruse.* Kezia returned to her list of potentially gullible women.

Half an hour later she retried the mail.com account. The Master had taken the bait. Not only had he committed the cardinal sin of responding to a mail from an account he'd never seen before, he'd confirmed his idiocy by placing all the other recipients in the CC box.

Kezia wondered if she should pass the list to Ross. The manner in which she'd obtained it might prove embarrassing for him. No, it was up to her to check the names. She didn't recognise any, except one.

Neville Devlin was a member of the Lodge of Integrity.

Chapter Twenty-two

Alex Thomas proved to be a business-like blonde with thick black glasses in her early forties. She had shoulder length hair and thin lips that Ross imagined never broke into a smile.

'Your task is simple,' said Thomas. 'You should arrange a team of approximately fifteen officers, at least four of them armed, and two female. We've identified a property on Unthank Road. You should expect to find between six and eight eastern European women, probably Poles, Romanians or Ukrainians, and a maximum of three men.'

'And I'm expected to organise this by Saturday morning?'

'It won't be any earlier. We're waiting for a certain fishing boat to leave Lowestoft on Friday afternoon. As soon as it returns, you'll get the call.'

Ross became uncomfortable. He didn't feel in control of this situation. 'What evidence do you have against these people?'

'Nothing we can share at present. Just detain everyone until my people arrive. Do not react to any request for lawyers.'

'Is that allowed?'

'These people are all illegals. We treat them as suspected terrorists until proven otherwise.'

'Even the women? Haven't they been trafficked?'

Thomas shot back a steely stare. 'You might think so. Assume nothing. One or two could be part of the gang. We'll bring in translators at the earliest opportunity.'

'Should we search the place after we've arrested the inmates?'

'No. Our people know what they're looking for. You just need to secure the property.'

Once Thomas disappeared, Ross assembled his team. Someone in the hierarchy had oiled the wheels, but it took him an hour and a half to contact the officers and complete the inevitable paperwork. Once he'd done that, he turned his attention to the property itself. The Land Registry recorded the owner as a limited company based in Birmingham. He guessed it would be pointless to check any further – experience told him he'd find sub-lets within sub-lets linked with false names.

He checked the intelligence database. One hit. Investigators suspected a resident of living off immoral earnings, but no further action had been taken.

'Shit,' was Ross's reaction.

The entry listed the suspect's name as 'Adrian Drogusha'.

Too close for comfort.

***

By lunchtime, Kezia had found employment in a burger bar. Minimum wage, maximum discomfort. That evening she wore an oversized uniform and had to smile at every customer, be they drunken lechers or gobby teenagers. The smell of burgers clung to her clothes, and she swore she would never consume one again. She longed to be back in the vegan paradise of the Green Haven Café.

She crawled onto to her couch enveloped in a miasma of burning meat and overcooked onions. The next morning, she would be back in a pub with her tablet, followed by an afternoon and evening slapping greasy rounds of minced flesh onto a hotplate.

At least she couldn't see a wolf lurking in the doorway.

***

The Saturday morning sun fought to escape the previous night's thunderclouds as Ross sat in his car watching the building on Unthank Road. The front garden, if it could be called such, comprised an expanse of gravel through which lay a slabbed path. Brown and blue wheelie bins provided the only cover. An access road ran behind the house. Ross had arranged for two armed officers to wait there for any flight out the back door.

His phone rang.

Thomas simply said, 'Go.'

He hit the hazard lights. Ten seconds later the three vans screeched into position. A policeman holding an enforcer, the standard portable battering ram, ran up to the door, an armed colleague at his side. Two more men with guns followed.

They didn't stick to the niceties. No knock, no ring on the doorbell, just two swings of the enforcer and the four men disappeared past the shattered door into the interior. Thirty seconds later two other figures darted into the house – one of them being Linda Stevens.

A radio message told other uniformed officers the situation was safe enough for them to jump out of their van and join the party. Ross followed, stepping aside to allow four young women to leave, all wearing dressing gowns and wide-eyed concern. Two WPCs accompanied the women.

Inside the front room two men sat on a sofa, staring up at the barrels of a pair of Glock 17s. Ross recognised one as Ardi Dragusha. The DI turned without speaking and left to explore the rest of the house. He met two more women coming down the stairs – Mirjeta Bardici leading the way.

Her eyes asked the question before her lips did. 'You help me please.'

Ross didn't reply. He watched the women depart followed by a male officer and ascended the stairs. He counted four bedrooms upstairs. The residents had locked two of the doors before the raid started, as evidenced by the splintered wood on the frames. It made sense – the two men would have been sampling the goods while imprisoning the other four women. Porcelain bowls under the beds reinforced his theory.

He looked inside the first room occupied by the men. A pair of handcuffs hung off the headboard, the key protruding from one of the wrist restraints. He guessed the woman had been secured to the bed. No such device in the last room. Either somebody trusted his bed-mate, or she lived in such fear that flight was impossible. Ross spotted what looked like a used condom lying on the floor. The prohibition on his searching suddenly looked like a blessing.

'Bastards.'

Ross wheeled round to find Stevens standing behind him.

'I'd chop their balls off if it was up to me,' she said.

'It's not up to us,' replied Ross. 'This is a Border Force investigation.'

'What're they going to do? Send the bastards back?'

'What's your solution? Apart from castration? Allow the British taxpayer to pay for their food and lodgings for a few years?'

Stevens wandered round the room. 'Sometimes I wonder what's the point.'

'We're well-paid street cleaners. What's the point of any job? Even doctors. The people they allegedly cure all die eventually.'

Stevens opened a drawer. 'You're more cynical than I am.'

'You're disobeying orders. We don't search. Even though one of them's Ardi Dragusha, who in my mind is still a suspect for the Susan Smith murder.'

She looked down. 'Two mobiles in here. Wouldn't you like to know who's he been contacting?'

Ross joined her. He put on a pair of gloves and pulled out the first phone. iPhone 7, expensive, a brand an egotistic pimp would own. The second, an Alcatel: the cheapest pay-as-you-go Tesco offered. He'd checked after the interview with Sy Mercer.

Dragusha allowed Mirjeta Bardici the freedom to go off with punters. If any of the women were permitted the freedom to sleep without restrictions, it would be her. The chances were, she shared the bed with Dragusha. But he wouldn't allow her a phone. It was too tempting...

Ross dropped the Alcatel into an evidence bag. 'Take this back to Bethel Street.'

Stevens probably guessed his request implicated her in the seizure, and in doing so he ensured she wouldn't rat on him a second time. Nevertheless, she pocketed the phone without complaint.

They left one of the uniformed officers guarding the house. Ross drove back to his flat and laid down on the bed.

He would never abandon his search for the killer of Susan Smith.

***

Thomas and her Border Force crew arrived late Saturday afternoon. Ross met Thomas in Bethel Street while three of her men travelled to Unthank Road.

'You know Ardian Dragusha is a person of interest in one of our murder enquiries?' asked Ross.

Thomas shrugged. 'Prime suspect?'

'No, we've arrested someone. But Dragusha isn't out of the woods yet. We found his DNA at the scene; he's got a motive and no alibi.' Ross refrained from admitting he might have removed an even more damning piece of evidence from the house in Unthank Road.

'We can probably stick him with a murder charge,' said Thomas. 'Or accessory to manslaughter at the very least. They've ditched illegals in the sea in the past to prevent us catching them. That's in addition to drugs and people smuggling.'

'Isn't he here legally? He's a Kosovan refugee.'

'He's probably never set foot in Kosovo. Dragusha's most likely an Albanian like his mates. He'll have used forged papers to get refugee status.'

'What about the women?' asked Ross.

'They're being questioned. I expect some of them will claim asylum. We'll maybe swap that for their witness statement.'

Ross refused to argue the morality of forcing vulnerable women to put themselves at further risk to gain a chance to live a normal life. Not with Thomas, anyway.

He felt relieved when the Border Force unit departed. They took the two men to a secure detention centre, refusing to say where. Uniformed officers escorted the six women to a safe house in the city run by a charity – Thomas expressed her satisfaction that all of them, including Mirjeta Bardici, were psychologically scarred victims.

Ross found Stevens and retrieved the Alcatel mobile. He switched it on – no password. Then he selected contacts. Only two: 'Si' and 'Red'.

He had no doubts. He held Susan Smith's phone.

And it didn't require an enormous amount of imagination to guess how Dragusha obtained it.

***

Kezia's fast-food hell didn't respect the Sabbath. While Ross idled in his flat wondering if the *Sunday Times's* reporting of the latest North Korean missile test meant any career ambitions might be pointless, she flipped burgers. She had a day off to look forward to, if lap dance training counted as a day off.

The Sunday trade was sparse, lacking the drunken louts who tormented her at closing time on Fridays and Saturdays. She'd decided to clean the hotplates when two women walked in. Kezia recognised one of them as Mirjeta Bardici. The other was dark-haired, slim, pale, wearing a long navy-blue coat. She wore black studs in her nose and upper lip.

Bardici stopped and stared at Kezia. 'I know you.'

The other girl tugged at Bardici's sleeve. 'Come on, Jeta, let's get some food and get out.'

Kezia didn't reply as she took their orders: two cheeseburgers, one with onion, one without. The outlet owner remained in the back, sorting out the day's takings.

'You catch killers,' said Bardici.

'Sure,' said Kezia. 'This is my second job. Where's your minder?'

'Police catch him. I am free.'

The other girl stood shaking her head.

'Something I wondered,' continued Kezia. 'This Brian guy you met on Fridays – what did he look like?'

Bardici shrugged.

Kezia pulled a five pound note out of her back pocket, 'This, and the burgers are free. If you tell me about Brian.'

Bardici grabbed the money. 'He losing hair. Nice looking but he have this thing on his face.' She tapped her cheek. 'Why you ask?'

'No reason,' lied Kezia. She'd now uncovered Brian's identity, and why he might have wanted to attack her.

Chapter Twenty-three

The Monday morning sun promised another warm day. Kezia boarded a bus to the riverside village of Wroxham and arrived at Vicki Mayweather's home just after eleven o'clock. The house was expensive, detached, and set well back from the road. Mayweather was in her early thirties, tanned, with shoulder-length brown hair. Even wearing a loose-fitting tracksuit, it was obvious she'd kept her dancer's figure. Kezia followed Mayweather through an IKEA furnished lounge into a spacious sunroom at the rear. Rubber mats covered the floor. A chrome pole reached from the centre of the floor to the ceiling.

Two women sat side by side on a wicker couch near the back door. The younger, perhaps eighteen or nineteen, had long auburn hair framing a face with green eyes and a small lipsticked mouth. Kezia guessed the other's age as mid-twenties. Mixed race, shoulder length hair, large gold earrings, intelligent brown eyes.

'Hi,' said the older woman. 'I'm Jazmin. Jazmin Adeyemi.'

'And I'm Izzie Reynolds,' the other one said. 'You must be Mary.'

'That's me. Mary Malone.'

Mayweather clapped her hands. 'Anyone for coffee?'

No refusals. Kezia sat down on an armchair. 'You two both from Hot Steps?'

'Yeah, right,' said Reynolds. 'Sounds like a nice earner. Dunno about you two, but I'm a student. I'm doing a creative writing degree at the UEA. I mean, you need some money to get by. And it'll be a wicked insight into, well, men and sex.'

Adeyemi laughed. 'Girl, you don't need that. Me, it's men and sex got me into this. Gotta kid, see, and I'm not letting her grow up like me. My girl's gonna get a good life. C'mon Mary, what's your excuse?'

'I need the money. I'm looking after my old Ma. She's a bit... you know... dotty.'

'Cool,' said Reynolds. 'What d'you *think* the guys'll be like? The punters, the ones that'll pay for the dancing?'

'Sleaze-balls,' snapped Adeyemi. 'Randy old men, cheating on their wives. Don't get your hopes up.'

Mayweather returned with a tray, four cups, milk and sugar. Kezia would have liked a biscuit but appreciated in this temple of the body beautiful such things were verboten.

'Listen, ladies,' Mayweather began, 'I've been tasked with getting you three up to the standard required of an exotic dancer. Also...' She looked at each of the trio in turn. 'I need to ensure you've got the right attitude.'

'Sure we have,' said Reynolds.

Mayweather shook her head. 'Convince me. First, let me lay it out like it is. What you're planning to do will stay with you for the rest of your life. Snooty people will look down on you. Expect some men to walk away when they find out.'

'Boring farts,' muttered Reynolds.

'I overheard your conversation,' said Mayweather. 'All of you are in it for the money. That's good. Sometimes I get girls who're in it for the dancing. Or want a husband. They're the ones I need to watch.'

She took a long drink of coffee and then continued. 'You have to set limits in this job and stick to them. This game's like swimming in the sea. If you just paddle in the shallows, you'll never get anywhere. If you go too far, you're lost.'

Kezia grinned. 'Sure, I get that. So how far do we have to go?'

'That's up to you. The fact is, the more you show, the more the dough. Understand?'

Kezia understood. She'd guessed that.

So did Reynolds, although for her this was a revelation. 'Miss Stewart told me I didn't have to go topless.'

'Sure, she's right. You don't have to do anything. In fact, you can sit all night with guys who want to get into your knickers and charm them with your theories about the works of Victor Hugo, but I wouldn't recommend it.'

Reynolds' hand trembled as she picked up her cup. 'You mean I should let them screw me? No way.'

'I never said that. There are three sorts of guys go to these clubs. There are the ones who go just to be one of the boys. They're embarrassed, they don't want to talk to you, they'll stare at you when you're on the pole, but they'd rather pull their toenails out than pay for a private dance. I say forget 'em.

'Then there are the lonely guys. Basically nice, all they want is company. If you've got the chat, you can spend some time with them, make a bit of cash. You'll make enough to eat but not to live well.

'Then you've got... What did you say, Jazmin? The sleaze-bags. Okay, that's a harsh term. Anyway, they're the ones who'll pay for your holiday if you treat them right. If they're with their mates, they'll be acting top dog, waving the fivers around. They'll want a private dance, and they'll sit there with their tongues hanging out, trousers bulging.

'These guys come back week after week. They soon learn which girls flash the flesh, even better... rub their butt or their tits against the punter.'

Reynolds' nervousness hadn't disappeared. 'Miss Stewart said there's no touching.'

'She's right again. They can't touch you. But you can touch them.' She paused. 'Within limits. No kissing and no use of hands. But you heard me right about tits and bum. Nude is good. And you're on film all the time.'

Reynolds sat with mouth open. Adeyemi looked at Kezia and shrugged. She'd met that kind of man enough times.

'What you're trying to do is make the sleaze-bags think you're up for it. That gives you another problem. They'll proposition you. Offer you big money to drop your knickers. Don't.'

'Depends on how big the money is,' said Adeyemi.

'Or how fit the guy is,' giggled Reynolds.

'It's up to you,' replied Mayweather. 'Just don't expect to work at Hot Steps again. Tom Vickery has no truck with prostitution. Or drugs, for that matter.'

The trainer looked at Kezia. 'Mary, you're quiet. Any thoughts?'

'No. Sounds cool.' *Sounds bloody awful, actually*. No way was Kezia becoming a lap dancer.

'Fine. Now I've told you about the guys. They're bad enough. The real bitch is the other girls.'

Reynolds' mouth had closed, now set in an expression of horrified curiosity.

'You're in competition. Some nights there will be more dancers than guys. There's a pecking order and you three will start at the bottom. You'll find there are cliques. Join one or die.' She stared at Kezia. 'This is no job for a loner.'

Coffee finished, the three girls changed into exercise gear. Reynolds sported a navy-blue leotard, Adeyemi a grey tracksuit. Kezia wore a T-shirt and big black knickers. Mayweather kicked off the training with floor exercises. To her shame, Kezia was the only one unable to do the splits.

They hadn't danced a step by one o'clock when Mayweather called a halt. Reynolds's lack of fitness was now as obvious as Kezia's inflexibility. Their hostess provided a lunch consisting of wholemeal bread, salad, and fruit.

Reynolds muttered a wish to go for a walk. Kezia interpreted it as a quest for chocolate. Adeyemi needed to check up on her daughter. Mayweather sat with Kezia in the garden, a cigarette in her hand.

'I can't read you, Mary.'

Sorry, I can't say the same about you. 'I'm not a book.'

Mayweather sent a plume of smoke into the air. 'I don't just train dancers. Vickery and the others hire me to weed out the no-hopers. Like Izzie. Please don't tell her.'

'What about Jazmin?'

'She's got balls. She'll smile and grit her teeth and do whatever it takes. I just hope she doesn't go the wrong way.'

'Wrong way?' Kezia already understood.

'It's too easy to take the money for extras. If Vickery finds out, all you've got to sell is your pussy.'

Time to pounce. 'Like Susan Smith?'

Mayweather stiffened. 'Why do you ask?'

'Friend of mine has a friend of a friend in the police. They mentioned she worked at Hot Steps.'

'Is that why you're here?'

Kezia could almost smell the suspicion. 'No. It's just when I mentioned I was going for a job, Julie, that's her name, she said the police were looking into her background – that's Susan's, not Julie's.'

'I remember Susan. Except we called her Trixie.' Mayweather stubbed out the cigarette on the edge of the bench. 'Stupid cow.'

'What went wrong?'

'She did. I'm not saying anymore. Except be careful. Play by the rules. That's if you ever start.'

'You think I'm not up to it?'

Mayweather spotted Jazmin returning. 'Prove me wrong,' she said.

***

Ross threw the mobile, wrapped in a polythene evidence bag, down on Mick Alder's desk. 'Found in Ardi Dragusha's bedroom. It's Susan Smith's.'

Alder stared at the phone. 'Bugger. You've had it dusted for prints?'

'They found Dragusha's and Susan's. This doesn't help the case against Jeremy Kendal, does it?'

'Doesn't weaken it either. We could keep quiet about it.'

'Doesn't it worry you we've got the wrong man?'

Alder picked up the mobile. 'This guy Dragusha – what does he sound like? I mean, how good's his English?'

'He's Albanian. He can hardly string two words together. Why?'

Alder swung round in his chair, a triumphant smile on his face. 'Because Kendal told us the mysterious stranger who allegedly handed back his hammer had a Norfolk accent. You remember? Besides, if he was shagging this Bardici bird as well he'd have come across Dragusha and recognised him.'

'Kendal was pissed. Dragusha could have rehearsed his speech.'

Alder pushed the phone back. 'For fuck's sake, don't do the defence's job for them. We've got the right man. Hide this in a drawer.'

Ross had a dilemma. He could leave the mobile with Alder, meaning it was the other DI's responsibility if the evidence was misused. Or...

He picked up the phone. 'Remember I've got this.'

***

Kezia's life for the rest of the week became routine: a morning spent digging up details of her mother's targets, an afternoon and evening frying and fending off drunks, the late hours flipping between recovery and raiding dustbins. Occasionally barking dogs blocked her activities, but no murders or angry neighbours interrupted her efforts. There was no time for exercise so her return to Vicki Mayweather's could prove embarrassing.

Ross's first task was a phone call to Nottingham.

'Cheryl Jackson?'

'Who's asking?'

'My name's David Ross. I'm a detective with Norfolk Constabulary. I – '

'How can I be sure you're who you say you are?'

'I've been told you smoke smuggled cigarettes. And you used to live with a girl called Trixie or Susan.'

Silence for five seconds. 'You're Jenna's mate, right?'

'Jenna?'

'Sorry, I can't help.'

She's worried. And I'm stupid. Kezia would have used an alias. 'Cheryl, please don't hang up. The woman who called herself Jenna is a key witness in our enquiries. That's not her actual name.'

'Christ. Who the hell is she?'

'Someone who's nervous of Tom Vickery,' said Ross. 'Just like you. I'm her friend. I suppose she mentioned me.'

'Sure. I'm still not telling you anything.'

'It's nothing about Vickery. It's all to do with Susan's death. My friend told me you cared about her. So please help me.'

A shorter pause. 'Depends what you're asking.'

'Okay, thanks.' Ross hesitated, wondering if she'd be happy with what he was about to say. 'I understand you and Susan were… Can I describe it as being in business together?'

'We were prostitutes. Okay? I thought Jenna or whatever her name is would have told you that.'

'She did. What I need to establish is if you ever entertained university students between 2008 and 2011.'

He heard her laugh. 'Jesus, we never asked them what they did. If they had the money, we'd have… What did you say?' Another giggle. 'Entertained them.'

'Does the name Keith Pritchard mean anything?'

'We never asked for names either.'

'The name Jane Nolan doesn't ring a bell then?'

'Sorry. But… Trixie once got hired as a stripper for a student do. She said one of them tried to rape her, but he was too pissed. After that we never worked alone on something like that.'

'Can you remember any details?'

'Sorry. All I can say is she was a bit traumatised and said if she ever met him again, she'd make sure he suffered.'

Ross glanced at the whiteboard as he put the phone down. McLeod had made a half-hearted attempt to clean it, but Pritchard's name was still legible. Then again, randy students who drank too much and regretted it the next day weren't an endangered species, as he knew from personal experience.

He tried to obtain an interview with Ardi Dragusha, but Thomas blocked it. He contemplated telling her about Susan Smith's mobile, but decided he'd been in enough trouble to risk more.

Ross returned to his growing in-tray. He had two active ongoing cases: shoplifting and burglaries. Mishra had made more progress on the former and had requested assistance from uniform to intercept a planned raid on a major department store in town.

On Wednesday morning his file on the burglaries increased in thickness. If he'd hoped it might divert his thoughts from Susan Smith's murder, he was going to be very disappointed. The report had been filed by PC Clifton Walker, the victim was a Mrs Sarah Consodine, listed as living on Rosary Road.

Ross knocked on Mrs Consodine's door without enthusiasm. He'd guessed she wouldn't rush into his arms, but he thought she might show some appreciation that a senior officer had turned up.

She looked at him as if he'd offered to sell her a week-old turd. 'It's you,' she said. 'I remember you from when that whore was killed. I don't suppose you've solved her murder yet.'

'We have a man in custody.'

'Well, we're no safer. The whores are still standing outside and now some hooligan has broken into my house. If I hadn't disturbed him heaven knows what might have happened.'

'There's a forensics team on its way. I trust that's okay.'

Consodine sniffed. 'I suppose. I'm not having them tramp through the dining room or upstairs, as he never went there. And I hope if they dust for prints then they'll clean up afterwards.'

'Did you provide us with a list of everything that was taken?'

'I've already told that black officer. Hasn't he written anything down? Typical, I say.'

'He has. I'm wondering if you've found anything else missing?' Ross had only skimmed Walker's report, but he'd no intention of admitting it.

'No. I've lost three toby jugs, and a silver picture frame with a photograph of my wedding. Of great sentimental value, I would add.'

Sentimental and Mrs Consodine didn't sit together in Ross's opinion.

'I met your chief the other day,' she said. 'A very pleasant lady. I believe her name was Mrs Forsyth. I told her we need to bring back hanging and corporal punishment.'

Any chance being a stuck-up, intolerant busybody might become a capital offence? 'Did the intruder cause any damage?'

'He forced a window at the back. I realise I should turn on the burglar alarm but Clemmie would set it off.'

'Clemmie?'

'My cat. Named after Winston Churchill's wife, of course. Now there was a politician. He wouldn't tolerate these immigrants selling drugs and prostituting themselves.'

'May I come in?'

'I suppose.' Consodine led him through an ill-lit hallway, walls festooned with paintings. They were all similar, images of a countryside Ross guessed was Tuscany. Her front room looked like the inside of an antique shop, dark mahogany furniture covered in jugs and figurines.

'You stated you disturbed the burglar. Can you please tell me exactly what happened?'

Consodine snorted. 'I've already told the constable.'

'Please humour me.'

304

'Very well. I was in bed. I'm a very light sleeper and I heard a noise. I tiptoed downstairs, and I saw a light. It turned out to be a torch, a small one. He was looking at my ornaments.' She pointed at a sideboard. 'Over there.'

On the floor lay several sheets of bubble-wrap.

'Are those yours?' asked Ross, pointing at the plastic.

'No, he brought them. At least he had the decency to wrap my valuables before he took them. I hope they will be returned intact.'

'I hope so too. Forensics will collect these and test them for prints and DNA. Please carry on.'

'I must have screamed. He picked up a bag and ran out through the kitchen.'

'Did you see his face?'

'If you expect me to run after a dangerous criminal you are very much mistaken. I just saw a silhouette as he was framed in the doorway. I felt he was not a young man.'

'Do you have any pictures of the stolen items?'

'Certainly not. I can describe them in detail. Please get your notebook out.'

Ross held up his mobile. 'I can record this more easily.'

'Certainly not. You should do things the old-fashioned way. As I was saying to Mr Warder recently – '

'I assume you mean Nigel Warder?'

'Yes, our next MP. He's a working-class boy who built up his own successful engineering company. That's the type of politician we need. They might let him stand in Norwich South. The sooner we can get rid of that awful Clive Lewis, the better. I mean, not only is that man Lewis a communist like Jeremy Corbyn, but he's – '

Ross guessed another racist comment was on the cards. 'I assume you met ACC Forsyth at the same event.'

'Yes, it was a fund-raising event at Mr Warder's house. Most of our city's leading citizens were there.'

'Did you meet a gentleman called Tom Vickery?'

'Mr Vickery... ah, yes, I was introduced to him. A successful entrepreneur, I believe. The sort of person we should be encouraging.'

Little do you know, you silly old bat. 'Right, yes... I'm acquainted with Mr Vickery – he's provided employment to many of our citizens, especially young people. You don't remember if a gentleman called Richard Carpenter was there?'

'The lawyer? Why, yes, he was. A most polite young man.' She looked wistfully at the ceiling. 'I can imagine how a jury could be swayed by him.'

'I'm sure.' Ross pulled out a notebook. 'Now, Mrs Consodine, please supply me with a description of the stolen items.'

***

While Ross exited the darkness of Sarah Consodine's house, Kezia's burner phone rang. An unfamiliar number.

'Hello?'

'Mary?'

Mandy Stewart. Kezia wondered if Mayweather had delivered a damning report on her performance and this was the brush off.

'Yeah. Is that Mandy?'

'Sure is. Vicki says you three are doing fine. Okay from your point of view?'

'Yeah, no probs.'

'The reason I'm calling is that Tom, that's Mr Vickery, is hosting a business function at his house. He's promoting his application to build some houses on a greenfield site. He needs some help to serve drinks, assist the delegates, that sort of thing.'

'Sounds cool.' More like terrifying.

'He doesn't want to use too many girls from the club.'

No doubt in case they embarrassed any of Tom's guests.

'We wondered if you, Izzie, and Jazmin might be interested. Ten pounds an hour, cash in hand.'

'Sure. When is it?'

'Thursday week. The tenth of August. It would be handy if you could come in a couple of days before for a costume fitting.'

Kezia's dodgy meter swung round towards red. 'Costume?'

'The site's near Caister St Mary. There's an old Roman town there so Tom's calling the development Imperial Grove and we thought it would be a fab idea to have the hostesses dressed as slave girls.'

Dressed, yes. Acting – no way.

***

At eleven thirty-five the same evening, Kezia crawled up the steps to her flat swathed in an aroma of fried meat. Sabina was waiting, an excited smile on her face.

'Wonderful news, Kezia!'

Kezia had suffered her Ma's wonderful before. Wonderful is a subjective word.

'They're holding a psychic evening at the church on Saturday, and the medium's dropped out due to unexpected circumstances.' Cue for a joke, but Kezia wasn't laughing. 'They want me to step in. This is our big breakthrough. What do you think?'

'What's it all about? An audience of strangers? You standing up the front asking if anyone's got a dead relative called John? That's not how we work.'

Sabina grabbed Kezia's hand. 'They're not strangers. You've done some work on a few of them. I've a good idea of who else might come, so I've got lots of names for you.'

'Ma – look. I've got a job. It's paying our rent. We're coming up to the busy end of the week and I can't get time off. I'll do what I can, but I'm bloody tired.'

Sabina now clasped both of her daughter's hands. 'I need this, Kezia. You need this. You have the same powers as me. You can see through the curtain as I can, only you still don't acknowledge it. That's what you are, a psychic, not some nameless lackey in a chip shop.'

Kezia wasn't going to point out she dealt in burgers. The smell wafting off her clothes was enough. Her mother was half-right. She wasn't cut out to stand behind a counter dishing out unhealthy food to unhealthy people. Yet neither was she content to participate in what was basically a confidence trick, even if her Ma was as convinced of the illusion as her victims were.

She's family. One last time… 'Okay, Ma, I'll chuck the job in and work on your audience. Give me the details.'

Half an hour later Kezia lay on the couch gazing into the darkness. She was troubled. Out in the wilderness, the wolves were gathering to mount another attack.

Chapter Twenty-four

Kezia used the central library in the Forum building to access the internet the next morning, despite its proximity to Bethel Street. She'd decided to claim a sudden illness had forced her to withdraw from the burger business. Something infectious would be best, a condition that might convince her employer that Kezia's motivation was consideration for him, and hence open the door for a return at a later date.

Her first task was to invent a rare disease. Lymphatic monocellular inflammation, so rare nobody's caught it yet. She then began to work her way through her mother's list.

***

It was ten o'clock on a cloudy Norwich morning, and crowds jostled their way through a city centre department store. A middle-aged woman carrying a large shopping bag headed for the exit. She was unaware she'd been spotted. Another woman had pointed her out to an assistant. 'She stole one of your clocks.'

The store's two detectives were waiting: one male, one female, both wearing navy-blue suits. Their target didn't look like the average shoplifter – but then, years of experience told them there was no such thing. She was smartly dressed, perfectly coiffured hair, possibly a manager at a nearby office. They stopped her at the door, asked to look inside the bag, before one of them triumphantly lifted out a small clock. Cue a look of shocked horror from the woman, the expected cries of denial, the hand raised to the mouth as the gravity of her situation kicked in.

A third detective arrived as they were escorting the bewildered woman to the back office.

'Detective Inspector Ross, Norfolk Police.' He flashed his warrant card. 'You can let this woman go. She's the victim of a shoplifting gang.'

'She pinched a clock,' said the female detective.

'No, someone dropped it into her bag. The same person who told you she'd stolen it.'

The accused woman stood perplexed for a second. 'What happens to me?'

'We don't need you anymore,' said Ross. 'And, ma'am, please in future watch your bag if you don't want to be a victim of crime.'

The male store detective spoke up. 'What about the person who set her up?'

'I expect my colleagues are dealing with her and the other five.'

'Five?' The male detective spun around seeking the evildoing quintet among the crowd.

Mishra arrived. 'Everything okay, sir?'

'Yes thanks, Kirsi.' He turned to the detectives. 'In addition to the elderly woman who pointed out the theft of the clock, there were two women with prams, a man carrying a sports bag, a woman with an identical bag, and a woman wearing a tight T-shirt and a mini-skirt with fishnet tights.'

'I think I noticed her,' said the male detective.

Mishra smiled. 'You were supposed to. Simply so you didn't notice anyone else. The guy with the bag and one of the women with the prams were the main thieves. The prams were swapped in the lift, the bags in the café so if you had spotted items being taken you wouldn't find them at the exit.'

The female detective grinned. 'You men are all the same. Your brains are in your trousers.'

Mishra glanced at Ross before turning to the male detective. 'Don't worry sir, you wouldn't be the first to be distracted by a pretty girl.'

Point taken, Kirsi.

Ross regained his composure. 'This gang have been operating across East Anglia for several months. If you can supply a copy of your CCTV, it would be helpful.'

Mishra and Ross joined McLeod in watching uniformed officers shepherding the gang into police vans.

'Good work, people,' said Ross. 'I think a celebratory drink might be in order. First, back to Bethel Street and paperwork.'

They reconvened at Ross's desk an hour later, ready to go to the nearby Coach and Horses.

McLeod patted paper files related to the shoplifters, now nestling in a cardboard box ready for the Crown Prosecution Service. 'Suppose you'll want us on the housebreakings next?'

'That's right,' said Ross. He pulled out a picture of William Pickersgill. 'This is our main suspect.'

Mishra gasped. 'He's the spitting image of Bill Potter. You remember, the neighbour you asked me to speak to about Kev Connor? The one I thought was a bit suspicious.'

Ross tapped the picture. This was turning out to be one of their better days. 'Let's not rush into this. We'll do a bit of digging – check if Potter and Pickersgill are one and the same. Then we'll get a warrant.' He smiled at his team. 'In the meantime, let's celebrate.'

***

Ross spent the first part of the following afternoon in front of a computer screen with a telephone in his hand.

William Pickersgill left Highpoint Prison in 2010, penniless and unemployed. In 2011, a rare vase from the time of the Ming emperor Xuande was sold in an Amsterdam auction house for ninety-eight thousand euros. The vendor was a private company based in Luxembourg. Pickersgill was suspected of stealing a similar vase before his capture, but in spite of appeals from the insurers, it was impossible to prove the stolen artefact was the same one appearing in the Dutch sale.

Ross rung DCI Steve Tavernier, a Met detective specialising in art thefts he'd met at a conference the previous year. He'd discovered Tavernier was involved in the investigation into the sale of the vase.

After the usual social niceties, Ross asked about the Chinese antique.

'They've changed a bit, but back then money laundering was rife in Luxembourg. Pickersgill could easily have set up a company to sell his stuff. There were probably other items we haven't picked up on yet.'

'How could he get the money out?' asked Ross.

'No problem. He could have moved the money into a Swiss bank and then transferred it back here. Claimed it as gambling winnings. HMRC wouldn't look too closely if the trail was complicated enough.'

'Do the Met know if Pickersgill changed his name?'

'Hang on.' Ross guessed Tavernier was checking his own systems. 'We've got a report he's now known as Potter. Living up your way as a matter of fact. I suppose that's not a surprise?'

'He's a person of interest. Someone's stealing expensive pots.'

Tavernier laughed. 'That's him, all right. Is he still using bubble-wrap? Cut into metre square pieces if I remember.'

'We found some at his last job.' Ross knew he'd got his man. 'Did Pickersgill ever show any tendency towards violence?'

'Not that we know. He was a villain all right. Would have sold his old grandmother, especially if she was a genuine antique. But violence... nah. Why?'

'There's a possible murder a few doors down. If it was murder, it was very clever.'

'Clever, yes,' said Tavernier. 'If he wanted to kill anyone, he wouldn't beat them over the head with an iron bar. Sophisticated, that's how he'd have done it.'

Ross finished the call with a promise to buy Tavernier a beer and sat back. This was the kind of case he dreamt about. He just needed to get a warrant and Pickersgill/Potter would be providing pleasure to Her Majesty once more.

His euphoria was interrupted when an angry looking DI Fliss Kemble stomped over to his desk. 'David, I want a word with you.'

Ross looked up. Kemble was in her forties with short blonde hair. Her face always had a flushed look – now accentuated by her obvious fury. 'Fire away.'

'In private.' She jerked her thumb towards a meeting room.

Ross followed her into the room. She slammed the door when he'd entered.

Kemble didn't wait to sit down. 'Why the hell didn't you tell me about the raid in Unthank Road?'

'I was working with Border Force. Need to know.'

'Didn't Devlin tell you we were watching the property? We'd a tip-off stuff was arriving on Saturday night. We arrived and uniforms were already there. No way were they delivering if they saw cops hanging around outside. Four months' work down the bloody pan.'

'No. Devlin didn't tell me. So maybe you should have a go at him, not me. And I'd guess that Border Force had already intercepted your shipment.'

Kemble slumped down on a chair. 'Shit, what a shambles. You knew there were drugs involved though, didn't you? You could have given me a heads up.'

Ross sat down opposite her. 'Yep. I was told drugs, weapons, people, and prostitution. Plus, hints of murder and other misbehaviour. I should have told the whole bloody station. Probably got it published in the *East Anglian*.'

Kemble put her head in her hands. 'Bloody Border Force. Them and the security services. Think they're God's gift.'

'Can you salvage anything?'

She sat back and looked at the ceiling. 'We've rounded up some foot soldiers. We wanted to trail the van. See where else it went after Unthank.'

'Did the foot soldiers include Red Stibbons?'

'Should have done. Little creep. We didn't find any stuff, so he's still free. Only a matter of time before we nail him.'

'Mind if I visit him? Unofficially, of course.'

Kemble stood up. 'Be my guest.' She paused in the doorway. 'And don't forget to tell me if you find anything out.'

Ross didn't waste any time. He was soon on his way to the Nest Lane Estate.

Every town has its Nest Lane; rated by the government as one of the most deprived areas in the UK, in a city ranked as one of the best to live in. Most of the residents would be decent, making the best of their lot, their back gardens neat and their houses clean. It was the others who dragged it down: the willingly unemployed, the addicts, those whose lives revolved round TV and the bottle.

Ross was surprised to find Stibbons's house appeared like one of the good ones – the front lawn was trimmed, the door newly painted, a contrast to the long grass covered in dog shit next door.

His knock was answered by a small woman wearing a track suit and thick-lensed glasses. 'Mrs Stibbons?'

She peered at him like he was a specimen in a jar. 'What d'you want?'

'Is Alfred in?'

'No.'

A voice drifted down from upstairs. 'Who is it?'

Ross smiled. 'Care to answer the question again?'

'You're a cop. He's innocent.'

'Sure. I need to talk to him about something else. You'll note I've come alone. If I need to, I'll bring the cavalry and I'd hate them to trample all over your nice garden.'

Mrs Stibbons shook her head and motioned him in. The front room was dark, heavy grey net curtains muting the daylight, black picture frames on cheap mahogany-effect furniture. A deep red and green carpet covered the floor.

Ross looked at the photos. A young boy at the seaside, no doubt Red Stibbons in his more innocent days, a fading black-and-white image of a smiling man with a toothbrush moustache clad in an army uniform, a younger Mrs Stibbons in a hat suggesting she was at a wedding. No sign of Mr Stibbons, if ever he existed. Were those the highlights of her life?

Red appeared. Smart, short haircut, clean white T-shirt, a fresh face with knowing eyes. For some reason Ross thought he looked like an estate agent.

Stibbons wove an American drawl into his Norfolk accent. 'Can't you lot leave us alone?'

'Not when there's murder afoot,' replied Ross.

'Murder. You can't pin that on me.'

Ross smiled. 'Your mum doesn't need to hear this.'

Mrs Stibbons folded her arms. 'I'm not leaving. If you're going to – '

'S'okay, mum. We'll go outside. Nothing to worry about.'

Red led Ross into a long narrow back garden. A concrete path led straight from the house, bisecting a well cut but weed-ridden lawn. On either side lay flowerbeds. Short walls allowed visibility of the neighbouring plots. On the left a mixture of grass and shingle on which was scattered a mass of children's toys. On the right the garden was unkempt, the only feature being a rotting shed at the bottom.

'My mum loves her garden,' said Red.

Ross wasn't going to get into a horticultural discussion. 'Susan Smith.'

'Never heard of her.'

'Try again. Maybe you knew her as Trixie. You were her pusher.'

A smug smile. 'Dunno what you're talking about.'

'You're a drug dealer. Doesn't matter if they didn't find anything the other day. They'll get you one way or the other.'

The grin didn't disappear. 'I'm too clever for that.'

'You're not. I found where you keep them.'

The smile disappeared for a second. Stibbons glanced towards the foot of the neighbour's garden.

Ross waved a finger towards the rotting shed. 'Hang on while I call the station.'

Red wasn't smiling any more. 'You can't! You'll need a warrant'n all that stuff.'

'Not for drugs. Of course, you could tell me about Susan Smith. Like what happened when you saw her on the night she died.'

'You recording this?'

'No, what you tell me is off the record. For now.'

'I didn't see her. Honest. Okay, Suze called me, but she was wanting a load. Like normally she can only take a bag of smack. Says she'll have the dough by the Saturday.'

'How much is a load?'

'Two centuries, like a couple of hundred quid. Reckon she was going to do a runner. Would've cleaned me out but, hey, business is business.'

'Where was the deal going to take place?'

'The pub at the top of Aylsham Road. I went there but she never showed. Didn't hang around, not with a stash like that in my bag.'

'Okay, you'd better not be bullshitting me.' Ross nodded, stared at the pusher, then walked back to the house. Red followed him up the path. 'You know your suppliers are out of action?'

Stibbons shrugged. 'One door closes, that's what they say.'

The old man who lived next door tottered out into his overgrown garden supported by a zimmer frame, cigarette in hand, rheumy eyes fixed on Red.

Ross hadn't any doubts about which door would be closing on Red Stibbons.

Once he got into his car, he called Kemble. 'If you're quick the stuff'll still be in the neighbour's shed.'

As he drove away the blue flashing lights were coming round the corner.

***

The next day Kezia continued her own online investigations, this time in the Wetherspoon's Glasshouse in Wensum Street, the continuation of Magdalen Street south of the river before the thoroughfare becomes Tombland.

As Kezia entered the pub, Ross and Mishra returned to Gertrude Road with an entourage of uniforms.

'Mr Potter,' said Ross when the householder opened the door. 'Or should I say Pickersgill?'

Potter/Pickersgill was in his late fifties, with a full head of unnaturally black hair, and a large nose.

'The name's Potter,' he said. 'What d'you want?'

'Police. DI Ross and DS Mishra. We've got a warrant to search your house in connection with a number of robberies in the area.'

'Search away, mate. I've got nothing to hide.'

Ross entered the house, followed by the other officers. The interior was like an antique shop; paintings on every wall, pottery and porcelain on every polished hardwood surface. He'd got an inventory of stolen items but trying to find them here would be like searching for a needle in a stack of other needles.

He decided the best tactic would be to hunt for just one of Sarah Consodine's items – a Royal Doulton Henry V toby jug, price circa £500. He'd obtained a picture and distributed this to the searchers. He also suggested they look for bubble wrap. While the uniforms began their quest, he confronted the suspect.

'Do you deny you were once known as William Pickersgill?'

'No point, mate, is there? Yeah, right, I was him. But I've given up me old ways, and I don't want you lot fingering me for everything what goes missing.'

'Do you have an alibi for Tuesday evening around eleven p.m.?'

'Yeah, I was bonking Julia Roberts.' He nodded to Mishra. 'Begging your pardon, miss. Julia comes over from Hollywood when she needs a class shag. Hang on... Tuesday? Nah, Tuesday's the night I service Joanna Lumley. Give her a call, mate. She'll sort you out.'

'You'll have to do better than that.'

'I'm a bloody single man without any mates. I was here, right? You prove different.'

'I've got some other dates. June the twentieth?'

'Listen to me, ya Scotch git. I never go out at night. Too many criminals what you lot haven't nabbed. I do me garden during the day, and I helps some of the others round here what ain't so nimble.'

Ross looked round. 'You've got a nice collection here. Cost a bit. How can you afford it?'

'You bloody Jocks are obsessed with money, ain't ya? I've got some savings. Not a lot, but I likes to be surrounded by beautiful things. You gonna arrest me for that?'

The uniforms came in, shaking their heads.

Potter/Pickersgill stood with arms folded. 'Ya see? Nuffing. Zippo. Now piss off and leave me alone.'

Ross's encounter with Stibbons had suggested a solution. 'Kirsi, take Constable Scrivens and visit Mrs Johnstone. She's the lady with a mobility scooter. Ask if she's got a shed and if so, can you look inside?'

The grin disappeared from Potter/Pickersgill's face. 'Here, you can't bother her! She's an old lady. Disabled'n all.'

'Tell you what,' said Ross. 'Maybe you're right. The sight of a police uniform might prove unsettling. Constable Scrivens, can you please stay with Mr Potter and ensure he doesn't leave while Kirsi and I visit Mrs Johnstone?'

Mrs Johnstone was pleased to welcome visitors and regale them with more details of her medical history.

'My shed?' she said at last. 'Well, of course you can look. I can't get out there because of my problems. In fact, the only person who goes in there is that nice Mr Potter. I think you'll find he's got the key to the padlock.'

Ross left Mishra discussing the events surrounding Mrs Johnstone's unsuccessful hip replacement and went back to see Potter/Pickersgill.

'I ain't got the key. And if I had, you'd need another warrant. And ya ain't gonna get one of them in a hurry and ya can't keep me here for long, so piss off.'

Ross walked back to the front door. As he expected, there was a single key sitting in a dish on a table by the entrance. 'No problem,' he shouted.

Mrs Johnstone's shed contained the normal items one might expect: a lawnmower, several flowerpots, a couple of jam jars, weed killer, canes, and a packet of fertiliser. What in other circumstances might come as a surprise were the three toby jugs, the silver photo frame and the large roll of bubble wrap.

'Nuffing to do with me,' was the excuse Ross received on his return. 'I might've touched the bubble wrap, ya know, when I get the mower out. Wasn't sure why the old bat had bubble wrap anyway.'

Ross arrested Potter/Pickersgill. The thief's immediate response was to fall back on 'No comment' to every question.

They hadn't got enough. This case wasn't over.

***

Kezia lay down on the couch. She'd finished her research and needed to debrief her mother. She was nervous. The psychic evening was looming like an onrushing tornado. It wasn't the thought of her Ma making a fool of herself, more the feeling Kezia herself was the potential victim.

Chapter Twenty-five

While Sabina perused the data on her audience, Kezia made the most of the continuing fine weather to walk into town for some clothes shopping. While her peers might head for Monsoon or Zara, Kezia strolled instead through the narrow alleys of Norwich Market.

She found nothing of interest, so she made her way along Gentleman's Walk, the pedestrianised street running beside the market. She passed the usual assortment of buskers: two girls playing saxophones, a youth bellowing out Ed Sheeran songs fronted by an array of never-to-be-sold CDs, the ever-present puppet man as well as two Jehovah's Witnesses and a flock of anti-vivisectionists.

A campaigner for vegan lifestyles thrust a leaflet towards her. She sidestepped him and a horde of Japanese tourists before turning into White Lion Street. A dog sitting beside a mound of blankets in a doorway gazed at her with a piteous expression. Even with Kezia's inability to name canine breeds, she could tell it was a mongrel. Like her, in truth.

The sight of the dog's companion cut her pessimistic navel-gazing short. Curled up in the corner of the doorway lay Sy Mercer, at his side an upturned baseball cap containing a few coins. Beside him sat a square of brown cardboard decorated with the words 'Hungry and Homeless'.

'You aren't homeless,' said Kezia.

Mercer's dark sunken eyes looked up. 'Shit, it's you.'

'Yeah. What's the dog called?'

'Dunno. Might be fucking Rover for all I care. It's a mate's. I'm guarding his patch. What d'you want?'

'Talk about Susan. A peace offering.' She threw a pound coin into the cap, then scanned the blankets for infestation before sitting down beside him. 'How are you doing, anyway?'

'Fucking awful. Bastards refuse to give me compensation. Say I had to live with Suze for two years before they'll fork out. It's a fucking injustice. The pigs won't even give me her stuff.'

'What stuff?'

'Clothes'n things. Her mobile. Then there's her locket. Worth a bomb.'

'Antique?'

Mercer wiped his nose on his sleeve. 'Dunno. It's gold, so it's gotta be worth something. Few weeks before Suze died… yeah, the day they done me for begging, she holds it up and says it'll keep us in good shit for years.'

'So how come she didn't sell it?'

'Dunno. She says that's not what we do.'

'Perhaps she expected the value to go up?'

Mercer looked up hopefully at a group of giggling girls. 'Nah. I dunno. C'mon, nobody's gonna give me shit if you're sitting there. Fuck off.'

Kezia accepted she should leave. She spotted a man scrabbling in his pocket for a coin as she stood up.

'I wouldn't bother,' she told him. 'He's got his own house and he'll only spend it on drugs.'

She didn't feel any guilt about losing Mercer some income.

***

'No comment.' Probably the hundredth time that morning.

Bill Potter stared at the clock on the wall. The only information he'd volunteered was he'd changed his name to Potter by deed poll.

'Come on, Bill,' said Ross, 'you must realise we'll get you in the end. Do everyone a favour and tell the truth.'

Potter whispered to the duty solicitor, then replied, 'No comment.'

Mishra tried to help. 'Let's recap. You're a known thief who specialises in antique pottery. We found stolen antique pottery in a shed to which you had sole access. Any jury will find you guilty. It'll go better for you if you confess.'

Another whispered conversation. This time the duty solicitor spoke. 'Mr Potter would like to point out Mrs Johnstone's assertion that only one key exists may be challenged. Mr Potter cannot be the first to have access and it would be simple for someone to create a duplicate.'

Ross conceded the solicitor might have a point. Not that he'd mention it.

Potter decided on a new strategy. 'You should check that Kev Connor if you want to make a collar.'

'Come off it,' said Ross. 'Connor couldn't tell the difference between a Ming vase and a chamber pot. Besides, Connor was toast when you pinched the toby jugs.'

Potter beamed. 'He had an accomplice.'

Ross pounced on this. 'If he did, you would seem the most likely candidate.'

'No comment.'

Half an hour later Ross terminated the interview. A further five minutes lapsed before Bill Potter walked out of Bethel Street.

***

The spiritualist church hall was around two-thirds full when the clock above the door showed seven-thirty. Kezia sat at the back while a florid woman in purple introduced her mother to the audience.

The wolves returned. No blood, but a fleeting glimpse of grey fur, teeth bared, the sleek shapes circling around her. The vision metamorphosed into the figure of Detective Constable Linda Stevens, followed by a tanned man with a prominent birthmark on his cheek.

'Hello Kezia. How's it going?' Stevens patted her companion on the arm. 'This is Joe Leadbetter. We've come to watch your mum. One false claim and we'll have her.'

At the front of the hall Sabina cleared her throat and began her pitch. 'Good evening, ladies and gentlemen. I'm very happy to have been invited here tonight. Let me begin by telling you about my background, which has undoubtedly contributed to my unique powers.'

No time to lose. 'Do you mind if I have a private word with Mr Leadbetter?'

Stevens and Leadbetter exchanged a glance.

'Why?' asked Stevens.

'It wouldn't be private if I told you.'

Leadbetter shrugged and nodded. 'Yeah. It isn't going to make any difference. You keep listening to the old bat.'

Kezia led the man into a small adjoining room, containing only six wooden chairs and a table. Posters for various events adorned the walls. She stopped, placed her palms either side of her head, shut her eyes, adopted an agonised expression and then spoke. 'Herbert?'

Leadbetter looked round to check if anyone else lurked in the room. 'Eh, what's this?'.

'Shut up, I'm speaking to your dad. Herbert? Oh, really.'

'I'm off.'

'No, wait. He told the hooker his name was Brian?'

Leadbetter paused, hand on the door handle. 'What's this?'

'Your dad's very disappointed in you. Calling yourself Brian and cheating on your wife. With a prostitute as well.'

'Who told you?'

'Herbert's telling me. I've got my Ma's powers, believe it or not.'

'You're lying. You saw me pick her up. Well, it's your word against mine.'

'I'm visualising a first aid room in a warehouse. A blonde girl... she's not English. What, Herbert? She's been trafficked. Oh dear, that means Joe's committed a breach of the Sexual Offences Act 2003. My, Herbert, what a clever man you are knowing that. You're not a dumbo like your son.'

'You stop that, bitch. You can't prove it.'

Kezia shook her head as if she emerged from a trance. 'Oh, wow, so weird. You're right, Brian – sorry, Joe. I can't prove it. Unless... Hey, suppose I got Mirjeta – she's the hooker, but you know that. I get her and maybe your mum and... why not?... your wife... all together, and they check times of when you left Chalk Hill Road on Fridays and when you arrived home?'

Leadbetter started to shake. Kezia feared she'd overdone it. He might attack her.

Instead, he slumped against the wall. 'What do you want?'

'You go back and tell DC Stevens you're convinced me and my Ma do have special powers and you'll testify to that. Invent something about your dad if you like. I'll support you. Nobody else need find out about Mirjeta.'

When they returned Stevens gave them the thumbs up. 'She's just put the noose round her neck. You listen.'

Sabina was in full flow. 'You won't be surprised to learn my ability to travel through the veil cannot be achieved without intervention from beyond. My guide is John Phillips, servant to the Duke of Devonshire around seventeen-thirty. It is he who waits for my call, he who finds the troubled spirits who wander the dark halls between life and eternity.'

'She's genuine,' said Leadbetter. 'I'm withdrawing my complaint.'

'What? We've got her.' Stevens stared at Leadbetter open-mouthed, then looked at Kezia. 'What's she done? Given you money? Something else?'

Kezia smiled. 'The truth from beyond the grave. Your grandfather sends a message as well. He wants to tell you the day in June 1991 you spent in Clacton with him and your grandmother is still one of his happiest memories.'

Stevens' mouth opened again. She clearly never noticed her cousin Margaret had mentioned the outing in a Facebook post.

While Sabina amazed the ranks of believers with intimate details of their lives, Kezia watched an angry Stevens and a worried Leadbetter depart.

She'd chased one particular pack of wolves away. She'd confirmed Joe Leadbetter had a solid alibi for the time of Susan Smith's murder.

Most significant of all, she was now certain Leadbetter was not the man who tried to blind her by the side of the Wensum.

**

Ross couldn't leave loose ends. On a sunny Sunday morning he returned to Wymondham, ringing on the O'Donnells' doorbell.

Mrs O'Donnell appeared. 'You again,' she said coldly.

'Is Walter in?'

'Why?'

Ross attempted a reassuring smile. 'I'd like a quick word. Nothing important.'

Her eyes narrowed. 'I in't trustin' you.' She turned to shout up the stairs. 'Walter, the police want you. What you done now?'

Walter appeared, bleary eyed, wearing a string vest and navy-blue track suit bottoms.

His attire didn't impress Mrs O'Donnell. 'Walter, what you be a-wearing!'

Ross grinned. 'Hi, Walter. Do you fancy a little walk?'

'Eh?' Walter glanced at Ross and then at his mother.

'A little friendly talk, that's all,' said Ross. 'Five minutes.'

Walter pulled on a black jacket that did nothing for the fashionability of his ensemble and squeezed past his mother, a suspicious scowl on her face.

'Thanks for coming out, Walter,' said Ross when they were out of earshot of the house. 'I've discovered you spun us a porky when we visited here before.'

'No!'

Ross kept smiling. 'You told us you were at your club. Only we've discovered you told us a big fat lie.'

'I was at my club.'

'Try again. We've got you on CCTV coming back from Norwich at eleven o'clock.'

This time Walter turned to ensure his mother couldn't hear.

'I was. Just didn't say which club.'

'You told us old Joe the barman would provide you an alibi.'

'Well… I guess old Joe'll back me up.'

Ross lost the smile. 'You realise old Joe is now likely to face a charge of obstruction. The same goes for you.'

'All right. I goes to Hot Steps. I buy a beer, watch the girls, then they make me leave, so I go up the Shades and have a few more beers.' Walter lowered his voice. 'If my mother find out, I'll be in trouble.'

Ross shook his head. *I've wasted a Sunday morning on this mummy's boy who's more scared of her than the police.*

Ross swung O'Donnell round. 'Do you realise what a bloody idiot you are?'

331

'I'm sorry. I din't think it would matter. You caught the bugger what done it, en't ya? Please, I won't do it again. I promise. Please don't tell – '

'Just shut up, Walter.' Ross's anger subsided. He now felt sorry for the snivelling creature in front of him. 'That night in Hot Steps. Did you see Tom Vickery?'

'Who?' Walter wiped a tear from the corner of his eye.

'The guy who owns it. Tall, balding.'

'No. I go in and have one beer. They let me stay for half an hour and then I'm out.'

'What time did you leave?'

Walter stopped shaking. 'About nine. Then I'm at the Walnut Tree Shades. You know the one – near the market. I remember a band called Four Kicks or something.'

'And you saw nothing suspicious at Hot Steps?'

'No.'

Ross decided he wouldn't get anything useful out of Walter. He was just about to tell this pathetic little man to go home when…

'I seen Trixie at Hot Steps last year.'

'What?'

'Don't shout,' pleaded whispering Walter. 'I seen her. I go there every so often, but I in't tellin' Ma.' He acknowledged Ross's nod and continued. 'She come in and ask to meet someone.'

'Tom Vickery?'

'I don't remember. All I remember is she make a scene and they chuck her out. This big guy, he come out the back and tell her to piss off.'

'Big, bald guy?'

'That's him.'

'Okay, Walter, this is important. When did this happen?'

'Oh, that would be… January last year. I remember, it was the Friday arter the New Year party at the social club.'

'And you're sure you saw Trixie?'

'Yes. She be a bit rough-looking from what I remember, but it was her. I hoped she be back but she in't now.' Another tear formed.

'Okay Walter, you've given us useful info.' *Vickery lied to me.*

Worry creased Walter's face. 'Will I have to come to court?'

'I doubt it.' Even if the Crown Prosecution Service decided Walter might prove a useful witness, Ross didn't believe Vickery would stand for it.

He'd need to find another way to prove Susan Smith had made contact with her former employer.

Chapter Twenty-Six

Mick Alder slammed the papers down on Ross's desk.

'Got him!'

Ross looked up. 'Who?'

'Jeremy Kendal. He's confessed.'

Ross read the statement. Susan Smith had taunted Kendal about his looks. He'd lost it. He'd found it hard to control his moods since his injury. Post-traumatic stress etcetera. He hoped the court would take his tragic sacrifice in the service to his country into account.

'No hooded man then?' asked Ross.

'He made it all up. Say what you like about Richard Carpenter, but he accepts when he's beaten. Kendal will get off lightly, no doubt. War hero, humiliated by a drugged-up whore, mental problems, that sort of thing. Hear you nailed the shoplifters and got a guy for the burglaries. Devlin'll be taking us out for drinks at this rate.'

Ross forced a smile. Richard Carpenter, freemason, friend of Tom Vickery, possibly linked to Susan Smith, had convinced a vulnerable man his only option was to offer a guilty plea. Ross had no choice but to be seen playing the game, helping the force hit its numbers, not rocking the boat.

Someone else would have to stand up for justice. He walked out of the station and strolled towards the market. When he was clear of eavesdroppers, he pulled out the burner phone.

'It's David. How are you?'

'Fine. I'm on a number twelve bus to Wroxham. I'm not giving up.'

'Stevens was swearing about you this morning. She said you got to Joe Leadbetter, and he's making the weirdest allegations about how you did it.'

'My psychic powers, nothing else. Why are you calling?'

'Jez Kendal has confessed. I thought I should tell you. You can stop this lap dancing nonsense now.'

Silence. Then she said, 'He didn't do it. I'm certain.'

'If it's any comfort, I don't reckon he did it either. I'm convinced his lawyer told him it was his only hope.'

'Richard Carpenter? The freemason?'

'That's him. I'm wondering if it's a cover-up.'

'Something you should know,' said Kezia. 'Your DCI's in the same lodge as Carpenter.'

'Devlin?'

'Yeah. I'm pretty sure.'

'How did you uncover that?'

'Psychic powers. What else? I can send you a list of other members.'

'Psychic powers, my arse. Keep the list for now. And take care... please. Phone me if you've got a problem.'

Ross returned to Bethel Street. McLeod was standing by the coffee machine.

'Hi, guv. Good news about Kendal, eh?'

Ross nodded. 'Right, great.'

McLeod looked around to make sure nobody skulked behind him. 'Another rumour. Devlin's asked the cyber boys to track down a computer hacker.'

'So? That's what they do, isn't it?'

McLeod grinned. 'Right, but this one's personal. Somebody got hold of the email addresses of all the people in his freemasons' lodge.' Worry suddenly crossed the DC's face. 'You're not one, are you? A mason?'

'No, and I didn't realise Devlin was one till now.'

He'd learned something else. Kezia was pretty smart with computers as well.

***

He couldn't resist it. Richard Carpenter's office was located in a street leading off Prince of Wales Road. Ross guessed once Susan Smith had approached Vickery, the club owner would have taken steps to ensure there was no repetition. It was likely this would take the form of physical intimidation, but Vickery would have a Plan B. He hadn't used violence against Walter O'Donnell, instead relying on his trusted lawyer. And that lawyer had his own case to answer.

The reception area was impressive. A red leather settee and a table on which lay some legal magazines of little interest to his clients were situated beside a fish tank, watched over by a prim receptionist in her forties. A certificate from Cambridge University hung on the wall confirming Carpenter's Doctor of Law degree.

'This is most improper,' were Carpenter's opening words. 'Assuming you've come to speak to me about Jeremy Kendal, I suggest you go through the CPS in future. Besides, I was under the impression DI Alder is now the SIO.'

Ross smiled. 'This is off the record, Mr Carpenter. I've come across some information that might assist your client.'

'My client, if you mean Mr Kendal, has agreed to plead guilty. There are clear mitigating circumstances which I hope the court will take into account. I can't imagine anything you can tell me would improve his chances. But please come into my office and have your say.'

He led Ross into a room rich with ostentation. Black leather replaced the red of reception. One wall was devoid of bookshelves and was instead plastered with certificates and commendations. Thick carpet muffled Ross's footsteps as he took a seat.

'Now, Inspector Ross, what is this new piece of evidence?'

'I've spoken to a witness who'll testify Tom Vickery threatened Susan Smith when she attempted to visit him in Hot Steps.'

Carpenter looked down at his desk and tapped his fingers on the surface. 'When was this?'

'After she returned from Nottingham.'

'Some time ago.' Carpenter tried to look uninterested. Ross knew different. Carpenter would only have known when the dead woman returned if Vickery had mentioned it. 'May I have the name of this witness?'

'Not yet. Witnesses have a tendency to change their story when Mr Vickery's concerned.'

Carpenter stared at Ross. 'Only because your attempts to fit up Mr Vickery have been uncovered in time.'

'Did you ever meet Susan Smith?'

'Pardon?'

'I asked if you ever met Susan Smith? I imagine you drafted some kind of letter warning her off. I just wondered if you delivered it personally.'

Carpenter's fingers stopped drumming for a split second. 'Inspector, I'm not going to dignify your insinuation with an answer. All I would say is that any work I do is confidential, and I wouldn't disclose it to you.'

'What about seven years ago?' Ross waited for a reaction. 'You remember... the lodge?'

Carpenter's fingers stopped moving. 'Which lodge are you talking about?'

Ross sat back. 'I believe you understand.'

Carpenter mirrored Ross's action. 'Your question... Is it in any way related to a data breach connected to my freemasonry lodge? Someone sent a mail purporting to be me and obtained a list of members, all of whom are respectable citizens and who would have nothing to do with prostitutes. Do you have any knowledge about that?'

'No, and did I infer your members associated with hookers?' asked Ross. He waited for an answer that didn't come. 'Something else you could help me with. Did you ever have dealings with a man called Kevin Connor? Ex-employee of Mr Vickery at Hot Steps?'

'Perhaps. I dealt with several of Mr Vickery's staff. Employment dispute, was it?'

'Assault. Seems a rival tried to offer Tom protection, and he sent Kev Connor round to prove he didn't need it. We felt Mr Connor was a little too assertive, but our key witness declined to testify. Probably didn't fancy a second trip to the Norwich and Norfolk casualty department. Remember?'

'No.' Carpenter almost didn't give Ross time to finish his question.

'Suppose I go to the CPS and ask to check their records? Would I find your name as defence solicitor?'

The calm facade was failing. 'Forgive me, inspector, but I can't be expected to remember every case I've worked on. Can you?'

'I might remember if I heard the subject had been murdered.'

'I understood Mr Connor died as a result of an accident?'

A slip-up. You do remember Connor. You've spoken to Devlin about him.

'The only reason I'm aware of Mr Connor's death is we monitor the local news for opportunities to assist relatives to seek compensation for professional incompetence. In his case he seems to have been responsible for his own demise.'

'In other words, you're an ambulance chaser.'

'Inspector Ross, you're walking on very thin ice. If you've shown an interest in my lodge, then you'll realise I have contacts who could make your life very difficult.'

'Might make my life easier. I could give up being a copper, become a vigilante. I'd enjoy dealing with the villains who get away with murder.'

Carpenter stood up and looked out of his window. Like Vickery's office, the cathedral spire dominated the skyline.

'Inspector, you seem to have an unnatural fixation with Tom Vickery. Let me tell you about Tom. He's a decent chap. Your Presbyterian prejudices may cause you to detest how he makes his money, but he's a man of principle. If you're loyal to him, he'll back you all the way. Perhaps in the past his activities have brushed the edges of the law, but he's now respectable.'

Ross laughed. 'Decent? Respectable? Strip clubs, dodgy building deals? You need to buy a dictionary.'

Carpenter waved his arm in the general direction of the Anglican cathedral. 'Look at this city. Pretty little place. It's got a castle, two cathedrals, quaint old buildings, two excellent universities, an old wall, lots of nice touristy things. It gets top ratings for good places to live. But cities are like people. You strip the skin off the most beautiful human being, and you see the same blood and bones and shit-filled intestines as the ugliest old crone.'

The lawyer sat down. 'You rank-and-file cops resemble beauty therapists, or perhaps unskilled cleaners. You keep the streets looking nice, sweep the dirt under the carpet. Me and Tom, we deal with the guts, where the real issues are. There would be a lot more drugs, illegal prostitution and low-level crime if it wasn't for Tom. If you care about this city, don't think about bringing him down.'

'Who's going to get justice for Susan Smith?' asked Ross. 'What's Tom doing for her?'

'I'll be frank,' said Carpenter. 'Susan Smith was collateral damage in a greater battle. She was dead as soon as she stuck a needle in her arm. Heroin would have got her if Jeremy Kendal hadn't killed her first. If I were you, I'd forget her and stick to crimes against decent people.'

'And how do you define decent?'

'That's your problem, Inspector. I think this meeting is at an end. I normally charge two hundred pounds an hour for advice, so if you want to continue our discussion, you'll need to put your hand in your pocket.'

Ross left, now convinced Carpenter knew more about Connor and Susan Smith than he'd suggested. There was also a niggling question rattling around his brain.

Was there another lodge?

***

Adeyemi was waiting in Vicki Mayweather's sunroom when Kezia arrived, already wearing her grey tracksuit.

'No Izzie?' asked Kezia.

'Says she's not well,' replied Mayweather. 'She's promised to come next week, but I'm not holding my breath.'

Warm-up routines, a few basic dance moves, more exercises – then onto the pole. Adeyemi was proficient, Kezia uncoordinated. Lunch came as a welcome relief.

'Pity Izzie isn't here,' said Mayweather. 'We could've played cards.'

'I'm useless with them,' said Adeyemi. 'My brother can do tricks.'

Kezia needed a morale boost. 'I can show you one.'

Mayweather produced a pack.

'Shuffle them,' said Kezia, 'and then pick one out. Don't show me.'

The older woman obliged.

'Okay, look at it. Focus on the card.'

The other two smiled.

'Red,' said Kezia. 'Low number.'

Mayweather turned the card round. 'Three of hearts. Good guess.'

'Try again.'

Adeyemi pulled out a card.

Kezia concentrated. 'Black. Picture card.'

Adeyemi showed Kezia the card. 'Queen of clubs.'

'Again.'

Mayweather's turn.

Kezia couldn't read her at first. 'I'm not seeing it... focus more... High red.'

Mayweather showed Kezia the ace of hearts. 'Clever. How come you can't tell us the actual card?'

'Can't. Like it's too vague. Although I was fairly certain the last one was an ace.'

Adeyemi went to check on her daughter.

Mayweather placed the cards back in the pack. 'You read minds, don't you?'

'Kind of. You were easier to read than Jazmin. Maybe she was more worried about her kid.'

'What else can you see?'

'You're unhappy. It's all about a woman.'

'Bloody hell, you're good.' Mayweather pulled out her cigarettes. 'Is it obvious? She's in a civil partnership, won't leave her partner. I mean she says she will but I'm thinking different. Nobody's going to pull the wool over your eyes.'

Kezia smiled. 'Trouble is, they do. Infatuation gets in the way, like a fog. I'm in too deep before I see what shits some men are.'

Mayweather returned the smile. 'You ever thought about riding a different train?'

Kezia shook her head. 'Thanks for the offer. You'd have made a great conductor, but I like the one I'm on.'

Mayweather pulled out a cigarette and twirled it around in her fingers. 'No problem. Please get in touch if you change your mind. Anyone on the horizon?'

'There's a guy, he acts interested, but… Like he's too wrapped up in his work and he's older than me, so…'

'Good guy? Single?'

'Suppose.'

'Don't give up. They're a rare commodity. So I've been told.' Mayweather lit up and blew a plume of smoke towards the ceiling. 'Has Mandy been in touch? About the party?'

'Yeah. Sounds like fun.'

'Take care. It's more dangerous than the club. There won't be cameras watching every room.'

'Mandy told us it was a respectable business function.'

'That's a contradiction in terms,' said Mayweather. 'Vickery might have changed but some of his old mates haven't. They'll be expecting something extra. I shouldn't be telling you this, but… Hell, I like you. Some of the girls were in a group they called the Premier League. All dancers, but Vickery also used them as hostesses for a private members club he ran in the city. Susan Smith was one. Mandy Stewart was in the League as well. The clientele was the rich, his mates or anybody he wanted onside. Basically, it was a posh knocking shop. They asked me, but I wasn't having any of it.'

'When was this?'

'Six, seven years ago. Around the time Susan left. Rumour was she was up the duff and Vickery paid for her to have an abortion.'

'So, what guys should I be scared of?'

Mayweather took another puff. 'When I say private, I mean private. Councillors, police, politicians, big business. Anyone who could ease Tom Vickery's path into high society. That means they're powerful and in some cases untouchable.'

'Why are you telling me this? Isn't Vickery a mate of yours?'

'Tom's a good guy. Might sound odd, but he's straight. Old school. If you're loyal to him, he'll look after you. Male chauvinist pig of the first order. He had a rough start in life, and he's done the best he can. Trouble is he's got baggage he'll never get rid of, and innocent people still get hurt. I don't want to see you caught up in all of that.'

'Thanks for the heads up.'

'No problem.' Mayweather blew a perfect ring. 'Please don't mention our little chat to Tom.'

Adeyemi came back in. 'All's well.'

'Good,' said Mayweather. 'We can get back to the pole now.'

Halfway through the exercises, Kezia wondered if anyone had suffered so much agony around a pole since Captain Scott and his doomed expedition.

***

344

Alex Thomas called Ross at two o'clock. She invited him to a secure detention unit near Great Yarmouth. From the outside it looked like a warehouse.

'This place isn't on the map,' she said when he entered. 'We run it in conjunction with the security services. The Albanian operation could be a front for terrorism so until we're sure it isn't, we keep the suspects here.'

Dragusha sat in a windowless room, chained to a ring on a steel table.

The prisoner rattled his chains. 'They treat me like animal, no?'

'You treated Mirjeta and the other girls no better.'

Dragusha spat on the floor. 'Pah. Whores. They deserve nothing.'

'Why did you want to talk to me?'

Dragusha nodded towards Thomas. 'She say I do murder. She lie. She say you say I murder Trixie.'

'So how come you had her mobile phone?'

'I explain. Mirjeta tell me Trixie have money. Lot of money. I want Trixie out. I want my girls on street, not her. I go talk to Trixie, say you go. You not need be on street.'

'I'm assuming you intended to beat her up and rob her. Scare her into leaving Rosary Road.'

'No. I no hurt her. I see men come out park – '

'Men? How many?'

'That Kendz, he come out first. Then other man. He follow Kendz.'

'Describe this man.'

'He wear black. Black hood. I no see face.'

Kendal had spoken the truth…

'Are you sure it was a man? Could it have been a woman?'

'He walk like a man. But who can tell in this country?'

'Okay, the men have gone. Then what?'

'I go find Trixie. She dead. I look for money. I find mobile. It cheap one, I know now. I keep, might be useful.'

'Why didn't you call an ambulance? Or the police?'

'You funny man? You come, you arrest me. I am illegal immigrant.'

'Did you see anyone else? A girl, perhaps?'

'I think I see someone running away. Could be girl.'

'What about the drugs? Who did you supply in Norwich?'

'No comment.'

Ross recognised they weren't going to get anything else out of Dragusha. He followed Thomas out of the room.

'What was that about a mobile?' she asked. 'We only found one phone and that was his.'

'The price of my cooperation,' Ross replied. 'Trust me.'

Thomas grinned. 'No sweat. Did he tell you what you wanted to hear? Sounded a bit unlikely to me.'

'It fits the facts as they stand,' said Ross. 'An inconvenient truth, as they say.'

***

The next breakthrough came on Tuesday morning. The proprietor of an antique shop in Long Melford in neighbouring Suffolk had suspicions over a seller, and the item in question matched a vase stolen in Norwich a month previously. The county's police apprehended the man, who unlike his supplier did not fall back on a tirade of 'No comments'.

Bill Potter again found himself in Bethel Street.

'Arthur Zaminski,' said Ross. 'Friend of yours?'

'No comment.'

'He fingered you as selling him a William Moorcroft Eventide vase. Two days after it vanished from a house in Newmarket Road.'

'He's lying.'

'Thing is, he said he met you in Ipswich. We've got CCTV showing you walking into a pub with a Tesco's carrier bag containing something about the same size as the vase. An hour later you come out empty handed. Mr Zaminski is now carrying the bag. '

'No – ' A whisper with the duty solicitor, then a few seconds rubbing hands with pursed lips. 'All right, you've got me. I'm guilty. My hand's up for all the jobs you mentioned, plus there's a couple you missed. I'm a poor old man and I need the money.'

Ross sat back. 'Thank you, Mr Potter. You've done the right thing.'

'That bloody Sarah Consodine. Should've known she'd be my downfall.'

Mishra smiled. 'You admit you've been involved with her before?'

'God, no. Only person who got properly involved with her was Lovejoy Lennie. That's what we called her husband. Bloody villain, but he got his punishment married to her. He was the dodgiest dealer north of London. Fakes, fixed auctions, you name it. Even rumours he dealt in smack to boost his income.'

'I suppose you worked with Lennie?' asked Ross.

'Sort of, tried to pass stuff onto him in the old days but he wouldn't pay anything near the value. When I read about the stuck-up cow in the paper rabbiting on about ladies of the night, well, I couldn't resist it. I guessed Lovejoy would keep some nice stuff for himself, so I'm thinking I'm having some of that.'

'Okay, Bill,' said Ross. 'We'll type up a confession for you to check and sign. Then we'll get you before the beaks as soon as possible.'

'What about bail?' asked the solicitor. 'Mr Potter is no threat to anyone and I'm sure he'll promise to stay at home.'

Ross shook his head. 'I don't believe we can trust him enough.'

Potter leant forward. 'Suppose I tell you about Kev Connor? Would that help?'

'Depends what you tell me,' said Ross. 'If it's something interesting then I might reconsider.'

'Okay. You've seen my work. I'm a careful man. Every job planned in advance.'

'I want to hear about Connor, not you.'

'Fine, I'm coming to that. See, I spent a lot of time on Rosary Road, you understand, checking out Mrs Consodine's.

I had to postpone the job for a couple of weeks after the murder 'cause you rozzers were all over the place.'

'Connor.'

'Right. It was the week before the prozzie got done. I was there three times, and every time I spotted Kev Connor on the way. Once I clocked him near the park. I reckon he was watching the girls.'

'Are you certain?'

'Yeah, absolutely. Even though he wore this hoodie, he'd a funny way of walking. Bloody good job he didn't see me.' Potter tapped his nose. 'But I'm smart, right?'

Ross stood up. 'Right, any smarter and we might not have caught you. Let me see about bail.'

Kev Connor: a violent thug who frequented Rosary Road with interest in prostitutes… a hooded man with an English accent.

Ross was certain he'd nailed Susan Smith's killer. The question now was who killed Connor.

***

Kezia, Reynolds and Adeyemi convened in Vickery's office at the back of Hot Steps at four o'clock. Kezia was relieved to discover Tom Vickery had declined an opportunity to watch the girls disrobing, especially as brassieres were off the menu. Instead, Mandy Stewart supervised an Asian woman who took their measurements then disappeared.

'Are you better now?' Kezia asked Reynolds when Stewart left the room. 'We missed you yesterday.'

'Yeah, I wasn't feeling well. Like it's a woman thing.'

'You still gonna do the dancing?' asked Adeyemi.

'Yeah… well, maybe. I'm not sure about the nude stuff but, you know, once I've watched the other girls do it, it'll be okay.'

Kezia opened the door to ensure Stewart wasn't on her way back. 'What about this party? Do we trust Vickery it's all above board?'

'It's proper businessmen, innit?' said Reynolds.

'They're the worst sort,' announced Adeyemi. 'Give 'em a drink and their hands'll be all over us.'

Reynolds shivered. 'Wonder what these costumes will be like?'

'Bet you won't confuse them with a burka,' answered Kezia. She heard Stewart's footsteps approaching the door. 'Watch out.'

'Right,' said Stewart. 'Listen carefully. Wear clean white knickers and remember they'll be on show. Frillier the better. You'll be picked up at the station at six o'clock on Thursday evening. Don't be late. There'll be four other girls there. The minibus will take you to Tom's house. Maya will be there to fit your costumes and make any last-minute adjustments.'

'Suppose we get delayed,' asked Reynolds. 'Where's the house?'

Stewart stared at the student. 'You will not be late. If you don't turn up, you won't ever work for us again. Understood?' The older woman turned to Kezia and Adeyemi. 'Same goes for you.'

Adeyemi put her hand up. 'Can we bring our mobiles? I'll need to check on my daughter.'

'You can take them on the minibus. When you get to Tom's house you will change in an outhouse and leave any personal possessions there.'

Adeyemi scowled. 'What time do we get back?'

'The function will end at midnight. You'll help tidy up and I'd expect you to be back at the station by two o'clock at the very latest. If you don't like it, speak up now.'

Adeyemi shook her head. 'Okay. No problem.'

'Right, now the ground rules. Tom's house is not Hot Steps. If a guy goes too far in the club, we get the penguins on the door to throw him out. The purpose of this function is to gain the support of these men for Tom's building project. If their hands wander, you'll have to deal with it. Don't piss them off.'

'You're saying they can grope us!' A hint of panic entered Reynolds' voice.

'No, I'm saying you deal with it. We'll have people there to help. These are respectable men, so they're not going to rape you. Just get a bit frisky, that's all.'

'So, what are we doing?' asked Kezia.

'Smile and serve drinks, that's all. Oh… and in the lounge you might have to sit on their laps and feed them grapes.'

God, this is going to be humiliating.

'Now, there will be a photographer there. He'll be trying to spot anything that appears a bit compromising, so if you notice him, try to act like you're a willing participant. Is that plain?'

Kezia decided it was very plain. 'In other words, Tom will blackmail them if they block his plans.'

Stewart smiled. 'Not a word I'd use. I'd rather say Tom will ask them to reconsider any adverse decision on the grounds they owe him an apology for abusing his hospitality.'

Great, sounds like I can add coercion, bribery, and corruption to my growing list of crimes. And no way can I tell Ross.

***

It was a wet Wednesday afternoon when Kezia set off for Norwich jail. The burner phone rang as she walked into Knox Road. Even at a distance of eight hundred feet, the entrance to the prison at the far end was intimidating.

'David?'

'How's things?' *He sounds concerned.*

'Fine. I'm off to visit Jez. Don't stop me.'

'No problem. Listen, I've found who killed Susan. It was Kev Connor.'

Kezia punched the air. 'Hey, that's so great. Are they going to let Jez out?'

'It's not so simple. The key witness is Mirjeta Bardici's pimp. He's got no reason to help us and even if he did nobody's going to believe a word he says.'

'What do we do?'

'I keep trying to implicate Vickery. You do nothing, unless...'

'What?'

'If you can get Kendal to change his plea, it might help him. But Kezia...'

'What?'

'Please drop this dancing idea. Pretend you've sprained your ankle. Things are going to get nasty, and I don't want you caught in the crossfire.'

'Yeah, okay.'

'Promise?'

No way can I break a promise to Ross. So don't make one. 'Sorry, I gotta go. Don't want to miss visiting time. You take care.' She ended the call.

Kezia blanked out the consequences of her decision and began the long walk down Knox Road towards the prison entrance. She took a deep breath, ready for the checks, the searches, the questions, and the haunting memories of her father waiting behind the dark red brick wall.

Fifteen minutes later she again met with Jez Kendal.

Kendal avoided eye contact. 'I'm guilty.'

'You're not,' replied Kezia. 'I know who killed Susan. What did your lawyer tell you?'

'How did you…?' Kendal's voice rose in pitch. 'You know who did it?'

'Yes,' she said. 'We reckon it's a man called Kev Connor.'

'Then why don't you tell the police? Arrest this Connor. Make him confess.'

'It's not that easy. Connor's dead. They reckon he died in an accident. The only witness won't testify 'cause it would only incriminate him further.'

Kendal put his head in his hands. 'Shit. I didn't want to confess. Mr Carpenter said it would be best. I'd be out in three years. I wouldn't even have to go to jail, just some special hospital. He reckoned if I didn't say I did it, then I'd get life and it wouldn't be fair on my mum.'

'What else did Mr Carpenter say?'

'He reckons I've got psycho-whatsit issues and I should say I don't remember killing Trixie. I should say she was making fun of me and it all went red.'

'Please, Kendz, your best chance is to tell the truth.'

Kendal stared at her. 'What makes you a bloody expert? Mr Carpenter knows the law. If he says I should plead guilty, then I'll plead guilty. I don't need no charity do-gooder messing up my life.'

'You're making a mistake, Kendz.'

He hung his head again. 'Just piss off, okay.'

'Okay, Kendz, I'm going to leave now. Is there anything you need?'

Kendal looked at her with frightened eyes. 'Make sure they put me in a jail near to my Mum. Please.'

'I'll do my best,' said Kezia.

She called Ross when she left the jail. Ross again tried to dissuade her from contact with Tom Vickery.

He knew who killed Susan. He'd worked out how he'd done it, and how Tom Vickery and his hangers-on had ensnared an innocent man to take the rap.

He still hadn't worked out why.

Chapter Twenty-seven

The minibus arrived at ten minutes past six. Under other circumstances, it would have been a pleasant evening. Four other girls joined them, introduced only as Gloria, Jeannie, Brandi and Mia. Kezia guessed the newcomers had worked as hostesses before – they all seemed to be aged around thirty, and she wondered if they'd recently retired from Vickery's clubs.

Kezia guessed she, Adeyemi and Reynolds were the freshest meat. She also felt the presence of Ross. He didn't want her to do this, and he'd be using the tracker on her phone to follow her. She'd thought about leaving the mobile behind, then realised it would cut off her primary source of help if problems arose.

Kezia had little idea of Norfolk beyond the city boundaries. She assumed they'd started heading west on the Kings Lynn-bound A47, then turned off the road in a southerly direction. She spotted a signpost to Wymondham. Half an hour after they left the station, the bus swung into a long driveway.

The route culminated in a circular car park at the centre of which stood a round marble fountain topped with a small gold statue of a Greek god who Kezia assumed was Eros. Ahead lay Vickery's house, a large modern brick construction. The vehicle stopped outside a triple garage set apart from the main building. Stewart led the seven women around the side and up a flight of external stairs.

The upper floor had been converted into a small studio apartment. It was plainly furnished, the walls bare of decoration, the kitchen area spotless. Kezia noticed no evidence anyone lived there. Their costumes lay on the bed, each in a polythene bag with a name handwritten on a label.

'No bras,' commanded Stewart.

Kezia pulled her outfit from its bag, a short, gold lamé-trimmed white dress with matching gold arm bands. More Greek fantasy than Roman. The fit wasn't perfect, a little too tight, although that might have been deliberate. Maya hadn't erred on the generous side with any of the costumes, and the seamstress failed to arrive as promised.

Vickery also provided footwear, gold sandals with ankle straps. After Kezia dressed, if such a term could be used, she looked at herself in a long mirror. Weird, but she'd do.

'Ladies,' said Stewart when they all sported the white and gold outfits, 'I'll remind you what your task is. Simple – serve wine, feed them grapes, and make the men think they're a bunch of ageing playboys. So flirt with them. When you pour the wine, use words like 'Can I tempt you sir?' or 'Can I increase yours by a couple of inches?'. Use your imagination.'

'Christ, that sounds like a bloody *Carry On* film,' said Gloria, a buxom redhead whose apparel appeared to be under more strain than the others.

Stewart shot her a withering look. 'If they don't want wine, we'll supply lager or soft drinks. You can get them from the kitchen. In the fridge.'

The sandal straps cut into Kezia's feet as she walked from the garage into the house. The entrance hall had a white marble floor. A pair of curved staircases led up into the two wings. Kezia wondered how long it would take one of the guests to suggest he and she should explore the upper storey. Ahead lay a space extending perhaps eighty feet towards the rear of the property where it transformed into a summer room. In the centre sat a six-foot-long model of Vickery's planned development enclosed in a large glass case. A woman with shoulder-length blonde hair wearing a low-cut cream top and split royal-blue skirt perched next to a grand piano in one corner. The melody of Billy Joel's 'Piano Man' drifted across. Caterers stopped stacking the tables around the edge of the room with cheeses, rolls and canapés, and leered at the newly arrived women.

Stewart snapped at the men. 'You're not paid to gawp. Carry on.' She pointed. 'The kitchen's to the left through that door.'

'Welcome!' Vickery's voice boomed behind them. He wore a white dinner jacket and bow tie. Kezia wondered if anyone would mistake him for a waiter. Bad move if they did.

The club owner opened his arms. 'What visions of loveliness. My God, those old Romans must have had a wonderful time. Come ladies, join me outside for a group photo.'

He ushered them through a set of French doors at the rear of the house like a hungry sheepdog guiding its flock towards the slaughterhouse. The group entered a courtyard paved in the ubiquitous marble and dominated by an oval swimming pool. A sunroom lay on the far edge, facing west to receive the last rays of the setting sun. Stewart assembled the women in front of this while Vickery squeezed in at the edge, his arm snaking round Kezia, his hand brushing against her right breast. 'This is nice, isn't it Mary?'

'Sure is,' lied Kezia.

A dark-haired man with a camera appeared and told them to say cheese. When he'd taken four shots, Vickery took his time to release his grip. Kezia forced a smile and seized the opportunity to glance inside the outbuilding. She noted a couch and a small table on which lay a telephone, an ashtray and a copy of *North Norfolk Living* magazine.

Vickery and his entourage left the seven standing by the pool. Jeannie, blonde, heavy make-up, bright red lips, watched the club owner disappear into the house. 'Done all right for himself, the old letch.'

Brandi, Afro-Caribbean, tall, slim, nodded. 'He's all right, old Vic. Never bothered me. Wonder who else is coming?'

Blonde, freckled, petite Mia smiled. 'Hope they're rich. Might be good for a bit of business.'

Brandi sighed. 'You're not still on the game, are you girl?'

Mia laughed. 'Why not? I'm choosy, though. Not like the old days.'

Kezia contemplated the old days as well. 'You remember Susan Smith?'

'Nah.'

'She was called Trixie. Left about seven years ago.'

Jeannie, brunette, the only one of the group whose costume strained more in the waist than the bust, whistled. 'Whew, there's a name from the past. She was premier league, wasn't she?'

'I never bothered with that shit,' said Brandi.

Gloria nodded. 'Me neither. I always went home alone. I made enough dancing.'

Mia screwed up her face. 'I could never make enough. Old Vic never wanted me for the league. Too short, I reckon.'

Reynolds saved Kezia from having to ask. 'What's this premier league?'

'Bit like this, only without clothes,' said Mia.

'And the rest,' added Brandi. 'Old Vic shipped the girls to some fancy house to entertain some high rollers. They never said who.'

'They weren't told,' said Jeannie. 'The punters never revealed their names.'

Gloria laughed. 'I bet they did know. Footballers, politicians, big business types. They'd have been in the paper or telly. Old Vic would've killed the girls if they'd talked.'

Something didn't seem right to Kezia. 'Not freemasons?'

'Some of them might've been freemasons,' said Jeannie. 'But I heard one girl mention Pablo Delmonte.'

Mia gasped. 'The City player? The one what got sacked for — '

'Yeah, him,' said Jeannie. 'Only guy I ever heard linked with the premiers. And I bet he wasn't a mason, not with a name like that.'

Kezia glanced at the telephone in the sunroom. *Could she?*

Stewart called over from the house. 'Come on. I need to show you where everything is.'

They suffered the lustful stares of the caterers once more as Stewart showed them the various locations where activities would take place. Kezia was relieved to hear the feeding of the grapes had been cancelled as Vickery wanted everyone where he could see them.

She, Brandi and Reynolds found themselves standing alone.

The rear doors remained open. Reynolds shivered as a breeze chilled the room. 'I'm not sure I want to do this anymore. It's demeaning. Like all these men gawping.'

'Babe,' said Brandi, 'it's when the men stop gawping you gotta worry.'

Reynolds folded her arms. 'I want guys to like me as a person, not a sex object.'

Kezia saw Reynolds's fear – a vision of a mouse flitted across her mind. Brandi acted too cool to register.

Brandi placed a hand on Reynold's trembling arm. 'Listen girl, I've done it all in my time and believe me, there's a helluva lot of tossers who can't see beyond my colour. I spent two months as a traffic warden, and folks don't see anything but the uniform. So we're all objects to some people, so fuck 'em, that's what I say. It's their problem, not mine.'

'But they're exploiting us.'

'Yeah, well, I flash my tits at some man an' he gives me money. As Aretha Franklin said, who's zoomin' who?'

Kezia refused to get involved in a feminist argument. The mention of exploitation reminded her of what she did for her mother.

The guests started arriving half-an-hour later. Mostly male, although some had brought partners, and five women appeared who Kezia identified as invitees in their own right. Most of the men wore suits and ties, although a smattering of the younger guests sported open-necked shirts. Long dresses appeared to be de rigueur for ladies, at least those who weren't carrying trays. And apart from two of the faux slave girls and four of the caterers, everyone present was white. Hardly a cross-section of society.

Within twenty minutes the crowd divided; couples and unattached females grouped together in one corner while unaccompanied males clustered together in the centre of the room. These men were polite, respectful... until the drink began to exert its influence. Hands began to wander, lips mouthed suggestive comments. Reynolds lasted until nine o'clock when she fled upstairs in tears, followed by an irate Stewart. Kezia wondered if she should follow suit. She visualised pigs, rams, rutting stags, sniffing dogs... A warning to be vigilant, not yet a precursor of danger.

The pianist played tunes from the seventies and eighties. Kezia recognised a few Beatles numbers, more Billy Joel, some Duran Duran. A group of men crowded round the piano, doubtless admiring the performer rather than the performance. The air became tainted with cigar smoke and middle-aged sweat.

A hand pulled at her sleeve. 'Here, love, give us one. And a glass of wine would be welcome as well, eh?' An obese man, red faced, wearing a grey suit with trousers too long, jacket too narrow, an aura of stale sweat, and a plain tie matching the colour of his cheeks.

'Why, sure, sir.' Big smile hiding a desire to punch him in his protruding belly as she poured the wine.

'You're the best looking one,' he slurred. 'D'you fancy a late supper afterwards?' His hand slipped down towards her buttocks.

'Be nice, Stanley.' The speaker was balding, but still possessed a charisma which even Kezia found intriguing. 'I'm sorry,' he said. 'Stanley's not used to wine. More a beer man, aren't you?'

'Piss off, Warder,' came the reply. 'We'll sort you lot out at the next election.' With a parting sneer, he walked away.

Kezia's rescuer executed a mocking wave at the departing man. 'Never ply a socialist with alcohol. Their principles are always the first casualty of drink.'

'Thanks. I take it you're a Tory?'

'Naturally.' He smiled and offered her his hand. 'Nigel Warder. Would-be parliamentary candidate. And you are...'

'Um, Mary Malone. Would-be dancer.'

'Very pleased to meet you, Mary. Would you mind if I said you are the most beautiful rose in this garden?'

Kezia's man meter had just left the green of hero and headed towards the red area marked sleaze-bag. She was, however, a little thrilled to realise he seemed to be telling the truth.

A hand reached across and lifted a glass from her tray. 'You don't mind, do you?'

Kezia turned to look at the newcomer. Handsome, a suit surely sourced from Savile Row, teeth like a toothpaste advert. She wondered if Stewart would let her keep this outfit. It transformed her into a man magnet.

'Richard, my favourite lawyer,' said Warder. 'Have you come to steal my jewel?'

The newcomer smiled at Kezia. 'I wish.' Then he turned again to Warder. 'You'd better apologise to Stanley. He's on the planning committee, remember?'

'Stanley and I will never be friends. He's an out-and-out socialist. The sort who believes the way to achieve prosperity for the masses is to remove the incentive from the only people capable of delivering the means to that prosperity.'

'He's no Corbynista,' said the lawyer. 'Otherwise, he wouldn't be here.'

'That doesn't mean anything,' replied Warder. 'Keep your friends close, and your enemies even closer. Remember?'

The other looked round before speaking. 'Tom wants us all to be friends. Until the next meeting, okay?'

Kezia suddenly felt she didn't exist. She mumbled an 'Excuse me' and swivelled to offer wine to a group who discussed Norwich City's prospects of promotion in the coming season.

'...One-all away to Fulham. Cracking result. Oh, thanks, love. I'll have a red.'

A whisper behind her. '... got that oink Kendal to confess. What the hell else could I do?' The voice belonged to the man known as Richard.

Richard... It must be Richard Carpenter.

'D'you do orgies?' Thin man, lined face, could be someone's grandfather, breaking off from his opinion on City's form to ogle Kezia.

'Sorry.' Sweet smile, fluttering eyelashes, aimed at what she imagined as a panting dog. 'Just wine and beer.'

A hand grabbed her arm. 'I recognise you.'

I don't know you. Problem is you're telling the truth. 'Sorry, sir, can't think where.'

'You're a waitress somewhere else.'

'That's it. Bet you can't guess where?' *You don't look like a Green Haven regular.*

The man held up a finger. 'Got it. Police do at the Maid's Head last Christmas.'

Coquettish bow. 'You must be a detective.'

He lifted a glass of red wine from her tray and leered at her. 'You bet, my dear. I'm a Detective Chief Inspector, no less.'

'Go on, Neville,' said the thin man. 'Tell her you'll take down anything she says.'

Shit. I'm talking with Ross's boss – keep smiling. 'I'll have to watch you boys.'

She prayed the wine would continue to dull Devlin's memory. He'd have seen her mugshot. It was lucky lipstick and mascara had transformed the sullen Kezia who scowled at their camera a few days before. She recognised another stroke of luck. His desire for her suffocated any further curiosity.

A change in the air. Drink fuelled emotion; lust, joy, occasional anger. It might have been the combination of smoke mixed with tangible testosterone and her own tensions, but Kezia's vision became blurred, a menagerie threatening to replace reality.

She had to keep in control. *Don't let your fear allow hallucinations to take over.*

Carpenter and Warder had wandered out of earshot, accompanied by Devlin. Kezia plotted a route through the guests to reach them, but they'd reached Jeannie's area.

'Premier league. Won't see those days again.' Kezia turned at the words. Three men, one the man known as Stanley. She moved closer.

'City haven't got the money. It's teams like Villa and Wolves'll be chasing promotion. We'll be lucky if we finish mid-table.'

Damn football. She handed out drinks to the group and moved on. The conversations became louder, some cruder, some inane. Kezia resumed her trips to and from the kitchen, eyes and desire following her all the time. Beasts floated across her mind, males jostling for leadership of the pack.

She quietened the visions by moving towards the area occupied by couples. She passed four women talking; power suits, expensive haircuts, manicured nails. Kezia picked up the contempt, disgust and arrogance aimed directly at her, accompanied by an unexpected glimmer of desire from one of the quartet.

Husbands projected lust and embarrassment; wives, jealousy, anger, amusement and sympathy. Kezia could deal with those. She smiled as glasses vanished from her tray.

But once she turned back, the other creatures came... not wolves, but something else. Big cats, somewhere in the mid-distance, watching. A faint smell of blood...

Why? Instinct drew her eyes to the far side of the room. Gloria was talking to Stewart. All smiles, female gossip... Stewart's face changed... serious, concerned. The club manager's stare fixed on Kezia.

'You got any white left, honey?' She didn't understand the words, no longer noticed the men in suits. They seemed now just blurs, with outstretched arms, hands brushing her body. Her attention fixed on Stewart, who trotted across to where Tom Vickery stood talking to a tall man in a cream suit.

'You, I asked if you'd got white?' A hand resting on her bum.

Focus... 'Sorry, sir. I'll go and get some.'

As she walked towards the kitchen, Vickery had deserted his companion. He and Stewart whispered together, but their eyes focused on Kezia.

Lions, moving in for the kill.

The caterers were still busy, preparing, washing up glasses, leering at the goddesses in their white and gold outfits. Kezia poured out six glasses of white and added them to her tray. She spied an exit from the kitchen to her right. She wondered if she should leave.

Pointless... the flat above the garage would be locked, she'd no idea where she was, and Vickery would have protection watching the house. Whatever trouble she'd landed in, she'd have to face it.

Stewart pounced as soon as she re-entered the main room. 'Mary, Tom would like a quick word.'

A brief wave of fear... she detected no outward indication of hostility. Instead Kezia read suspicion, concern.

Stewart led the way through a doorway into what looked like Vickery's private study. Bookshelves lined the walls. Kezia spotted a full set of Dickens, the plays of Shakespeare, a variety of volumes designed for coffee tables. A collection intended to impress rather than read. The red carpet was thick and expensive. Vickery sat behind a large desk on which lay a silver model ocean liner. Two chairs, red leather, sat on her side of the desk. He emanated the same aura as Stewart. The lions did not intend to kill, but they would if it meant their pride survived.

'Shut the door after you, Mandy,' commanded Vickery.

Stewart walked out. Kezia felt naked as Vickery's eyes moved up and down her body. It wasn't lust, it was control.

She took a deep breath, letting the oxygen bring her back to full consciousness.

'Why did you ask about Susan Smith?'

'You mean Trixie?' Kezia put on her most nonchalant expression. 'I'm a mate of Sy Mercer. You know, Trixie's boyfriend.'

Vickery obviously didn't recognise Mercer's name. Just as well – no-one would want to be Sy's mate.

'You're lying. You're a fucking journalist.'

'No. It's, like, I was speaking with Sy and I say I want to get some cash and he says, 'Why don't you try lap dancing' and I say, like, 'Come on', and he says Trixie used to make a lot when she worked at Hot Steps so – '

'So a woman gets murdered and you want to follow her example?'

'Nah, like who wants to get killed? Trixie fucked up, right? Got into drugs and things.'

'Did he tell you why Trixie left Norwich?'

'Dunno. I suppose she got into drugs and you gave her the boot. Won't happen to me, Mr Vickery, I promise.'

Kezia saw the lion calm down and vanish like the Cheshire cat.

'Sit down.'

She carefully lowered herself onto the nearest chair, pulling the short skirt as far down over her thighs as possible.

'I like you, Mary. You're a lousy dancer but a looker. End of the day that's what the punters want.'

Kezia tried coquettishness. 'Thank you, Mr Vickery.'

'What did the others tell you about Susan?'

Careful. Gloria has probably reported the conversation in its entirety.

'Not a lot. They said she was premier league. I'm not sure what they meant.'

'Shit!' Vickery banged the desk. 'Gobby bitches.' He stared at the door for five seconds before his smile returned. 'Mary, let me give you some advice. You probably think I'm a dirty old man. Maybe I am. I like looking at pretty girls, but that's all I do… look. You work for me, I watch your back. All I ask in return is you're loyal, and what happens in Hot Steps stays in Hot Steps. Okay?'

'Yes, Mr Vickery.'

'Susan messed up. I tried to help her, but she went her own way. All this talk about the premier league… All I'll say is some writer once said the past was another country. Do you understand what that means?'

'No,' lied Kezia.

'A few years ago… let's say I allowed the girls a bit more freedom. Additional opportunities to make money, you understand. Big mistake, as I've found to my cost. Today, you dance, you go home. Anyone gives you hassle, I'll step in. But no drugs, and no selling your services outside the club. Am I making myself plain?'

'Yes, Mr Vickery.'

'Good. And I'd advise you to stay clear of any so-called friends of Susan. They're bad news.'

Kezia's confidence had grown. Danger was a mere shadow now. 'Thank you, Mr Vickery. I've finished with Sy Mercer, anyway. He tried… you know...'

Vickery nodded.

'In fact, I wondered if it might be him that killed her. I reckon he could be violent.'

Vickery laughed. 'Don't worry. They got the bastard who did it. Some crazy ex-squaddie.' He stood up and walked to the door. 'I'm not paying you to brighten up my office. Off you go and watch out for wandering hands.'

He rested his own palm on her lower back as she smiled at him and left.

David Ross has it all wrong.

Vickery had not ordered the death of Susan Smith. And he hadn't a clue who did.

Chapter Twenty-eight

Ross left the station car park and returned to his empty flat. It seemed darker, more drab, dirtier than he remembered. The sink overflowed with unwashed dishes; discarded clothes littered the bedroom floor. The smell of rotting food lingered like a malevolent spirit.

He should go out. Find a bar, talk to women, get his life back. Join a society, book a proper holiday. Club 18-30 – he still almost qualified. Maybe he should quit the police as well: an occupation gazing at the dark underside of humanity, oozing evil and deceit. He'd lost faith in everyone, even himself.

Christ, he'd become besotted with a woman who'd turned out to be a thief, liar and a confidence trickster, and who was now plunging headlong into a career of vice. She was too dangerous. By her own admission, she'd never sustain a relationship. And her age... What, over ten years younger than him? A gypsy as well. Not to mention the weird visions. Kezia had to be mentally ill. Certifiable, even.

He tried to block her out. He filled the sink with hot water and a few drops of washing up liquid, then dropped in the first plate. After he'd cleansed every piece of filth from the crockery, he'd leave this prison of a flat and buy a take-away curry. Lamb Madras, perhaps. A bottle of Cobra to go with it.

Sod that, sitting at home, all alone. White plates, the colour of tombstones, filled the drainer as he contemplated going to a restaurant. *Yeah, right, sit there and stare at all the happy couples holding hands. Guaranteed to cheer you up, you pathetic saddo.*

Don't daydream about Kezia. Focus on Susan Smith – who killed her?

Simple, Kev Connor. Devlin would need a lot of convincing. The DCI kept mentioning Occam's Razor – the simplest explanation was usually the correct one, which meant nailing Jez Kendal.

Assuming Connor proved to be the murderer, then why? Even William of Occam would agree that as a thug for hire, somebody paid him. Someone with money, someone whose fortune or reputation could be destroyed by Susan Smith.

Unless... Border Force expected a third male in the Unthank Road house. Dragusha's boss – a crime lord who wanted to dominate street prostitution in Norwich. Such a man would have the resources to hire a killer and even buy Richard Carpenter.

But why the prolonged assault on her face? Most contract killers would finish the job and leave. It wouldn't be to hide her identity. Anyone with sense would assume the police had her fingerprints in their records.

Drugs? Suppose Susan threatened to expose her supplier? Red Stibbons's number was the last one she dialled. Stibbons's story sounded genuine and hadn't changed under interrogation. But... who supplied Stibbons? Had Susan found out his – or her – name? Ardi Dragusha was associated with one source. There might be others. For example, Sarah Consodine – the widow of Lovejoy Lennie, suspected heroin smuggler. Was it by chance that Susan's beat lay directly outside her home?

Kezia... it always came back to her. She'd infected his mind like a drug. He couldn't shake her off. Why had Connor attacked Kezia? Perhaps Connor worried she'd seen him? But she hadn't... had she? If so, why had she kept quiet?

His mind raced. Was Kezia involved somehow? Had she lied to him, played him along? Half-Russian... might there be some family connection to the Albanians?

Ross couldn't get her out of his mind. Would she still try to prove Kendal's innocence? He accessed the iPhone tracker, and it didn't take long to find Kezia's location.

Vickery's house.

He had to get out. Walk, breathe in fresh air, think.

Ten minutes later he stood on the street. His body had escaped, but his thoughts remained trapped by his obsession with Kezia.

Connor discovered her identity, where she lived. Perhaps he'd followed her after killing Susan, but that made no sense. He'd have slain Kezia on the spot.

Then William of Occam's philosophy hit him like a sledgehammer.

Old William's methods told him who paid Connor. A delve in the databases at Bethel Street might confirm whether they killed him as well.

**

Kezia continued to circulate, forcing a smile despite rampant chauvinism and ill-fitting shoes. One of these leering, pawing, lusting creatures might have ordered the murder of Susan Smith. She tried to read them, but she only sensed the harbingers of desire and contempt. The comments turned more vulgar, the hands more active. Relief came at ten o'clock when the sound of a gong muted a hundred conversations and a single piano.

'Gentlemen.' Vickery stood by the front entrance to the room flanked by Mandy Stewart and Richard Carpenter. 'I beg your attention for a few minutes.'

He waited till the last whispers died down, and every eye had turned his way.

'You represent the best of Norwich and Norfolk society. You are the leaders of our community, and it's a privilege to welcome you to my humble home.'

Vickery stopped the consequent smattering of applause by raising his hand.

'Our county, our beloved Norfolk, has an undeserved reputation as a backwater. The butt of a thousand jokes. Taken for granted by the government, abandoned as a lost cause by the opposition. The home counties get paid for prestige and self-interest, the north gets it share out of sympathy and political influence, but we get nothing but scraps and derision.

'I want to change this injustice, but I need your help.' He stopped and looked around, arms outstretched. 'We must be seen as leaders. Innovators. The county that points towards the future and reaches it before all others.'

Vickery paused to take a drink of water and soak in the appreciative murmurs from the throng. 'What are the major problems our beloved Norfolk faces? Indeed, not just us, but our entire country.'

Kezia listened, impressed. *God, this is profound stuff for a strip club owner.*

'Not enough housing. Rising energy costs. Fear of crime.'

I'm not hearing any mention of poverty or prejudice.

'Imperial Grove will address all of those. A mix of executive and affordable homes.'

Yeah, all houses are affordable if you've got enough money.

'Nothing new, you may be thinking. But this will be different. The environment will not just be carbon-neutral, but carbon positive. Every house will have solar tiles on its roof, connection to a ground source heat pump, triple-glazed windows, the highest level of naturally sourced insulation in the walls. Every property will benefit from a dual water supply – a communal rainwater harvesting system for toilets and washing machines and mains for drinking and personal use. There will be a sewage pre-treatment plant where we will extract methane to generate electricity.'

Vickery waved to his right; at whom was about to become clear. 'Nigel's given us a steer on the crime reduction angle. A managed CCTV network will cover all properties and entrances to the development. Every home will be fitted with toughened glass and specialist locks.

'Although we plan to build on a flood plain, each building will be on stilts, as will the access roads, to ensure not only security from flooding but also ease of disabled entry. All waste material will be recycled where possible.'

Even from a distance, Kezia perceived a different truth. Vickery intended to withdraw from many of his pledges once construction was underway and irreversible.

Vickery paused and took a drink of water. 'I'm aware we're planning to develop on a site of archaeological interest. We'll sponsor any necessary survey, and we'll assist the university authorities as much as possible.'

You mean bribe them to cut corners.

'Together we can put Norfolk on the map as a world leader in sustainable construction. It will be our legacy.'

More applause. This time Vickery let it run for several seconds.

'I've known some of you a long time. Many of you were around when I started in the property business, and I've got you to thank for my success. My first job involved knocking down Chapelfields Lodge and building a block of flats.'

Chapelfields Lodge. A building. No connection at all to freemasons. Had Cheryl Jackson got it wrong?

'I'll never forget the good times we used to have in the old house but time moves on.' Vickery paused and looked round as if he tried to spot particular people in the crowd.

He's sending out a warning. Support me or your past will bury you.

The speech resumed. 'As I said, time moves on. We've come a long way since then. Nigel here had just graduated from law school. Junior clerk or something and look at him now. He's a promising politician and senior magistrate, but then he had to run the family heating business in his spare time. In fact, you were very much hands on in those days. Isn't that right, Nigel? Bit like some of you lads tonight, eh?'

Kezia picked up on Vickery's subtle smile.

He's describing Nigel Warder – a man capable of fixing a gas boiler to make it appear faulty.

Kezia stared at Warder, or rather the beast within. If I can see it, he'll be thinking about the lodge, remembering what he had to do to keep his guilty past a secret. A magistrate who Susan Smith might have recognised the day Sy Mercer appeared before his court – the same day Susan announced her locket was worth a fortune. She recalled the image of the young Cheryl Smith. A child who inherited her looks from her father.

Calm down, girl.

She had to get through this evening, then phone Ross. Kezia carried on serving wine, fending off advances, ignoring sore feet, smiling, and acting like a walking Greek Barbie doll.

The visions came again. Her gaze settled on the far side of the room, where Vickery, Devlin and Warder huddled in conversation. Warder didn't look at his companions. Instead, he scanned the throng. He stopped when he spotted Kezia.

Kezia visualised the wolf as its hungry eyes fixed on hers. Blood dripped from its jaws. Then it transformed back into Warder, now clicking on his mobile. *He wasn't calling, he was searching...* Visions came in bloody waves. She wouldn't be allowed to leave. Nobody here would take her seriously if she attempted to expose the magistrate. She had to call Ross. The building by the pool represented her best hope.

Men propositioned her as she hobbled towards the French doors. The sun had set since she last ventured outdoors; the only light was the glow from the house.

Two guests stood by the water smoking. 'Hi, babe,' said one. 'Want some company?'

She ignored them and headed for the summerhouse.

Thank God, it's unlocked. She slipped inside. A powerful smell of chlorine hit her, suggesting the space contained the equipment used to clean the pool; an antiseptic odour, the sort she imagined you'd get in a mortuary. Kezia couldn't see the telephone in the darkness. It took her a minute to locate it and for her eyes to adjust sufficiently to make out the characters on the keypad. Her trembling hands punched Ross's mobile number.

Unobtainable. Either he'd switched it off or he'd reached somewhere without coverage. A figure slipped into the corner of her mind – a grey monster, sniffing, hunting her down.

What's David's home number? Concentrate… subtract one, reverse, double. Five seconds' desperate mental calculation elapsed. *Got it.* It took her two attempts to key in the right digits.

Woman's voice – the lazy bastard hadn't been bothered to record his own reply. 'We're ever so sorry but we're not able to answer your call just now.' *Too bloody calm* – the realisation hit Kezia that she listened to the former Mrs Ross, even now conspiring to oversee the downfall of a potential rival. 'Please leave a message after the beep – ' *Hurry up, you stupid cow…* 'and we'll get back to you as soon as possible.'

Too late. The wolf approached too fast, wading through a lake of blood. She glanced through the window. The men had gone. The figure moved purposely towards the summerhouse.

Beep. 'David, it's me. I've worked out who killed Susan. And Connor. It was – '

The door opened. A strip light above exploded into light. Nigel Warder stood, hand on the switch. He lunged and ripped the phone from her grasp.

'You shouldn't let your ex-partners use social media,' he said. 'I've found your picture, Kezia Lee.'

'Big deal,' she said, fighting the fear threatening to paralyse her. 'What's it to you?'

'You've found out too much,' he said. 'Asking about Trixie and finding out about the premier league.'

Kezia took a pace back from the blooded vision, almost tripping over the table. 'Not a lot you can do. Too many witnesses.' *More a prayer than a statement.*

'Too many with something to lose if you gab. I clocked the way you looked at me. You know the truth.'

'I'm guessing you're Cheryl's dad.' She told herself to stay strong, aware her voice betrayed her. 'That's Trixie's girl, by the way. Trixie came to your court with Sy Mercer and recognised you. She tried to blackmail you, right?'

'Right, and she's dead. They've assumed some washed-up army type killed her.'

He took a step forward.

'You… you're lying,' Kezia stammered. 'You paid Kev Connor.' She looked round for a weapon. 'I suppose you said you'd give him an easy time in future if he worked for you.'

'More likely I'd give him two thousand pounds, but you can't prove it.'

The wolf still threatened, bloodlust in its eyes. 'That's fine. You can let me go now.'

'No way. You'll blab to the police and they'll start digging. Tom shouldn't have mentioned I used to be a heating engineer. The cops will take another look at the boiler.'

He took another step towards her. She spotted a tub to her right – chlorine granules. Hardly dangerous. A small trowel sat behind it – it might do some damage.

'Back off,' she screamed. 'You can't keep me here forever.'

She edged towards the trowel. Warder anticipated the attempt and moved to his left.

'I've no intention,' he said. 'You lured me here with some cock and bull story about politics then tried to seduce me. I fought you off but must have stunned you, after which you staggered out and fell into the pool. Delayed concussion. A terrible accident.'

'Someone'll see.' She shouted now. Her last hope was a curious guest.

'Not if I wait till the end to chuck you in. Tom'll back me up.'

Warder made his move. Kezia brought her knee up. Warder blocked the attempt with his fist and drove her towards the wall, pinning her neck with his other arm.

She thrust him away, but he proved too strong. He pushed at her throat.

'If you strangle me...' she croaked, 'they'll discover it's murder.'

Warder eased the pressure for a second. 'They won't. You'll pass out, then I'll drop you in the pool. The police will put it down as a sex game gone wrong. There's a hundred men in there and it might have been any of them.'

Grab his balls.

Warder guessed her intention, pressing hard against her. One hand grasped her right arm, the other reaching for her neck. She tried to loosen his grip but failed.

Headbutt.

Too slow. He lowered his forehead to meet hers, the collision stunning her for long enough to let him grasp her throat.

Warder squeezed harder. Kezia raked her fingernails down his face. They were too short to break skin. She gripped his wrist with her left hand and fought while her world dissolved into a red mist of blood and fire. For a second nothing existed but the pain and a longing for breath or release. Then she half-saw, half-felt, a vague presence emerging through the crimson curtain towards the sunroom.

Tom Vickery.

The club owner opened the door. 'What's happening?'

Warder released his grip. Kezia slumped to the floor clutching her throat, every gasped breath an agony.

'Tom, meet Kezia Lee. Dirty little gyppo thief, con artist and spy. She knows all about the premier league. She'll ruin us. You let her go, you can forget about Imperial Grove and all your fine plans.'

'Can't have that,' said Vickery, looking at Kezia.

'We need to silence her,' said Warder. 'Permanently.'

Kezia forced a smile. 'Like you silenced Susan Smith.' Her voice had reduced to a croak.

'What?' Vickery turned to Warder. 'What's she saying?'

Kezia pointed a wavering finger at the magistrate. 'He got Kev Connor to kill Susan. Not just kill her.' She paused, waiting for the pain in her throat to subside. 'Destroy her face so her own mother wouldn't recognise her. He feared I witnessed the murder which is why Connor tried to blind me. Then he killed Connor to keep him quiet.'

Warder laughed. 'She's talking rubbish.' It was so obvious he lied. Even Vickery should be able to understand that.

'I'm not. If you kill me, Ross'll be after you. I've left him a message. He's got the tooth – Cheryl's tooth. It'll prove you're the father. He'll find out – '

Vickery pushed his friend aside. 'Shut up, you stupid bitch.' He turned to Warder. 'We need to sort this out. Right now.'

Kezia couldn't spot anyone outside. The two men blocked her route to freedom.

Only one looked like a wolf.

'Get out,' said Vickery, pulling Kezia towards him. 'And keep your gob shut or else.'

'What?' Warder stared at his companion. 'She'll – '

Vickery held the door open and relaxed his grip. 'Mary, I'm paying you to entertain my guests. Kindly do so.' He smiled. 'Oh, and please don't mention this unpleasantness to anyone inside. I'd hate to spoil anyone's evening.'

Kezia staggered out the summerhouse and stood trembling in the chilling air until she could breathe normally. Fighting nausea, she stumbled into the function room in a daze. Her tray still sat on the table where she'd left it, but it now contained nothing but empties. Men made remarks, but she never heard or even noticed them as she returned to the kitchen, managing to only shatter one glass on the tiled floor. Her mind had morphed into a kaleidoscope of conflicting images: mad dogs, wolves, and something else... intangible but not threatening.

'Kezia!' A familiar voice broke through her confusion.

She turned.

Ross stood in the doorway, an incongruous knight errant clad in a Hobgoblin beer T-shirt and jeans. 'Are you okay? Why's your neck red?'

She began shaking. 'It was Warder. Tried... Tried to strangle me. He killed Connor. He paid Connor to kill Susan. She was one of the premier league. Upmarket whores run by Vickery.'

He wondered if he should gather her into his arms. He decided he had to act the policeman. 'I know. I've got reinforcements coming. Where is he?'

'Outside. With Vickery. Vickery saved me – no idea why.'

Ross marched out into the swimming pool area, with a barefoot Kezia trailing behind. She'd abandoned her shoes by the kitchen door.

Vickery stood outside the summerhouse, a cigar clamped in his mouth.

He laughed. 'I don't recall inviting you.'

'That's why I missed out on the dress code. Besides, I'm here on official business.'

'I suspected as much. You'll no doubt wish to speak to Mr Warder. He's waiting in the pool room. I can guarantee he'll cooperate.'

'I thought he was your mate?'

'Was, inspector, was. An important word.' Vickery looked at Kezia. 'You might not believe it, but I protect my girls. It was fortunate I spotted Nigel running out after the young lady. I won't shed any tears for him. Susan deserves justice.'

Ross jerked his thumb backwards towards the house. 'What'll happen when some of those guys get their names mentioned in court. The premier league, that's what this is all about, isn't it?'

Vickery didn't appear worried. 'How did you find out it was him, Inspector?'

'Simple. I found a witness who observed Connor leave Old Library Wood immediately after Kendal. Someone must have told Connor Kezia was in the area and might have seen something. The same someone would have known her address. The only person I know for certain fits that category is Warder. I checked him on the internet and discovered he started off his working life as a heating engineer. That's how he had the expertise to dispose of Connor. He rigged the boiler, so it looked like an accident.'

'Perhaps he was just angry at what Connor did to Trixie? He was a decent man.'

'Was. An important word, you said. I'm guessing messing her up was part of the deal. Warder would expect us to put her picture on the front page of the papers to ask if anyone recognised her. He had access to conviction records, so he could confirm her prints weren't on the system. He couldn't risk one of his old mates recognising her and coming forward. Best to tip off the boyfriend and hope the press lost interest after a couple of days.'

'What a team.' Vickery looked from one to the other. 'Holmes and Watson, but I'm still not sure which one's the master detective.'

Ross glanced back towards the function room. 'Sorry if this spoils your development prospect.'

Kezia didn't need any psychic abilities to spot the detective lied.

'A minor setback. I predict Nigel will show his patriotism and save the country the cost of a trial by pleading guilty.'

'Why should he do that?'

'I suspect you'll gather enough to hang him. And he won't want his family to suffer the embarrassment of a trial. He's got two children. At private school, may I add.'

'And you'll pay the fees?'

'The least I can do for a former friend. He worries me, though. Some of my associates have met with nasty accidents in prison. If he's careful, he'll be all right.' Vickery turned towards the sunroom. 'When your men arrive, can I ask they come round the back? I don't want to ruin my guests' evening.'

Half an hour later other police arrived, although Devlin had suddenly become invisible. Ross contemplated ordering them to tramp through the house but decided against it. You didn't antagonise Tom Vickery for no reason. He knew the warning that the club owner's people could get to Warder even in prison represented an indirect threat to Kezia and himself.

Kezia stood outside wearing Ross's jacket. She still shivered. 'Thanks for coming.'

'No problem. As soon as I realised about Warder's involvement, I got nervous Vickery was behind it and you were in danger.'

'Vickery had no idea. Trust me.'

He put an arm round her shoulders. 'We'd better be going. You need to see a doctor. Tell them you want to change, then I'll get the police surgeon to check you out. I'll have to get started on the paperwork as soon as possible.'

Mandy Stewart opened the apartment for Kezia to change. In the main house festivities continued as well as could be expected with two hostesses missing and murmurs of a police raid. Kezia left the Greek goddess costume behind. It felt soiled, a reminder of a life she'd avoided, a life that sucked in Susan Smith and spat her out.

Ross said nothing for the first five minutes of the drive back.

Finally, he said, 'Why the hell did you go there tonight? I told you to stay clear of Vickery. You might've been killed.'

'So? I nailed Nigel Warder. You should be grateful.'

'Crap. I was ready to arrest Warder. I'd worked it out. I didn't need you to get in the bloody way.'

Kezia stared ahead, biting her lip for a full minute.

'What would you have done?' she said. 'What proof did you have?'

'I – ' *She spoke the truth. All he had was circumstantial.* 'We'd have looked at the boiler again. His DNA might have been on it. Then we've got the DNA from the tooth.'

'Might. Might. That's all you'd have. A shitload of mights. I got you a fucking confession.'

It was Ross's turn to stay silent.

Kezia blinked first. 'Sorry. I should thank you for coming to rescue me.' She grinned. 'Even though you didn't have to.' Except she'd prayed he would. 'By the way, ignore the message on your phone.'

'No problem. Kezia, I'm only cross because I...' He couldn't reveal the truth. 'I feel responsible for what happens to you.' He paused while he negotiated the turn onto the A47. 'Let's say we solved this together.'

'A team,' she said, regretting the words as soon as she spoke. It smacked of a desire for a closer relationship, even commitment. He didn't deserve that.

'Sure,' was the last word Ross uttered on the drive back to Norwich.

Chapter Twenty-nine

Kezia slept in until noon.

Ross had waited two hours until the doctor confirmed her fitness to go home, then taken her back to Magdalen Street. She sensed he'd wanted to embrace her, but she understood why he wouldn't. Kezia remained forbidden fruit, and Ross didn't wish to get chucked out of the Eden of Bethel Street by the omnipotent God also known as Alison Forsyth.

Kezia resigned herself to falling back into her old life – she wouldn't see or hear from Ross again. It had been fun, occasionally scary, and she'd laid to rest the ghost of Hester Boswell as well as getting a measure of justice for Susan Smith. Her first task would be to contact the burger bar and tell them antibiotics had vanquished her lymphatic monocellular inflammation. Her Ma rode high, but things would change. They'd be on the road again before long. Perhaps north this time, Scotland even, where an entire nation of Rosses waited to greet her, hopefully lacking the baggage that came with the individual she'd never forget.

She'd put two killers in jail and saved an innocent man, although she wondered whether Jez Kendal's life would get any better. She'd shared a kinship with Susan Smith. Fate forced both of them to operate on the edge of society, living on their wits, exploited and exploiters. They differed in that one had wandered too near to the precipice, but Kezia realised even she'd strayed too close for comfort.

The guilt that had haunted her for years seemed to have gone, replaced by a mere nagging concern that an existence flipping burgers and raiding bins comprised a waste of her talents.

Maybe she should speak to Ross one more time – just to get some career advice, nothing more. Hell, she only looked for an excuse.

He's not the one for you. Don't think about him again.

Kezia never did what people told her, and they included herself.

***

Ross also slept in. He'd finished the paperwork and ensured a custody sergeant locked Warder in the cells of Bethel Street. He'd let the legal people decide which magistrates the self-confessed murderer would appear before.

Warder's creative confession stated he'd met Susan Smith in a bar, with a consequent one-night stand. No doubt Vickery would produce witnesses who'd back up the unlikely tale. Warder allegedly hired Connor when she'd tried to blackmail him. He just wanted Susan frightened and had been horrified when he found out about the murder. Connor then demanded money with menaces to keep quiet, so Warder, in fear of his own life and those of his family, believed his only option was to eliminate the violent thug. Richard Carpenter would claim poor Nigel Warder was the victim in all of this – if Vickery allowed Carpenter to represent his old friend.

No mention of Castlefields Lodge or the premier league. Kezia's name never appeared in any statement or report – the only person who might want her involved was DC Linda Stevens. The local press refused to risk the wrath of Tom Vickery, and the nationals had already lost interest in the deaths of two nobodies on the edge of England.

Ross failed to uncover anything that would stick to Vickery, and in truth he didn't want to. Vickery was legit now, if owning a strip club and skimming the surface of out-and-out bribery could be described as legit. He recognised that, as far as Warder was concerned, Vickery acted as judge and jury. And given his contacts in the criminal world, even the executioner if he wanted.

Devlin, on the other hand, was implicated. The DCI was tainted, and he knew it. Alison Forsyth would discover he'd blocked the investigation and kept an innocent man in jail because he wanted to protect his friends. A move to another force might save him.

Ross opened the curtains. The sun brightened his flat, a new day, a fresh start. Time for a clean-out. He would get a life, join an internet dating site, take up ballroom dancing, whatever it took.

A few weeks later he returned to Rosary Road. An organised group of residents were cleansing Old Library Wood of the ghosts and shadows haunting it. The prostitutes and drugs might soon be a distant memory. He should consign Kezia, and Heather, to the same fate.

Ross strolled into the tranquillity of the park. He saw no spectres, past or present. Children laughed, lovers strolled hand-in-hand while small dogs chased balls across newly mown grass. He gazed at the clear blue sky, determined to end his infatuation with the crazy red-haired gypsy girl.

If Kezia stood beside him, she'd have pointed out the pigs fluttering high above.